In a Heartbeat

CAROL ROGERS

Published by Gresham House Press

Paperback ISBN: 978-1-0684271-1-4

In a Heartbeat

CAROL ROGERS

Gresham House
PRESS

old but she felt older. Could she really blame David if he had met someone younger, more vibrant and prettier than her? She wasn't much fun to be around, she was aware of that. She vowed inwardly to make more effort to get her marriage back on track.

She brought herself back to the moment remembering that it was time to wake up the kids. They needed to get showered and dressed and have breakfast before they left for school. The twins were just ten years old. Mia was a pretty, clever girl and, like her parents, had ambitions to go to University. She had just started learning French and Spanish and had already progressed much further than her peers. Matthew, or Matty as they called him, was a typical boy. He loved football and played for his school team. He was very mature for his age and was realistic in accepting that academically he was never going to excel like his sister, but he loved sport. He was a good all rounder. As well as football he enjoyed swimming, cricket, tennis and rugby. As long as he was competing in something sporty, Matty was happy. Sadie and David were proud of their children. They were contented, well grounded kids and rarely caused them any problems. She hoped that the tangible tension between her and David wouldn't upset them. It made her more determined than ever to work harder at her relationship.

She knocked on Mia and Matty's bedroom doors. "Come on kids, you're going to be late for school. Get yourselves out of bed and dressed and come down for breakfast." She heard Mia grumbling under her breath. She had never been very good at getting up. Sadie repeated herself, this time more urgently. Matty called out "Ok Mum, I'll be down in a minute."

Sadie knew he would be the first one down. His tummy would be rumbling and he would be looking for his breakfast. He was always hungry. She assumed it was because he played so much sport. He needed the fuel to keep him going. She laid the table with bowls, cereal, orange juice and was already preparing toast and scrambled eggs when the kids came downstairs. It was important for her to ensure that they had a good breakfast inside them before they left for school.

The twins attended the same private school in Brentwood. Both her and David had done a lot of research on what were the best schools in the area and had been pleased with their choices. They had attended a pre-prep school until they were seven years old and were now in the third year of prep school. There were so many sporting options for Matty, and Mia was thriving academically. Sadie was grateful that , as parents, they were in a financial position to be able to give their children the best education.

After breakfast, she grabbed her car keys and ushered the kids out to the Range Rover parked in the drive. ' 'Come on kids, we're going to be late." The school was only five miles from home but she liked to allow at least half an hour to get there. The traffic was always pretty heavy at this time in the morning and she hated rushing. "Have either of you got anything on after school today?" she asked.

"I'm playing in a football match Mum but it's a home game, so I shouldn't be too late' said Matty. "Oh no", said Mia. "That means I've got to wait around for you to finish the game".

"That's ok", said Sadie "We can both watch the game, and then why don't we go out for some tea afterwards? I don't think Dad will be home tonight. He has an important meeting in Paris today. So why don't we treat ourselves - perhaps a pizza?"

"Oh yeah!" said Matty. "I'll be starving after the game, pizza will be great. "Mia nodded in agreement but secretly thought how boring it would be to have to watch a whole football match. It really wasn't her scene.

After Sadie dropped the twins off at school, she headed into town. She had decided to have a look round the shops and buy some new clothes. She always seemed to be wearing jogging pants and sweatshirts these days. She had a nice figure but it was always hidden under baggy clothes. If she wanted David to take more notice of her, then she needed to remind him of how attractive she could be when she made the effort. She headed into John Lewis and made her way to the lady's fashion floor. It had been so long since she had been shopping for clothes that she felt spoiled for choice. She chose a handful of dresses to try on and selected six to take to the dressing room. Four of the six fitted her well and flattered her slim figure. After paying for her dresses, she made her way to the lingerie department. She looked for something sexy. Something to excite David. She finally settled on a black negligee. That should do the trick, she thought to herself.

When she got home, she noticed that there was an answer phone message on her mobile from David. "Hi Sadie. I'm really sorry love but the meeting went on longer than I thought. I don't think I will make it home tonight, so just go ahead and have dinner with the kids. I'll book an early morning flight and I'll see you tomorrow."

She felt disappointed but not really surprised. She had a feeling that he wouldn't be home. He was in Paris, why would he want to come home when he could spend the evening there? She hoped that he would call her back again before she went to the school for Matty's football match. But he didn't.

She presumed he was just too busy. She convinced herself that there was nothing to worry about. David loved her and the children. He wouldn't cheat on her would he?

By the time she got to the school, the match had already kicked off and Mia was standing sulkily at the edge of the pitch pretending to watch the game but taking sneaky looks at her new phone at the same time. Both her and Matty had plagued their parents to have a phone like all their friends. They had finally relented and gifted them one for their tenth birthdays.

"Hi Mum. I didn't think you were coming, I was getting worried", said Mia. "Oh sorry sweetie, I should have texted you. I went shopping this afternoon and then I was waiting to see if dad was going to call again. He had left a message on the answerphone to say that he wouldn't be home tonight, but I wondered if he would ring again".

"And did he?" asked Mia. Sadie shook her head. "I expect he is still really busy. You know what dad is like. He won't stop until his work is done for the day. He will be home in the morning though, so you will see him when you get back from school."

"He goes away a lot doesn't he?' said Mia. "We hardly ever see him Mum. "Sadie was thinking of how to answer, when she surprised her and left her lost for words. "Mum, you and dad aren't going to get a divorce like Jessica's parents are you?"

"No sweetheart, of course not", she answered quickly. "Look let's concentrate on watching the game. We're here for Matty, and don't worry, dad and I are fine." Just at that moment, there was a huge cheer from the pitch. Matty had scored a goal. Sadie clapped and cheered. "Hoorah, well done Matty" she shouted. Mia clapped politely wishing that they would blow the final whistle. She was bored.

She was a very bright and intuitive ten year old, and had known for a long time that her parents were unhappy.She was aware of what her mum had been through in the past and she wished that there was something she could do to make things better. She had tried to discuss her concerns with her brother but he was completely blinkered. He told her not to be silly, there was nothing wrong. All parents argued. It was normal.

The match finally finished with a score of three to the home team and two to the away team. Matty ran off the pitch towards his mum and sister. His face was bright pink and sweaty and he was puffing and blowing, but he was elated that his team had won. "Did you see my goal Mum?" he said excitedly.

"Yes darling, well done!" she exclaimed.

"We're through to the next round now. If we win our next match, then we'll be in the final."

"I'm really proud of you darling. Let's go and have that pizza. You must be starving". At last, thought Mia. She found watching football so boring although she was secretly proud of her brother. She decided not to tell him though. She thought his head was big enough already!

Three marguerita pizzas, and three large helpings of ice-cream later, Sadie and the kids arrived home. She had enjoyed spending time with them listening to their endless chatter about what was happening at school. She thought it was hilarious that their friends referred to them as the M & M's - just like the sweets of the same name. She was happy that they enjoyed school so much and had made so many friends - friends from good families who had similar backgrounds to them. Their parents were mostly professionals in business, or the medical profession. One of Matty's friends had a famous pop star dad, although Sadie had never heard of him. According to Matty he had an album in the charts but Sadie had to admit that she wasn't really into pop music these days. I need to get with it, she thought. I'm becoming boring and middle aged!

"Right come on kids. It's 9o'clock. It's time you were getting ready for bed", she said. "You can have half an hour of watching some TV if you manage to get into bed within the next fifteen minutes", she added.

They both raced up the stairs into their respective bedrooms. They had their own TV's which saved many arguments on who wanted to watch what. Matty called out to Mia that he was going to catch up on last night's football.

"That will make a change", said Mia sarcastically. "I've got a Disney film I want to watch."

"Rather you than me ," said Matty. "That's for little kids."

"Well it's better than boring football. That's all you're interested in!"

"Just you wait and see, I'll be a famous footballer one day and it will be me on the TV!"

"In your dreams!" said Mia.

Sadie could hear the kids winding each other up and sensed an argument brewing. She called upstairs, "Right you two, that's enough. One more word and you'll be straight in bed."

That seemed to do the trick. When all was quiet and she was happy that they had turned off their TV's and fallen asleep, she poured herself a glass of wine and sat down in her favourite armchair. She felt tired. It had been a busy day.

She was looking forward to seeing David tomorrow. She had missed him. He always got a taxi from the airport so she didn't have to worry about picking him up. She decided she would have a leisurely bath once she had taken the kids to school and take her time in getting ready. She guessed that he would be home around midday. She was going to prepare a nice lunch and they could catch up on their news before the twins came home. After a second glass of wine, she felt in a reflective mood. Her thoughts took her back to everything that had happened to her since her heady days at University and how different her life was now.

As she got into bed and drifted off to sleep, the unwelcome, dark intrusive thoughts invaded her mind as they often did late at night. She thought of the day that changed her very existence. The day that she stopped being the old Sadie. The day that would haunt her for the rest of her life. "I'm so, so sorry," she whispered as she finally succumbed to the darkness and tumbling sensation of sleep.....

Chapter 1

2010

Sadie was 19 years old and in the second year of her degree course at Liverpool University when she first met David. He was studying Law and she was doing a Batchelor of Arts degree. She was having lunch in the restaurant one day when he approached her table and asked if he could join her.

"I hope you don't mind," he said. "But I'm trying to avoid someone. If he thinks we are lunching together, then perhaps he'll get the message".

Sadie thought it sounded a strange thing to say but invited him to sit down.

"No of course not, be my guest", she said. He sat down opposite her. She couldn't help but notice how good looking he was. He was the atypical tall dark and handsome guy that attracted attention.

"Do you mind me asking who it is you are avoiding?" She hoped that he didn't think her too forward for questioning him.

"Oh it's just this guy that's on my course" said David. ""He follows me everywhere and quite frankly, It's driving me nuts. I've known him for over a year now. He was a good friend to me in the beginning but he is getting a bit too clingy and I don't know how to get rid of him without upsetting him. He talks endlessly about how wealthy his family is and how they live in this huge house in Cheshire. He wants to be a lawyer in his father's law firm. He is obviously very clever but he is just so full of himself.He is trying to impress but, as far as I'm concerned, it's having the opposite effect".

"Oh dear,' said Sadie. 'That's a difficult one. I woudn't want to upset him either. Perhaps, he is just lonely. I'm sure he is a nice guy, otherwise you wouldn't have made friends with him in the first place".

"Well, you are very gracious and understanding in saying that, and by the way, I'm David," he said as he outstretched his hand – David Burns. "Hello David, pleased to meet you, I'm Sadie - Sadie Connel. "

"What a pretty name," he said.

"Thank you, it was my grandmother's name. Everyone called her Sarah but I prefer Sadie".

"Well Sadie it is then", he said. He had noticed the Scottish lilt to her voice and asked what part of Scotland she was from.

"Just outside of Edinburgh", she answered. "We don't have such a broad accent as people from other parts of the country, such as Glasgow for instance."

"I noticed that. It's very attractive."

"Thank you. And where are you from?" she asked.

"My family home is in Brighton, Sussex. We have a house quite close to the sea. I was born and brought up in Brighton so I have never lived anywhere else until I moved here."

"What made you choose Liverpool?" she asked.

"It had the course that I wanted to do and I thought it was about time that I spread my wings", he laughed.

"What about you? Why not Edinburgh Uni?"

"Similar reasons really", said Sadie. "I haven't regretted it for a second. The lecturers here are great and I love the city."

"Well that's something we have in common straightaway." I'm really enjoying my course too, and Liverpool is such a cool place" he said.

"Are you having lunch?", he asked.

"Yes, I've ordered shepherds pie. They'll bring it over when it's ready" said Sadie. "That sounds nice, do you mind if I have the same?"

"No of course not," she said, thinking how very polite he was.

He got up from the table and went across to the counter to order his lunch. She watched him and thought to herself – mmm, he looks as cute from the back as he does from the front. She felt the stirring of butterflies in her tummy. Was it just the hunger, or was it something else?

Sadie hadn't had many boyfriends before she started at University. All the boys she had met seemed only interested in one thing and that wasn't attractive to her. Yes, of course she looked forward to falling in love with someone and being intimate with that special guy one day. But she hadn't met anyone yet who made her feel that way. Perhaps David could be that guy? she thought.

She pulled herself away from her daydreams just as he returned and took his seat opposite her again. "Well, that's lunch ordered and I'm having apple crumble and custard too. I've got a couple of heavy lectures this afternoon so I need to keep my strength up" he laughed.

"What will you do about your 'friend' then?" asked Sadie.

"I'm going to tell him that I'm busy with studies and I've got a girlfriend, so I don't think it's fair to string him along. I just haven't got the time to spend with him at the moment."

"Oh so you have got a girlfriend then?" She tried to keep the disappointment from her voice.

"No not yet but I'm hoping too", he said mysteriously. It had not escaped him how beautiful Sadie was. He noticed her bright blue eyes, lovely smile and pretty blonde hair and thought to himself that he had never felt so attracted to a girl like her before. He wanted to ask her out but decided that now wasn't the right time. He thought it would be better to wait a day or two and see what happened.

They ate their lunch making polite conversation, both feeling strangely awkward and lost in their own private thoughts.

"Well, it was lovely meeting you Sadie. I hope we can meet up again soon", he said after they had finished lunch.

"I'm usually in here most days", she answered. "I'll look forward to it".

"Enjoy your lecture", she called out as he left the restaurant. He turned, smiled and gave her a wave.

Well that was strange, she thought. She had hoped that he was going to ask her out on a date but perhaps he hadn't found her attractive. Perhaps he had found HER boring. She was also confused by his story about the annoying friend. Why would this guy be so obsessive about him? She decided not to analyse the situation any longer. If he was interested in seeing her again, then he would seek her out. She wasn't going to worry about what might happen. For now, she had work to do in the university library so she made her way up to the second floor and found a quiet space where she could concentrate and make some notes for her assignment which was due in the following week.

She went to bed that night thinking about David. He had a powerful magnetism which seemed to draw her in. She had never experienced these feelings before. She felt strangely excited. I hope I see him again tomorrow, she thought as she drifted off to sleep.

Sure enough David was sitting at the same table when she walked into the restaurant the next day. "Over here", he called out. She didn't want to appear too keen as she answered.

"Oh hello David. It's nice to see you again. Did you manage to talk to your friend?" she asked. By the way what's his name? I don't think I've seen him before."

"Yes I did" he said. His name is Alan - Alan Burgess. I told him that I wouldn't be around as much anymore as I had a girlfriend. I told him that it was you. I hope you don't mind?" She looked at him in astonishment. "Well that was a bit forward," she said. "You haven't even asked me out yet!"

"Well we can soon change that. What are you doing tonight?"

Sadie answered, trying not to sound too keen. "Well I should be working on my assignment. It's due in next week and I'm only halfway through it".

"You'll have plenty of time to finish it. Come on it's just a date. We can go out for dinner or just a drink, if you'd prefer not to have a late night" he said pleadingly.

"Ok you win. But let's just have a drink, then perhaps I can do some work when we get back".

"Deal!" said David, grinning from ear to ear.

She spent a long time getting ready for her date that night. They were only going to the student bar but she wanted to look her best. She chose to wear a pretty pale blue maxi dress which complimented her blue eyes and her favourite white pumps. She wore her hair loose and curly round her shoulders and applied only the lightest of make up. She looked at her reflection in the mirror. Mmm not too bad, she thought. I'll do! She walked into the bar and David was already there, sitting at a table in the corner. The sight of Sadie took his breath away. She looked amazing.

"Wow, you look lovely Sadie", he said.

"You don't look so bad yourself", she said, looking at his strong arms and chest under a crisp short sleeved white shirt. He really was a good looking guy, she thought.

One drink turned into two, then three and before they knew it, it was 10.30pm. They had spent the entire evening chatting, laughing and putting the world to rights. Sadie had never felt this comfortable with a guy before. They seemed to have so much in common. Both were the only child of parents who had given them wonderful happy childhoods. They had both attended good schools and had a great education.

David spoke to her about his dreams and aspirations to be a successful lawyer, and she told him that she had always wanted to be a teacher. "I like the idea of teaching little ones", she said. "Getting involved at the very start of their education and watching them grow. That would be so wonderful."

David looked at her fondly across the table. She really was a special girl, he thought. He couldn't wait to get to know her better. The future suddenly looked brighter.

He walked her back to her accommodation at the end of the night. "Surely you're not going to do any work now are you? It's very late, I'm sure it can wait until tomorrow", he said. Sadie smiled up at him and looked deep into his eyes. Before she knew what was happening, he had swept her into his arms and they were kissing passionately, completely lost in one another. She opened her front door and they tumbled inside entwined in each other's arms.

They walked towards the bedroom and laid on the bed, stroking and caressing each other. David's voice was hoarse with passion.

"Sadie, you are so beautiful, I want you so much". She couldn't believe what was happening. She had only known this man for a couple of days and here they were about to make love.

She wanted him too but something made her stop.

"David, I think it's too soon. I am really attracted to you, but we hardly know each other. Let's wait until we are both sure, plus I don't want to get pregnant and I'm not on the pill".

"It's ok, I've got a condom," he said. She thought how convenient it was that he had come prepared. He must have known that this would happen.

"Please, let's just wait. We have plenty of time. I don't want to rush things". David understood and, although he had wanted to make love to her, he respected the fact that she wanted to wait. It said a lot about her and just made him long to be with her even more.

Despite the awkwardness of the moment, they kissed passionately once again and agreed to take things a bit slower. After saying a loving goodnight to one another, they arranged to meet in the restaurant the next day for lunch.

She found it difficult to sleep that night. Her thoughts kept straying to the events of the evening. She had loved being with David. She really fancied him and it had been difficult to stop their lovemaking. But she knew it was the right thing to do. They needed to get to know one another properly first and then it would happen naturally. She had to concentrate on working towards her degree for now. That had to be her priority.

David's head was spinning. He knew that he hadn't known Sadie for very long but he felt that he was already falling in love with her. He had been disappointed and a little frustrated that they hadn't been intimate tonight but he knew that it would happen one day. Now that he had met her, he didn't want to lose her. He longed to hold her in his arms again and looked forward to seeing her tomorrow. He finally fell asleep dreaming of her and looking forward to a future with her.

Chapter 2

From that first date onwards, Sadie and David were inseparable. They met every day for lunch and spent most days in the library studying together. They helped one another with revision and had agreed that their studies must always come first if they were to get their degrees.

Alan was often around and would make a beeline to join them. Sadie liked Alan. He seemed a gentle soul and he was obviously lonely. She persuaded David to be kinder to him and include him whenever they met up with friends in the student bar.

They would try and get together with everyone at least once a week and have a night off from studies. They had also discovered a lovely little Italian restaurant in town so they would manage another date night once a week where talking about work was completely off the menu and they would just enjoy each other's company.

Life was good. Sadie knew she was falling in love with David and he had already said the 'L' word to her. They had given in to their passion one afternoon when they had gone back to her apartment with the intention to study. Temptation took the better of them and they ended up spending the rest of the afternoon in bed. Their lovemaking was gentle and tender. Sadie didn't think it was possible to be so happy. David was an incredible lover. His touch made her tingle with warmth and unbelievable pleasure. She longed for him time and time again until they were both physically exhausted and their passion gave way to a deep and contented sleep.

Needless to say, there was no work done that day. They laughed about how their plans for the day had taken an unexpected but glorious twist. They had taken the next step in their relationship and agreed that perhaps now, if they were going to have a future together, it was the right time for them to meet each other's parents. The University was about to close for the Christmas break, so they decided that this would be a good opportunity for both families to be introduced to one another.

"We could arrange for the parents to meet when they come to pick us up for the Christmas holidays and then take them to our Italian restaurant", said Sadie.

"That sounds a good idea. It will certainly be easier than trying to arrange something in one another's homes", said David.

She laughed "Yes it could be difficult bearing in mind your parents live in Sussex and mine are in Scotland!" She had learned that David's parents were considerably older than hers and they were now retired. His father had also been a solicitor and his mother was a nurse. When they married, they had decided not to have any children. They wanted to travel and just enjoy being together without the responsibility of looking after a family. When David's mum was in her early forties, she was shocked to learn that she was four months pregnant. Although David's arrival wasn't at all planned, the moment she held him in her arms for the first time, she was smitten.

Just like Sadie, David had been adored by his parents and had enjoyed an indulgent childhood. Although they tried not to spoil him, there wasn't much that they denied him. Sadie thought that they sounded really nice people. She was looking forward to meeting them and she felt sure that they would get on well with her parents.

Sadie's parents were both teachers and were still working. Her mum, Mary, taught history in a grammar school in Edinburgh and her dad, Rob, taught maths at a private school just outside the city. She telephoned her parents that night. Mary answered the phone.

"Oh hello love, how are you?" she said in her soft Scottish accent. "I'm fine Mum. Actually I'm better than fine. You know I have been dating David for a few months now?"

"Yes, how is it going?" she said. "Really well. I think I am falling for him. We get on so well and have such a lot in common. I want you and dad to meet him and his parents. How would you feel about that?"

"It seems a bit soon love. Are you sure it's a good idea to meet his family now. Isn't it better to wait a little longer?" she said.

"No I don't want to wait.We are both sure how we feel and it's important to us that our families get along. We wanted to take you all to our favourite Italian restaurant in Liverpool. You'd love it there and I'm sure you will like David's parents too. They are retired now. His dad used to be a solicitor and his mum was a nurse. Their names are Susan and Colin and they sound really lovely Mum. Please say yes - please" she begged.

"Let me speak to your dad love. It's up to him. When were you thinking of all this happening then?"

"We thought it would be a good opportunity when you come to pick me up for the Christmas holidays. David's parents are picking him up too, so we could make it on that day", she said.

"Ok, I suppose that would make sense. If it's really what you want. But I don't want you to get hurt love. What if things don't work out between you? You are still so young. You've got plenty of time to fall in love. I don't want you rushing into anything".

Mary felt concerned for her daughter. She knew nothing about

David. What if he was stringing her along. Their daughter meant everything to Mary and Rob. They had been unable to have any more children, so she had always been extra special. Mary knew that they had spoiled her. Now that she was an adult, she found it difficult letting go. It had been hard enough when she left home to go to University. She wasn't prepared for the possibility of her having a serious relationship - not yet.

"I'll speak to your dad and I'll call you back in an hour or so", said Mary. She knew that Rob would agree. Whatever made his daughter happy, made him happy but she needed a bit of time to think about it.

"Thanks Mum, you're a star. I'll wait to hear from you then. Love you." "And I love you too" said Mary as she ended the call.

True to her word, Mary rang her daughter back later that day. "You win" she said jokingly. "Dad is happy to meet David and his parents. So, I guess it's a done deal. I usually end up agreeing with whatever he says! Just let us know as soon as possible when it's likely to be Sadie. We've got quite a few things going on in the next few weeks".

"Oh that's great Mum, thank dad too won't you? You won't regret it. David is lovely so I'm sure his parents will be too", she said.

"Ok love. I'll wait to hear from you then".

"David is at a lecture this afternoon, so he'll ring his parents this evening. I'll let you know what they say", she said.

She was deep in thought making notes for her next assignment, when David knocked at her door. "Hi sweetheart. I've spoken to the parents and they are up for it", he said excitedly.

"Great, my parents are too so let's set a date for when we pack up here and then we can book a table at the restaurant", she said.

Sadie was looking forward to the Christmas break. She had been working really hard. It would be nice to spend some time at home enjoying mum's cooking and getting all her washing done. If nothing else, her time at University had taught her to appreciate her mum a lot more. She would miss David but it was only for a few weeks and it might be good for them to spend a little time apart to reflect on their relationship. She was sure of her feelings. She knew that David loved her, but her mum was right, she was still very young. There was plenty of time before either of them needed to think about committing to spending the rest of their lives together.

They decided on 12th December as the day they would pack their belongings and leave their student accommodations for the Christmas break. After checking with both sets of parents, they booked the restaurant for 2pm. That would give them all enough time to travel from their respective homes.

Over the next ten days or so, they were both busy completing their latest assignments and getting prepared for the new term in January. They also went Christmas shopping together to buy presents for their families. "What would you like for Christmas sweetheart?" said David one day.

"Oh I don't need anything", she said . "Let's agree not to buy each other a present. Money is a bit tight for both of us. We'll wait until we graduate. We can treat ourselves then - perhaps a week's break in Scotland. You have never visited Scotland. You would love it. We could hire a car or even camper van and I could show you the sights", she said excitedly.

"That sounds a great idea and typical of you my darling - sensible and practical as well as beautiful" he laughed.

She joined in his laughter. "Well, thank you kind sir!" she said. "But it would be nice wouldn't it and it will give us something to look forward to?"

It was the morning of the 12th December. Sadie and David had heard from their parents and they were all on their way. "Once we have loaded our stuff into both cars, we'll set off for the restaurant", said David as she was gathering a few clothes and the family Christmas presents and packing them into a large holdall.

"We can walk round," she said. "It will only take ten minutes or so and it might break the ice a bit before we all sit down to dinner".

"Don't worry, sweetheart, it's going to be fine. I'm sure the four of them will have plenty to talk about. You know what these "oldies" are like" he laughed. "They'll probably be talking about us when we were children and how lovely we were! Knowing my mum and dad, they will probably bring a few photo albums with them and they'll bore us all to death with memories of my first words, the day I took my first steps, my first day of school etc. etc."

She laughed out loud. "Oh no, God forbid. That's the sort of thing my parents would do too. We'll have to steer the conversation away from that subject if it comes up. I get so embarrassed when my parents talk about my childhood. Listening to them, you would think I was a saint. All I can say is that they didn't know the half of it!"

"I won't ask" he said laughing.

Sadie's parents arrived first and were introduced to David. 'I'm very pleased to meet you", he said politely. He shook Rob's outstretched hand and attempted rather an awkward embrace with Mary.

"We are pleased to meet you too" said Rob. "Sadie has told us so much about you".

"All good, I hope? He laughed. "Of course", Mary added, smiling at her daughter. Luckily Colin and Susan arrived shortly after, and once all the introductions and pleasantries were exchanged, the six of them made their way to the restaurant.

As Sadie and David had expected, the meal was as fabulous as ever. The conversation flowed naturally and they were relieved that there was no mention of childhood experiences and luckily no photo albums. Both sets of parents seemed to get on very well much to their relief.

The parents seemed happy to know that they were serious about one another but agreed that they should both concentrate on achieving their grades and graduating before there was any talk of engagements or marriage.

David laughed at the suggestion. "We haven't even thought about that yet, have we Sadie?"

"No, not at all," she said. "One step at a time. We both need to find work after we graduate and then we need to save up. It will be a couple of years at least I should think".

Mary didn't know what Rob or David's parents thought about that. But personally she felt relieved that they weren't going to rush into anything. She quite liked David. He seemed a nice lad but there was just something about him. Something she couldn't put her finger on.

She wanted Sadie to be really sure before she made any commitment to him. If they were going to wait a couple of years, then that was good as far as she was concerned. She hoped that she was wrong but she couldn't shake off the uncomfortable feeling that she had. Was there more to David than meets the eye?

The four parents agreed to split the cost of the meal between them and thanked them both for arranging such a lovely lunch. "It was really nice of you all to come. Sadie and I have enjoyed your company", David said.

"Well we had better get going, we've got a long journey", said Rob, glancing at his daughter.

"My stuff is all ready to put in the car Dad. I just need to say goodbye to David . Give me a few minutes".

David took her hand and led her outside. "I'm going to miss you so much sweetheart. I know it's only a few weeks but what am I going to do without you?" he said sadly.

"I will miss you too darling but we've both got a lot of work to do. This is a big year for us. Our final exams are looming. If we both want good results then we've got to put the work in. A few weeks with no distractions will give us the opportunity to do that. Also it's Christmas and we both need to spend time with our extended families. The time will soon pass and then we can be together again".

"My wise, beautiful girlfriend. You are always so logical and sensible and you are quite right as usual!" he said laughing. She smiled fondly at him. He looked like a little boy who'd had his sweets taken away.She loved him so much. He seemed so vulnerable somehow.

After saying goodbye, I love you, multiple times, they finally tore themselves away from each other and together with their parents walked back to where their cars were parked. Once all their stuff was packed in, they left in convoy with Rob's car leading the way until they reached the motorway. They continued to wave frantically to one another out of the back windows until they split to go their separate ways.

Sadie was surprised how much she actually enjoyed the Christmas break back at home. It was lovely spending quality time with her parents and having the opportunity to catch up with other family members and some of her friends that she had gone to school with. She had also managed to do some work in preparation for the new term. She spoke to David every day. She missed him like crazy, but it was good to hear that he was also enjoying his time at home and he seemed to be getting thoroughly spoiled by his doting mum! "Honestly Sadie, mum is running around like a headless chicken looking after me. She is such a great cook. I swear I've put on a stone since I've been at home", he laughed.

"My mum is the same. We are very lucky to have such lovely parents", she added. ' Nice that it is to be home though, I can't wait to see you sweetheart", he said. "When are you going back?'

"I'm going to get the train next week . Now that I haven't got the Christmas presents to carry, my bag is much lighter so I'll manage. I don't really want to drag mum and dad down again. It's a bit of a stretch from Edinburgh. They are insisting that they drive me back but I'll be fine on the train. I'd much rather do that", she said.

"I'm doing the same", he said. "I plan to be back in Halls by the 10th January".

"That sounds good. Let's travel back on the 9th. Term starts on the 12th so that will give us a few days to get settled back in again. I can't wait to see you", she said.

"Me too. I've missed you so much." he replied.

After she had finished her call, Sadie went to find her mum who was baking in the kitchen.

"I've just spoken to David, Mum, and we've decided to travel back to Liverpool on the 9th January. No arguments but I'm definitely going to take the train. David is too. It makes sense. There is no point in you driving down if you don't need to. I haven't got much to carry, so it will be fine" she insisted.

Mary dreaded the thought of her daughter leaving. She had loved having her at home again. She still felt concerned about her relationship with David and had discussed it with Rob a few days ago.

"Don't be silly love. He seems like a really nice guy and he obviously thinks a lot of our Sadie. You are just being over protective. I don't think anyone will be good enough for her in your eyes", he said kindly.

"It's not that Rob. Of course I want her to be happy, get married and have a family. But I'm not sure that David is the right one for her. There is something about him that I just can't put my finger on. Don't you think that it's strange that he doesn't seem to have many friends and Susan said that he has never had a proper girlfriend prior to Sadie? I just wonder why. He's a very handsome young man".

"Well isn't that a good thing?" he questioned "It means that he isn't a jack the lad type who would be likely to stray", he added.

"Yes, maybe", said Mary. "But let's put it this way - I won't be upset or surprised if the relationship fizzles out."

"Don't let Sadie hear you say that!" Rob was surprised by his wife's concerns. He had liked David when they met. He appeared to be a decent guy and was very ambitious. Rob was impressed by his aspirations to be a lawyer and was in no doubt that he would do well in the future. Sadie would have financial security and that was important to him.

David's parents were similarly sad to see him going back to Liverpool. They had enjoyed their time with him. He had been quiet but his mum, Susan, had put that down to him missing Sadie. Her and Colin had really taken to Sadie from the minute they met her. They could see that she was a lovely young girl and obviously had a close family who thought the world of her. She seemed kind and thoughtful and she was very pretty.

Susan felt that David had made a good choice. She was beginning to think that he would never meet a nice girl. He had always excelled academically at school and was a popular boy with both the staff and the other kids but he never asked for friends to come over for tea or a sleepover after school as did most of his peers. He seemed to be quite content with his own company and spent most of the time in his room reading.

Susan worried about him when he was growing up. He didn't show any interest in sport like most of the boys. From a young age he had decided that he wanted to be a lawyer in London, and that remained his main focus. He would read books and watch films centered around high profile court cases and dreamt of being rich and successful one day. Colin didn't share his wife's concerns and tried to reassure her that David was just different. He was proud of his son, especially as he wanted to follow in his own footsteps and study law.

"We can't influence him to be someone he isn't, Susan", he had said to her. "He is a bright and clever boy. We should be encouraging him in his dreams for the future. Not all boys like football, rolling around in the mud, or chasing girls. He has ambition. He knows what he wants to do when he leaves school. That's a rare quality in kids these days", he said proudly.

Susan agreed that she was probably over reacting and promised her husband that she would try and understand her son better and accept him for who he was.

As David progressed through Junior School and Grammar School, he continued to excel. He achieved 3 A grades in his A level exams and after researching the best University for the course he wanted to do, he applied to Liverpool.

David had found it difficult to settle into University life at first. He enjoyed the course but was overwhelmed with what was expected of him in order to fit in with the other students. He avoided the many parties and social events which were a big part of university life. He knew that he was different to the other guys on his course. They would constantly brag about their sexual exploits, sharing intimate details of their conquests. They teased him constantly and called him a swat.

"You need to work less and concentrate on having some fun Dave", one of them said.

"It's not all about sex", David replied. "Well, what else is there?" laughed the other guy. With that he left the room and that's when he met Alan for the first time. Alan had been listening to the banter and approached him.

"Don't listen to those idiots", he said. "I doubt that any of them will get their degrees. They're not taking their course seriously. In fact it wouldn't surprise me if they get kicked off", he added.

David nodded and told Alan that he was heading to the restaurant for a coffee. "Do you want to join me?" he asked.

"Yep that sounds good", said Alan.

Once they started talking, they were surprised to learn how much they had in common and it was quite clear that they both shared the same ambition to be successful lawyers. David told Alan how he fancied Corporate Law. "It's the highest paid legal specialism, and that's what I want. I want the power and the financial rewards that it will bring".

"It's good that you have such clear plans of what you want to do. I'm not sure yet," answered Alan. "I'm very interested in Criminal Law but dad wants me to join his firm after I graduate and specialise in Family Law. Mind you, we've got at least a year completing our Legal Practice Course after graduating before we have to decide on our specialisms, so I may well change my mind by then", he said.

David knew that there was still a long road ahead before he could even think about earning a reasonable salary. After finishing his exams he knew he would need to join a Law firm who would be happy taking him on as a trainee solicitor for a year before he was fully qualified. He and Alan continued chatting about their hopes for the future and family backgrounds. David felt that he had found a friend - someone on his level and someone who wasn't obsessed with screwing every girl in sight.

For the first year of their course, they became good friends. They tended to hang out together and made a point of avoiding the parties and drunken antics of the other students.

It was just before David met Sadie in year two that things changed between them. Alan had become very dependent on him. He wanted to be with him constantly. David began to feel uncomfortable. He felt confused about his feelings for him. He decided that it would be better if they didn't see so much of one another. He made his mind up that he would speak to him about it - soon.

Chapter 3

It was the start of a new term. Their final year. David and Sadie were back in Liverpool after the Christmas break. They were so happy to be together again. They agreed that it had been hard to be apart for those few weeks but that this was going to be THEIR year. They would pass their exams, get their degrees and go away on their promised holiday to Scotland. But first, there was lots of work to do. Final exams were scheduled for April and May with results being announced in June. They weren't sure of the date of Gradation Day but it was likely to be at the end of June.

They were both excited to be entering this stage of their lives together. They had so much to look forward to. They accepted that the first couple of years were going to be difficult while David was completing his qualifications and Sadie would need to look for a teaching position, but they were young. They had the rest of their lives to fulfil their dreams.

The first few months of the year passed in a flurry of revision, lectures and assignments. The final exams were on the horizon now. It was exciting on the one hand but terrifying on the other. Alan would often join Sadie and David during quiet times in the library when they were revising. Sadie noticed that David acted strangely around him. He was pleasant to him which pleased her but he seemed distant and unwilling to engage in conversation with him.

She spoke to him about it but he dismissed her concerns.

"It's fine between us, he just irritates me sometimes, that's all. He is such a know all".

"That's unfair David," she said. He's very kind and thoughtful and he has been a good friend to you", she said crossly.

He shook his head. "You don't really know him," he said "Let's just forget it. I don't want to argue with you, sweetheart. We're both feeling under pressure with the exams looming. Let's have a break this evening and go out for a drink - just the two of us. It will do us good to have some quality time together".

Sadie agreed and said that she would meet him in the student bar later.

As she got ready to go out that evening, her thoughts turned to the situation between Alan and David. They had been friends for nearly two years but their relationship puzzled her. David was obviously very fond of Alan so why was he sometimes so unpleasant to him. It was a side of him that she never saw when he was with her and she had to admit that it disturbed her. Alan really was a kind soul as far as she was concerned and although he was obviously very clever, she never felt that he presented himself as a know all.

In fact, he was always willing and eager to help them if they were finding any aspects of their coursework difficult. There was never any expectation from him for thanks or appreciation. He genuinely seemed happy to help. She decided that it was probably better if she didn't mention how she felt to David.

Whatever it was between him and Alan, she wouldn't get involved, especially if it was going to cause further tension. She loved David and the last thing she wanted was for them to argue, especially now, just before final exams.

By the beginning of June exams were over and final coursework and presentations were handed in. Now it was just a case of waiting for the results. They both felt quietly confident but were also aware that it didn't pay to be too complacent. On the other hand, Alan was convinced that he would get a First. He had worked hard, he hadn't struggled with the exams and his coursework was always on point.

"I told you that he was a know all didn't I?" said David.

"He's just confident that's all", she answered. "It sounds like you are a bit jealous of him", she added.

"Of course, I'm not. It's just that he thinks he is so perfect. It gets a bit wearing sometimes," he said.

"Well we haven't got that long to wait before we all discover our fate. So why don't we just enjoy the next couple of weeks before results are announced. Let's go out tonight. Shall we book a table at the Italian?" "Good idea", said David. "Just us two", he added.

"Yes, just us two", she answered with a sigh.

They both enjoyed the next few weeks relaxing and planning what their future would be following graduation. David had already written to a firm specialising in Corporate Law in London. They had emailed him and agreed to see him for an interview with a view to offering him a part time position as a student solicitor. They told him that it would be subject to him completing a two year Legal Practice Course which he could also do part time. He thought that It sounded a great proposition. He appreciated that he wouldn't be earning much for a few years, but if he could start off working in London, that would be the place to be for future employment. He wondered how Sadie would feel about moving nearer to London with him and approached her for her reaction.

"I would be up for that darling. I am sure I would find it easier to get a teaching job nearer London. "she said. "But I think we should try and find somewhere to live first. We're going to have to rent to start with, as money will be tight. Perhaps we should look at different areas outside of London that you can commute from. The properties will be much cheaper."

"Yes, I think you're right sweetheart. We can register with a few estate agents and see what comes up."

Exam results were posted on the student portal in the third week of July. When the day finally came, Sadie, David and Alan had agreed that they would look at them together to give each other moral support.

"We'll look for yours first Sadie", said David.

"Oh dear, I suddenly feel very nervous", she said.

She scanned the lists of students and clicked on her name. It took a minute for the results to appear. She looked twice then looked twice again - she had a first class honours! It was beyond her wildest dreams. She expected to pass but not at such a high level. She was ecstatic and whooped with joy.

"Well done darling. I'm so very proud of you. All that hard work has paid off", said David enveloping her in his arms.

"Yes, congratulations Sadie" said Alan. "You deserve it", he added.

"Now it's your turn David" she said. He felt apprehensive as he selected his name from the list of law students. He hesitated as he looked long and hard at his results "Wow, I've got a First too", he declared excitedly.

Alan completed the hat trick. Sadie and David had never doubted that he would. "We must all go out tonight and celebrate", said Sadie. "I'm going to ring mum and dad, they will be so excited".

"Yes, I'll ring mine too", said David. "Alan, we'll see you in the student bar later. Is that ok?", said Sadie.

"Yeah, I'll look forward to it. Well done you two!" he said as he left the room. He was going to ring his family too. I hope they will be proud of me, he thought to himself.

The atmosphere in the student bar that night was electric. The emotions evoked over the last three years of studying were tangible. Students sat in little clusters, laughing and drinking, enjoying the moment. There were some who were more subdued. Sadie guessed they were probably the casualties - those who hadn't made the grade and would have to re-take their exams. She thought it was sad. She would have hated to be in that position but at the same time, she guessed that they probably hadn't put the work in. No pain, no gain, she thought to herself.

It wasn't long before the consumption of alcohol led to some more raucous behaviour from some of the students. "Come on you lot", one of them shouted. "Let's make some noise!"

Sadie, David and Alan found themselves being dragged up on to the floor, linking arms with their fellow students and singing along with 'We are the Champions' at the top of their voices. This proceeded many more spurious renditions of bawdy rugby songs before the night ended. They had a great time.

Alan had left much earlier complaining of a headache. Too much red wine! Sadie thought. As her and David left to go back to their accommodation. They linked arms and agreed that this had been the happiest day of their lives. They had each other, they had passed their exams. This was just the start of their journey together. They felt truly blessed.

It was Graduation Day. The parents were on their way to Liverpool. They all had hired their gowns and mortarboards and had already had some professional photos taken ahead of the ceremony. They had been told to be ready to enter the main hall of the University at least half an hour before proceedings began.

"I hope my mum and dad are here soon, otherwise I won't be able to speak to them until after the ceremony", said Sadie.

"Mine are here already, and my brother and sister", said Alan. "I spoke to them briefly before they left to get a coffee. I'll see them once it's over".

"I've already told my parents that it will be better if we meet up after the ceremony and that they should go straight to their seats.It will be less stressful", said David. "I don't want them fussing around me, and I know they will".

"You're probably right", agreed Sadie. "I should have told mum and dad to do that too".

"Well, I think they will have to," he said, just as they heard a call for all students to take their places in preparation for entering the grand hall.

As they walked slowly and proudly into the hall, Sadie looked at the rows of seats facing the stage. Some were already occupied. She quickly scanned the seats to see if her parents were already there. She noticed David's parents in the third row. They smiled and gave a subtle wave. The hall was hushed in almost regal silence as the students entered and took their seats. The senior lecturers and members of staff sat quietly on rather uncomfortable looking wooden chairs on the stage. The scene was set.

Once all the guests had arrived, the ceremonies would begin. The students were informed that there would be a number of speeches before they would be asked to come up and receive their degree certificate - or rather a rolled up piece of paper. They had been told that the original certificate would be given to them later in the day.

After the speeches, the graduates names were called out and they were invited up one by one to receive their degrees. Friends and family in the audience clapped and cheered as each graduate received their awards and congratulations from each of the dignitaries on the stage. Sadie glanced across the rows of seats as her name was called out and saw her mum and dad sitting in the row behind David's parents. She noticed that her mum was holding a tissue up to her face. Oh no, she's crying, she thought to herself, as she turned her attentions to accepting her certificate and shaking hands with everyone on the stage.

David and Alan were much further down the list than her, so she had already taken her seat when it was their turn to go on stage. She made sure that they could see and hear her as she enthusiastically joined in with the cheering and clapping as they accepted their degrees.

The whole ceremony lasted about one and a half hours. Sadie felt hot and sticky by the time they were able to leave the hall and greet their family and friends. I'll be glad to get this bloody robe off as soon as all the photos are taken, she thought to herself. After every conceivable pose possible in their graduation robes and the traditional throwing of the mortarboards in the air picture, the photos were done.

"Thank goodness for that", exclaimed Sadie. "I'm so hot. Let's go and look for the parents", she said to David.

Alan had already left them to look for his family. "I'll see you later", he called happily.

Sadie and David found their parents sitting together at one of the many tables that had been put out in the gardens. They were all sipping prosecco and eating the sandwiches which had also been provided as refreshments for the guests.

"Oh there you are, you two", Rob called out. "Come and join us". Everyone seemed to be talking at once. There was so much excitement from all four proud parents. They both went from one to the other being hugged and kissed to within an inch of their lives!

"Thank you everyone", David said breathlessly as his mum finally released him from her grasp. "I think me and Sadie need a proper drink after all that. Right Sadie?"

"Yes please", she said. I think a large gin and tonic is what I need'.

"Yes, and I've got a very cold beer with my name on it waiting for me", he said laughing.

As he went off to the student bar for drinks, Sadie sat down with the parents. "Thank you all for coming. It means a lot to us for you all to be here", she said. They all agreed that it had been a lovely afternoon and continued to wax lyrical about how proud they were of her and David.

"We'll need to get some more photos before you take off your gowns", said Mary. "Oh yes please", added Susan. "I want one to frame that I can put on my sideboard for everyone to see. "We'll get one of just you and David and then one of each of you with your own mum and dad", she said excitedly.

After Sadie and David had finally finished their drinks and had a few sandwiches, the obligatory photos were taken before everyone agreed that it was time to hit the road. Both sets of parents had long journeys to undertake and Sadie and David were exhausted and eager to remove their robes and wear something cooler. The day had been long and very hot but also very successful. It was an occasion that none of them would ever forget.

Later that evening they both reflected on the day and especially on the connection that they noticed had formed between both sets of parents. "I heard my mum and yours exchanging phone numbers", she told David.

"Really", he said. "I wonder what that's all about?" he questioned.

"I've no idea, but they obviously got on very well. Perhaps they just want to keep in touch, especially as we are planning on moving in together. They'll probably be checking in regularly to make sure that we are looking after one another", she laughed.

"Well at least they'll know each other well by the time we get married", added David.

"Married? But you haven't asked me yet", she said coyly.

"Funny you should say that", he answered. With that, he knelt down and produced a small box from the pocket in his shorts.

"Is that what I think it is?", said Sadie, trying to keep the excitement from bubbling up inside her.

"I know that we won't be able to get married for two years, sweetheart. But you know how much I love you so – this is it. Sadie Connel, will you do me the honour of becoming my wife?" She looked at the beautiful white gold ring with a cluster of diamonds sparkling in the light. The excitement of the day and now this, finally caught up with her as tears of joy trickled down her face.

"Of course I will my darling. I love you too – so very much!" He slid the ring on to her finger. It fitted perfectly, and then he swept her into his arms, kissing her passionately. "Right young lady. We need to celebrate", he said.

"Oh no darling, no more partying, it's been a long day. I'm ready for bed now".

"That's exactly what I mean", he said laughing, as, holding hands, they walked quickly towards Sadie's room.

The next morning they woke up on a high from their night of passion. Sadie was still feeling giddy from David's unexpected proposal. She didn't believe that anyone could be this happy as she snuggled into his naked body.

"Good morning sweetheart", David said sleepily. "And good morning to you too, future husband", she said laughing. "I suppose we should get up and face the day. Parents to inform and all that", he said.

"Do you think they will be happy that we've got engaged?" she questioned. "You don't think that they would have preferred we wait a little longer?'.

"To be honest, sweetheart, I don't really care what they think. We love each other. We want to be together for the rest of our lives. That's all that matters to me. I hope they are happy for us, but WE are happy and that's what's important."

After a lazy, long breakfast in bed and lots of coffee, they both decided to call their parents individually and break the news of their engagement.

"We must let Alan know too", said Sadie. Talking of which, I wonder what happened to him yesterday? He said that he would see us later when he left to find his family. But there was no sign of him after that. "I hope he is ok".

"Why wouldn't he be?" questioned David. "He's a big boy, he can take care of himself."

"I know", she said. "But I thought that he was going to introduce us to his family. He talks so much about them."

"They would probably have bored the pants off us anyway", he said sarcastically. Sadie decided not to answer. She didn't like the way that he seemed to continually put Alan down, especially in front of her. She suggested that they meet later after she had spoken to her mum and dad. "Perhaps we can go for a walk. It's such a lovely day."

"Sounds good sweetheart. See you later", he said as he made his way back to his room.

Mary answered her mobile and was pleased to see that it was her daughter calling. "Hi darling. I was hoping you would call today. Have you recovered from all the excitement yesterday?"

"Only just", she answered. "But I have some more exciting news for you and dad."

Mary already had a feeling about what her daughter was going to tell her. She noticed yesterday that her and David seemed closer than ever. She wouldn't deny that she liked David. But there was still something about him that she didn't trust.

"Well I wonder what that can be?" said Mary, desperately hoping that she was wrong.

"David asked me to marry him yesterday evening and - I said yes!" she said, hardly containing her excitement. "He has bought me the most beautiful engagement ring and it actually fits! Oh Mum, I'm so very happy. I hope you and dad will be too?"

Mary beckoned Rob over to listen in on the conversation. "Did you hear what your daughter just said?"

"Yes I did. Congratulations darling. Your mum and I are delighted. Aren't we Mary?"

Mary shook her head vigorously as she looked at Rob, safe in the knowledge that Sadie couldn't see her disappointment. Turning back to her call, she said "Yes darling we are very happy for you. If you're sure that's what you want. You are only twenty remember."

"We won't get married for a couple of years Mum. We both have to get jobs first and David won't be fully qualified for another two years anyway. It's going to be a long engagement, so don't worry you won't have to pay for a wedding just yet", she laughed.

Mary felt uneasy but managed to cover the uncertainty in her voice. She didn't want to burst Sadie's bubble. She was obviously very happy and she loved her so much She wanted to support her, so if that meant putting her own fears to one side, then she would do it for her daughter.

"Mum and dad were thrilled about our news, David", she said when she met up with him later for their walk. "Yes mine too", he said. "They think you are a wonderful girl and that I am a very lucky man", he said proudly.

"Aww that's nice", she said. "I think mum was just a bit concerned that it might be a bit soon but I told her that we won't be getting married for another couple of years and she accepted that."

"Well, it might not be that long," he said. "I might qualify earlier if I work super hard." "Well let's just wait and see", she said .

"In the meantime, why don't we plan our trip to Scotland? I did mention it to mum and dad and they thought it was a great idea for you to see my home country. We could hire a motorhome and then we don't have to worry about accommodation. There are so many lovely places to see, especially up in the Highlands. What do you think?"

"I think that sounds a brilliant idea. There is nothing to stop us going in a couple of days. We'll enquire about the hire of the motorhome, chuck a few clothes in a case and set off." He had driven a van before, so he felt sure that a motorhome wouldn't be that different.

Later that evening they bumped into Alan in the student bar. "Where did you get to yesterday?" Sadie asked him. "We were looking forward to meeting your family."

"Oh they didn't stay long", he answered. "My little sister was hot and very bored, so they set off home more or less as soon as the ceremony was over". He sounded disappointed. Sadie felt very sorry for him. The picture he had painted of a very happy close family who were supposedly very proud of him, didn't seem to exist in reality. They should have been with him, celebrating as a family. All the other students had their friends and families with them right up until the end of the afternoon. He said that, after his parents went home, he had gone back to his room alone and watched the TV until bedtime.

"Oh that's so sad Alan. You should have come and found us. You would have been very welcome to sit with us and our parents. They would have liked to meet you. We've told them all about you", she said smiling broadly.

"That's kind of you to say Sadie but I wasn't feeling great anyway so it was no big deal". She could see that he didn't mean a word of it. David didn't say anything but just listened to their conversation, looking slightly awkward. “By the way”, David said suddenly looking directly at Alan. ‘Me and Sadie are engaged to be married. I proposed last night and she accepted”.

Alan’s expression was one of complete shock as he turned to Sadie and said “Are you sure this is what you want Sadie?” She was taken aback.

“Yes of course. Why woudn’t I? We love each other.”

He said no more. Without even looking at David, he turned on his heels and walked out of the bar.

“Alan”, she called. “Come back, what’s wrong? Please don’t leave. We can talk about this.” David just shrugged his shoulders and turned to her.

“I told you he was weird. Just forget about him. Don’t let him spoil our happiness. We’ll go away on our holiday to Scotland. I’m sure by the time we get back, he’ll be fine. He’s probably still upset about his family not supporting him yesterday. He’ll get over it.”

Sadie wasn’t so sure. There was something really troubling Alan and she didn’t think that it was anything to do with his family.

Chapter 4

Following their trip to Scotland, they arrived back in Liverpool in the middle of August. It had been a holiday they would never forget. They laughed constantly and made love every day. They marvelled at how beautiful the Highlands were. They had seen the most incredible scenery that took their breath away. David loved driving the motorhome and told Sadie that they must do it again one day.

"Once we are settled and we both have jobs, we must definitely do it again", he had said. She agreed. She felt happy and relaxed. She had enjoyed their trip so much and they had got on really well. She couldn't wait for their new life to start in London.

They decided to look for somewhere close to London that they could rent and settled on Chelmsford in Essex. It looked like a nice area with plenty of schools and David said he could easily commute to London from there. He registered interest with several estate agents for a fully furnished flat in the Chelmsford area and Sadie started emailing some of the primary schools to enquire whether they had any vacancies for teachers. She was aware that it was coming up for the new term in September, so it was unlikely that they would be looking for staff now, but decided it was worth a try.

They hadn't seen Alan since David had told him of their engagement, so they headed to his room to see how he was and to tell him of their plans. They knocked on his door but there was no reply. “He’s probably down in the student bar”, David said. “Let’s go. I’m sure he’ll be there.”

They were about to leave when the door next to his opened. “If you are looking for Alan, he’s gone”, said his neighbour. “He packed his stuff and told me that he was going home to his parents. Apparently he is going to work in his Dad’s law firm”, he continued.

“Did he leave a forwarding address? “asked Sadie.

“No, not with me. I didn’t really know him that well. He was a bit of a loner, but they would be able to tell you in the admissions office I’m sure. They keep a record of student’s personal details,” he answered.

“Ok, thanks”, she said . “We’ll go and see them.”

As they walked away, David turned to her and said “If Alan had wanted us to know that he was going home, then he would have told us and he would have given us the address. He has my mobile number and he hasn’t attempted to call or message, so I guess that says it all. I don’t think we should try and find out his parent’s address. If he wants to contact us then he will. We’ve got enough to think about at the moment. Let’s just concentrate on our future and let Alan get on with his”, he said slightly impatiently.

She nodded but felt uneasy. Alan had obviously been upset by the news that her and David were engaged. She was fond of Alan and had hoped that they could all continue to be friends after University. She didn’t know what to think but David was right, they had a lot to deal with at the moment. Hopefully, Alan would get in touch with David once he was settled back at home.

The next few weeks were a whirlwind. They managed to find a lovely two bedroomed flat in Chelmer Village which was a bus ride away from Chelmsford. David had already done a recce and was happy that the journey to London was doable. He also followed up with his previous contact with the Corporate Law firm and arranged an interview.

Luckily the flat was available immediately, so they began the painstaking task of packing everything from their student accommodation into boxes and black bags. David hired a van to take all their belongings and various pot plants. They were amazed at just how much stuff they had accrued over the last three years! On the final day, Sadie had to confess to feeling a bit emotional. She had loved her time at University. She was going to miss the familiarity of her daily routine. She was going to miss the city. She was going to miss it all.

David wasn't quite so sentimental. He felt ready for the next chapter in their lives. He had enjoyed University life but it was time to move on. As they drove off in the van with the contents of their lives shifting around in the back, he didn't spare a backward glance. Sadie, on the other hand, felt herself struggling to hold back the tears. She told herself not to be so silly. She had her whole life in front of her and the future looked good. She was going to marry the love of her life and he would take care of her. She knew that with certainty, so why was she feeling apprehensive?

She dismissed her negative thoughts and reached across and squeezed David's hand "It's exciting isn't it darling? Our first home together. I can't wait." He smiled and squeezed her hand back. "It's going to be awesome sweetheart."

They arrived in Chelmsford quicker than they had expected and made their way to the estate agents to pick up the key for their flat. The estate agent ran through the details of the rental agreement and after they had signed on the dotted line and received directions, they set off to Chelmer Village. They were really impressed by how pretty the village looked as they drove in. The flat was easy to find. It was in a quiet cul de sac on the first floor and it had a pretty little balcony overlooking the gardens at the front.

"Oh David, it looks perfect", said Sadie excitedly.

"It certainly does sweetheart. I think we've cracked it here and the rent is really affordable too. I've got a good feeling that everything is going to turn out alright for us. Let's get inside".

As they entered the front door, they were surprised at how big the lounge was. It was open plan to the kitchen which had lots of fitted cupboards, a washing machine and a dishwasher. It was separated from the lounge area with a huge island which had six high backed stools around it. Just off the hall there were two double bedrooms and a lovely bathroom with a walk in shower.

"Blimey, I didn't expect it to be quite as nice as this", he said . "This will be fine for us until we can afford to buy our own place."

"That could be a while, added Sadie. "I've got to find a job and you won't be earning much for the next couple of years until you are fully qualified. But, as you say, this is perfect until then and the village looks nice too."

Once they were reasonably settled and most of their boxes had been unpacked, Sadie checked her emails to see if she had any replies from any of the schools she had written to. Most of them had replied and, as she expected, they said that they were fully staffed, thanked her for her interest and wished her well for the future.

As she opened the last one, already deciding that it would be another rejection, she was pleased to see that it wasn't an absolute 'no'. It had been written by the secretary to the Head Teacher at a primary school in Chelmsford and whilst the school was fully staffed at the moment, they informed her that there would be a vacancy for a teacher to take the reception class at the start of the next new term in January. The email requested that Sadie contact the school to discuss this further.

She was delighted and called out to David who was busy re-arranging furniture in the lounge. "David, I've had an email from this primary school in Chelmsford. They are looking for a teacher to start in January and they have asked me to contact them." "That's brilliant, sweetheart. No chance of anything in September though?"

"No they are fully staffed but they want to see me so let's wait and see. I'll call them in the morning and find out a bit more," she said.

She felt excited and couldn't wait to tell her mum. "I'm just going to ring mum David. I was going to anyway, just to let her know that we've arrived safely and that we're settling in. She'll be thrilled to hear that I may have a job too."

"I'd better contact my folks too", he answered. "I promised that I'd let them know once we had moved in."

Mary had just got in from work as her daughter rang. "Hi darling, have you arrived? Is the flat nice? Is everything ok?

"One thing at a time Mum", she said laughing. "Yes, yes and yes. Everything is fantastic. The flat is fabulous, much nicer than we imagined and it's in a lovely village. I'm sure we are going to be very happy here", she added.

"Oh that's good, I've been thinking about you all day."

"I've got some more news too Mum. I've had an email from a primary school in Chelmsford that I wrote to and they want to see me. I'm going to ring them tomorrow. They haven't got a vacancy yet but there will be one in January and it's for the reception class which is what I wanted."

"Really, darling – that's fantastic. You will let me know what they say after you've spoken to them won't you?" she said excitedly. "Wait until I tell your dad. He's not home yet. He will be so pleased for you. How is David?" Mary asked.

"He's fine. He has got an interview with a law firm in London next week and that sounds very promising. We can't believe how everything is falling into place for us Mum. It's so exciting."

Mary agreed. She was so pleased that both her and David had the promise of work on the horizon. Hopefully they would be able to save some money for a deposit for their own home in a couple of years. Her and Rob had already discussed the possibility of helping them out financially when the time was right. She would talk about it with Susan at some point, she decided. She didn't want to tread on her and Colin's toes if it was something they had considered too.

David's parents were also delighted to hear their news when he rang them later that evening and had wished both him and Sadie good luck for their upcoming interviews. As the light faded and darkness fell, Sadie realised just how exhausted she felt. It had been a tiring day.

"I'm ready for bed David. We can crack on again in the morning."
"Yes, I was thinking the same thing", he said. "Let's go and try that new bed out", he said laughing.

"Not tonight Josephine", she giggled. I'm going to bed to sleep. I'm afraid anything else is off the menu!" They both laughed and hugged each other.

"I love you so much my funny girl," he said .

The next morning, Sadie awoke with renewed energy. The bed turned out to be very comfortable and they both slept soundly.

"We need to get some food in", she said. "Yes, I thought about that. Let's do an online shop until we sort out where the local supermarket is", said David. "I think ultimately we are going to have to buy a little car to get around."

"Can we afford it?" she asked.

"I've got a few thousand pounds in my savings account. It won't buy us a Porsche but I'm sure we can find a little runaround to suit us. Once I start working in London, I'll be fine getting a bus to the station in Chelmsford, but you'll need a car to travel to your school, sweetheart", he added.

"Well, I haven't got the job yet but yes, you're right, I will need transport I suppose.

Later that morning, Sadie telephoned the Head Teacher's secretary. She felt nervous and a little apprehensive as the phone was answered. "Hill Park Primary School. How can I help you?" said a very officious voice at the end of the line. "

"Oh, hello, is that the Head Teacher's secretary?" Sadie asked. "Yes it is, who is it calling?"

"My name is Sadie Connel. You very kindly answered my email a couple of weeks ago when I was enquiring if you had any vacancies for a teacher."

"Oh yes, I remember. Hello Sadie. Is it ok if I call you Sadie?" she asked kindly. "

"Yes of course," said Sadie, feeling pleased that she was sounding less terrifying. The Head Teacher, Mrs Wendy Marshall, has asked me to arrange an interview for you. Is that ok?"

"Yes, that's great. When can I come in and see her?" Sadie asked. "She has space tomorrow in the afternoon. Is that too short notice for you?" the secretary enquired.

"No that's absolutely fine", she answered, already panicking at how she was going to get there.

"Shall we say 2pm?"

"2pm it is then" Sadie answered. "Thank you very much. I'll look forward to it."

She ended the call with her head spinning. Tomorrow! What was she going to wear? How would she get there? I'll have to find out if the school is on a bus route and I need to go and find something suitable in my wardrobe, she thought.

David was busy putting all the shopping away that they had bought on line when she entered the kitchen. "Guess what?' I've got an interview tomorrow at Hill Park Primary School" she said hardly able to contain her excitement. "I'm just going to see if it's on a bus route."

"I'm sure it will be", David answered, smiling at her lovely face flushed with happiness. "Once I've sorted this shopping out, we'll look together. Don't worry, if needs be you can get a taxi. One way or another we'll get you there darling. I'm so happy for you."

To Sadie's relief when they looked into it, the school was easy to find and there was a bus that left down the road and stopped right outside the school. She had already chosen a two piece suit in navy blue that she decided to wear with a white blouse. She'd had it ages and had been tempted many times to take it to a charity shop but something made her hang on to it. This was obviously the occasion she thought!

The next morning she spent time preparing for her interview. She did some research on the school so that she was prepared for any questions that she may be asked. She discovered that the latest Ofsted rating on the school was superb and their website was informative and comprehensive. Sadie was encouraged to see that the school seemed innovative in providing a wide variety of subjects including music, sports and even outdoor classrooms. She had always felt passionate about giving kids the best possible access to as many opportunities to learn in the early years of their education, and this school seemed to have it all.

After saying goodbye to David, she set off to catch the bus. She was nervous but felt confident that she was prepared for her interview. Sure enough the bus route was direct and the bus stopped just a short distance from the school. She quickly found the secretary's office and knocked gingerly on the door. "Come in", a voice called.

"Good afternoon, I'm Sadie Connel. I've come to see Mrs Marshall for an interview", she said to the very smart, smiling woman behind the desk.

"Hello Sadie, I'm Mrs Marshall's secretary. We spoke yesterday. Please come this way." She followed her into a small office where the Head Teacher was sitting waiting. She got up straight away and shook her hand gesturing for her to sit down opposite her. "I'm pleased to meet you Sadie', she said kindly. "Thank you for coming."

"Well, thank you for seeing me. I was delighted to hear from you." She thought Mrs Marshall looked kind and almost motherly. She proceeded to explain that one of her reception class teachers was leaving at the end of the next term and that they would need to replace her. She had seen Sadie's email and read her CV and was very impressed with her education history.

"I see that you obtained a first class Batchelor of Arts degree, Sadie. That's very impressive. You must have worked very hard indeed."

"Yes, I did, thank you. I've always wanted to teach. My parents are both teachers, so I guess it's in the genes," she laughed. "I especially want to teach reception. I think that small children are like little sponges, eager to soak up everything around them and, I'm sure that to have the privilege to teach them right at the beginning of their education journey would be so rewarding."

"Well said, Sadie! "answered Mrs Marshall. That's exactly what I believe and I would expect nothing less from my teaching staff. You sound the ideal candidate for the job. I admire your attitude and you certainly have the right qualifications for teaching. What I am going to put to you is this – If I offer you the position, would you be able to start after half term in October? That way you can work alongside

Miss Bennet, the current teacher, and be eased in gently. It will also be good for the children to meet you ahead of the new term. How would you feel about that?"

"That would be fantastic," she answered, trying to hide her obvious excitement. "I'm not working anywhere else so I'm available any time. Half term will suit me fine." After chatting generally about the school and Sadie asking a few pertinent questions about the curriculum, Mrs Marshall said that she would be in touch within the next four weeks to finalise details regarding the contract of employment etc. Sadie shook her hand once again and thanked her for her time. She walked from the office smiling like the cat who got the cream. The teaching job sounded perfect for her and she really liked what she had seen of the school. She couldn't wait to get home and let David and her parents know the good news.

"I'm home darling," she called out as she entered the flat. David appeared from the kitchen looking disheveled and wearing rubber gloves.

"We've had a leak under the kitchen sink. I think I've fixed it now but I could have done without it," he said, obviously annoyed. "I really wanted to spend time this afternoon preparing for my interview. I've only got a couple of more days until I go up to London." Sadie wondered for a moment whether he had forgotten about her interview.

"Oh I'm sorry, sweetheart I didn't ask you how it went at the school", he said finally.

"Yes I was beginning to wonder", she answered a little sulkily. "It went very well. I've been offered a position teaching one of the reception classes for the January term but the Head Teacher wants me to start after October half term so that I can be introduced slowly and the children get to know me. The present teacher is leaving at Christmas so I will be replacing her," she said.

"That sounds amazing Sadie. If I get offered a job too, then we can start earning some money at last. I told you everything would work out well didn't I ?"

He walked towards her and took her in his arms and told her how proud he was of her. He had said all the right things, so she didn't know why, but she felt a bit deflated. Was he as excited for her as he was making out to be? Sometimes she was aware that he could be a little bit selfish and that everything was all about him. Oh it's probably me being a bit sensitive she thought to herself.

As predicted, her mum and dad were over the moon when she phoned them with her news. She held the phone away from her ear as they whooped and cheered and exclaimed at how clever she was.

Sadie had always appreciated her parents. They had showered her with love all her life and continually encouraged her to follow her dreams. She hoped that, one day, her and David would be as good at parenting their own children as her Mum and Dad had been in caring for her.

She did wonder about the future. Would they have children? Would they always be as happy as they were now? Would her dreams for the future be fulfilled? So many questions were whirling round in her head. She didn't have the answers but she was determined to live life to the full and do everything possible to make those dreams come true.

Chapter 5

It was the third week in October. David had been working as a trainee solicitor with the law firm in London for two weeks. At his interview, they had been impressed with his qualifications and his motivation and agreed that he could work with them for three days a week whilst he studied for his Legal Practice Course. David told them that he was really keen to specialise in Corporate Law so they were happy for him to be involved with some of the more straightforward cases as part of his training. Sadie had never seen him quite so happy. He was absolutely loving his job and seemed to be handling the extra studies on his non working days with ease.

He told her that he was determined to complete his course ahead of the predicted two year time frame. He was out to impress his employers and aimed to be fully qualified and handling his own cases by then.

Sadie was impressed by his determination and didn't want to dampen his enthusiasm but she secretly doubted the reality of his aspirations. There was still a long road ahead and there was always the possibility that he might not make the grade or he may even change direction. He had always been fixed on the idea of Corporate Law, but she questioned whether it would be the right choice for him. She hoped that her concerns were unfounded for his sake. Meanwhile, she was looking forward to her first day working at the school. She had already spent an afternoon there and had met the rest of the teaching staff. They had all greeted her warmly and made her feel welcome. She had been given a tour of the school so that she knew roughly where everything was and had met some of the children.

She was pleased that the school was an advocate for school uniforms and thought how smart all the children looked in their red sweaters and grey trousers and skirts with white shirts and matching red and grey striped ties.

She had also met Miss Bennett who she would be replacing next term. Her first name was Laura and she told Sadie that she was leaving to get married. Her fiancé had been offered a job in Germany so they were moving there permanently. Sadie thought they would work well together. Laura seemed to share the same ideas as she did and they were of a similar age.

"On your first day I'll introduce you to the class and I'll tell them that you are going to be their new teacher," Laura had said. "They don't know that I am leaving yet. I think some of them might be a bit upset so if they know that you are replacing me and they see how nice you are, it will soften the blow. These little ones do tend to get attached to you. Obviously there has to be boundaries and they have to be shown that you are there to teach them and you are not their mummy, but it's difficult. They are so young and dependent on you. It's hard for us as teachers too. You can't help but get attached to them."

"I can understand that," answered Sadie. "I am sure I would feel the same in your position. But don't worry I will look after your little class for you and I will do my very best to be as good a teacher as you have been." Laura smiled and thanked Sadie for her kind words. Before she left, they agreed to meet an hour before school started on her first morning and go through the lessons for the week together.

On the morning of her first day, she kissed David goodbye. It was one of his study days so he was working at home. "Wish me luck," she said as she hugged him.

"You'll smash it sweetheart. I don't doubt it," he said. "I'm sorry that you have got to get the bus again" he added. "I've seen a little car that will be ideal for you. I was going to tell you tonight and I thought we could go and look at it together. It's on the forecourt of the garage in the village. It's a Fiat and although it's quite old, it hasn't done many miles and it's in great condition."

"Can we afford it?" she asked. "Yes, just about, and anyway you need to have a car," he said. "You get off and have a great day and we'll go and look at it later."

She felt quite excited at the prospect of having her own car. She had to admit that it was a bit of a pain having to wait for buses all the time and it would give her some independence.

Her first day at the school was everything she hoped it would be. She had met with Laura before class and together they had planned the lessons for the coming week. When Laura told the class that she was leaving at the end of term, some of the children looked really sad. One or two of them started to cry softly. Sadie stood at the front of the class and told them not to be sad. She said that Miss Bennett was going to get married and was looking forward to an exciting new life.

She told them that she was going to be their new teacher and that they would be having fun and learning new things every day. Soon the children were chattering excitedly about the prospect of having a new teacher and, after encouragement from Laura, they said perfectly in unison -"Welcome Miss Connel and thank you for being our new teacher." Sadie thought it was very sweet as she fought to keep the tears from her eyes.

By the end of the day, she had learned most of the children's names and had already noticed those who were going to be more receptive to learning. She couldn't wait to work with all of them and show them how much fun their lessons were going to be. They're going to be my little sponges! she thought happily to herself.

David was waiting eagerly at home to hear how she had got on. "It was amazing David. The kids were absolutely lovely and although they were a bit upset at first when they knew Laura was leaving, they soon cheered up and I think they really liked me."

"Why wouldn't they?" he answered. "You are going to be an amazing teacher and I'm going to be the best lawyer in London. "We're the dream team!", he laughed. "Now, let's go and buy you that car."

Sadie loved the little car as soon as she saw it. As David had said, it was absolutely immaculate and had only forty thousand miles on the clock. The man at the garage said she could have a test drive if she wanted but David had spent half an hour looking over it inside and out and he was satisfied that it was good to go. It also had a year's MOT and had recently had new tyres. With a bit of haggling, he managed to knock the price down by two hundred pounds which was an extra bonus. He shook hands on the deal and said to the man in the garage. "We'll get it taxed and sort out the insurance and pick it up tomorrow, if that's ok?"

"Fine by me", said the man. "I'll take it off the forecourt and park it round the back in case anyone else shows any interest in it."

Sadie went home on a high. She couldn't believe that David had spent his savings on buying her a car. "Thank you so much darling," she said squeezing his hand. "It's going to give me my independence. I can do the shopping myself – no more on-line orders and I'll be able to drive to and from the school without waiting at draughty bus stops. I'm such a lucky girl."

"You are more than welcome sweetheart and I'll be able to drive it sometimes too, won't I?" he said laughing.

"I'll think about it!" she said.

The next day after school, they made their way to the garage to pick up the car. They were delighted to see that it had been washed and polished ready for them to take away. David paid the man in the garage with his debit card and thanked him for washing the car. "All part of the service sir", he answered.

"Right Miss Connel, you're in the driving seat", said David as he opened the door for her to get in.

"It's been ages since I last drove. I hope I haven't forgotten how to do it," she said nervously.

"It's like riding a bike, you never forget," he said. She pulled away from the garage with a jerk but once she had got used to the gears and the feel of the steering, she felt much more confident.

"Well done", said David as they pulled up outside the flat. "You drove very well." "Thank you darling and thank you again for my lovely little car. I couldn't be happier if it was a Porsche," she laughed.

"One day it will be! One day, sweetheart", he answered.

Sadie couldn't believe how much easier her life was now that she had a car. She didn't need to leave for work so early and it meant that she was able to take anything in that she needed for the class without having to carry heavy bags. She was loving her job and the children really seemed to be responding to her.She planned to introduce games that helped them to use their imagination and encourage resourcefulness. For one of the games she thought of arranging the children into small groups, asking them to decorate a large cardboard box with paints and materials to create their own den or fairy castle. She knew that kids loved the competitiveness of team games and would enjoy the opportunity of winning the task.

Laura was very impressed with Sadie's teaching skills. She didn't really want to leave the school but she knew that Sadie was going to do a great job of taking over her class. She would enjoy the last few weeks that she had left safe in the knowledge that the children would be in good hands.

Sadie thought she had met all of the other teachers but one day, in the staff room, Peter, one of the 2nd year teachers, introduced her to Lisa who taught one of the first year classes. Lisa explained that she had been off sick for six weeks so her class had been taken by a supply teacher.

"It's lovely to meet you Sadie. I understand that you are taking over the reception class from Laura", she said.

Sadie noticed how very pretty Lisa was. She had beautiful brown eyes and jet black hair down to her shoulders. She wondered how old she was. It was difficult to tell. "This is a great school. I'm sure you will be very happy here", said Lisa. 'Oh, I already am", she answered. "The kids are great and the staff are lovely. They have made me feel so welcome."

"Yes, they are a lovely bunch", Lisa said. "I wouldn't want to work anywhere else."

"How long have you been here?" Sadie asked.

"I was probably your age -twenty?" she said.

"I'm nearly twenty one" said Sadie.

"I'm twenty four so, yes about four years now", said Lisa.

They continued chatting happily whilst they had their lunch break. Sadie was surprised how naturally the conversation flowed between them. She felt that she had known her for ages. She hadn't made many close friends at university so It was lovely to find someone that she felt she could talk to so easily.

Lisa was nice. She seemed really interested to hear about Sadie's life. How she had always dreamt of being a teacher, her life growing up in Scotland as a child and how she had met David.

"Do you have a boyfriend?" Sadie asked.

"Yes I do. His name is Mark and he's an accountant. We met at a bar in Chelmsford two years ago and we moved in together six months after that. It was a bit of a whirlwind romance," said Lisa."We keep talking about getting engaged but it hasn't happened yet. I actually don't know what I would do without him. I haven't really got any family - a few distant cousins and a brother who lives in Australia, but I don't hear from him.

We were never really close. Both my parents were killed in a motorbike accident the first year that I was at Uni. They had always been keen bikers from the day they first met and had never had an accident before, but on this one day, they were hit head on by a lorry that had a blow out and careered into them. The only comfort I have, is that they were killed instantly. They wouldn't have known anything about it."

"Oh Lisa, that is awful. I'm so sorry. I can't imagine how terrible that was for you to lose both parents together in such a tragic way" said Sadie.

"Thank you, yes it was really hard, especially as I had just started at Uni. I nearly gave up on continuing with my studies but I thought how proud mum and dad would be of me if I got my degree, so I did it for them."

"That was a really brave thing to do" said Sadie. "I'm not sure that I could have done it. I really admire you. I'm sure your parents would be very proud of you."

She didn't really know what else to say. She felt really moved by Lisa's story and was tempted to throw her arms around her but, she had to remind herself that she had only just met her. Perhaps she would be embarrassed by such an outward show of affection from someone she barely knew. After chatting for a few more minutes,

Sadie glanced up at the clock and was surprised to see that it was time for her to go back to her class.

"I'd better get back now", she said. "It's been lovely talking to you Lisa. Perhaps I'll see you tomorrow at lunchtime and we can carry on where we left off," she laughed.

"I'll look forward to it", she said. Have a good afternoon!"

Sadie told David all about her meeting with Lisa when she got home. "I feel like I've made a really good friend, David. She is such a nice girl. I'm sure you would like her too. Her boyfriend is an accountant and they live together in a flat in Chelmsford - so not far away." Perhaps when I get to know her a little better, I could invite them both round for dinner one evening. It will be good for both of us to make some new friends. What do you think?" she asked.

"Yes, sounds good, sweetheart. Oh and by the way", he added. "Guess who rang me at work today?"

"I've no idea", she answered. She wasn't ready for the answer he gave her and sat with her mouth open in surprise as he said - "Alan."

"Oh at last. I'm so happy that he contacted you. I often think about him. How is he?"

"He sounded fine. He has left home. It didn't work out for him working with his dad. He also realised that he wants to specialise in Criminal Law so he has got a similar position as I have in London.

"Really? I'm very surprised. I thought that he was dead set on working for his dad's firm. He spoke about it all the time."

"I know he did but I did tell you right from the beginning that a lot of that was him bragging. I think the truth of it is that he didn't really get on with his parents. Look how they behaved at his graduation. Leaving early the way they did. If they were as close as he said they were, they wouldn't have done that."

"I agree. I felt really sorry for him that day. Poor Alan, how did you leave it with him?"

"He wants to come and see us. He's got a studio flat in London but he said it's tiny - not enough room to swing a cat apparently."

"Yes of course he can come and see us. I hope you told him that?"

"I said I would speak to you first, but yes, of course I did," he answered.

Before they went to bed that night, he agreed with Sadie that he would ring Alan the next day and invite him down to spend the weekend with them.

She met with Lisa for lunch the next day and found herself telling her all about Alan. How David had befriended him as a first year student and then seemed to withdraw from him after he met her. She felt comfortable sharing her thoughts with Lisa. She was a good listener and like her, she thought it was strange how David's attitude towards Alan changed so drastically.

"He told me that Alan was a show off and became a bit clingy and dependent on him and that's why he didn't want to continue the friendship," explained Sadie. "The strange thing is I didn't get that impression of him at all. I found him to be kind and caring. I really liked him. Anyway, the good news is that he has been in touch with David recently and he is coming to see us. I'm so pleased. He has always seemed a bit of loner and, apart from us, he doesn't seem to have any other friends."

"What a shame, poor guy," said Lisa. He sounds a really nice person. David should be happy that he has such a good friend. They are hard to find these days," she said.

Sadie noticed how sad she looked as she said that and wondered if she had been hurt by a friend in the past.

"I don't think I will ever fully understand what makes a man tick," she said unexpectedly. "Mark knows I love him. I'm always telling him but he is so insecure. He worries if I'm not home at the same time every evening. He wants to know where I am and who I'm with. He even questions what I am wearing."

Sadie suddenly felt concerned. She thought that Mark sounded a bit controlling and that wasn't healthy. "Are you sure that you're alright?" she asked Lisa. He shouldn't really be telling you what to do."

Lisa suddenly brightened and looked directly at Sadie.

"Oh it's not like that. He just cares that's all. I've got used to his funny ways. It's fine. We are very happy."

Sadie wasn't so sure that she was being completely truthful but decided not to press her anymore on the subject. She hardly knew her after all. She wasn't in any position to pass judgment on her relationship.

Lisa never spoke about her relationship with Mark again. They continued to meet for lunch every day. They were becoming really good friends and would spend ages chatting but never about Mark.

"How did your weekend go with Alan?" Lisa asked. "Oh he didn't come after all. He said that something had come up and he couldn't make it. David was working anyway so it was probably for the best. We've re-arranged for next weekend."

"We're going away next weekend too", said Lisa. "It's Mark's birthday so we've booked a little cottage in Suffolk. We're having a romantic weekend, just the two of us."

"That sounds lovely. It will make a nice break. The kids here are lovely, but they are a bit full on aren't they?", she laughed.

"They certainly are but for me it's the best job in the world," said Lisa.

"I couldn't agree more." said Sadie. "I've only got a couple of more weeks until I take over from Laura then the little darlings will be entirely in my hands, and then they had better watch out!"

They both laughed knowing that was going to be far from the

truth. Sadie loved the little ones in her class and couldn't wait to be their full time teacher.

As he promised, Alan arrived at their flat the following weekend. They assumed that he would be coming on the train but he turned up in a posh car that he said his dad had bought him as a graduation present. Sadie was so pleased to see him and thought that he looked really well and seemed different somehow. He looked smart and had his hair cut in a modern style.

She had always thought of him as a bit of a geek - in the nicest possible way. But for the first time, she noticed that he was actually very good looking.

Alan hugged her closely and shook David's hand. "Thank you for inviting me guys. It's so good to see you after all this time," he said cheerfully.

"You too Alan. We've missed you," said Sadie.

David nodded in agreement but didn't say anything. "Let's crack open a bottle to celebrate," she said. David looked surprised. "It's a bit early for that isn't it?" he said.

"It's never too early. We haven't seen Alan for a while. I'm sure he has lots to tell us. Haven't you Alan?"

"Yes, it will be great to catch up with you both," he answered.

Whilst David went to the fridge for a bottle of wine, she invited Alan to sit down. "Your flat is lovely Sadie. So neat and tidy and it's big isn't it? My place is like a rabbit hutch but living in London that's all I can afford for the time being. The good thing is that it's a bus ride away from where I work, so I guess it's a good trade off."

"Tell me", she questioned. "What happened between you and your dad? I thought you were going to work in his Law firm?"

"I was, and I did for a while," he answered. "But we fell out. I told him that I wanted to specialise in Criminal Law and not Family Law which is what he wanted me to do. He didn't agree with that and he gave me such a hard time that I decided to leave.

I haven't been entirely honest with you and David about my parents. I know I created this picture of us being this happy and close family, but it just isn't true. I was never quite good enough for my dad, both socially and in the workplace. Because I didn't conform to his ideal of how his son should be, he treated me like a second rate citizen. Mum wasn't much better. She walks in dad's shadow. I think deep down she is afraid of him and won't do anything to cross him. He bought me the car and gave me a few thousand pounds and watched me pack my bags and leave. He seemed to be relieved that I was going."

"Oh Alan, that's terrible. I'm so sorry that you have been treated this way - and by your own family. It's unforgivable," she said sadly. "I thought it was strange that they didn't stay long for your graduation. They should have shown you how proud they were of you and celebrated with you, just as the other families did with their kids. They don't deserve you Alan. You are clever and you are a lovely guy. It's their loss."

She was suddenly feeling really annoyed and mindful of how lucky her and David were to have such loving, caring parents. David entered the room with the wine and some glasses on a tray. He had heard some of the conversation, but decided not to mention it. Instead he suggested that they enjoy their drink and then go for a walk around the village.

"How about we go to the local pub for lunch after our walk sweetheart", he said to Sadie. He turned to Alan. "You'll like it in there Alan, the food is great." Alan smiled. "Sounds good to me," he said.

The weekend passed quickly. Sadie really enjoyed Alan's company and as he was leaving on Sunday afternoon, she urged him to visit again soon. David had been very pleasant and polite during his visit but she was aware, once again, that he was distancing himself from their friend. After he had left she decided to speak to him about it.

"Did you enjoy seeing Alan again", she asked. "He seemed different. Much happier in his own skin somehow. Did you think so too?"

"I guess so, yes", he answered. "It's probably because he has broken away from that family of his at last."

"Did you hear the conversation I had with him when he first arrived. You were in the kitchen getting the drinks, but I wondered if you had picked up on any of it?" she said.

"Yes I heard some of it but I chose not to mention it. I don't really want to get involved in his family dynamics," he answered.

"But he is our friend David. I'm sure he would have liked you to show him some support."

"Sadie I don't want to discuss this anymore," he said crossly. "Alan has his life and we have ours. He needs to sort out his own problems and it sounds like he is on the right track anyway. He's enjoying living in London and he's loving his job. You don't need to worry about him."

She was taken aback by his response and felt like she had touched a nerve. She chose to walk away from what could have been a potential argument and went into the kitchen to prepare dinner. She only saw this side of him when Alan was around.It puzzled her but she decided to let it drop. They were in love and very happy. She didn't want anything to spoil that.

Chapter 6

It was three weeks before Christmas. Sadie and David had discussed how they would celebrate it as well as her 21st which was the day after Boxing Day. They agreed that it would be nice to invite both sets of parents for Christmas.

"David, Why don't you ring your mum and dad and ask them if they would like to come. Tell them that they can have our room and my mum and dad can go in the spare room. We'll be ok on the sofa bed in the lounge, won't we?", she asked.

"Yes of course, it will be kind of romantic".

"Not with the parents next door it won't!" she said laughing.

When she rang, she was surprised when her dad answered. "Hello love, it's good to hear from you. Your mum was going to ring you soon to see what you were thinking of doing for your 21st?" he said.

"Actually I'm ringing about Christmas, Dad. David and I would like you to join us and his parents at our place for Christmas."

"That sounds nice love, but will you have room for us all? Wouldn't it be better if you came up here? We've got more space than you. David's parents would be welcome too."

"I suppose we could", she answered. "Let me speak to David about it. He will have to check with his parents too."

"Of course, think about it and give us a call back. You can speak to your mum then. She's out shopping at the moment."

"Thanks Dad. I will."

When she spoke to David he agreed that it would probably be better to go to her parents despite the long journey up to Scotland. They didn't really have enough room in their flat. It would have been a bit of a squash in their small kitchen cooking a Christmas dinner for six people.

He was quite surprised when his mum said that her and his dad would love to join them all.

"That sounds lovely David", said Susan. "Your dad and I were just going to have a quiet one here. I really liked Sadie's parents when we met them. I'm sure we will all have a nice time together. I've got Mary's phone number. I'll give her a call and find out what we can bring for the dinner. I'm not going empty handed", she added.

Sadie rang her mum later to check that she was happy about them all going for Christmas and that it hadn't just been her dad getting carried away. She assured her that she was delighted they were going and that she didn't want them to bring anything other than themselves.

"Well, Susan is insistent apparently", said Sadie. She told David that she is going to ring you to find out what she can do to help, so be prepared! she laughed.

"Now what about your 21st?" said David later that evening. "We've got to celebrate the big birthday. "You didn't celebrate yours", she said. "All we did was go out for dinner, so that will be enough for me too. We could invite Lisa and her partner Mark, and we can ask Alan too," she said excitedly.

"Are you sure. Don't you want a party or a trip up to London to see a show – something special?" he asked.

"No, it's kind of you darling but I would much prefer a quiet evening with our friends. I know that you haven't met Lisa and Mark yet. I haven't met Mark either but he sounds quite a nice guy and Lisa is lovely. We could go to a posh restaurant. I'd enjoy that much more than a party and anyway who would we invite? We don't know enough people," she said laughing. "I'll speak to Lisa about it at work tomorrow and take it from there."

The next day at school, Laura spoke to the children in the class and reminded them that she would be leaving to get married and moving to Germany at the end of term. "Miss Connel will be taking over from me and I want you to be good boys and girls and make her feel welcome. She has some great lessons planned for you next year. You're going to have the best fun with her." she told them.

Sadie was going to miss Laura but she felt really excited knowing that she would be having sole responsibility for teaching the children from next term. She had been working on lots of different ideas for lessons to stimulate and motivate them. She wanted them to enjoy coming to school and learning new things. It was a challenge that she looked forward to. She met Lisa as usual at lunchtime and told her about her plans for her 21st. "We're going up to my parents in Scotland for Christmas but we will be home for my birthday, the day after Boxing Day. I wondered if you and Mark would like to join us for dinner at a nice restaurant in Chelmsford? I don't know which one. We don't really know many restaurants in town but we'll do some research on line and see which ones are recommended."

"That sounds great", answered Lisa. "We would love to join you. It's a special occasion, and I think it's about time that our other halves met each other don't you?" she said.

"I was also going to ask you how you feel about having a girly day out shopping after we break up. I want to get a new dress for Christmas and something that I can wear for my birthday. It's been ages since I went shopping. I can't remember the last time I bought anything new."

"I'd love to," said Lisa. I just need to check that Mark hasn't got anything else planned first."

Sadie felt rather puzzled. She hadn't mentioned any particular day. So why would she need to check with Mark, she wondered.

"I was thinking of the Saturday after we break up if that sounds ok?" she said. "We could make a day of it and have lunch out."

"I'll let you know tomorrow but that sounds good. I do really want to come," she said. Sadie thought that she seemed a bit reluctant to commit and felt it was strange that she would need to speak to Mark first. David never minded her going out on her own. In fact he encouraged it. It gave him the opportunity to study quietly at home without her chattering or the radio blaring!

She spoke to him about it later and told him how strangely Lisa reacted when she asked her to go out shopping with her. "It does seem a bit odd", he agreed. "Perhaps Mark likes to have her all to himself when they're not working at weekends".

"I don't think it's that, because to begin with, I didn't mention a particular day. I just hope he is not one of those control freaks. There are other things she has said about him which makes me think he could be."

She felt concerned about her friend and hoped that she was wrong in her assumptions. She would wait and see what Lisa said tomorrow.

The next day she met with her in the staff room as usual. After they had exchanged their news from the morning classes, Sadie asked her if she had thought anymore about their proposed shopping trip.

"Oh yes, sorry I nearly forgot", she said. "Mark is quite happy for me to go out shopping with you but I will need to be home by 5pm at the latest if that's ok? We usually sit down to eat at about 6pm and he does like to have his dinner on time." she laughed rather awkwardly.

"He is a bit of a stickler isn't he?" said Sadie. Once again, she felt a little uneasy. This man definitely seemed to be controlling Lisa. She didn't like the sound of him and wondered if she had made a mistake in inviting him to her 21st celebration.

"I also spoke to him about your birthday meal and he told me to thank you very much for inviting us. We would love to come. He can recommend a lovely restaurant that he takes his clients to sometimes if you would like to have the details," Lisa added.

"That's great, I'm glad you're going to come. David is looking forward to meeting you both and it will be good to meet Mark too," she said. Let me know the details of that restaurant and I'll ask David to give them a call."

She went back to the classroom deep in thought about her friend. On the one hand she seemed really happy in her relationship and Mark obviously loved her very much but he was clearly manipulating her to some extent. She just hoped that there wasn't more to it and that Lisa really was ok.

Later that evening, she asked David if he had contacted Alan to invite him out for the meal on her birthday.

"Yes I rang him", he said "but he doesn't think he will be able to come. It sounds like he's got a date. He just said that he had already arranged to go to the theatre with a friend that evening. He was really sorry and said to thank you very much for inviting him."

"On a date!" exclaimed Sadie. "Well that's a turn up for the books. I didn't know he had a girlfriend - good for him!"

She was disappointed but also pleased to hear that Alan was obviously coming out of his shell if he had started dating. "I told you that he seemed different when we saw him that weekend didn't I?" she said. "He was more self assured and happier than he ever was at Uni."

"He just said it was a date. It could be anyone, not necessarily a girlfriend. It could be a work colleague," said David.

"What makes you think that?" she asked.

"I don't know. I'm just saying that's all. We shouldn't just assume," he added.

She thought it better not to pursue the conversation further. She would never understand David's attitude towards Alan but he clearly had issues with him. It puzzled her but she decided that if he wanted to talk about it then he would. She wasn't going to pressure him.

It was the last day of term. The school was adorned with sparking Christmas decorations. There was a huge tree in the main hall covered in twinkling lights and glittery baubles, and in each of the classrooms, the children had decorated the walls with paintings of what they love most about Christmas. Sadie was amazed at some the artwork her little ones had produced and marvelled at their imagination and creativity. She smiled at all the different versions of Father Christmas and the reindeers each one with it's own special charm. Some of the paintings from the really young ones were just splashes of colour but the classroom looked lovely and bright and very festive.

She had decided that there would be no lessons in the afternoon but instead she was going to organise some party games. She had also bought each of the children a small selection box which she was going to hand out at the end of the day. She wanted to make sure that It was going to be a last day of term full of fun! Sure enough, the children had an amazing afternoon. Sadie, Laura, Peter and Lisa together with some of the other teachers had joined forces to arrange lots of games for them and the surprise gift of chocolate selection boxes prompted lots of cheers and very smiley faces. Laura spoke to the children for the last time and said that she was going to miss them very much but reminded them that Miss Connel would be looking after them. Some of the children had bought her small gifts and Good

Luck cards. Sadie felt quite emotional as she noticed how Laura was struggling to hold back the tears. She was obviously very fond of the children. It was hard for her saying goodbye. Sadie had also bought Laura a small gift. She had been so kind and supportive of her over the past few months and she wanted to show her appreciation. Laura carefully opened her gift which was wrapped in pink tissue paper. It was a silver bangle. Sadie had noticed that Laura wore silver jewellery and thought it would be something to remember her by.

"Oh Sadie, it's beautiful," she said. 'You shouldn't have spent your money on me. It's so sweet of you." "It's my pleasure", she answered. "You have been so kind and I feel much more confident to take the class now after your guidance these past few months. I really wish you luck in your new life abroad and in your marriage. You deserve all the happiness in the world."

Laura couldn't contain her tears any longer as she hugged Sadie and said goodbye. "I'll keep in touch, I promise", she called out as she left the classroom for the last time. "Yes, make sure you do", Sadie replied as she disappeared down the corridor.

As she left the school that evening, she felt happy and content. She was working her dream job, she had an amazing fiancé and she had made a really good friend in Lisa. The future was looking good. She was even looking forward to Christmas which surprised her. If someone told me last Christmas that I would be spending Christmas with four 'oldies' then I wouldn't have believed it, she thought to herself.

But first she had her girly day with Lisa to look forward to on Saturday. She had arranged to meet her in Chelmsford around 11am as Lisa lived just walking distance from the town centre.

'I'll be waiting outside Debenhams", Lisa said. You can park your car fairly close by. There's a big multi storey so I'm sure you will be able to get in there." she said.

"That sounds perfect Lisa. I'll see you on Saturday. I'm looking forward to it so much." "Me too", she answered.

Later that evening after dinner, Sadie and David sat down together on the sofa with a bottle of wine. "It feels good to know that I'm not working now for a couple of weeks", she said as she put her feet up on his lap.

"Yes, lucky you. I've got to work flat out in order to take Christmas Eve off so that we can travel up to Scotland. I've got so much work to do before then," he said wearily.

"You don't speak much about your job. You're still enjoying working in London aren't you. You don't have any regrets?" she asked.

"No none whatsoever. They are giving me more and more responsibility and seem to really like me. I can see a real future there. It's just difficult juggling work with the extra study, but I'm determined to qualify next year and then I can start earning some real money." he answered.

Sadie wondered if he had made any friends in the workplace. He had never mentioned anyone specifically and she knew that he ate his lunch at his desk which was something she discouraged him in doing.

She told him that he should go out for a walk, get some fresh air and recharge his batteries but he chose not to take her advice and said that he didn't want to get involved with having to make small talk with his colleagues. He preferred his own company and just wanted to focus on work.

Yes, stubborn, she thought to herself. His mum had told her that, as a child, he had always been a loner. He hadn't had many friends and preferred to be on his own, even then. It appeared to Sadie that he hadn't changed at all as far as that was concerned.

The wine flowed freely and she suddenly felt very romantic. It was usually David that made the first move but tonight she was going to show him just how sexy she could be. She stood up from the sofa and slowly removed her jumper, her bra and then her jeans and panties. As she stood naked in front of him, David pulled her towards him as she tugged at his trousers and undid his fly. "I want you so much", she whispered as David removed his trousers and pants and laid on top of her.

Their lovemaking was slow and gentle as if they didn't want it to end. He kissed her breasts hungrily as she arched her back towards him asking for more. They were lost in the moment exploring each other's bodies as if it was their first time.

"That was amazing sweetheart", said David softly. "You were really sexy tonight. Shall we go to bed for a repeat performance?" he laughed. "That's just what I was going to say", she answered.

It was a bitterly cold but bright morning when Sadie set off to meet Lisa. The sky was a clear blue despite the frostiness in the air and the winter sun was like a beacon adding to the brightness off the day. She scraped the thin layer of ice from the windscreen and thought how lucky she was to have her own little car. It gave her the freedom and independence for days like this and David was only too happy for her to go out and enjoy herself with friends. It gave him the opportunity to study quietly at home without any interruptions.

She wondered if Mark was as understanding and hoped that he wouldn't be giving Lisa a hard time. She managed to park the car in the multi storey car park that Lisa had recommended and was surprised at how few places there were left. I guess people are Christmas shopping, she thought. She walked to Debenhams and checked her watch. She was right on time and decided she would wait just inside the doors to keep out of the cold until Lisa arrived. She marvelled at how pretty the streets and the shop windows were with their Christmas displays and smiled at all the hustle and bustle of shoppers coming and going laden with bags full of presents and rolls of colourful Christmas wrapping paper. What a fuss for just one day, she thought, but then reminded herself that she hadn't done any shopping yet. She would have to arrange a day out with David to get presents for the parents. She decided she would speak to him about it when she got home.

Twenty minutes had passed and Lisa still hadn't arrived. Sadie thought about ringing her just as she suddenly appeared puffing and blowing.

"I'm so sorry Sadie. I know I'm late. We were a bit slow in getting up this morning. By the time I had cooked Mark's breakfast and showered and dressed, a couple of hours had gone. I do apologise. Have you been waiting long?"

"No not at all and I didn't mind, it's been quite entertaining watching everyone dashing around doing their Christmas shopping. I hope you haven't been rushing to get here. You sound out of breath. Couldn't Mark have cooked his own breakfast though?" she added.

"I don't mind. He does love his bacon and eggs at the weekend." Sadie thought what a selfish bugger he was. He could have cooked it himself knowing that Lisa was going out. However, she decided it was better not to voice her opinions to Lisa.

"Well you're here now, so let's go and hit the shops", she said laughing. They linked arms and set off down the high street. They spent a couple of hours popping in and out of various clothes shops looking at dresses. Sadie eventually found a lovely black and white print dress which she thought would be nice both for Christmas and for her birthday and decided she would try it on.

"What about you, Lisa?" This is nice". She held up a pretty deep pink dress with short sleeves. "It's a size 10. It's your size and the colour would really suit you. Go on try it", she urged her.

"Yes it's lovely", she answered, "but I don't like the sleeves. I would prefer long sleeves, especially now it's getting colder."

"But you'll be indoors when you're wearing it," said Sadie. "Long sleeves may make you too hot. "Just try it on - for me. I'll be in the cubicle next door trying on my dress. You can give me your opinion and I'll do the same for you."

"Ok then," Lisa sighed. "You win. I'll pop out and show you when I've got it on." Sadie looked at her reflection in the mirror twisting and turning to make sure the dress was a perfect fit. She was pleased to see that it not only fitted her really well , but it looked lovely on her. Mmm, not bad. I'm definitely going to get this one and maybe I'll see if there is anything else I like, she thought to herself. Before she took the dress off and changed back into her own clothes, she thought she would pop her head round the curtain of Lisa's fitting room to show her the dress and see how she was getting on. She was beginning to wonder why she was taking so long.

As she opened the curtain, she saw her standing in just her bra and panties. The pink dress was on the floor of the fitting room. Sadie's eyes went directly to her shoulders and the tops of her arms. She recoiled in horror at the sight before her. She had angry red marks on her shoulders and ugly black bruises on the tops of her arms. Before she could utter a word, Lisa snapped angrily

"What are you doing coming in here? I told you I would show you the dress when I had it on. You have no right to intrude my privacy like this." Sadie couldn't comprehend what she was seeing and hearing from her friend. This couldn't be happening.

"Did Mark do this to you?" she asked. Lisa shut the curtain in her face. "Of course not", she said. "I'm getting dressed now. I'll be out in a minute."

When she eventually emerged from the fitting room, Sadie could see that she had been crying. "Look, let's not argue Lisa. I care about you. You are my friend. Let's go and find somewhere quiet for lunch and let's talk - please?" she urged.

"And just so you know", said Lisa, "it's nothing to do with Mark. I had a bit of an accident. I fell off a step ladder." Sadie knew she was lying. She doubted that you would get injuries like that from falling off a step ladder but she was aware how sensitive the situation was. She didn't want to antagonise her. She wanted to help her. She would find somewhere they could sit and talk. She needed her to know that she was there to support her no matter what.

Without speaking another word, the two girls left the shop and found a restaurant which was just off the High Street. Sadie looked through the windows. it looked relatively quiet. "Let's go in here. We need something to eat and drink. We need to talk."

They found a small table for two in the corner and ordered a couple of lattes. Sadie asked the waiter to give them some time before they ordered lunch. "Yes, that's fine", he said. "We're not very busy today. Everyone is out and about doing their Christmas shopping", he added with a smile.

Sadie turned to Lisa, struggling to find the right words to say. "What really happened Lisa? I'm not stupid. There is no way that you would get those bruises that I saw from falling off a step ladder."

Lisa looked downwards as if she was finding it difficult to make eye contact with her friend. "I'm sorry I snapped at you. I was just a bit shocked that's all."

"I understand Lisa. I'm not upset about that. I'm upset that whatever has happened, you have chosen to keep it from me", she said sadly.

"Ok, you're right, I didn't fall but I'm embarrassed to tell you the truth. Promise me that what I am about to tell you, stays between you and me. It's private. I don't want anyone to know. I didn't want **you** to know", said Lisa. Sadie noticed the colour rising in her face as she continued.

"Mark and I have an adventurous sex life and sometimes it leads to our intimacy becoming somewhat physical. I know it sounds odd and I don't expect you to understand, but he likes rough sex."

"To the extent where he hurts you?!" No, you're right, I don't understand!" said Sadie angrily. "Sex shouldn't be violent Lisa. Not if you truly love one another. I appreciate that it is nobody else's business what goes on in the bedroom between two consenting adults. But honestly, there has to be a line drawn when your partner is inflicting pain on you. They are serious bruises that you have there. Mark shouldn't be allowed to get way with it."

"Mark loves me and what makes him happy makes me happy. If you don't mind, I'd rather not talk about this anymore. I don't want you to mention it again - please." Sadie could see that she meant it. Their day out had already been ruined. She decided that, as far as she was concerned, the subject was closed - for now at least. They would have their lunch and try and enjoy the rest of the afternoon, but from now on she promised herself that she would be keeping a very close eye on Lisa.

They parted company having enjoyed a lovely lunch and a glass of wine. She was pleased that Lisa seemed a lot happier. They wished each other a Happy Christmas and said their goodbyes.

"I'll see you and Mark at the restaurant on my birthday, don't forget", she called out as Lisa turned to leave. "I wouldn't miss it for the world", she replied.

Sadie was still deep in thought about what Lisa had told her when she got home. David was in the kitchen eating beans on toast. "Hi sweetheart. I've missed you. Did you have a lovely day? Show me your new dress then", he said with a mouthful of food.

"I've missed you too", she answered. "As for my day, it wasn't quite what I expected, and no I didn't get a new dress although I found one that I really liked."

"Oh why not? I thought that was the idea of going shopping today. And why wasn't it the day you expected?" he said feeling puzzled. She sat down opposite him and poured herself a glass of wine. She recounted the events of the day and watched as his expression changed when she told him about Lisa's bruises and the explanation that she gave for having them.

"Do you believe her?" he asked.

"I'm not sure, she answered. "There may be an element of truth in it. I know I'm a bit naïve but I have heard of couples that enjoy rough sex. But honestly, David, her bruises were really bad. It was if her arms had been restrained or gripped tightly, and her shoulders looked really sore too. I want to believe that she is telling the truth but I can't help feeling really concerned about her. I promised her that I wouldn't tell anyone else about this and she asked that I never mention it again so please keep it to yourself. You will won't you?" she pleaded.

"Of course, sweetheart, I promise you my lips are sealed. It's not really any of our business anyway is it? Let's just concentrate on us for now. We've got Christmas coming up and we're off to Scotland in a day or two. It's going to be great spending time with the oldies, don't you agree?" he laughed. "Before that though, we're going into Chelmsford tomorrow, we'll get some presents for the parents, and you're going to get that dress you liked, young lady." '

"What did I do to deserve you?" she said as she threw her arms around him.

Chapter 7

It was the morning of Christmas Eve. They had spent an hour or two getting everything ready and loading up the car in readiness for their journey up to Scotland. There were bags of Christmas goodies and presents for the parents on the back seat and a suitcase for their clothes in the boot. Luckily the weather forecast promised a fine frost free day so they were looking forward to a pleasant journey. They agreed that they would share the driving and have a couple of stops along the way to ease the boredom of driving on the motorways.

Sadie was still feeling troubled about Lisa but she was determined not to let it spoil Christmas. She told herself that she would be seeing her in a couple of days and could check on how she was then. She had also spoken to David about Alan and asked him if he knew where he was going for Christmas. She doubted whether he would be going to see his family and she didn't like to think of him being on his own. He told her that she worried too much about everyone else.

"Alan will be fine", he said. "He'll probably spend Christmas with his new friend." She thought he sounded a bit cynical and wondered if he knew more about Alan's friend than he was letting on. "Did you find anything else out about who it might be?" she questioned. "No I didn't. It's none of our business Sadie. I'm sure he will tell us in his own good time."

"Well I'm going to ring him in the New Year and see if he wants to come and visit us again. You never know, he might bring his mystery friend with him", she laughed.

David looked at her shaking his head. "You don't give up do you?" he said smiling.

The journey to Scotland went quicker than they both expected. The roads were surprisingly quiet and the weather remained fine. Mary and Rob were surprised as they pulled up on their drive. They didn't think they would be there for another couple of hours at least. Mary rushed out to greet her daughter hugging her tightly. She had been looking forward to seeing her so much.

"We didn't expect you quite so soon, darling. You must have had a good journey with no hold-ups". She turned to David, smiling. "It's great to see you both. Come inside, I'll put the kettle on." Sadie immediately felt the enveloping cosiness of home as she walked into the hallway and was met with the most amazing smells coming from the direction of the kitchen. Her mum was a great cook and was always so organised when it came to preparing Christmas dinner. She would have all the baking finished and preparations for dinner completed by Christmas Eve.

She was looking forward to the luxury and contentment that being at home always brought her. She missed the comforting familiarity of it all more than she realised. Her dad emerged from the kitchen wearing one of her mum's aprons.

"I've been peeling the spuds", he laughed. She rushed towards him and hugged him tightly. "Hi Dad, I've missed you and I'm glad to see that you are still following tradition and helping mum with the vegetables", she said laughing.

"Hello young man", said Rob shaking David's hand vigorously. "It's good to have you both here. Your mum and dad will be joining us soon. Susan rang Mary an hour or so ago. They had just stopped for petrol and said they expected to arrive within a couple of hours."

After they had enjoyed a cup of tea, Mary wanted to hear all the news. How was the flat? How were they getting on with their new jobs? Rob laughed and told her not to bombard them with lots of questions.

"They've had a long journey love. We can here all their news after we've all sat down to dinner and we're relaxed. We'll open a bottle or two and then we can have a proper catch up."

David thought how lovely Sadie's parents were. It was no surprise to him that Sadie was the loving and caring person she was. Mary and Rob were great role models as parents and they obviously loved their daughter very much.

"Oh here they are", said Mary as she looked out of the window to see Susan and Colin's car drawing up on the drive behind Sadie and David's. Rob went to the door to greet them. "Welcome, it's lovely to see you. How was your journey?" he asked.

"Oh it was fine thank you Rob", answered Susan. Mary took their coats and greeted them warmly. "Come and sit down. I've lit the log burner so it's nice and cosy in the lounge." Colin approached his son and shook his hand and kissed Sadie on the cheek.

"Good to see you both", he said. Susan kissed her son and hugged Sadie. "We've been looking forward to this so much", she said. "It was really good of your mum and dad to invite us."

Sadie felt that it had seemed a bit uncomfortable when David's parents first arrived. She had thought to herself that it wasn't really surprising as both her and her mum and dad didn't really know them. But once the evening meal was over and everyone had sat down with a glass of wine, she was pleased to see that the atmosphere seemed more relaxed. Mary and Susan were chatting away quite happily about what cookery programmes they were currently watching on TV and Rob and Colin were contemplating whether or not to open a bottle of brandy.

"Looks like the oldies are getting on ok", said David as they both went out to the car to bring everything in. "Yes, it's good. I did wonder at first. It all seemed a bit awkward to start with didn't it?" she added.

"How about we leave them all to it soon and have an early night. I don't know about you sweetheart, but I'm shattered after that long journey and we've got a big day tomorrow," he said.

"I was going to suggest that anyway", she answered. "I'm tired too. It's been a long day."

Christmas morning brought about a big change in the weather. Blue cloudless skies had been replaced with dark sombre clouds and heavy rain. Sadie awoke early, disturbed by the wind rattling the open window in the en-suite. She tiptoed out of bed trying not to wake David who was lying on his back snoring like a lion. After closing the window, she decided to go downstairs. She knew what her mum was like on Christmas morning, she would have been up since the crack of dawn preparing the turkey and laying the table. She opened the kitchen door and sure enough, her mum was there mixing stuffing and doing unmentionable things to the turkey in readiness for it going in the oven.

"Happy Christmas Mum" she said as she crept up behind her and encircled her in her arms.

"Happy Christmas to you too darling", Mary answered. "You're up early. Couldn't you sleep? Wasn't the bed comfy?" she added sounding worried.

"Mum, the bed was great. It was the wind and rain that woke me up. It's not a typical traditional picture of Christmas when you look out of the window is it? What happened to the clear skies and smattering of soft snow on the ground?" she laughed. "Well we can't do much about the weather darling, but we will have a lovely day despite that. Your dad has dug out all your old board games for us to play after dinner. He's determined that we play Monopoly, so I'm just warning you to be prepared!" It made her think of all the Christmas's in the past when a game of Monopoly would almost cause them to come to blows over who had the most money in the bank and the best properties to barter with. It was always good fun. She told her mum that she quite liked the idea of following tradition and playing it again today.

"I'm glad to have you all to myself for a little while this morning Sadie. I haven't had the chance to talk to you properly. Is everything alright between you and David? Are you happy?" she asked.

"Yes David and I are really happy Mum. I don't want you to worry about us. We're getting along fine. He's very kind and thoughtful. I'm lucky".

"I think he is the lucky one', added Mary. "I just hope he appreciates you and doesn't take you for granted. You are such a sweet girl."

"You're just biased", she laughed. "Seriously though, sometimes I feel that you don't really like David - that you think he's not good enough for me", she said sadly.

"I do like him Sadie. I can see that he is a good person and it's clear to me how much you love one another. It's just that I've always felt that he is never being entirely honest about his past. It's like he is keeping secrets. He never talks about having any friends. Have you ever met any of his friends?" she asked.

"He just prefers his own company - apart from me of course" said Sadie laughing. "Not everyone has lots of friends, certainly not really close friends. Look at me for instance. I don't keep in touch with my old school mates. Since I moved to Chelmsford, I haven't heard from any of them. I'm just happy that I met Lisa. She is a great friend and one that I know I will always have. Next time you come to see us, I'll introduce you. She is such a lovely girl . You will really like her, "she said.

"I'm so pleased. It's important to have friends outside of your relationship. Someone you can talk to and have fun with. I'll look forward to meeting her one day," said Mary.

Sadie felt sad as her thoughts turned to Alan. She looked at her mum and said "David does have one friend – in fact I am friends with him too. Do you remember us telling you about Alan? David met him during the first year of Uni. They were really good mates but the friendship fell apart for some reason and I've never understood why. We both still see him. He's a lovely guy but David is so cold towards him. I have tried to talk to him about it, but he just shuts me down. Alan came to visit us a month or so ago and although David was perfectly pleasant and cordial with him, I could sense the atmosphere between them. I've decided I'm not going to question him anymore about it. If something happened between them then he clearly doesn't want to share it with me. I have to respect that."

"But it's not healthy to keep secrets from one another Sadie, especially as you are getting married. He should tell you what is bothering him with regard to Alan. How are you going to continue a friendship with someone under those circumstances? Isn't it better if you just stop seeing Alan? It sounds like that is what David wants," said Mary.

"I suppose you're right but I really like him and I feel sorry for him. I think he will be very upset if we lose contact – and so will I."

"It worries me that David is behaving like this towards a friend Sadie. I wish that you could get to the bottom of it. It's clearly worrying you. Wait until Christmas is over and you've been out for your birthday and then try and pick a moment to talk to him."

"I'll think about it Mum but let's not talk about it anymore. It's time to get that turkey stuffed!!"

After the conversation with her mum, she went back upstairs to get showered and dressed. David was sitting on the edge of the bed. "Happy Christmas darling! Have you been helping your mum in the kitchen?"

"Happy Christmas to you too", she answered. "Yes we've been doing some stuffing", she laughed. He swept her into his arms kissing her passionately. "Have we got time to go back to bed?"

"No, I can hear your parents moving about next door. I think we should get ready and go downstairs," she said.

"Spoilsport", he said laughing. She showered and put on her new dress and applied some make up. "Wow you look gorgeous", said David.

"You look smart too", she said as she looked him up and down. He really is a good looking guy, she thought to herself.

"Right Miss Connel, let's go down and wow the oldies."

The rest of the day passed with them enjoying the most amazing Christmas dinner, lots of alcohol, wonderful presents and some very amusing party games – including Monopoly! Sadie thought how great it was that everyone was getting on so well. David's parents turned out to be really good sports and happily joined in with all of Rob's silly party games. He even got them involved in his version of charades which had everyone giggling like school children.

You can always rely on good old dad to keep everyone entertained, she thought to herself. It turned out to be a really wonderful day. As the day drew to a close and they had finally exhausted most of the board games and had consumed more than enough food and drink, everyone sat back in their chairs enjoying a cup of tea.

"Mary and Rob, Colin and I would like to thank you for your kind hospitality," said Susan. "We have had such a great time. It's been ages since both of us have laughed so much. We must return the favour soon. We would love it if you came to visit us. If you plan a trip in the summer, we can enjoy spending some time at the beach. We're just a stone's throw away." "Well we have enjoyed having you – all of you", said Mary as she turned and smiled at Sadie and David. "We would love to come to Brighton and visit you – wouldn't we Rob?"

"You bet", he said laughing. "'I never could resist a stick of rock and a candyfloss."

Once Susan and Sadie had helped Mary tidy up the kitchen and all the washing up had been done, everyone made their way to bed. Sadie and David wanted to make an early start in the morning and his parents were keen to get on the road before late morning. "Wasn't it a great day?" she said to him as they snuggled up in bed.

"It was fun wasn't it?" Who would have thought that the oldies would be so entertaining", he laughed. "It will be good to get home though and we've got your birthday to look forward to now," he added. "Your mum and dad have given me their present to you. They want you to have it on the morning of your birthday. I have no idea what it is but it's in a fairly small box. I've also got something for you from my mum and dad."

"Oooh how exciting", said Sadie. "I am a very lucky girl." "And I'm a lucky guy", he said as he took her into his arms.

After emotional goodbyes, they set off from Mary and Rob's house. They were both strangely quiet on the journey home, lost in their own thoughts. Sadie was thinking about Lisa and Alan and hoping that, in their own ways, they had enjoyed Christmas. David was, as usual, thinking about work and the amount of studying he had to catch up on. He was determined to finish his course within the next six months so that he could complete his qualifications. His one goal was to qualify and start earning money. Him and Sadie needed to buy their own home and whilst they loved the flat, he knew that they needed to get on the property ladder as soon as possible. This time, the journey home took a lot longer. There was a lot of traffic on the road and the wind and rain were slowing them down. When they finally pulled up outside their flat, it was really late and they were exhausted.

"I'm going to give mum a quick ring to let her know we've arrived safely and then I'm going straight to bed", said Sadie.

"I'll be right behind you darling. I'm shattered too", he said.

The next morning she woke up to a chorus of 'Happy Birthday to you' and a little pile of presents on the bed. David started singing, "You're 21 today, 21 today, you've got the key of the door, never been 21 before." "Stop, please stop", laughed Sadie. "You are going to be a great solicitor darling, but a singer - definitely not!"

"Hey you. You don't recognise star quality that's your trouble," he said grabbing her and kissing her.

"C'mon then, open your presents. Let's see what you've got", he said inpatiently. He handed her the small box first. "This is from your mum and dad". Sadie opened the box and stared at the beautiful necklace which was nestled on a small cushion. It was white gold and it had a pendant shaped as a heart which was covered in diamonds.

Sadie couldn't believe how beautiful it was. Inside there was a little card which read:

"To our darling daughter Sadie. You will always be our brightest diamond with the biggest heart. Sending all our love on your special birthday, Mum and Dad"

Sadie wiped a tear from her eye as she read her parents moving message to her.

"Their great aren't they?", she said.

"Yes you are very lucky, you have amazing parents – just the best", he said. He really meant it. He had loved spending time with Mary and Rob. They were lovely people. He cared for his parents too, but he didn't have the close relationship that Sadie had with hers. He was sure that they didn't really understand him - that he wasn't the son they would have wished for.

Susan and Colin had bought Sadie pretty silver earrings. "Oh they're lovely David. I'll wear them tonight. How kind of them. I'll ring them later and thank them."

"Right, it's my turn now", he said as he handed her another box – slightly bigger this time.

"This looks interesting", she said. She carefully unwrapped the paper removing the pretty bow which was tied around it. Inside was a beautiful watch. She had remembered admiring it in a jewellery shop window when they had been out Christmas shopping, but never for one minute did she expect David to buy it. It had been VERY expensive.

"Oh David, you didn't? It was such a lot of money – you shouldn't have!" she exclaimed.

"You deserve it sweetheart. Do you like it?" "No, I LOVE it", she said. "Thank you so much, darling."

After all the excitement, David cooked a lovely breakfast which they had in bed. "You are really spoiling me", she said. "Well there is a way you can repay me", he said laughing as he wrapped his arms around her and pulled her back under the covers.

After a lazy, loving morning in bed, Sadie finally got up, had a shower and dressed for the day. She telephoned both sets of parents thanking them for their beautiful gifts and then decided that she would call Lisa to make sure that she was still coming to the restaurant later.

"Hi Lisa, it's Sadie. How are you? Did you have a lovely Christmas?" she asked.

"Hi Sadie. Yes we had a great time, thank you. We went to Mark's parents for the day and got thoroughly spoiled". She thought how bubbly and happy she sounded and felt relieved. "Just checking that you're still on for tonight", she asked. "Yes, of course. We are both looking forward to it. Happy Birthday love. Are you having a good day so far?"

"Fabulous. I have had some lovely presents and David cooked me a breakfast, which is something he would never do normally. He's been great. I feel very loved".

"So you should Sadie. I love you too. You're a great friend", said Lisa. "We have a gift for you as well. I'll bring it with me tonight."

"You shouldn't have. It will just be nice to see you, and to meet Mark at last. We'll be there around 7pm. We can have some drinks in the bar first before we sit down to dinner."

"That's great. See you later!" said Lisa cheerily.

Sadie and David arrived at the restaurant a little ahead of time and found a quiet table at the bar. "You look lovely tonight birthday girl", he said. "That new dress really suits you."

"Thank you darling, and thank you again for making today so special", she answered.

He reached across the table and took her hand just as she spotted Lisa walking towards them, followed by Mark. She noticed how pretty Lisa looked. She was smiling and holding a bouquet of flowers along with a huge helium balloon with a big 21 printed on it. She thought Mark looked nice – though not quite what she had expected. She had imagined him being drop dead gorgeous and very tall but, in fact he was quite ordinary looking with glasses and only an inch or so taller than Lisa. She dismissed her negativity and told herself that she shouldn't judge a book by it's cover.

"Happy Birthday lovely lady!" exclaimed Lisa. "Sorry about the balloon but I just couldn't resist", she laughed. "This is my boyfriend Mark," she added as she stood to one side so that Mark could greet Sadie.

"I'm really pleased to meet you", he said kissing her softly on the cheek. "Lisa has told me so much about you. You have been a good friend to her. Lisa finds it difficult to socialise and meet new people,' don't you honey? It's really great that you both get on so well." he added.

Sadie looked at Lisa wondering how to reply. She thought it was a bit unkind of Mark to put her on the spot like that. She chose to ignore his comment and just smiled politely as she turned back to Lisa.

"I love the balloon and the flowers are beautiful - thank you so much." "We've bought you a little gift too, haven't we Mark? Is it still in your pocket?" she asked.

Mark put his hand in his jacket pocket and pulled out a long narrow box. "It's nothing exciting but I hope it will always remind you of the first day that you started teaching your own class. I got it engraved too," said Lisa. Sadie opened the box to see a beautiful silver pen. It had been engraved with the words 'Think of me with every word you write, love Lisa.'

" Oh Lisa that's so lovely. I will use it every day. Thank you both. It means a lot." She hugged her and out of courtesy, she quickly kissed Mark on the cheek. After they all sat down at the table, David stood up and asked everyone what they would like to drink. Mark answered straightaway and said that he and Lisa would have a vodka and coke but made no move to accompany David to the bar.

"I'll come with you" said Sadie.

As they both stood at the bar waiting for the drinks, she turned to him and whispered "I know we've only just met him but I don't think much of Mark.Why didn't he offer to help you with the drinks and why is he speaking for Lisa? Did she really want a vodka and coke or is that what he wanted her to have? It's exactly as I guessed. He is controlling her. I'm sure of it."

"Well whatever it is. It's none of our business sweetheart and I'm not spoiling your birthday celebrations because of something you think is happening. We'll have our drinks and our dinner and we'll try and enjoy ourselves, ok?" he answered.

The rest of the evening passed pleasantly. The meal was beautiful and surprisingly the conversation flowed well. Mark spoke a lot about his job and was interested in how David was progressing with his studies. When it came to Lisa he seemed to be very attentive asking her frequently if she was ok. "I'm fine Mark. The food is delicious. This restaurant was a good choice. We must come here again," she answered. Sadie wondered if she had over reacted earlier. Whilst she still had her doubts about Mark, he seemed very friendly and obviously cared for Lisa very much. David was right. Their relationship was none of her business. She told herself that she wouldn't get involved. As long as Lisa seemed happy and well, then that was all she cared about.

At the end of the evening, they all parted company making a promise that they would meet up again soon. Mark had paid his half of the bill and had bought another round of drinks so she had to admit that she was beginning to warm to him. As they both turned down the road towards their flat, Lisa called out "See you next term lovely lady".

"I'm looking forward to it", Sadie shouted back. "Night, night both of you", she added.

"Well that turned out to be a really lovely evening didn't it?" she said on the journey home. "Perhaps I was wrong about Mark after all."

"Perhaps, he said. "I'm still not sure. When you and Lisa went to the Ladies, he was talking in quite a derogatory way about her. It made me feel very uncomfortable."

"What did he say?" she answered, suddenly feeling concerned. "He was talking about you and how lovely you looked in your dress and then he said that Lisa didn't really have any dress sense and that he often had to tell her what to wear. He said that she had embarrassed him in front of clients on many occasions because she was inappropriately dressed."

"What does he mean – inappropriately dressed?" she said angrily.

"He said that she often looked scruffy."

"Scruffy! – how dare he?" I've never seen Lisa looking scruffy, far from it. She is always immaculately turned out even when she is in her jogging pants. I wished that I looked as lovely as she did all the time. She is such a beautiful girl, inside and out. What on earth is she doing with that creep?"

She was really angry now and chided herself for beginning to think that Mark was a nice guy after all.

"I wish I hadn't told you now. Look at you, you're all wound up. This isn't how I wanted your birthday celebrations to end."

"I'm glad you told me. I'm going to be keeping a close eye on Lisa from now on. If he hurts her in any way, I won't be responsible for my actions."

She would be lying if she said the conversation she had with David about Mark hadn't put a damper on her birthday, because it had. With David snoring contentedly beside her, She struggled to put all thoughts of Lisa out of her head, spending hours trying to calm the feeling of panic that was overwhelming her and preventing the solace of sleep. When she finally drifted off, her dreams were dark, vivid and menacing.

Chapter 8

For Sadie and David the following year was full on. David's ambition to be completely qualified within two years had been realised and he had been offered a full time post as a Corporate Lawyer with the same company in London. He was already handling some important cases and travelling extensively across London advising clients on corporate transactions as well as offering strategic advice to businesses looking to restructure for increased efficiency and profits. He was absolutely loving his job and his employers were impressed with his knowledge, know how and his natural talent in dealing with the clients - some of whom were notoriously difficult. Sadie was very proud of him and admitted to herself that she had been wrong in doubting that he would succeed. He had achieved his dream and because of that, they were now much more comfortable financially and feeling in a better position to take the next step of buying their own home.

They had also discussed marriage and were both in agreement that there was no reason to wait now that David was working full time. Sadie was also loving teaching. Her class were so eager to learn and loving the variety of lessons that she planned for them. Seeing their happy little faces every morning, gave her so much pleasure. She called them 'her little sponges' which amused them greatly. She tried to make every day different and exciting and whenever the weather was fine, she would teach outside in the fresh air. They would learn about nature, search for different flowers, leaves, rocks and acorns and how to grow flowers from seed. They loved Sadie as much as she loved them. There was never an occasion where she would have to chastise a child for bad behaviour. It just never happened in her class. She was really proud of that.

Her success and popularity as a teacher hadn't escaped the Head Teacher, Mrs. Marshall. She could see that Sadie had a natural talent in working with such small children. She appreciated that she was young, soon to be married and guessed that, at some point, she would want to have her own children and perhaps move house. She just hoped that she woudn't lose her to another school. She was a real asset and a very popular member of staff.

She knew that her and Lisa were very close which pleased her. She was aware that Lisa had some issues in her relationship in the past and often wondered if some of her sick leave absences were in some way connected. At least she had Sadie looking out for her now and she had to admit that Lisa hadn't been off sick once during the last 10 months. She hoped that things between her and her partner were more settled now.

Sadie and David were going to speak to both sets of parents to see how they would feel about them getting married quite soon. They were both in agreement that it would be a small registry office wedding with only their parents and some close friends as guests. It seemed silly to spend thousands of pounds on a wedding when that could go towards a deposit on a house of their own. They had decided to stay in the same area because of Sadie's job and had already started looking at larger properties in Chelmsford.

When Sadie telephoned her mum and dad she was surprised to learn that they were completely in agreement and not only that, but they had spoken to David's parents to see how they would feel about joining with them in giving Sadie and David twenty thousand pounds to help with the deposit on a house. They couldn't believe that their parents were being so generous and so understanding. Sadie had been convinced that her mum, in particular, would have insisted on her having the traditional white wedding in a church with lots of guests. It was a relief to know that there wouldn't be any arguments on who should or shouldn't come to their wedding.

Apart from their mums and dads, they decided to invite Lisa and Mark, Mrs Marshall from school and her husband, her colleague Peter and his wife and of course, Alan. They hadn't heard much from Alan throughout the year. It transpired that he didn't have a girlfriend as Sadie had imagined. He said that he wasn't in a relationship. He was just enjoying his job and going out occasionally with friends from work. David didn't speak of Alan unless Sadie mentioned him. She thought it was a shame that they couldn't resume their friendship but had decided long ago that it wasn't any of her business. She had accepted that David was a bit of a loner and completely dedicated to her and his job. That seemed to be enough for him and she accepted it. The wedding was planned. The registry office had been booked and the guests invited. Everyone who had been invited had accepted their invitations so now all that remained was for Sadie to buy her dress. She had also asked Lisa to be her bridesmaid which she was thrilled to agree to. With just two weeks to go until the big day, Sadie and Lisa had arranged to go into town to choose their dresses. There was a lovely bridal shop that Sadie had ear marked for a visit, so she had telephoned the shop to request an appointment for a fitting. On the day of the appointment, she had arranged to meet Lisa outside the shop. When they entered the shop their eyes went to the vast rails of bridal gowns.

"Goodness me Lisa, how on earth am I going to choose a dress from all of these? They all look lovely." Lisa agreed, as a middle aged woman dressed in black approached them from the back of the shop.

"Good afternoon ladies. I understand you have an appointment to try on some wedding gowns?"

"Yes please", said Sadie. Also we will be looking for a bridesmaid's dress for my friend." "Of course", said the woman. "We'll concentrate on you first though, shall we? Did you have any particular style in mind."

"Something classic and simple", she answered. It will be a registry office wedding so I don't want a big flouncy princess dress," she said laughing.

"That's fine. I'll pull some gowns from the rails that I think you may like and I'll bring them into the fitting room, if you would like to follow me."

Sadie and Lisa couldn't stop themselves from giggling. The woman was so terse, not at all friendly and seemed to be looking down her nose at them.

"What a snooty bitch" exclaimed Lisa when they went into the fitting room. "You would think that she would be more pleasant. After all, you're here to buy a wedding dress. It's special. She should be making YOU feel special."

"Oh well, we're here now. We'll look but if there is nothing that we both like, then we'll go somewhere else," said Sadie. The woman eventually entered the dressing room as she was sitting waiting in her bra and panties.

"I've found six dresses that I think you will like. If they don't fit you, we can alter them, so don't worry about that", said the woman.

"Well the wedding is in two weeks, so there probably won't be time for alterations will there?" asked Sadie. "Oh my goodness, no. Usually our brides come in months before the day. You have left it rather late!" she exclaimed.

"Well show me what you've got and we'll take it from there," said Sadie feeling slightly irritated. She tried on all of the dresses. There was just one that fitted her perfectly.

Lisa exclaimed "Oh Sadie you look absolutely beautiful! It's perfect on you. That has got to be the one." She looked at her reflection in the mirror. She agreed with Lisa – it was perfect. It was simple and classic with a sweetheart neckline. It fitted her petite figure beautifully and had a small train. She loved it. She didn't think she would find anything else that would be so beautiful.

"Yes, this is the one. I'll take it," she said to the woman.

"A good choice my dear. You look stunning. I'm sure your husband to be will be overwhelmed when he sees you wearing it," said the woman a little more kindly. "Do you want to look at veils?" she asked.

"No definitely not a veil, but perhaps a little headdress or flower or something for my hair," she answered.

The woman showed her a selection of headdresses and ornate flowers for her hair before she spotted just the one she liked in the window. It was like a head band and it was covered in pearls and diamante's . It was really pretty and she thought it would look nice if she chose to wear her hair down. "I'd like that one please" she said to the woman as she pointed towards the window.

"Are you sure you don't want to try any others on?" she asked. "No, I'm quite sure, thank you," said Sadie.

"Right Lisa, it's your turn." How do you fancy pale green silk? You have such lovely dark hair. I think it will really suit you."

"That sounds nice. I just want you to have everything you want on your special day- you deserve it more than anyone I know," said Lisa squeezing her hand.

"Aww bless you. You are such a true friend. I love you, you know that don't you?"

"Yes and I love you too", said Lisa.

It turned out that it wasn't so straightforward for Lisa finding the right dress. There was nothing in green silk that either fitted or suited her, so they settled on a pale pink gown which was similar in style to Sadie's. She looked stunning. Sadie thought how very beautiful she was. She wondered if she would ever get married one day and would it be to Mark? She still wasn't sure about him but had to admit that Lisa seemed much happier these days. More than anything she hoped that she would find the happiness that she had found with David. She felt so lucky to have him in her life. She had to pinch herself to believe that he was soon to be her husband.

It was a cold but sunny day in late October when Sadie woke up on the morning of her wedding day. She shivered as she left the warmth of her bed and reached for her fluffy dressing gown and slippers. She looked at the clock beside the bed. It was 8am. I've got plenty of time, she thought to herself. The wedding was due to start at 1.30pm and the car was coming for her at 1.15pm. She could hear her parents speaking in low mumbles in the bedroom next door and smiled. She was so happy that they were here with her on her special day.

David, as tradition dictated for the groom, was staying with his parents in the hotel that they had booked for the reception. She had kissed him goodbye last night and had laughed when he held her closely and whispered in her ear. "See you tomorrow, wife to be. Don't be late!"

She looked out of the window. She could see signs of a slight frost and congratulated herself on making the decision to go back to the bridal shop a few days earlier to purchase two white furry stoles for her and Lisa. We don't want to be seen shivering in the wedding photos, she had thought to herself. Lisa was due to arrive around 9am and they were both having their hair and make up done. Lisa had insisted on paying for it as a special treat.

"You want to look stunning for David don't you", she had said. "Not that you don't always look lovely," she added. She was really touched by Lisa's kind gesture and agreed that they should both make the most of being pampered and enjoy the experience. She could hear her Mum in the kitchen as she closed the bedroom door and went to see what she was up to.

"Oh you're up darling. I was going to bring you breakfast in bed. It's your wedding day. I want to spoil you," Mary said. "There is champagne in the fridge for later, so when you and Lisa are dressed ready to go, we'll have a little toast. It will help settle your nerves - and Dad's", she laughed. "Honestly Sadie you would think that it was him getting married. He's in the bedroom now stressing about which tie he should wear and whether or not he should re-write his speech. I wouldn't mind but he has already re-written it twice!" "Oh bless him," said Sadie. I'm sure whatever tie he chooses it will be fine, and if I know Dad, his speech will end up being totally spontaneous and intermixed with some of his usual silly jokes. Dad has always been good at public speaking. He shouldn't put so much pressure on himself. I'll go and speak to him and tell him not to be nervous. I have every faith in him." She knocked gently on the door of the spare bedroom. "Is it ok if I come in Dad? Are you decent?" She could hear him laughing as he said "Yes, I'm decent. Come in love."

"What's all this that mum tells me? She said you're a bit stressed about the wedding."

"Yes, I am a bit, love. It's an important day for you and David. I just want to make sure that everything goes to plan for you. I can't make up my mind whether or not I should change my speech," he said.

"If I were you Dad, I would just let it come naturally. You don't need to write anything down. You'll know what to say when the time comes. I've never known you to be lost for words," she laughed.

"Ok love, you're probably right. I'll wing it then."

"Good plan. Now what about this tie?" She looked at the variety of ties on the bed and chose one with a navy and pink stripe. "This will be perfect Dad. It will go with your navy blue suit and the pink will pick up the colour of Lisa's dress."

"What would I do without you, my beautiful daughter," he said. Sadie smiled and looked lovingly at his handsome concerned face.

"I love you Dad. If David and I can be half as happy as you and mum have been throughout your marriage, then I will be blessed." She hugged him tightly and then before emotions got the better of her, she turned and said "Right let's go and see how mum is getting on with breakfast. Lisa will be here soon and then the pampering begins!" she laughed.

Lisa arrived just after 9am. Sadie had already showered, washed her hair, and put her new silk dressing gown on and was sitting in the kitchen with her mum and dad. After greeting Lisa at the door she ushered her into the kitchen.

"Mum, Dad - this is my best friend Lisa." Mary and Rob stood up and, one at a time gave her a warm hug. "It's so nice to meet you at last," said Mary. Sadie has told us so much about you. You're every bit as beautiful as she said you were."

"Thank you Mrs Connel. That's very nice of you. It's good to meet you too."

"It's Mary and Rob, please. You're like family, so no formalities here," said Mary squeezing Lisa's hand.

They all sat chatting for over an hour at the kitchen table before Sadie realised the time. "The hairdresser and make-up lady will be here soon Lisa. Let's finish our coffee and get things ready. The flowers are also being delivered at 12." She suddenly felt a bit panicky for the first time that morning. It seemed like everything was now in full swing and the realisation that she was actually getting married, finally hit her.

As they both headed for the bedroom, Mary turned to Rob. “Isn’t Lisa a lovely young lady? She is so pretty and seems a really kind and loyal friend to Sadie. I’m so pleased that she has found such a good friend especially as she is living so far away now. At least I know that she will always have her support, should she need it in the future.”

“Yes, she certainly is a lovely girl, every bit as nice as Sadie said she was”, answered Rob.

“What do you mean about Sadie needing her support in the future though?” he added. “Well you know,” she answered. It’s just if there are any problems between her and David or anything goes wrong at work. I wasn’t referring to anything specific. It’s just good to know that she has a real friend in Lisa.”

“You’ve always doubted David, haven’t you?” he answered. I’ve never understood why, Mary. He’s a great lad. He works hard, and he loves our daughter, that’s plain to see. Try and put your negative thoughts to one side. I know you have Sadie’s best interests at heart love, but just be happy for her and let’s make today the best of her life. Deal?” he said.

“Of course, I don’t want anything to spoil today darling. I’m sorry, I guess I’m just one of those boring over protective Mum’s!” she laughed.

The two girls were ready, make up and hair were finished and dresses were on. Sadie looked at Lisa and felt so proud of her. She looked absolutely stunning - the perfect bridesmaid. As for Sadie, Lisa had shed a tear as she emerged from the bedroom. She couldn’t believe how beautiful she looked. Her dress was perfect and the pretty headdress was just the right choice to highlight her beautiful blonde hair which fell to her shoulders in soft waves. They both carried bouquets made up of pink and white roses and their white fur stoles were a perfect accessory on what was a chilly day. They made their way into the living room where Mary and Rob were waiting excitedly for them to make their grand entrance.

There was a gasp from Mary as they entered the room and Rob was struggling not to cry as they both looked at their beautiful daughter. "Sadie you look absolutely gorgeous", said Mary. She was also desperately trying to hold back the tears. "And Lisa sweetheart, you are simply beautiful," she added smiling kindly at her.

"Wow, What a pair of beauties!", said Rob. David will wonder what has hit him", he laughed. "Well, let's crack that bottle of champagne open, shall we? We've got twenty minutes or so before the cars are here – plenty of time."

"Good idea Dad", said Sadie. I think we're both a bit nervous now, aren't we?" she said smiling at Lisa.

Rob poured the champagne and raised his glass. "Here's to us having a wonderful day and cherishing every moment. I couldn't be prouder of my daughter and her lovely bridesmaid and I mustn't forget my darling wife who is also looking pretty damn gorgeous I have to say!"

Rob looked lovingly at Mary admiring her pretty silk dress and matching fascinator and thought how lucky he was to have enjoyed so many years of happiness with her by his side.

"Here, here Dad" said Sadie. "Mum you look lovely – every inch the mother of the bride, and Dad you don't look so bad yourself. That tie was a good choice wasn't it?" she laughed.

The two wedding cars arrived right on time. David had booked two silver Mercedes. One was for Sadie and her Dad and the other was for Lisa and Mary. Lisa and Mary left first, leaving Sadie and her Dad to spend a few minutes on their own in the flat.

"Sadie, you know how very much your mum and I love you, don't you?" said Rob as he felt his emotions getting the better of him. "I just want this time to say that we are always going to be here for you, no matter what. I know that today I will be relinquishing my responsibility for caring and protecting you to David. He will be your husband, your next of kin and the person who will take care of you and love you, and I'm happy that you have found your soulmate in him, but for as long as we're going to be around, we'll be there too. I don't want you to forget that."

"Oh Dad, you and mum are still young, you're going to be around for years and years yet. I can never imagine my life without you both and I appreciate you more than you'll ever know. I love David, of course I do, but it doesn't take away the love I have for you and Mum. You are the best mum and dad in the world."

Rob took her in his arms and kissed her cheek. "Thank you darling. Right, shall we go and get you married now?" he said laughing, but trying not to let her see him wiping away a tear.

Lisa and Mary arrived at the registry office five minutes ahead of Sadie and Rob. As Mary took her seat beside David's parents, Lisa waited outside for Sadie and her dad to arrive. She had chosen one of her and David's favourite songs for her entrance – Whitney Houston's rendition of Greatest Love of All, and as the music started Lisa, followed by Sadie and Rob, made their way into the room. Sadie was delighted to see that Alan was there and sitting beside Mark, Mr and Mrs Marshall and Peter and his wife.

Everyone turned to look as the wedding party entered. There were hushed whispers of 'she looks beautiful' and 'wow' as she walked towards David. He turned to look at her. He almost fainted at the sight of her. He had always thought her a beautiful woman but today she looked amazing. He smiled and bent forward to kiss her lightly on the lips and whispered in her ear.

"You are so beautiful darling, I love you." She looked at his handsome face and his beautiful eyes filling up with tears and thought how very lucky she was. This really was the happiest day of her life and, like her Dad said, she was going to cherish every moment of it.

Once the ceremony was over and everyone had arrived at the hotel, Sadie and David felt more relaxed. It had been an emotional afternoon for both of them and now it was time to eat, drink and enjoy being with their guests. Sadie was delighted that Alan had come and couldn't wait to grab a few minutes alone with him and catch up on his news. Mr and Mrs Marshall together with Peter and his wife seemed to be enjoying talking to both sets of parents but she noticed that Mark was completely occupied in keeping Lisa to himself.

He seemed to be isolating her from everyone else. She knew Lisa very well by now and she knew that she would want to chat to the other guests but he was making it very difficult for her. She decided that she would introduce her to Alan. If Mark didn't like it, then it was too bad. Alan was on his own and she knew that he would be very interested in talking to her.

She grabbed Alan's hand and led him to the table where Mark and Lisa were sitting. "Alan, this is my best friend Lisa. Lisa this is Alan. I've been wanting you to meet each other for a long time. You are both very important to me and I would love you to be friends."

"Hello Lisa", said Alan. "It's good to meet you. I've heard a lot about you from Sadie. You looked lovely today by the way," he said.

"Thank you . That's very nice of you to say. It's good to meet you too," she answered. Sadie glanced quickly at Mark, as Lisa and Alan shook hands. His face said it all. He was smiling at Alan but his eyes were like cold steel. She knew that he was pissed off but she didn't care. Lisa had every right to talk to anyone she wanted to.

She just hoped that Mark wouldn't make a scene. At that moment David walked across the room towards her.

"Oh there you are Mrs Burns. You're wanted darling - Mr and Mrs Marshall would love to speak to you and Peter would like you to meet his wife. Can you come and have a word with them?"

"Yes of course", she said, smiling at the strangeness of being addressed as Mrs Burns. "I want to speak to everyone before we sit down to dinner. I was just introducing Alan to Lisa."

She noticed how David avoided making eye contact with Alan but simply smiled and said "That's good. Please help yourselves to a glass of bubbly - you too Mark", he added.

Sadie walked over to where the Marshalls were sitting with their parents. They stood up as she approached and Mrs Marshall hugged and kissed her, exclaiming how beautiful she looked and what a lovely service it had been. "It's lovely to have you here," she answered. "Have you all had a glass of bubbly yet? We'll be sitting down to dinner soon, you must all be starving - I know I am," she laughed.

After she had chatted to Peter and been introduced to his wife she made sure everyone had a drink and wandered back to see how things were going between Alan and Lisa. She was pleased to find them both deep in conversation. Mark was still sitting next to Lisa looking very displeased. She noticed that he seemed to be knocking back the champagne. There were three or four empty glasses in front of him and he looked as if he was about to get up and get another one.

Luckily at that moment, the Restaurant Manager announced that dinner was about to be served and requested that everyone take their places at the tables. She breathed a sigh of relief. She still didn't trust Mark not to make a scene. She hoped that by sitting down to dinner, his mood would lift. Alan was seated between David's Dad and Mrs Marshall so Mark would have Lisa to himself on the top table.

Thankfully, dinner went smoothly. The food was great and Rob's speech was predictably the highlight of the day.

He had everyone in fits of laughter recounting some of his funny stories from Sadie's childhood one minute, and then as he became more sentimental about her and his happy marriage to Mary, it was more about fighting back the tears. He had such a special way of connecting with people. Sadie had often thought that was what made him such a good teacher.

David also stood up and thanked everyone for coming and making their day so special. He thanked Lisa for being such a beautiful bridesmaid and lastly paid a loving tribute to Sadie. "I want to thank my gorgeous wife for making me the happiest man in the world today. This is just the start of our journey through life together. I can't think of anyone else that I would rather make that journey with."

"He then turned to Sadie, raised his glass and said "I propose a toast to my beautiful bride. I love you darling."

"I love you too, Mr Burns", she answered as she took his hand and squeezed it tightly. She felt overwhelmed with the emotion of the day and the outpouring of love. Right at that moment, she couldn't imagine that life could get any better than this. There were no dark clouds, no negative thoughts – just hopes and dreams for the future with her new husband.

Chapter 9

After the wedding, David surprised Sadie by telling her that he had booked a honeymoon in the Canary Islands. He gave her just two day's notice to dig out some summer clothes and get her suitcase packed. She hadn't expected a honeymoon. They were busy house hunting and in the process of applying for a mortgage and money was tight. But David was insistent that they should have a break in the sun before all the hard work of moving house was upon them. They had spent their wedding night in the hotel which was lovely and she would have been quite happy with that but, she wasn't going to turn her nose up at a week in the sun.

Both sets of parents had gone home having spent a few days in the hotel too. Sadie and David were pleased to see that they had all formed a close friendship. Rob and Mary had been to Brighton and stayed with Colin and Susan earlier in the year and now they were talking about going on a cruise together next summer.

Sadie had managed to catch up properly with Alan after the wedding breakfast. He told her how much he was enjoying his job. After qualifying, he had chosen to specialise in Criminal Law which was always his dream and he was still living in London.

He hadn't mentioned having a girlfriend so she had decided not to ask him. He was happy and seemed more confident in himself and that was the main thing. When he left to go back to London after the wedding, he had said to both her and David that he would keep in touch and would come and see them again once they had moved into their new house. She hoped that he would keep his word but felt unsure. Both him and David had been very cordial towards each other but she sensed there was still something which remained unspoken between them.

She had also spoken to Lisa the day after the wedding. Mark had been very quiet during the reception. He was obviously not having a good time. She just hoped that he wouldn't have taken it out on Lisa when they got home and decided to call her. The phone rang for a couple of minutes before Lisa answered. "Sorry Sadie I was in the loo. How are you doing Mrs Burns?" she laughed.

"I'm great thank you love. How are you? I didn't get to speak to you much at the reception. Alan seemed to be monopolising you. I hope Mark wasn't getting jealous. He didn't look very happy."

"No, I'm sorry about that. I was going to call you today anyway. He does tend to get jealous if he thinks there might be another guy interested in me. He was convinced that Alan was coming on to me, but that couldn't have been further from the truth. He wasn't interested so much in me but we found that we shared a common interest in science fiction. We were talking for ages but there was nothing else to it. I couldn't convince him though and we had a massive row when we got home," she said.

"He didn't hurt you did he?" asked Sadie feeling concerned. "No, I'm fine. It was just a row. He'll get over it," said Lisa rather unconvincingly.

"Honestly Lisa, I don't know how you put up with him. You know you could do so much better don't you? Alan for instance," she said.

"Alan is a lovely guy, but not for me Sadie. I love Mark. I know he can be difficult but I am as much to blame. I know I let him down sometimes. I should consider his feelings more and not be so selfish."

"Lisa you are the most unselfish person I know! You are not to blame for anything in your relationship. Mark wants to control you. He wants to own you exclusively and that's just not normal behaviour. I wish that you could see that," she said, suddenly feeling angry.

"Well let's just agree to disagree Sadie. Me and Mark are happy. You don't need to worry."

She ended the call by telling her that David had booked a week away in the Canaries and that she would ring her when she got back. Not for the first time, she felt worried. Why couldn't Lisa see that Mark was a control freak? Why was she so blind to it? She suddenly felt an icy cold fear sweep through her and shivered inwardly.

If he lays one finger on her, I'll bloody kill him! she thought to herself, trying to control the urge to call her back and tell her to pack her bags. She knew that Lisa wasn't prepared to talk about it anymore. She needed to try and respect that, but it was hard - very hard.

Mrs Marshall gladly agreed for Sadie to take a week's leave to go on honeymoon. She said that Peter was going to take her class until she came back. David had also requested a week off with his company. She felt excited at the prospect of enjoying some warm sunshine. It was early November and it was cold and miserable. She had packed her shorts, bikinis and summer dresses in anticipation.

"It's going to be just what the doctor ordered," said David as they were waiting for the taxi to take them to Stansted Airport. "A whole week of relaxation - just what we need", he sighed. "It will be all systems go when we get back. We've got to give notice on the flat and start looking seriously for our own house, so let's make sure that we recharge our batteries and make the most of that sunshine!"

She was looking forward to house hunting but she was under no illusions that it was going to be straightforward. Moving house never was in her experience. When she had lived with her parents they had moved several times because of their jobs. She remembered how stressed they had all been and the endless boxes which had to be packed and then unpacked again. It was exhausting. She knew David was right. They must make the most of this holiday and she was going to do her very best to do just that! They couldn't believe how quickly their week in the sun went. They enjoyed every minute. The hotel was superb. The weather was fabulous. They had eaten glorious food and drank lots of wine and made love at every opportunity - even late at night on the beach in the soft glow of the moonlight. It had been every bit as perfect as David said it would be. Sadie felt glowing and relaxed and now they were home, ready to face the next step in their lives and find somewhere to live.

She returned to work the day after they got home. As she entered the classroom, she was met with a little chorus of 'Good morning Mrs Burns'. She clapped her hands in surprise as she looked at the eager smiling faces before her. "So you know that I was away getting married do you?" she laughed.

One little girl put her hand up and said, "Mrs Marshall told us but you're not going to Germany too are you?" she asked, her little face creasing in concern.

"Oh bless you, no I'm not going anywhere Millie", she answered the little girl. "I'm back now and I'm staying," she said reassuringly.

The rest of the day was spent with her having lots of questions from the little ones about her wedding day. Did she have a long white dress? Did she have a party? What was her husband's name? Is he a nice man? It was amusing and very sweet, but she needed to concentrate on getting the children focused again. She guessed that they probably hadn't done very much learning over the past week. Knowing Peter he would probably have just made sure that they had lots of fun.

"Right children, it's back to work now. It will be the Christmas holidays before we know it, and we've got a lot of work to do before then." She watched as they sat upright hanging on every word she was saying . In that moment she realised more than ever that this was the job she wanted to do for ever.

When it came to lunchtime, she walked down the corridor to the staff room hoping to see Lisa, but she wasn't there. Peter was sitting there eating his sandwiches. "Hi Peter", she said. "Have you seen Lisa?" "I think she is off sick", he answered. "I haven't seen her for a week or so. Mrs Marshall will probably know," he answered.

"Ok, thanks. I'll go and see her," she said feeling uneasy. "Oh and thank you for taking my class for me," she added. "I hope they were good?"

"They were little stars but they missed you", he said. "How was the honeymoon?"

"It was great thank you Peter. So lovely to spend a week in the sunshine. I'll see you later."

She knocked gingerly on Mrs Marshall's door. "Come in", said the voice from within. "Oh Sadie, it's you. How are you? How was your honeymoon. You look absolutely glowing. You must have had some lovely weather."

"It was great Mrs Marshall," she answered.

"Oh please call me Wendy, Sadie. I feel like we know each other well enough now and Mrs Marshall sounds so stuffy", she laughed.

"Ok, Wendy – I wondered if you knew where Lisa is. Is she off sick?" she asked.

"Yes, she called in sick last Monday. A tummy bug I think," she said.

"That's odd". She was feeling fine when I last spoke to her – the day before I went away. I'll give her a call when I get home this evening to see how she is."

Sadie was really worried now. Something didn't feel right. She couldn't wait for the end of class so that she could speak to Lisa. When all the children had gone home, she sat in the classroom and wondered about ringing her before she left for home. She thought it would make sense to speak to her now. If anything was wrong , she could walk to her flat from the school and be there in minutes. The phone rang for a couple of minutes before she answered "Hello" in a very quiet timid voice.

"Lisa, it's me. I'm at the school. Mrs Marshall said you have been off sick all week. What's wrong. Are you ok?"

"Oh Hi Sadie. Did you have a lovely holiday?"

"Don't worry about that at the moment. What's going on? And be honest with me. I'm not listening to any stories about a tummy bug. What has Mark done to you?" There was an eerie silence on the other end of the phone. She hear Lisa take a deep breath as she answered.

"We had a fight – it wasn't Mark's fault. I had been talking about Alan and what a fascinating conversation we had about science fiction. Mark isn't interested in it at all so it was nice for me to converse with someone who shares my interests. It was like I was rubbing his nose in it. I should have known better. I'm aware of how jealous he can be. He got very angry and accused me of fancying Alan and asked me if I was planning on seeing him again. I told him how ridiculous that was and he just lashed out – he didn't mean to. He caught the side of my face and I've got a black eye. I didn't think it was appropriate to come to school looking like that and people were bound to ask questions. But Sadie before you say anything, I'm fine now. The bruises are fading and Mark and I have made up. He said that he would never react like that again. He is really sorry."

Sadie took a moment to absorb what Lisa was telling her before she answered.

"I knew it, I just knew it", she said. It was only a matter of time before he hurt you again and don't think that I was fooled for one minute when I saw those bruises on your arms and you said it was down to rough sex. He is a control freak and a bully and he is going to keep doing this to you unless you do something about it. You've got to leave him Lisa. You know he isn't going to change. I fear for your safety. I love you, you're my best friend. I can't bear to think of you suffering like this. You are a beautiful person, inside and out. You deserve so much better than this." She was struggling to hold back the tears but she was angry – so angry. How dare he? He was a monster. She had to get Lisa away from him somehow.

"Look, why don't you come and stay with us for a few days?" she asked. "We can talk about this properly and decide what to do. What do you say?"

"No. I know you have my best interests at heart and I appreciate it I really do. But Mark and I will sort it out. I need to try and be less selfish and consider his feelings more. I have to take responsibility for a lot of our problems", she answered. Sadie was gobsmacked. How could Lisa be so naïve?

"Well I can't force you but I want you to know that I will keep my phone beside me 24hrs a day and you have got to promise me that you will call me at any time if you're in trouble. Promise me?"

"I promise", said Lisa. "But I will be fine and I'm coming back to school on Monday so I'll see you then, ok?"

Sadie had no alternative other than to accept what she said , but driving home that evening she felt scared for her friend and feared that this situation wasn't going to end well.

She spoke to David about what had happened over dinner and a glass of wine that evening. David was worried about Sadie. He felt that she was getting too involved in her friend's relationship, although he did agree with her that Lisa should pack her bags and leave Mark. It was a difficult situation. She clearly cared for her friend very much and could see how Mark was manipulating and controlling her.

"I know how much you care for Lisa, darling. So do I, but you can't tell her what to do. All you can do is carry on being her friend and be there to support her, if and when she needs you. You'll drive her away otherwise.She's an intelligent woman. If and when she decides to leave Mark then it's got to be when she is ready. I suspect a lot of what is driving her reluctance to talk about it, is fear. Fear that he may leave her or hurt her in some way. He's an arsehole, there is no doubt about that, but honestly Sadie, I don't think there is much else we can do about it at the moment", he said.

"I know you're right", she answered, but I feel so helpless and I'm terrified that he is really going to hurt her one day."

"Well, like I said, just be vigilant and be there to support her if she needs you. Try not to worry too much, "he added. She nodded in agreement but couldn't shake off the feeling that Lisa was in danger. She hoped that she would be back at school on Monday. She would talk to her again. Maybe she could make her see sense.

David had registered with a few estate agents in town and had identified several properties for them both to look at. They decided to arrange viewing appointments at the weekend when they would have more time and could see them in daylight. The nights were dark and dreary now. It was proving to be a cold , wet Winter. They conceded that it probably wasn't a good time of year to be looking for a house but they were keen to find something and move in early in the New Year. They had given three month's notice on the flat in agreement with the landlord so time was of the essence.

The first house that they looked at was very close to town and had been empty for a while. It was a semi detached Victorian property with beautiful sash windows and large airy rooms with high ceilings. It was definitely in need of some TLC but they could both see the potential. The kitchen was small and galley style, but David was quick to realise that they could knock out a wall to create a large family kitchen and dining area. The garden at the back was huge and overrun with weeds but it backed onto farmland and was completely private. After the viewing, they looked at each other smiling.

"I know it needs a lot of work, but I bloody love it!" David exclaimed. "Me too!" said Sadie excitedly. "If we get it for a good price, we should have enough money left to make a few improvements and the rest we could do over time," she said.

"Well we've got a couple more to look at so let's not make a decision yet"he answered. Deep down he just knew that they had found their ideal home. It had felt right from the moment they went through the front door and he guessed that Sadie had that same feeling but he didn't want to rush into anything just yet.

They were disappointed with the other houses they looked at that day. They were just not what they wanted - modern and beautiful inside but completely soulless. They had arranged some more viewings which they agreed they would still go ahead with, but it was obvious to both of them that the first one was the one to beat. That evening they talked constantly about all the improvements they could make to turn it into their dream home. Sadie didn't think it was possible to get so excited about buying a house.

"In time, we could even add an extension to the back of the house, there's masses of room," she said. "Steady on," laughed David. "We haven't decided to buy it yet – have we? Or have we?" Let's make a decision by Monday and if we do go ahead, we'll put a cheeky offer in. Do you agree?" "I agree", she answered.

By the time Sunday evening had come and they had viewed the

other properties on their list, they both agreed that house number one was the one! David said that he would ring the estate agents from his office in the morning and make an offer below the asking price. The fact that they had a mortgage in place and they were first time buyers with nothing to sell was in their favour and he knew that they had more than a good chance of getting it. He said that he would ring Sadie's mobile at lunchtime and let her know the outcome. She left for school that morning with butterflies in her tummy. She was excited about the house and also anxious about Lisa and whether or not she would be back to work today. Luckily the morning passed quickly. The children were engrossed in their latest project of drawing and painting pictures to illustrate each letter of the alphabet. Sadie told them that the best pictures would be displayed on the wall in the corridor outside the classroom.

She smiled at some of their efforts. Little Marcus had drawn his version of a gnome under the letter N and looked puzzled when Sadie pointed out that gnome began with a G! "Don't worry Marcus. He's a beautiful gnome and it's a very hard word to spell. We will be doing more work on spellings next year when you're a little older, so you mustn't be upset. You are a good boy for choosing such a clever word – well done". She was happy to see that Marcus didn't mind that he had made a mistake and happily carried on painting his gnome.

When it came to lunchtime, she made her way to the staff room. She was looking forward to seeing Lisa and was still eagerly waiting for a call from David about the house. She saw her by the sink filling the kettle to make a cup of tea.

"Hi lovely, I was hoping you would be back today. How are you feeling?" she said looking earnestly into her face. She could see a faint bruise under one of her eyes which Lisa had tried unsuccessfully to cover with make-up.

"I'm absolutely fine, thank you Sadie. How are you? I've missed you," she answered. "Let' s go and sit down over there in the corner", she answered. "We've got a lot to catch up on. As they took their tea and sat down she wondered about mentioning the fact that she could see the bruises under Lisa's eye but decided to wait and see if she mentioned it first.

Before she could get a word in edgeways, Lisa wanted to know everything about the honeymoon. Was it a lovely hotel? Was the weather good? Did they do any sightseeing?

She seemed to be bombarding her with questions, almost in an effort to avoid her bringing up the subject. She told her that they had a lovely holiday and that, since they had been home, her and David had found an amazing house and that they were going to put in an offer to buy it. Lisa was delighted and even more so when she heard that the house was much nearer to town and that they would be living closer to one another.

"Sadie, that's fab news. We'll be able to meet up more. It's so exciting!" She wasn't convinced by this burst of enthusiasm from Lisa. She seemed a bit hyper and over excited - not her usual self at all. She decided to bite the bullet.

"Now, that's enough about me. What about you? I know you have tried to cover them with make up, but I can see your bruises Lisa. I can't believe he hit you in the face enough to cause bruising like that. Did he hurt you anywhere else?"

At this point Lisa's apparent happy mood crumbled. She started weeping quietly. Sadie led her from the staff room and away from prying eyes. "Come on my love let's go outside and round the back of the school. You can tell me all about it." Once they were outside, Lisa's body began to shake with loud sobs.

"You were right Sadie.I think that Mark has a problem. He has always had a short fuse and like I've told you before, he doesn't like it if anyone pays me attention. But he is even jealous of our friendship. He wants me to stop seeing you. He thinks that you are turning me against him.

"Well, he's right there!" exclaimed Sadie.

"I know I shouldn't have come back to school today. Peter and a couple of the other teachers noticed the bruise under my eye. I just told them that I opened a cupboard door and it hit me in the face. That seemed to satisfy them. I just couldn't bear to be at home on my own for another day. Mark is out working and when he comes home he is often in a foul mood because he is tired. I can't seem to do anything right.He criticises how I dress, my cooking. He says that I don't keep the place clean, and then when we go to bed he expects me to be intimate with him.

Last night he forced himself on me, Sadie. He has never done that before. It was something that I never want to go through again. I just don't know what to do." With these words Lisa started crying again.

"That's rape! You've got to leave him Lisa. There is nothing else you can do. He is going to destroy you bit by bit. You can't teach this afternoon. You need to go home and pack a bag and I'll pick you up after school. You can stay with us until you decide what you are going to do. I'll speak to Mrs Marshall. She'll understand. She is very fond of you and she knows that you are having relationship problems. It will be fine, I promise. Off you go and I'll see you later."

They hugged one another and Sadie gently wiped away her tears. As Lisa walked away, she turned and waved and Sadie blew her a kiss. She didn't know how she would get through the rest of the afternoon after this and she still hadn't heard from David. She walked back to the classroom, her mind in turmoil.

When she had the chance to check her phone, she could see that

David had tried to ring her twice and he had left her a message 'Offer in on the house. They are going to get back to me this evening. Fingers crossed xx' She texted back saying that she would be bringing Lisa home with her tonight and that she would explain when she saw him. She hoped that he wouldn't be cross. She knew that he felt she was too involved in Lisa's problems, but surely he would realise that she couldn't just leave her there with Mark. Not after what he had done to her.

Lisa was ready and had a bag packed when Sadie arrived. She seemed calmer and resolute that she was doing the right thing. She had written a note for Mark and left it on the kitchen worktop. She didn't say where she was going but just that she needed a few days away on her own. She asked that he didn't try and contact her. She wanted some space to figure things out. She hoped that he would understand.

When Sadie and Lisa arrived home, David was already there. He smiled sympathetically and gave Lisa a hug. "I got Sadie's message. I'm so sorry Lisa. It sounds like you have had a rough time. I can't believe that Mark could be so cruel. He must have a screw loose or something. You're welcome to stay here for as long as you like. As it happens, I have to go away on business for a few days, so it will give you the opportunity to spend time with Sadie and work out what you are going to do in the long term."

Sadie was puzzled and turning to David she said "Going away? You didn't tell me?"

"I'm sorry sweetheart, I didn't find out until today. They want me to go down to Bristol and see a client who owns a company and is planning a merger. He needs advice on drafting contracts and negotiating agreements. It's a good opportunity for me to prove myself. It could be the start of more cases like this. I didn't want to turn it down."

"No, of course not. I'm just surprised that's all. It seems a bit sudden. They could have given you a bit more notice."

"It doesn't work like that, I'm afraid", he said. Sometimes these cases call for an immediate response. Anyway it's good that you will have Lisa for company", he added.

"Have you heard from the estate agents yet?" she asked.

"Well that was going to be my next bit of news. They have accepted our offer!" Sadie squealed with delight. "Really?" she said.

"Yes really, and the good news is that they think it will go through quickly as there is no chain involved. We should be in just after Christmas!"

"Oh I am so happy for you both. That's brilliant news," said Lisa. "You both deserve this so much and I can't tell you how much I appreciate you letting me stay here for a while. I'm sure that me being away will help Mark to see that I'm not prepared to put up with his behaviour anymore and that if he wants me back, then he will have to change."

"I don't think he will ever change Lisa and I wouldn't even consider going back to him. You need to move on and make a new life for yourself," said Sadie feeling surprised that she was even thinking of going back.

"Well let's all go out to the pub in the village and get something to eat", said David. I think we all need a drink too. It's been an eventful day!"

Chapter 10

David left for Bristol early the next morning. Sadie drove him to the station leaving Lisa still in bed sleeping. They hadn't mentioned Mark again since yesterday evening although Lisa said that she had lots of missed calls from him and he had left several messages saying how sorry he was and that he wanted her to come home. She had managed to persuade her to stay for at least the time that David was away, and to rest. She telephoned Mrs Marshall and informed her that Lisa was staying with her and that she wouldn't be coming back to school for the rest of the week.

Mrs Marshall was extremely understanding and obviously concerned for Lisa. She told her not to worry and to tell her that she would arrange cover until she felt ready to come back. As she left for school that morning, she hoped that Lisa would be ok on her own until she got home. She knew that deep down, she was ready to forgive Mark despite her promises that she wouldn't go back to him. She felt completely helpless and wondered what else it would take before she realised what a bastard Mark was. She thought how ironic the saying 'Love is Blind' was. It certainly was in Lisa's case.

When she got home that evening, Lisa had made a Spag Bol for dinner and had tidied the flat. She seemed much brighter and looked more rested. Sadie asked if she had heard anymore from Mark. She said that he had been texting her all day but she had refrained from answering him. "That's good Lisa. Let him stew in his own juice for a while. I don't want you to go back to him, you know I don't, but I also know you. You're thinking about it aren't you?" she said feeling worried.

"He seems genuinely sorry Sadie. He even said that he would go to anger management classes. He recognizes that he has issues. He wants to be a better person. He also mentioned getting married."

"It's just words Lisa. People like him don't change. He may be fine for a while, but I guarantee that it won't last. He will revert to his old ways eventually, but I can't make you leave him. I can only advise you. If you want to go back to him, then it's your decision, but don't expect me to be happy about it."

She suddenly felt weary of the whole situation. David was right. She had become too involved. It was affecting her own relationship. They should be together now, celebrating the prospect of buying their own house. She wondered if he had chosen to take the case in Bristol to escape the drama of it all.

David telephoned later in the evening. He sounded happy and she thought maybe a little bit intoxicated. "Is it going well?" she asked.

"It's going brilliantly Sadie. I'm in the hotel bar with my client now." Another couple of days should do it and then I'll be home. I've also found a solicitor to handle the purchase of the house and there should be a surveyor going in within the next couple of weeks, so it's all systems go there too. Exciting times eh? How is Lisa doing?" he asked.

"She is fine. She looks so much better already. But I think she is seriously considering going back to him. He is so manipulative but she just can't see it. He is promising her all sorts and she is falling for it hook line and sinker. No matter what I say, she obviously can't get him out of her head. I don't get it, I really don't. It's not as if he is some hunky stud. God knows what on earth she sees in him!" Sadie felt exasperated and David could sense her frustration.

"Well, I hate to say, I told you so. If she decides to go back to him, there is nothing you can do about it. Like I've said before, you can only be there to support her if she needs you. Ultimately, It's not your responsibility. She needs to make her own decisions. Have you spoken to your mum recently? Perhaps she can advise you. She would want to know that you are going through this, you know she would. Give her a ring. It might make you feel better and look at things differently."

She agreed. She would ring her mum at the first opportunity when Lisa wasn't around. She went to bed that night feeling a lot better. David was right. She felt lucky that she had such an understanding and caring husband. She would be lost without him.

The next morning she woke up to mouth watering smells coming from the kitchen. Lisa was cooking bacon, eggs and mushrooms for breakfast. As she walked into the kitchen in her dressing gown, Lisa said

"Oh good, you're just in time. I was just going to call you to come and have breakfast before you have your shower. You should go to work with a nourishing meal inside you. I always cook breakfast for Mark before he goes to work."

"I usually make do with porridge and a piece of toast. That's enough for me", said Sadie. And David has cereal. He's not a big fan of cooked breakfasts. But it's very kind of you lovely. It looks delicious, thank you."

She asked Lisa what her plans were for that day. She said that she fancied having a long walk so she planned to get the bus to the big park near town and walk round the lake.

"I might even take some stale bread and feed the ducks," she said. "I'll have dinner ready for you when you get home. Do you like pork chops? I noticed there are some in the freezer. I can get them out and make a little roast dinner."

"That sounds yummy. You're spoiling me Lisa".

"It's the least I can do. You're putting me up and you won't accept any money. I just want to show my appreciation. You are such a good friend." Sadie felt touched by Lisa's words. She was such a sweet girl. If only she would feel brave enough to end her relationship with Mark and move on. If only......

Sure enough, when she arrived home from work, Lisa had prepared a lovely meal.

"I could get used to this", she laughed as she sat down to eat her dinner "I'm starving actually. I don't know what's wrong with me lately, I can't stop eating!"

"Perhaps you're pregnant" said Lisa laughing. "I've heard that could be one of the first signs."

"Oh don't say that. We're going to be moving house soon, that's the last thing I need and I'm on the pill anyway, so it can't be that. How was your walk today? Did you manage to avoid getting wet? It's been a miserable day, I thought you would probably change your mind about going out."

"No, I still ventured out and I was lucky, I managed to stay dry. I enjoyed it actually, it helped clear my head and decide what to do." Sadie felt her heart sink.

She guessed what Lisa was going to say next.

"I spoke to Mark today. We had a long conversation and he has promised me that, if I come home, he is going to make an appointment to see a counsellor and if they recommend it, he will enrol on an anger management class. He is genuinely sorry Sadie. He was almost in tears. I truly believe that he is going to change."

Sadie could see that she meant it. She was definitely going back to Mark and nothing she would say was going to dissuade her. In that moment she realised that she had to let her go. She wasn't going to stop her. Whatever happened next was out of her hands.

"Ok love, it's your decision. When are you leaving?"

"I'm going back tonight. Mark is going to pick me up at the end of the road. He didn't want to face you. He is so ashamed of his behaviour. I just wanted to thank you - and David. You have both been so kind and understanding. I wouldn't have got through this without you," she said.

"I will always be here for you Lisa. Please don't forget it and never be afraid to contact me at any time if you need me - day or night. Are you planning on going back to work then?"

"Yes I spoke to Mrs Marshall this morning. I'm going back tomorrow. She was really pleased to hear from me."

"That's good. The children will be pleased to see you. I'm sure they have missed you," said Sadie.

Lisa packed her things and left at 7pm that evening. Mark had texted her to say that he was waiting in the car at the end of the road. Sadie hugged her tightly and said she would see her at school tomorrow. As she walked down the road towards Mark, she prayed inwardly that she was going to be ok. As far as she was concerned she would never trust Mark again. She didn't believe a word that he said, but there was absolutely nothing she could do about it. After checking in with David to see how he was getting on in Bristol, she decided to ring her mum. She hadn't spoken to her in a while. Both her and her dad didn't even know about the house. She had been so involved with Lisa's problems lately that she had neglected everything and everyone else. She hadn't spoken to Alan since the wedding either. She made a mental note to contact him too in a couple of days.

"Hi Mum", she said as she heard her warm, comforting voice

on the end of the phone. "Sadie, I've been thinking about you. We haven't spoken for ages. Is everything ok?"

"Yes, I'm fine Mum. I'm so sorry that I haven't rung you before now. It's been one thing after another here."

"Oh dear, nothing bad I hope", said Mary feeling worried.

"No, mostly good," answered Sadie. "I'll give you the good news first." She proceeded to tell Mary all about the house and that their offer had been accepted. "We should be moving in just after Christmas", she said excitedly.

"That's wonderful news love. It's gone through quickly hasn't it?" said Mary. "I'm so happy for you. The house sounds really nice and it seems like it has a lot of potential. It could be your forever home."

"Yes, maybe. It's in a great area, and in time we will be able to extend on it. It's got a huge back garden." "Wait until I tell your dad. He will be thrilled. He's working late at the school tonight otherwise I'm sure he would want to talk to you and hear all your news."

She then went on to explain everything that had happened with Lisa. Mary listened, sighing and tutting intermittently as she described how Mark had hurt her both mentally and physically.

"Why on earth has she gone back to him after what he has done?" said Mary incredulously. "Lisa is a lovely girl. She doesn't deserve to be treated like that. I knew there was something odd about that man when I met him at the wedding. My instincts are usually right. I'm sure you tried to stop her love, so don't blame yourself.'"

Mary sensed that Sadie was feeling guilty, that she hadn't tried harder to prevent Lisa from going back to him.

"There was no stopping her Mum. She was determined to give him another chance. God knows why, but she still loves him."

As they ended their call, Mary told her daughter that she would ring her again in a few days to see how things were. They also agreed that they needed to decide what to do about Christmas. Sadie said that she didn't think David would want to go anywhere this year. They would be very busy preparing for their big move. She knew that his parents had invited them to Brighton along with Mary and Rob but she wouldn't commit until she had spoken to him.

Mary was surprised to learn that David was away on business. She wondered, as did Sadie, whether it was because of the situation with Lisa. His business trip probably gave him the excuse he needed to avoid getting involved. She still felt slightly uneasy when it came to David. She knew that Rob didn't understand. He couldn't see that there was anything to be concerned about. David loved Sadie, he was hard working and he was always very pleasant and polite whenever they met. As far as Rob was concerned, Mary was being paranoid. He had concluded that in her eyes, there was never going to be anybody good enough for their daughter.

When Rob came home from work, Mary relayed the news from Sadie. He was thrilled to hear that they had found a house that they wanted to buy.

"See I told you didn't I? That lad is such a hard worker. They would never have got a mortgage if he hadn't qualified so quickly and look at the jobs he is getting already. He travels all over London seeing clients. He must be earning really good money now," said Rob.

"Well apparently, Sadie said he is away on business in Bristol which brings me to her next piece of news." She proceeded to tell Rob what had happened with Lisa and how worried Sadie was about her. He was horrified to hear that Mark had abused her and said that, knowing what a sweet and caring girl their daughter was, he could understand the concern she had for her friend.

"Poor Lisa", said Rob. I really liked her when we met her at the wedding. Such a pretty girl. What on earth is she doing with a man like that? She should run a mile." "I know", said Mary. "I think Sadie tried really hard to convince her to stay with her and David until she found somewhere else to live but, after a few days, she decided to go back to him. Apparently he has promised to change and says he will see a counsellor and enrol in an anger management class. Sadie isn't convinced and, from what I've heard, neither am I. Men like Mark don't usually change."

"Well, doesn't it make you glad that our Sadie has found herself a great guy in David when you hear stories like that? You really must stop worrying. I know you still have your doubts about him, but just look at how happy he makes our daughter and how well he is providing for her. I know she is in safe hands with him and that makes me happy. You should be too love. Promise me you'll put all these negative thoughts aside once and for all. What would Susan and Colin think if they knew that you doubted their son? Just think how hurt they would feel."

"I know and of course I wouldn't want to hurt them. I won't mention it again, I promise," she answered.

David returned from his business trip to Bristol the day after Lisa left. He was surprised to hear that she had gone back to Mark after what he had done to her but said to Sadie that there was nothing else she could have done. He could see that she was very upset and tried to reassure her that Lisa knew what she was doing and that she would be fine. If Mark was going to get the help that he said he was, then perhaps they could turn their relationship around. There was obviously a lot of love between them. With professional help and support, they could be happy again.

She pretended to agree rather than getting into a difficult conversation. She was aware that David was losing patience with the whole situation. He begrudged the fact she had got herself so involved. It was easier not to talk about it with him.

David was on a high after his trip and spent the whole evening telling her every detail of the contract that his client had made with the company who were behind the takeover and how he had negotiated on his behalf to get the best deal. She was really happy for him and loved the fact that he was totally absorbed in his job. He asked her how things were going at school and he laughed when she told him the story about little Marcus, his picture of a gnome and how he thought it was spelt with an N .

"Bless him" said David. "That's so sweet. He sounds a real little character. You are so good with the children Sadie. You're going to make a great mum one day." She smiled at the irony of David's words. She hoped that she was wrong, but she had a strong suspicion that she might already be pregnant.

She hadn't been feeling too well for the last couple of days and, at first, had put it down to all of the emotional upset with Lisa, but there were other signs. Her boobs felt sore and tender and, when she wasn't feeling sick, she was eating for England! Her appetite had always been good but now it was off the scale. Biscuits, chocolate, crisps – things she would never have eaten before. She just couldn't get enough of them.

However, at the same time, she told herself that it couldn't be possible. She was on the pill. She thought back to her honeymoon and the night that her and David had made love on the beach. They were both very drunk that night and she had been sick before she went to bed. She began to wonder – could that have made any difference?

As much as she longed to have children, now just wasn't the right time. They were about to move house, there was so much to do. What would her parents say? What about her job? She wasn't ready – not yet. She decided not to say anything to David. She would go to the chemist in her lunch hour tomorrow and buy a pregnancy test. Until then, she would try and not think about it.

David was very eager to make love when they went to bed that night. She felt tired and distracted. There was so much on her mind, but he had a way of getting her to respond to his touch. He knew exactly how to arouse her. Soon she was lost in the passion of the moment. All her worrying thoughts disappeared. For now she was in her safe place – in the arms of the man she loved.

Whilst they were having breakfast the next morning, she mentioned that she had spoken to her mum and she was asking what they were going to do for Christmas. She had said to her that they might just stay at home , there was so much to do before the move. He agreed but suggested that they go to his parent's just for Christmas day and come home on Boxing Day. "One day won't make a difference, sweetheart and it will save you having to cook, especially if half of the kitchen is packed in boxes by then!"

"I guess so", she said. "I'll ring mum tonight and tell her that we are going then. Will you let your Mum know too, or do you want me to ring her?"

"I'll call her", he answered. I'm due to speak to her anyway. I haven't rung her for a few weeks so I'm probably in the dog house," he laughed.

Sadie managed to slip out from the school during the morning break time and go to the chemist in the high street and get a pregnancy test. She decided that she would wait until she got home that evening before she did the test. She was keen to see Lisa at lunchtime and didn't want anything else to distract her. Lisa was sitting eating a sandwich when she entered the staff room. She smiled and jumped up to greet her.

"Hi Sadie, it's good to see you. Are you ok?"

"Yes, I'm fine but are you ok?" she answered.

"I'm great, I really am. Mark and I have sorted out our problems and I think, for the first time, we really understand one another. Those few days away from him seemed to do the trick. He has made an appointment to see a counsellor privately next week. He is really making an effort. He even cooked breakfast for ME this morning. I couldn't believe it! I'm so grateful to you Sadie. If it wasn't for you, I don't think Mark and I would be in this position now. He also asked me to apologise to you for the things that he said about you. He knows you are a good friend to me and that he had no right to ask me to stop seeing you."

As she listened to Lisa's excited account of Mark's promises to her and looked at her pretty smiling face full of hope, she just felt sadness. She didn't believe a word of it. She knew, at some point, his empty words would break Lisa's heart once again. But there was nothing she could do. She took her hand and squeezed it tightly.

"I'm so happy for you lovely, I really am." She hated herself for not being brave enough to say what she really felt. But Lisa was happy – for now. She decided not to do or say anything that was going to spoil that for her.

When she got home that evening, she was relieved to see that David had texted her to say that he was working late and wouldn't be home for dinner. He said that she should go ahead and eat without him. It would probably be bedtime before he was back. Normally, she would have been disappointed but she now had the opportunity to do her pregnancy test without him being around. Her hands were shaking as she followed the instructions on the box and peed on the stick.

She waited nervously for the result to appear. It seemed to take ages. She covered her eyes, afraid to look. When she finally took her hand away, she gasped in disbelief. There were two double vertical lines – she was pregnant! She was stunned – she didn't know what to think – she didn't know how she felt. She should have been ecstatic. But she just felt numb.

She wondered if she should tell David just yet. It could be a mistake. These tests weren't 100% accurate after all. She wanted to be absolutely sure and decided that she would make an appointment with the doctor and ask for a blood test. She thought that would be the best way of getting a definite yes or no. She went to bed that night waiting for David to come home and wondering how she was going to explain to him why she was going to the doctors.

'I'll think of something' she thought to herself as she drifted off to sleep.

When she woke up the next morning, David was lying beside her snoring. She hadn't heard him come to bed and wondered what time he had got home. She gave him a nudge and he opened his eyes, looking at her quizzically.

"Morning sweetheart. Are you ok? Did my snoring wake you up?"
"Yes you were snoring but I was awake anyway" she answered. "I didn't hear you come in last night. What time did you get home?"

"Yes, sorry, it was late. I should have texted you again. I think it was about 1am."

"1am! What on earth were you doing until that time?"

"I had a lot of paperwork to catch up on after my trip to Bristol. I was lucky to have caught the last train, otherwise I would have been stranded in the office overnight," he said.

"Are you going in this morning?" she asked.

"Yes I am but I'll leave it until later. I think I deserve a bit of a lie in."

"Ok. I'm going to get ready for school now but just to let you know that I'll be a bit late home tonight. I'm going to book an appointment at the doctors. I think I may have a stomach bug. I've been feeling sick lately. There's a lot of viruses around at the moment. A lot of the kids are off school with sickness."

"Oh poor you", he answered. Do you want me to come with you? I can finish work early. They owe me some time off."

"No, I'll be fine darling. I'm sure it's nothing to worry about. I'll see you tonight for dinner, ok?"

She hated herself for lying but she had no choice at the moment. She didn't want to tell him she was pregnant and then it turned out to be a false alarm. She needed to be sure. She also remembered that she had to ring her Mum about Christmas. She told herself that she would call her when she got back from the doctors.

The day passed quickly. The kids were engrossed in their Christmas projects which meant that Sadie wasn't under any pressure to keep them occupied. When she saw Lisa at lunchtime, she still seemed happy and bubbly. She didn't tell her that she thought she might be pregnant. David should be the first one to know and, if it was true, she needed time to process it herself. She was struggling to make sense of her feelings. Part of her felt excited at the prospect of having a baby but it just wasn't the right time. They were about to move house. She had just taken on her first class at the school. He mind was muddled with thoughts of how she would cope.

Luckily she had managed to book an appointment at the GP surgery that evening after school. She was going to see one of the nurses for a blood test first and the receptionist said, if necessary, she would see the doctor when she got the results. As she pulled into the car park, the nerves began to kick in. This was actually happening – she was about to find out if she was pregnant! She touched her stomach and she wondered – could there be a baby inside me? It seemed surreal.

The nurse was really nice and could see that Sadie was nervous. "I'm going to take a blood test which will confirm whether or not you are pregnant . I know it will give you peace of mind, but I have to say the pregnancy tests on the market nowadays are very accurate. I would be surprised if it wasn't positive", she said.

Sadie smiled and said that she understood. "I'm sure you are right, but I don't want to tell my husband until I can say definitely." "I completely understand", said the nurse. After she had taken the phial of blood, she asked her to take her shoes off and lay on the couch. "Can you lift you top up a bit Sadie and just pull your skirt down a little bit. I'm just going to feel your tummy." There was hushed silence as the nurse gently pushed low down on her tummy.

Sadie watched her as a smile spread across her face.

"Well young lady, I know we have to wait for the blood results to come back, but I'm pretty sure that you are pregnant from my examination. I'm not a doctor but I've seen countless women in the early stages of pregnancy and I would say that you are between six and seven weeks.

"How can that be when I'm on the pill?" said Sadie.

"Did you miss taking it one day or were you unwell at all?' enquired the nurse.

"Well there was one occasion when I had drunk too much alcohol. I was on my honeymoon and I was really sick that night. Could that be it?"

"It may well be. I guess we will never know though. These things are unusual, but they do happen. Are you going to go ahead with the pregnancy if it is positive? You're not under any pressure you know. If you don't want this baby, you have the right to a termination." said the nurse. "Oh God no!" exclaimed Sadie. "It wasn't planned, but I would never, ever do that. It's a surprise that's all. I just need to get my head around it."

The nurse gave her a broad smile and told her not to worry. The blood results would be back in the morning and she said she would ring her and let her know the results straightaway. She had already decided that she wouldn't say anything to David that evening. She would talk to him when she had heard back from the surgery, and let him know the results one way or another.

As soon as she got home, he was waiting for her with a worried expression on his face. "How did it go at the doctors darling? Are you ok? Is it a stomach bug?"

"The doctor thinks it probably is. He gave me a thorough examination. My blood pressure was fine and I don't have a temperature. He told me to be careful what I eat for the next few days and get plenty of rest. So there's nothing to worry about," she lied.

"I'm just going to have scrambled eggs on toast tonight. I don't fancy a big dinner. Is that ok with you darling?" she asked.

"Of course it is", he said. Actually I had dinner at lunchtime. You'll never guess who with," he teased.

"No, who? Tell me," urged Sadie.

"It was Alan. He rang me in the morning and said that he would be in the area at lunchtime. He was seeing a client at 2.30pm so he wondered if we could meet for lunch beforehand. He took me to this lovely Mexican restaurant – and he paid!'

"Really? How lovely. I've been thinking of him lately. I was going to suggest that we all try and get together before we move house," said Sadie.

"I don't think we will be able to darling. He is working on a big case at the moment and then there's Christmas. I said that we would contact him once we had moved into the house and he could come and help us with some painting," he laughed.

"That was a bit cheeky, but I have to say, it's a good idea. We're going to need some help. What did he say? Did he mind?"

"No, he said he would love to. He enjoys decorating apparently. He says he has completely modernised his flat since he has lived there and it looks lovely now. He was thinking about moving, but he's changed his mind. His flat looks so swish now."

She quizzed him all evening about Alan. What was he up to? How was his job? Did he have a girlfriend?

He said that they didn't talk about anything else other than work and that he had no idea whether or not he had a girlfriend. He could see how happy he was in his job though and, like him, he seemed to be moving up the ladder pretty quickly and was earning a lot of money.

She was so pleased to hear that David had not only met up with Alan but that he had appeared to really enjoy his company. She hoped that the strangeness she had seen between them on previous occasions had gone. She looked forward to Alan being a big part of their lives again. She missed him.

She had a sleepless and restless night thinking about what tomorrow would bring and what her blood results would reveal. As she got out of bed in the morning, she suddenly felt very strange. Her legs were wobbly and her head was throbbing.

"You ok darling?" said David feeling worried. He hadn't seen her like this before.

"I feel a bit sick and shaky," she answered. Before he could get around the bed to help her, she had run to the bathroom. He could hear her vomiting into the toilet pan.

"Sadie what's wrong? Do you think it's the stomach bug?" he asked. She lifted her head and grabbed some tissues to wipe her mouth. "Yes, I'm sure it is. Don't worry, it's nothing serious. I'll be ok in a minute.

"Well I think you should have the day off today and spend it resting in bed. I can ring Mrs Marshall for you. I'm sure they will manage without you for one day." He looked at her pale face and could see that she was shaking. He gently sat her on the bed, pulled her legs round and brought the covers up around her.

"Make sure you stay there. I'll get a glass and a jug of water, and I'll make you some toast. Just keep hydrated and sleep. I'll get home early tonight to take care of you, but keep your phone beside you. If you need me at all, just call me - promise."

"I promise," she said weakly. "I'm sure I'll be ok after some rest. I didn't sleep well last night."

He set off to work but was feeling concerned about Sadie. She was never unwell. This stomach bug had hit her hard. He decided he would ring her at lunchtime and see how she was feeling. If she was no better, he would come straight home. Mrs Marshall was very understanding when he had called to say that she wouldn't be well enough to come in. She hadn't known her to have a day off sick since the day she started at the school. She asked David to wish her well and told her not to worry. If she still wasn't feeling any better by tomorrow, she would arrange for another teacher to take her class.

Meanwhile, she started to feel a bit better. She ate the toast that David had made for her and had a couple of glasses of water. The sickness seemed to have passed so she got up, put her dressing gown on and went through to the lounge. She was about to turn the TV on and watch some daytime television, when she heard her phone ringing in the bedroom.

As she picked up her phone a voice asked "Hello, is that Mrs Burns?" She recognised that it was the nurse from the GP surgery.

"Yes it is", she answered.

"I'm Nurse Jackson. I saw you in the surgery yesterday for a blood test. We have the results through now." Sadie took a deep breath and sat back in the chair waiting nervously. "I am very pleased to tell you that your pregnancy has been confirmed. I have arranged an appointment for you on 8th January at 11am to see the midwife. You will be under her care from then on, unless there is a need for you to see the doctor. Congratulations!"

She listened carefully trying to absorb the news without over reacting. "That's great, thank you Nurse Jackson. I'll write that appointment in my diary so that I don't forget. I appreciate you ringing me so quickly."

"You are welcome my dear. If you have any problems or any questions to ask, please don't hesitate to ring the surgery. If I'm here, I'll be glad to help. If not, one of my colleagues will take care of you. Bye for now."

She ended the call and sat wondering what to do next. She would have to tell David now. She knew he wanted children. They had discussed it, but whether he would be happy to know that she was pregnant so soon after they had got married, she wasn't so sure. He was ambitious. He had big plans for his career. At times she had wondered if his strong desire for success was more important to him than she was. He could be selfish and self centered sometimes. How would he cope with a new baby disrupting his routine? She dismissed the feelings of negativity spinning around in her head and decided that, until she spoke to him and gave him the news, it was pointless to speculate.

She turned the television on and made herself some lunch. She told herself that she was going to stay on the couch all afternoon and rest just like she had promised David she would. She noticed that he hadn't telephoned her to see how she was and presumed that he was probably busy, so decided to text him and say that she was feeling much better. He quickly replied and said that he had been about to ring her and was pleased that she was ok now. He said he would try and get home early and that he would get a takeaway to save her cooking.

Sadie sent him back a thumbs up and heart emoji and laid back on the couch closing her eyes. Within minutes, she was fast asleep, her dreams a jumble of vivid images of babies crying and someone trying to chase her. She woke with a start to hear David opening the front door. She looked at the clock. It was 7pm. She had been asleep for five hours!

She looked up at his smiling face looking down on her and decided not to waste any more time. "Hi David. I'm glad you're home. Sit down, I've got something to tell you."

Chapter 11

David sat in stunned silence as she told him the whole story from when she suspected she was pregnant and taking a test, going to the surgery for a blood test and finally having confirmation that morning to say she was definitely pregnant - probably between six and seven weeks.

He asked her why she felt she had to pretend to him that she had a stomach bug. Why hadn't she told him the truth? He was hurt to think that she had kept it from him.

"I'm sorry David. I thought I was doing the right thing. If it had turned out to be a false alarm, then you would have been disappointed. I wanted to be absolutely sure before I told you. You are happy about it aren't you?"

She noticed his shocked expression and feared that he was upset with her.

"Of course. It's just a complete surprise that's all. It's the last thing I was expecting." With that, he jumped up and moved towards her with his arms outstretched. He took her in his arms and said "It's good news darling. I admit It's a bit of a shock but I just need to get used to the idea. I thought we were going to wait a couple of years before we had a family."

"Me too. I'm on the pill. I thought that would prevent me from getting pregnant, but apparently it can happen, although it's unusual.

I've got an appointment with the midwife in January. Will you come with me? I'm sure we will find out more then."

David agreed that he would come to the appointment with her and that they were not going to tell anyone about the pregnancy, including their parents, until after the first scan, just in case anything was to go wrong.

"The trouble with my mum is that she is very clever at sensing things," said Sadie. "Dad says she's like an old witch!" "Well you had better brush up on your acting skills darling. We can't tell her. We can't tell anyone. It's too soon."

She agreed wholeheartedly and said that she would do her best to distract her mum from any awkward questions at Christmas by talking about the house move and asking for her advice on home furnishings. "She likes to think that she is helping. That should do the trick," she said.

That night as they lay in bed, David placed his hand on her stomach. "I'm sure you have a little bump there already," he said stroking her gently.

"I know. I noticed it this morning. I shouldn't be showing yet, but you can definitely see something. I just hope that my clothes are going to fit me for the next couple of months, otherwise people are going to put two and two together."

"I am happy about it darling, I really am. I'm sorry that I didn't show it when you first told me. I just couldn't believe it that's all," he said.

"I know. It took me a while to process it too. I just hope we will be able to cope. There is so much going on in our lives at the moment. I do realise that it's bad timing."

"We will cope. We have each other and I'm sure our parents will help once the baby is born. I don't want you to worry. Leave the worrying to me. You've got a little one growing inside of you, and he or she needs to be your priority now. It will all be fine." He kissed her lips gently and held her close. "Now go to sleep Mrs Burns. We'll talk more about it tomorrow. You need to rest."

The next morning she felt much better and decided that she was well enough to go back to school. She got dressed in a blouse and one of her looser skirts. She was happy that she looked her usual smart self and that nobody would notice the swell in her tummy. The children were really pleased to see her and were eager to show her what they had been doing whilst she was away. They had finished their alphabet project. She was impressed with their creativity and said that they would spend the afternoon displaying their works of art on the wall outside the classroom. She told them that next week they would start making Christmas decorations and cards for their parents. This was met with a cheer from the kids. They always loved the run up to Christmas. They didn't have to do much work and they had so much fun. They felt lucky. For them, Mrs Burns was the best teacher in the world!

Sadie made her way to the staffroom at lunchtime. She felt exhausted after a busy morning with the children and was looking forward to sitting down and eating her lunch. Lisa was pleased to see her.

"Hi Sadie. Are you feeling better? Mrs Marshall said you had a stomach bug. I didn't think you would be back today. These bugs can be nasty. I must admit you look a little bit peaky."

"I'm much better now, just a bit tired that's all. I haven't been sleeping that well," she said. "How are things with you lovely?"

"Fine. Me and Mark are getting on really well. He is really trying, Sadie. He hasn't lost his temper once since I moved back and is much more considerate and understanding. That's how he was when we first met. I feel like I've got the old Mark back."

"I can see from your face that you are much happier. You look absolutely glowing. I'm really happy for you."

Lisa went on to say that her and Mark had decided to go away for Christmas. "We haven't been abroad on holiday since we first met so, we've taken the plunge, and booked a week in Tenerife."

"Good for you!" She was genuinely pleased for her friend. It was good to see her so upbeat and positive again.

"I guess you and David will spend Christmas getting ready for moving house, won't you? Have you got a date yet?"

"No, but it looks like it will be the second week of January. Everything seems to be progressing well, so that's what we're aiming for. We're going to David's parents in Brighton for Christmas Day and then home for Boxing Day. We'll probably start the task of packing boxes then."

"I don't envy you. Moving is so stressful but it will be worth it. The house sounds really lovely," said Lisa.

"It is, but we've got a lot of work to do. David wants to take a wall out downstairs and install a new kitchen as soon as we move in. We've got the money to do that and we'll decorate and buy some new carpets, but that will be it for a while. We'll have to save up before we can make any other improvements."

As the girls continued to chat happily, the bell rang to signify the start of afternoon classes. Sadie walked back to her classroom, looking out of the window at the heavy rain and dark menacing clouds. It was only 1.30pm but the bleak blustery sky gave the impression of nightfall. She shivered and pulled her cardigan across her chest to keep warm. She felt tired and could feel tension building in her neck which usually resulted in one of her bad heads.

She wondered how she was going to keep her secret until after Christmas. There was still two weeks to go. She prayed inwardly that she could at least get through the afternoon without being sick. It seemed that the normal expectation of morning sickness wasn't going to apply to her. She felt nauseous most of the day. It was something that was difficult to hide. She was aware that she looked 'peaky' as Lisa had said. Without plastering her face in make-up. She wasn't going to be able to blame it on a stomach bug for much longer.

David had told her that he would be late home that night so she took herself off to bed after a light supper of salmon and salad. Strangely enough, her ferocious appetite had waned and now she was finding it difficult to eat anything at all without feeling sick. She wondered how on earth she was going to be able to get through Christmas. Her mum was bound to notice that she wasn't herself, and just the thought of eating Christmas dinner made her shudder. She hoped that she could cope with it somehow.

David was adamant that he didn't want anyone to know about the pregnancy until after the three month scan. She respected his wishes and she knew he was right. She realised that there was always the chance of miscarriage during the early weeks. It was wiser not to tell everyone if there was a possibility that something might go wrong.

The next couple of weeks were a challenge for Sadie. Luckily, she found a way to cope with her nausea by drinking huge amounts of ginger tea and snacking on ginger biscuits. It did ease her symptoms and her appetite started to improve. The biggest problem was her expanding waistline. She had read some books about the milestones of pregnancy and had found a pregnant belly size chart which not only amused her but shocked her. According to the chart, her belly size was that of a fourteen week pregnancy and she was only ten weeks. Her clothes were beginning to feel tight now and it was getting harder and harder to know what to wear.

She decided that she would have to go shopping for some clothes in a larger size. So after school one day, she drove into town and bought herself a few pairs of wide leg trousers with elasticated waists and some loose tops. She looked at herself in the fitting room mirror. She looked good. The loose style hid her tummy. She hoped that nobody would notice her weight gain.

School was about to break up for the Christmas holidays. Sadie had managed to conceal her pregnancy. Even Lisa hadn't noticed. The sickness also seemed to have passed and she was feeling much more like her old self. She was more hopeful that she would be able to cope with Christmas now and, if her mum asked any awkward questions, she would be prepared.

On the last day of term, there was a big Christmas party for the kids in the main hall. Lisa, Sadie and Peter together with some of the other teachers had prepared a buffet of sandwiches, sausage rolls and cakes and Mr Marshall was manning the disco. The hall was decorated with balloons and Christmas decorations that the children had made themselves, and there was a huge tree with lights and glittery baubles on the stage. She looked around wistfully at the children dancing and enjoying themselves and wondered what she would be doing at this time next year. Life was going to be very different, she knew that. She hoped that having this baby wasn't going to change her relationship with David. He was saying all the right things, but she still wasn't convinced that he was really happy about the pregnancy. He was becoming more and more involved with his work. Sometimes she felt that he didn't have enough time for her. Would a baby push him even further away? She loved him so much and now that they were going to have a child together, she should be deliriously happy. But something - she didn't know what, was holding her back.

As the day came to an end and the children had gone home, she said her goodbyes to Lisa and wished her and Mark a lovely holiday in Tenerife.

"Make sure you enjoy yourselves and get a good tan. I'll think of you basking in the sun while we're shivering in the cold here." she laughed.

"We will. Thanks Sadie. I'll call you when we get back. If you need any help with your packing, Mark and I will be happy to come over and give you a hand."

"That's kind of you but we've done a fair bit already. I think we'll be fine. Just go away and enjoy being together. You've got a lot of time to make up."

"Thanks Sadie. You are such a good friend. I'll see you soon." Lisa kissed her on the cheek and waved goodbye as she walked out of the school gates with a skip in her step. Sadie and David arrived in Brighton early on Christmas morning. Both sets of parents were eagerly awaiting their arrival and welcomed them with home made hot sausage rolls and glasses of bucks fizz. Sadie wondered how she was going to avoid drinking alcohol without arousing suspicion. She hadn't considered that one! The only thing she could think of was to say that she hadn't fully recovered from the stomach bug and that alcohol wasn't agreeing with her at the moment.

It seemed to work.

Rob, in his usual jokey fashion, said that it would mean all the more for them, although Mary was more concerned.

"Didn't the doctor give you anything to help," she said. "You should be feeling better by now."

"I do feel much better Mum. I'm eating well. It's just that if I drink alcohol, it upsets my stomach. I'm sure it will pass. A lot of the teachers at school have had it, and it's taken them a few weeks to recover. Honestly, I'm fine. Stop worrying," she said.

'Well, I must admit you look really well", Mary answered. "Susan has cooked an enormous Christmas dinner so we were hoping that both of you would be hungry."

"We're famished, aren't we David? We've been starving ourselves all week for this," she laughed. David nodded in agreement and said. "I can't wait. Mum always cooks an amazing dinner." David was right – the dinner was huge and absolutely delicious. There was turkey, ham and beef and masses of vegetables and crispy roast potatoes, followed by Christmas pudding and trifle. Sadie was amazed and pleased that she was able to eat it all without any feelings of nausea and relieved that the conversation at the table centred around their impending house move, with no further mention of her health.

All four parents were keen to hear their plans for the house and when they were likely to move. Rob and Colin offered to come and help with the move but David insisted that they would manage.

"You remember our friend Alan from University? Well he's going to help us and he said that he'll do some painting for us. It seems like he has a flair for it. He's just re-decorated his place in London. I haven't seen his flat but, it sounds like he has transformed it. It might be better if you all come to see us when we've finished the kitchen. We're having a wall knocked down, so we'll be in a bit of a mess for a while."

"That's good of Alan to offer to help," said his dad. "He's a nice lad. I was talking to him at the wedding. He's like you David – very ambitious."

"Yes he is", answered David. He's very driven. His career is all important to him and he loves living in London. We lost touch for a while but I met up with him a couple of weeks ago and he treated me to lunch." "Well, as long as you're sure. Rob and I were happy to come and help you, weren't we mate?" said Colin. "Yes we were but it sounds like you've got it covered. Just let us know if you change your mind nearer the time," said Rob.

Later in the day as everyone was relaxing after dinner and recovering from Rob's obligatory party games, David and Sadie were in the kitchen washing up. They spoke about the obvious friendship that had formed between their parents, and how amusing it was listening to them laughing and chatting together. They seemed totally relaxed in each other's company. More than anything, they were grateful that it helped to steer away any chance of an awkward conversations which might reveal their secret.

"I think we've got away with it," said David.

"I hope so," she answered. She didn't tell him that she had noticed her mum giving her some quizzical looks over dinner. She felt sure that if not today, it was only a matter of time before she started asking questions.

"I think we should start to think about going home once we've finished here," he said. The roads might be icy if we leave it too late and you look tired darling. You've done very well today but I think you need to get home to bed."

She nodded in agreement. "Yes. I must admit, I am really tired now. I've eaten far too much. Look at the size of my tummy now!" she laughed. "You've got an extra mouth to feed don't forget," added David "You've got an excuse."

When they went back into the lounge, their parents were engrossed in a game of cards. "Come and join us," said Colin.

"I think we need to get going Dad," said David. The roads might be icy. I don't want to leave it too late. We've had a great day. Thank you all for your company and for your lovely presents."

Susan and Mary looked disappointed.

"Why don't you stay the night and go home in the morning?" said Susan. "We don't see you often and Mary and I will worry about you driving home in the dark, won't we Mary?"

"Yes we will," she agreed. "You can rest tonight and make an early start in the morning. That would make more sense."

Sadie looked at David. She didn't know what to say. If they stayed for another night, she knew that her mum would question her. Luckily David came to the rescue.

"It's kind of you Mum, but I've got to pop into work tomorrow. I know its Boxing Day but I need to pick up some important paperwork for a meeting the next morning. We'll be fine. If we leave now, we'll be home by 9pm." Sadie was relieved. She knew that he had just made up the story, but it seemed to convince them.

However, as they said their goodbyes, Mary took Sadie to one side. "I'm not going to embarrass you in front of everyone love, but I think I've guessed what's going on. All I'm going to say is, as soon as you are able to speak to me, I'll be waiting. Ring me as soon as you can. I love you."

"Thanks Mum. I love you too."

She was convinced that her Mum had guessed that she was pregnant, but she also knew that she woudn't say anything to the others. She would wait until she was ready, Sadie was sure of that. She decided not to tell David. It would only stress him out and there wasn't long to wait now. As soon as she was sure that her pregnancy was progressing as it should be, then she could tell everyone. That time couldn't come soon enough for her. She hated lying.

They arrived home just after 9pm. There hadn't been much traffic on the road. David didn't really expect there to be. it was Christmas night. Most people were at home enjoying the festivities. Sadie had slept most of the way home and as they pulled up outside their flat she rubbed her eyes and turned to him.

"I'm so sorry darling. I haven't been much company for you have I? I tried so hard to keep awake. I know you don't like driving in the dark, but I couldn't keep my eyes open." He laughed and reached across to hold her hand.

"I could see you struggling to keep awake but I was fine, honestly. I had plenty to think about which kept me occupied. You can't help feeling tired sweetheart. Let's get you inside. I think a nice hot shower and an early night is just what you need. I'll unpack the car. Off you go."

She gladly agreed. She hadn't felt such tiredness before. She couldn't wait to get into her own bed and snuggle under the covers. She didn't remember David coming to bed. She must have fallen asleep as soon as her head hit the pillow.

The next morning, he walked into the bedroom carrying a tray with hot buttered toast and marmalade and a couple of mugs of steaming hot coffee, just as she was waking up.

"Hello sleepyhead. Happy Boxing Day," he said laughing. He looked at her tousled hair, which she was busily pushing back from her face, the smudges of eye make up on her cheeks, and thought , even now, how beautiful she looked.

"Feeling better?"

Sadie smiled at her husband. "I feel a lot better thank you darling. I must look a mess though. I can barely remember getting into bed last night. I was exhausted. I don't remember removing my eye make up either. Is it all over my face?"

David laughed. "Well let's just say, you could give a circus clown a run for it's money this morning."

"Oh no, is it that bad?" she said as she reached across and picked up a mirror on the bedside table. She burst out laughing. "You're right, I do look like a clown. I need to get up and sort myself out before you decide to run a mile. You're not really going in to work today are you?" she asked.

"No, that was just something I made up for the 'oldies' otherwise they would have made us stay another night. I thought we could pack some boxes today. We could make a start in the lounge."

"Good idea," she said. "We'll see if the pub is open and we can book a table for dinner later. That will give us most of the day to get on."

By the end of the day, they had managed to fill a number of boxes and had started to work in the kitchen emptying cupboards and boxing up things that they knew they wouldn't use for the next few weeks. Luckily the pub was open and they had managed to book a table for 7pm. Sadie was pleased that she felt much better and, although she didn't want to tempt fate, it seemed that the sickness she had been experiencing had gone and her appetite was back. In fact she felt ferociously hungry and could hardly wait for her dinner later.

They arrived at the pub feeling very happy with their day's work and looking forward to their meal. David was amazed that she managed to eat three courses. He looked across the table at her beautiful face. She was blooming. Pregnancy suited her. He had to admit to himself that it wasn't what he wanted - certainly not yet - but there was no turning back. He would have to accept it. He hoped in time,that he would feel as happy about it as Sadie was. 'Why does life have to be so complicated,' he thought to himself.

He returned to work the next day and left Sadie still sleeping. When she woke up she decided that she would spend the day getting some more packing done. As she showered and dressed, her thoughts turned to Lisa. Her and Mark would be home from their holiday in a few days. She looked forward to speaking to her to find out how she was. However hard she tried, she wasn't convinced that Mark had changed. He might have brainwashed Lisa in believing it, but it would take more than his empty promises to convince her.

She also knew that she wouldn't be able to hide her pregnancy much longer. Her bump was quite noticeable now. The new school term started on the 5th January and her appointment with the midwife was on the 8th January. If she could keep up the pretence until after the appointment, and all was well, she was going to tell everyone about her news. She knew David wanted to wait until after the three month scan, but she was finding it too stressful now. She hoped that he would understand and decided that she would talk to him about it that evening when he got home from work.

By the time David got home, she was exhausted but very happy with how much packing she had done.

"Wow, you've done well sweetheart," he said. "There's not much left to do now. Just the last minute bits and pieces, and I've got some good news. We're exchanging contracts on the 12th January, so I can arrange to hire a van and we can move in on the 13th January."

"I hope that's not a Friday?" she laughed.

"No it's a Wednesday," he said smiling.

"That's good news," she answered. "We should know more about the baby by then too. Don't forget my appointment with the midwife."

"I haven't forgotten," said David. "In fact, I've already booked the day off." "That's great, darling thank you. I've been thinking. I know you said that we should wait until after the 3 month scan before we told everyone, but the way my waistline is expanding, I don't see myself being able to conceal it for that long. If the midwife reassures us the pregnancy is going well, how would you feel if we told everyone after the appointment?"

"I suppose it makes sense, he answered. "I understand how stressful it is for you and that's the last thing you need. Let's wait and see what the midwife says and we'll make a decision then."

Sadie was relieved at David's response. She felt the pressure lifting from her shoulders. She hated keeping secrets and it was exciting to think that, in a week or so she would be able to share her good news with everyone. She thought of her Mum who was probably waiting anxiously for her to call, and decided that both her and her Dad would be the first ones to know.

Chapter 12

It was the morning of the 8th January. Sadie and David were on their way to their appointment with the midwife at the hospital. During the journey, Sadie reflected on the events of the last week. She had spoken to Lisa on her return from holiday and was relieved to hear her sounding so happy and upbeat. She described how Mark had taken her out for a romantic meal one evening. The restaurant was really busy but despite that, to her great surprise, he got down on one knee and proposed to her.

She had to admit to feeling more than a little surprised at Lisa's news, but hearing the excitement in her voice pleased her. Perhaps she had been wrong about Mark after all. Maybe he was making the effort to change. She was happy for her friend and told herself that she would try and be more understanding and, for now, give him the benefit of the doubt.

Sadie spoke to Mrs Marshall on the first day back at school and had asked her if she could take the day off on the 8th January. She made up a story about her and David having to go to the bank to sign some papers regarding their mortgage application. She hated lying to her. She was such a kind and caring person. She hoped that when she was able to explain properly and tell her the truth, she would understand. Sadie loved her job. She didn't want to say, or do, anything to jeopordise that.

They arrived at the hospital ten minutes ahead of their appointment and were shown where to sit in reception until they were called in to the midwife. Sadie felt the butterflies stirring in her tummy and her heart starting to race. She hoped that the midwife would tell her that everything was going well with her pregnancy and that it was safe to tell everyone. The last couple of weeks had been difficult. She was sure that people were noticing that she was putting on weight. It was getting impossible to hide it now.

After five minutes, the midwife appeared from one of the offices down the corridor and called her name. “Mrs Burns, I can see you now. Can you follow me please? Your husband is welcome to come in too.”

They both stood up and followed her down the corridor. David squeezed her hand and whispered “You ok? You’re not nervous are you.”

“I am a bit,” she answered.

“Not long now,” he said.

The midwife introduced herself as Angela and told her that she would be looking after her throughout her pregnancy. She asked her to lay on the couch and, much to her surprise, said that she was going to give her an ultra sound to check on the pregnancy.

“I didn’t think I would have a scan until I was 12 weeks,” Sadie questioned.

“You’re not far off that now are you? Your notes tell me that you are approximately 10 weeks so, as you are here, we might as well do it now and get an accurate picture of how advanced you actually are. I must admit, just looking at you, I would say you are nearer to 12 weeks anyway.”

She lay on the couch and looked at the monitor next to her. She couldn’t believe that in a few minutes, she was going to see the image of her baby. She smiled at David. His face was full of concern. She reached across and held his hand, as the midwife spread gel on her tummy. Sadie asked what it was for and she explained that it helped to prevent air pockets which could block the sound waves that create the images. Sadie was fascinated as she looked at the fuzzy picture on the screen. She couldn't see anything resembling a baby and asked Angela if everything looked ok.

"Yes, I'm sure it is. I just want to ask one of my colleagues to come in and check something. Don't worry, everything looks fine."

She suddenly felt panic rising in her chest and turned to David.

"Something must be wrong", she said. "Why is she getting someone else to look at the scan?"

"I'm sure it's just a formality," David answered. "She said it was fine." However, he had to admit that he also felt concerned. He had noticed the midwife's puzzled expression as she looked at the images. Sadie was right. Why was she getting her colleague to come and look? Something didn't feel right. The door swung open and Angela walked back into the room followed by another midwife. "Sadie, this is my colleague, Sandra. She is just going to check something out for me. Is it ok if she takes a look at the scan?" she asked. Sadie nodded and attempted a smile but she was shaking inside afraid of what she was going to hear.

"Yes I agree with you Angela," the other midwife said. "Are you going to give this lovely couple the news or shall I?"

"What is it?" said Sadie. "Please tell me, what's wrong?"

"There's nothing wrong my dear. Not unless you have any objections to having two babies rather than one," said Angela smiling broadly.

"Two!" exclaimed David.

Sadie felt numb. She was trying to take it all in. It had been difficult enough accepting that she was pregnant. But two babies – twins – how did that happen? Angela asked both her and David to look again at the screen as she carefully showed them two small images with two heartbeats.

"Can you see now?" she said. "Two perfectly formed babies. I would say that you are approximately twelve weeks pregnant and everything looks absolutely fine. Congratulations, you are carrying twins!"

They left the hospital, still reeling from what had just happened. Sadie was clutching the ultra sound photo of their two babies and struggling to comprehend that they were actually growing inside her. David had hardly said a word. She could see that he was in shock.

"I can't believe it, can you?" she said. The colour seemed to have drained from his face as he answered.

"No, that was the last thing I was expecting. How are we going to cope with two babies? I thought that one would be difficult – but two!" he exclaimed.

"Well, I guess we will have to. It wasn't what I was expecting either," she answered. "But I must admit, it is exciting and it does explain why I have been putting on so much weight. Wait until we tell our parents. They are going to be gob smacked." she added.

"I'm gob smacked! I'm going to need a stiff drink when we get home."

Sadie laughed and put her arm around his waist. "But you are pleased aren't you?" she said.

"I will be", he answered. "I just need time to get my head around it that's all."

David was true to his word and poured himself a large whisky as soon as they got home. For once, Sadie was disappointed that she couldn't join him but remembered that her mum had always told her that a cup of hot tea with lots of sugar was good for shock. She would have to forget about alcohol now, at least for as long as she was carrying such precious cargo. Now that the news had began to sink in, she was already thinking ahead about everything they would need to buy for the twins. The midwife had told her that it was a bit too early to be able to tell the sex of the babies, but had booked her in for another scan at 5 months when the babies would be bigger and the images would be clearer.

For now, she would have to be patient and wait. She hoped that they would be girls, or at least one of them would be a girl. She had always liked the name Mia. That's what she would call her if she was lucky enough to have a daughter, she decided. Sadie looked across the room at David who was already on his second whisky. The colour had returned to his cheeks but he still looked shell shocked.

"You've hardly said a word darling. Are you ok?" she asked.

"Yeah I'm fine - just a lot to think about that's all. It's going to be an expensive few months what with getting the house done and buying two lots of everything for the babies. We might have to shelve a few things we wanted to get for the house. Money is going to be very tight."

Sadie could see that he was genuinely worried.

"It's ok, we've got the rest of our lives to work on the house. It doesn't have to be done straightaway and at least we will have enough bedrooms. We would really struggle if we had to stay here."
"Well, I definitely want to get the kitchen done and open up the space, if nothing else. We'll need that done more than ever now."

"Let's not worry too much about all that now. Let's just celebrate our wonderful news and let it soak in. I feel so lucky. I've got you, a lovely new house and I'm carrying our two babies. What more could I wish for?" she said cradling her tummy. He smiled at his wife fondly. She was blooming and looked so happy. He didn't want to burst her bubble but he couldn't help how he felt. Their lives were going to change dramatically. He wasn't sure that he was ready for it.

Sadie decided to telephone her mum and dad later in the evening after they had eaten. David said he would call his parents too. They agreed that it was only fair that the four of them were the first to hear their news. Sadie was surprised to hear her dad's voice at the end of the phone. '

"Hi Dad. You don't usually answer the phone. Is mum out?"

"Oh hello love. We were just talking about you and wondering if you've got a date yet for moving. Mum's here. She's just popped to the loo. Are you ok? There's nothing wrong is there?" said Rob.

"No Dad", she laughed. "Everything is great and, yes, we do have a moving date. That's one of the reasons why I'm ringing." "One of the reasons? That sounds mysterious. What's the other reason?" he asked. "If you go and get mum and put the phone on speaker, I can talk to you both together and fill you in."

Mary was quick to come to the phone as Rob called her from the kitchen.

"Sadie's on the phone love. She's got some news for us." he said.

"Hi Mum, I was just telling dad, we've got a date for the move. It's the 13th January." Mary and Rob joined together and whooped with delight.

"That's brilliant news Sadie. I expect dad told you that we were wondering when it would be. It's gone through very quickly and you're lucky. You haven't had any problems, have you?" added Mary.

"No, everything has gone very smoothly and we've almost finished the packing. Apart from David having to hire the van, we're more or less done. I think he is going to ask Alan if he can come and help to carry some of the heavy boxes and the furniture as I can't really do that now."

There was a stunned silence on the other end of the phone and then her dad said "What's wrong? Have you hurt your back or something?"

Mary looked at her husband and just shook her head. She waited for Sadie to speak but she didn't say anything.

"Are you pregnant love?" she asked.

Rob looked at his wife with surprise.

"Mary, what on earth made you ask her that?"

"It's true isn't it Sadie?" she said.

"Yes it's true. I think you guessed at Christmas didn't you Mum?"

"I suspected that you might be, but I didn't say anything to your Dad. Did I love?"

"No she didn't, Sadie. I must admit, I wasn't expecting this news quite so soon. How do you and David feel about it? Are you happy?" Rob asked.

"It wasn't planned, but yes we are happy. There's something else I need to tell you." Mary and Rob wondered what on earth their daughter was going to tell them now. One shock was quite enough for one day.

"I'm not having one baby," said Sadie. "I'm carrying twins. We had a scan today and that's when we found out. We're still coming to terms with it. You can imagine what a shock it was for both of us."

"Blimey!" Rob exclaimed. "I'm going to be a grandad twice over!" For once, Mary was speechless. She usually knew exactly what to say to her daughter, but this was something she just wasn't prepared for.

After they had ended their call to Sadie and asked her to promise to ring again soon to let them know how she was, they sat down with a cup of tea. Mary was still trying to come to terms with the news. Part of her felt happy to know that they were going to be grandparents. It was something that she had always looked forward to and two babies were a true blessing, but she was worried for Sadie.

Everything seemed to be happening too soon. In her opinion she had got married too soon and now she was having a family too soon. Her and David had just bought their first house. Sadie was just getting settled into her job and they didn't know many people in Essex. Who was going to be there for them once the babies were born? David couldn't be relied on. He was far too immersed in his career. Mary couldn't imagine him being around much to help her.

She turned to Rob who was deep in thought. "Well that was a bit of a surprise wasn't it?" she said. "How do you feel about it love?" she asked.

"Probably much the same as you," he answered. "How are they going to cope? It's going to be a huge commitment for both of them both financially and practically. Sadie is going to have to stop working. I know she will get maternity pay for a year, but she might not be able to go back to work at all with two kids to look after."

"If only we lived closer Rob, then we could help. I know it's a lot to think about, but perhaps we should consider retiring and moving down south to be closer to them. I know we had decided to work a few more years but we need to be there for our daughter. She is going to need us love."

"Let's just think about it Mary. That would be a big step for us. Our life and our friends are here. I'm not sure that's the right decision for us right now," he said. "We'll sleep on it and talk about it tomorrow, ok?"

"Yes, I know. We need to give it some serious thought before we make any rash decisions," Mary answered.

"I wonder what Colin and Susan will make of it when they hear the news?"

"Much the same as us, I would imagine," said Rob. "I'm sure we'll speak to them soon, and we'll find out. Let's not worry about it now.

It's time for the news." With that he got up and turned on the TV. Mary smiled at her husband as she took the mugs out to the kitchen. There was never anything that would stop him from watching the evening news.

As for her, if there was one thing that she was absolutely sure of, it was that she wouldn't be getting much sleep tonight.

Sadie went through to the bedroom after her call with Mary and Rob and found David dozing on the bed. "That's the whisky," she said as she gave him a gentle nudge. "It's sending you to sleep. I thought you were going to ring your mum and dad. I've spoken to mine." "And", said David sleepily. "What did they say?'

"Not a lot. I think they are pleased but they were very surprised to say the least," she answered.

"I'll call my folks a bit later when the effects of the whisky have worn off. I must admit, I do feel tired. Do you mind if I have a little sleep, sweetheart?"

"No. it's fine. I'm going to get the dinner on. I'll wake you up when it's ready."

Typical David, she thought as she walked into the kitchen. He's tired, how does he think I feel? She admitted to feeling a little bit annoyed with him. It was times like this that he showed his selfish side. She loved him so much and appreciated that, in so many ways, he was the perfect husband. She told herself that she should be more understanding. Today's news had affected both of them. David was obviously struggling with it more than she was.

He finally rang his parents later that evening after dinner. Sadie listened as he told them how she had found out she was pregnant but hadn't told him straightaway. He said that he had been shocked but was just coming to terms with it when they found out that she was carrying twins. She hoped that he would tell them how happy he was but he just sounded worried. There was no excitement in his voice, just concern about how they would cope.

It made her feel like she should be apologising to him, that it was an inconvenience for her to be pregnant when it wasn't planned. She felt hurt and betrayed. She wondered what Susan and Colin would be thinking after that conversation. After he ended the call, she asked him. "What did your Mum and Dad say? Were they pleased to hear that they are going to be grandparents? Only from what I heard, you didn't sound very happy as you were telling them."

"I just told them that I was worried that's all, and they understood that. But yes, of course they were pleased," he said.

"Look David, I understand that it's a lot to take in and that you're concerned about the finances and how we will manage with two babies, but can't you just be a little bit excited? I think we're lucky. Some women never get the chance to have one baby let alone two. I'm going to need your support for the next 6 or 7 months. If you're not on board with this, then I need to know now."

Sadie suddenly felt the frustration building up inside her. David could be so annoying sometimes.

"Of course I am sweetheart. I'm sorry, I've upset you. That's the last thing I wanted. Please don't worry about me. I am genuinely happy about the twins, I really am. And of course I will be here to support you – always." David took her into his arms and kissed her passionately. She felt the warmth of his touch and led him into the bedroom. "Are you sure we can?" he asked. "It won't hurt the babies will it?" "No it won't hurt them." She laughed as she said "Let's make the most of it before I start resembling a beached whale."

The next day, Sadie had decided that she would get into school a little bit earlier and speak to Mrs Marshall. She had hated lying to her about why she had taken the day off. It was time to tell her the truth about her pregnancy. Sadie knocked on her office door and heard her say, "Come in."

"Good morning Wendy," said Sadie. "Can I have a quick word before classes begin?"

"Yes of course, my dear. How are you? Did you get everything organised at the bank yesterday?"

"That's what I want to talk to you about, Wendy. I'm afraid that I told you a little white lie. I didn't have an appointment at the bank. My appointment was at the hospital with the midwife. I'm so sorry that I couldn't tell you. But David and I wanted to know that everything was alright before we told everyone. Apart from our parents, you are the first one to know that I'm pregnant."

"I must admit Sadie, I thought you were, so did Lisa, but we didn't want to say anything until you were ready to tell us yourself," said Wendy smiling.

"Really", said Sadie. I thought I had got away with it, especially by wearing my baggy clothes", she laughed.

"Call it women's intuition my dear, but we guessed a few weeks ago. Many congratulations, I'm delighted for you and David as I'm sure everyone will be. Did the midwife say everything is progressing well?"

"That brings me to my next piece of news," said Sadie. "We're having twins!"

"My word, how wonderful!" Wendy exclaimed. "That's fantastic. You must be thrilled to bits."

"Well, I have to admit it was a bit of a shock, especially for David. He's still trying to process it and, David being David, he's worried about how we're going to cope."

"You are going to be amazing parents, and you'll cope. You're not the first couple to have twins. It might be difficult for the first few months but you'll get through it and it will be lovely when you have two little ones running around."

"Thank you for being so understanding and supportive Wendy. I'm going to work right up until the last minute which will give you enough time to find a replacement for me. But I want you to know that I intend to come back after my maternity leave. I love it here. I don't ever want to leave," she said. She could feel herself choking back the tears at the thought of not being able to carry on working at this wonderful school.

"Well, let's wait and see, my dear. Your life will be very different once the babies are born. You may find it difficult to come back to work," said Wendy. "You know how much I value you. I don't want to lose such a good teacher, but you'll need to put your family first." Sadie smiled fondly at Wendy and said she had better go and welcome her class for the first lesson. She decided that she would talk to David about the possibility of finding child care for the twins once they were born. She didn't want to give up her job and she didn't want to let Wendy down.

As she entered the staff room at lunchtime, Lisa welcomed her with open arms. "Hey you", she called. "I hear that you have some exciting news for me.' She saw Sadie's surprised expression and laughed.

"It's ok, I bumped into Wendy in the corridor earlier. She just said that you had something to tell me. But I think I've guessed. Sadie hugged her friend and said, "Yes Wendy told me that both of you had been making assumptions", she said laughing. "I honestly thought that I had got away with it."

"Those baggy trousers and loose tops you were wearing were very nice but they couldn't hide the fact that your tummy seemed to be getting bigger every day, said Lisa laughing. "I could see that you weren't eating very much so it wasn't because of that. I didn't want to say anything. I knew that you would tell me as soon as you could. You're absolutely blooming Sadie. Are you feeling ok? How far gone are you?"

Lisa listened intently as Sadie told her about the visit to the midwife and her advising that she have an ultra sound scan. When she told her that the scan revealed two babies, she jumped out of her seat and clapped her hands with excitement. "That's amazing. No wonder you were putting on so much weight. Oh Sadie, I'm so happy for you. What wonderful news. I bet David is over the moon isn't he ?" she asked.

"Well, I wouldn't say that exactly," said Sadie. "I think he is in shock. It wasn't planned. I was still on the pill. One baby would have been a surprise,. Now that we know there is two, he's worrying about how we will cope and how we will manage financially."

"Really? Why is he worried about finances? He's earning good money now isn't he? It will be fine and he shouldn't be saying things like that to you now. You need him to be strong and to support you. You're the one having these babies and you're the one that will have the majority of the work in looking after them."

Lisa felt cross and more than a bit surprised in hearing David's reaction to the pregnancy. He always seemed so devoted to Sadie. It sounded out of character.

"Anyway, enough of me," said Sadie. "I want to hear all about this surprise engagement. Show me your ring then." She stared in amazement as Lisa held out her left hand. The ring was stunning. Mark had done well. It had obviously cost a lot of money.

"What a gorgeous ring, Lisa. I'm so happy for you. Are things still going well between you?"

"Yes, really well. We're talking about getting married next year. We're both really keen to start a family too, so you never know, we might end up being pregnant together," she laughed.

"Well unless you are intending on doing it soon, I don't think so lovely. These two will be here in six months or so. It seems surreal when I think of it like that. Six months is going to fly by. I just hope that we've got the house in some sort of order before then. It's hard to believe that we'll be moving in a few days.

David is going to ring Alan today. He said that he would come and help us, so David just wants to check to make sure he's still available. I'm not going to be able to lift anything so I'll probably just be on duty making tea and sandwiches."

"We can come and help you too," said Lisa. It sounds like you might need it."

"It's kind of you Lisa, but the three of us will be fine. You can come once we are settled." Sadie had already decided that she didn't want Mark to be there on their moving day. She was pleased that he was obviously making the effort with Lisa, but she didn't like him and she still didn't trust him.

The rest of the day seemed to be an endless stream of congratulations from the other teachers and the office staff. Sadie had decided not to say anything to the children until nearer the time. They were settled and happy now. She didn't think it would be fair to upset them with the thought that she would be leaving them in a few months. That was the one thing she was dreading. As hard as she'd tried not to, she had become very attached to them. They were a lovely group of kids. So eager to learn and so bright and gifted. She smiled and thought to herself how funny it was that she still referred to them as her little sponges!

Chapter 13

It was the day of the move. Alan arrived at 8am and he and David went to pick up the van. By 11am, after a couple of tea breaks and a round of bacon sandwiches, they were on the road. Sadie felt a little sad at leaving their flat. It had been a great first home for them but she was excited at the prospect of moving into their own house. David had already arranged for the builders to start work on knocking the wall down and installing a new kitchen for the following week and they had measured up and ordered new carpets for the sitting room and the bedrooms. Alan said that once all the building work was finished, he would book some time off work and come and help with the decorating. Sadie was so pleased to see him and David getting on well. It seemed that whatever differences they had before, had been resolved.

There had been one awkward moment when Sadie told Alan about her pregnancy. He seemed shocked and even more so when she told him she was having twins. He had looked at David waiting for him to say something, but David just laughed and said that he was shocked too and that he didn't realise he was such a super stud. Sadie didn't find it funny and looking at Alan's face, he didn't either.

"Is that all you can say David? How about – Yes it's great news isn't it. Sadie and I are very happy", she said feeling more than a little irritated.

"I was only joking sweetheart. You knew that, didn't you Alan?" Alan just smiled and squeezed Sadie's arm.

"I'm very happy for you Sadie. Just make sure you look after yourself. Carrying twins is a huge responsibility. Take no notice of David. He's always had a strange sense of humour."

She changed the subject , deciding that David was just in one of his silly moods. By the time they arrived at the house, they all agreed that they should find somewhere to eat before they unloaded the van. Sadie had noticed a nice pub on the way as she followed in the car, so she suggested that they go and check it out. She was feeling really hungry by now. A quiet sit down and a lovely lunch was just what she needed.

Conversation over lunch centred around David and Alan talking about work. Sadie looked across at David and noticed how animated he became once he was talking about his job. It's a shame that he can't be like that when he is talking about us and our babies, she thought to herself. Alan had also become a little distant from her since their previous conversation. She wondered if her news had upset him. Perhaps he thought that it might change their relationship and their friendship in some way. She hoped not. She really liked Alan. He was a good friend. As far as she was concerned, he would always be a big part of her life. She wondered why he hadn't met a nice girl. He was good looking, intelligent and had a great job. If only Lisa was still single, she thought wistfully.

By early evening, she was exhausted. She found Alan and David in the garden putting all the boxes they had unpacked into the shed.

"Do you two mind if I excuse myself and go to bed? I'm absolutely shattered", she asked.

"No of course not, sweetheart", said David. It's been a long day for you. We've almost finished anyway. The only boxes that we haven't unpacked are those with kitchen stuff in and we figured it wasn't worth emptying all of them until the builders have finished. We 've got enough basic things to use until then. Alan is going to be heading off soon too, aren't you?" he said turning to Alan.

"Yes, I've got a long day tomorrow", he answered.

"Thank you for everything you've done today Alan. We couldn't have got through it without you" she said, hugging him tight.

"Oh don't be silly, it's my pleasure and don't forget to let me know when you are ready to start decorating , and I'll come over and stay for a few days. Between us, we'll soon get it done", he said smiling.

The next few weeks were even more hectic and disruptive than they both had expected. The builders were very good and turned up every morning at 8am to start work but the mess was indescribable. Sadie felt her lungs were bursting with continually breathing in the dust. It was impossible to keep anything clean and she couldn't remember when they had last eaten a proper meal. They were surviving on microwave meals and snacks. Sometimes they had no running water for hours at a time. It was horrible and Sadie was beginning to wonder if they had made a mistake in even thinking about having the work done whilst she was pregnant She was sure that it couldn't be good for the babies either. She wasn't eating properly and resting as she should. David, as usual, escaped most of it as he spent most of his time at work, sometimes even staying late in the evenings.

It seemed endless, but finally the work was done. While David was at work one evening, Lisa came over to help Sadie clean up and unpack the remaining boxes of kitchen equipment into their new and very smart kitchen units. She was amazed at how big it was now that the wall had been taken down.

"It's fabulous Sadie", she said. "It looks like something out of Ideal

Home Magazine. You and David must be so pleased with it."

"Yes, we are. But more than anything, I'm pleased that the work is done. I don't think I could have put up with it for much longer. At least I can start cooking proper meals again."

"Yes, I noticed your smart new eye level oven and ceramic hob. I'm really quite jealous," said Lisa.

"Well, you'll have a kitchen like this one day when you and Mark get married," she said.

"Are you thinking of buying your own house?"

"Yes, we've started looking already actually, but anything we like is out of our price range. It will probably have to be a 'doer-upper' but I'm not sure I'm keen on that idea." said Lisa. "More than anything, I really want a baby. Seeing you pregnant has made me really broody, and now that Mark and I seem to be back on track, I think it could be the right time."

"Well, what does Mark think about that idea?" Sadie asked. She couldn't imagine that he would share Lisa's enthusiasm. It would mean him not having her to himself anymore. She was convinced that was his problem. He was controlling. He wanted her exclusively. Having a baby would change all that.

"Oh he's keen too - I think. Well he says he is. He just wants me to be happy", said Lisa.

After she had gone home, Sadie thought about what Lisa had said. She wasn't at all convinced that Mark was on board with them having a baby. He was just telling her what she wanted to hear. Once again, she felt the familiar feeling of concern for her friend. She hoped that Lisa would think again. Perhaps it was just a flight of fancy on her part. She certainly hoped so.

The following weeks passed quickly. Alan kept his word and took some time off to come and help David to do the decorating. They managed to paint the walls and ceilings in the hall, kitchen and lounge within three days and had started on the bedrooms ahead of the new carpets being fitted. The transformation was incredible. Sadie couldn't believe how a lick of white paint and some new soft furnishings could change a house so dramatically. Lisa had also helped Sadie with hanging new curtains and had offered to make some new cushion covers to match.

"I don't know how we would ever have got so much done in such a short time, if it wasn't for our friends," she said to David one evening. By now, she was feeling huge and finding it more difficult to move around.

"I feel like I haven't been much use now that I'm getting so big. Lisa and Alan have been absolute stars. We will never be able to thank them enough."

"Yes, they've been great", added David. "We'll make sure we take them out to dinner or perhaps invite them round here for dinner one evening to thank them properly."

"Good idea. We'll wait until after the scan next week and we'll sort something out," she answered.

The only downside is that we'll have to invite Mark too. I just don't like that man. I wish that Lisa was single. Her and Alan are such a good match. Nothing would make me happier than to see those two get together."

David looked surprised and paused as he answered. "There you go, matchmaking again. You'll never convince Lisa to leave Mark and Alan is quite happy on his own. He's got lots of friends. He's not lonely and he loves his job. Not everyone wants to get married and have kids, Sadie. We're all different. You need to accept Alan for who he is."

"I do accept him as he is", she answered, feeling a little under attack by his words. "I just said that him and Lisa would make a good match, that's all. I'm sorry, I didn't mean anything by it. Just forget that I said anything."

Sadie decided that she had obviously touched a nerve with David. She wouldn't mention it again. They both had so much to look forward to. From now on, she was going to concentrate on their own relationship. David was her world. He would always come first.

The day of the scan arrived. David had taken a few hours off from work to go with her, and Sadie had told Wendy Marshall that she would be back at school in the afternoon. Peter was going to cover her morning classes.

Angela, the same midwife they had seen before, greeted them warmly as they were directed into her surgery. "Hello Sadie and David. It's good to see you again. My, you've grown a bit around your tummy since I last saw you," she said to Sadie smiling. Are you keeping well?"

"Yes I feel fine," she answered. "Just a little tired that's all. We've recently moved house and been very busy, so I'm putting it down to that."

"Well, yes, that would make you tired, plus the fact that you are carrying around what looks like two very big babies. Don't forget that," she laughed. Have you felt any movement yet?"

" I think so yes," Sadie answered. It feels more like a flutter, almost as if I have wind in my tummy."

"Right, let's get you up on the couch and we'll have a look and see what's going on, shall we?"

Angela went through the same procedure as last time, as Sadie and David looked intently at the monitor. This time, they didn't need any direction. They could see their babies clearly. Both of them were moving and kicking their legs almost in unison. Angela smiled and turned to Sadie.

"They both look absolutely perfect. Do you want to know the sex of them?" she asked.

"Yes please", said Sadie excitedly. David squeezed her hand and nodded. "Out of interest", said Angela. "Do you have a preference?"

"I would love a little girl, but I expect David would like boys, wouldn't you David?" She looked across at her husband. He looked so vulnerable somehow.

"Boys would be nice", he said. "But as long as both babies are healthy, then that's the main thing."

"Right answer," said Angela laughing. "Well, I'm delighted to be able to tell you that you're both going to be happy, because you have one of each. One boy and one girl - perfect."

They both gave a cry of delight as they continued to watch their son and daughter wriggling around on the monitor. Sadie couldn't contain her tears of joy any longer as Angela handed her a tissue.

"Congratulations, both of you. It looks like you are going to have an instant family. One of each is ideal. I don't think they are identical, which means that they started life as two separate eggs that were fertilised separately. They will probably have different personalities and may not necessarily look alike either. It's going to be a very exciting time for you both."

Angela booked a follow up appointment for four weeks and told Sadie to try and rest and make sure that she continued eating a healthy diet. As they both left the hospital, David turned to Sadie and said

"It's great news isn't it sweetheart? A boy and a girl. We're so lucky." She thought that it was probably the first time that he had really shown any emotion or excitement since she first found out that she was pregnant. She held his hand tightly and smiled up at him.

"Yes darling, we are very lucky. I am so happy and I'm glad that you are too. I know the next few months are going to be expensive, and I know you're worried about that. We've got a lot of equipment and clothes to buy, but I can get a lot of things second hand on eBay and other similar sites. We'll manage somehow." "I'll have to get mum to start knitting again!" he laughed. "She used to knit things for me when I was little. She'll enjoy that,"

"Good idea, I'll ask mine too," added Sadie. It will keep both of them out of mischief!"

"By the way,' What do you think of the names Mia and Matthew?"

"Mmm - Mia and Matthew – yes I like those names. Mia and Matthew it is then!", he answered.

Sadie suddenly felt a closeness to David that she hadn't felt in a while. He seemed so much happier and relaxed. She hoped that his earlier doubts about the pregnancy had vanished once and for all. She knew that once the babies were born, he was going to be a great dad. She just needed him to believe it himself.

As they arrived home, she said "Do you think we should invite the parents down now that we've got the house straight? If we leave it much longer, I'll be so huge, I won't want to see anyone, and we did promise them at Christmas."

"I was thinking the same," said David. Let's ring them tonight. We can tell them about the scan and fix a weekend for them to come." "They'll have to book in somewhere to sleep though. We probably won't be able to sort the other bedrooms out for a while. Decorating and furnishing the nursery must be our first priority."

She smiled and thought to herself that he would never even given the nursery a thought a few weeks ago.

"Yes, let's call them tonight," she answered. The news that Sadie's twins were a boy and girl rippled through the school like wildfire. She was overwhelmed with the lovely comments and good wishes from her colleagues. Lisa, as expected, whooped with delight and hugged her tight.

"Sadie, it's such great news. One of each, it couldn't be more perfect. I'm really jealous now and even more broody than I was before. Wait until I tell Mark. He will be thrilled for you too."

"Well, don't put pressure on him Lisa. If he doesn't feel ready to have a baby yet, then you need to respect that. You're both getting on so much better. You don't want to spoil that do you?" she said.

"I understand what you're saying", Lisa answered. But it's my life too and I want to have a baby more than anything. Mark will understand. I'll talk to him again."

She decided not to say anything else to her friend. She had promised herself and David that she wasn't going to interfere in Lisa and Mark's relationship anymore. They needed to sort it out themselves. Despite her decision, it was difficult not to get involved. She cared for Lisa so much, but she couldn't risk suffering the stress of worrying about her. She needed to concentrate on looking after herself and her babies.

Over the next couple of weeks, ahead of the visit from the parents, Sadie and David started working on the nursery. It was a large double bedroom , so there was plenty of room for two cots, wardrobes and a couple of dressers which they had ordered on line. Sadie had also started buying a few clothes for the babies, mainly sleep suits and little vests which someone had told her was all you needed in the early weeks. She was so tempted by the pretty little dresses and cute romper suits she had seen in the shops, but decided to resist buying anything like that until the babies were born.

They had decided on a pale lemon for painting the walls and brightly patterned animal curtains and matching cot bedding. When the room was finished, Sadie looked around at their handiwork. The room looked better than she could have ever imagined. In that moment, the realisation that, in a few months, there would be two little people sleeping in there, suddenly overwhelmed her. How will the birth be? Will it hurt? Would she be able to cope with feeding two babies? So many questions that she couldn't answer were filling her thoughts. For the first time in a while, she longed for her Mum's love and reassurance.

The weekend visit from 'the oldies' as David called them, was like a breath of fresh air, especially for Sadie. Her and David had been working so hard on the house, she didn't realise how much she needed a break from it all. Susan and Mary had come laden with gifts for the babies and Rob and Colin brought a couple of bottles of champagne to celebrate the good news. Listening to their excited chatter about becoming grandparents, lifted her spirits. They absolutely loved the house and were amazed by how much work had been done in such a short time. They had all booked into a bed and breakfast nearby insisting that Sadie rested and had a break from household chores over the weekend. The two mums had been speaking on the phone ahead of their visit and decided that they were going to prepare some meals for the freezer which would save Sadie having to cook as her pregnancy progressed. Colin and Rob were assigned to the garden which still resembled a jungle despite David's efforts to clear some of the weeds and old bushes.

It was a busy weekend but a productive one. Sadie and David couldn't have been more pleased with everything 'the oldies' managed to do for them. The garden looked 100% better and the freezer was stacked with neatly labelled containers full of individual dinners of shepherds pie, beef stew, chicken curry and fish pie. On the last evening, David suggested that they crack open the champagne and order a takeaway.

"Thank you all so much for everything you've done this weekend," he said smiling at the tired but happy faces of their parents. "Sadie and I are so grateful. Let's have that drink while we are waiting for the food to arrive."

Sorry, sweetheart, but I think it's going to have to be a cup of tea for you," he said laughing.

"Ok, don't rub it in," she said nudging his arm. She patted her tummy and said, "Wait until these little ones are born, then I'll give you a run for your money!"

When Mary and Rob arrived home, they spoke about the weekend and how lovely it had been. "Sadie looks really well, doesn't she?" Mary said as she was pouring out a cup of tea for them both. "I can't believe how big she is already. It wouldn't surprise me if she has those babies early, you know. It's a shame that I didn't get the chance to speak to her and tell her that you and I are thinking about retiring early and moving down to be closer to her. We were all so busy, there wasn't the opportunity. Also, It probably wouldn't have been appropriate to talk about it when Colin and Susan were there."

"No," agreed Rob. "It wasn't the right time. We need to speak to both of them when they're on their own and when everything has settled a bit. There is so much going on for them at the moment."

"Do you think we should mention it to Susan and Colin too?" Mary asked.

"Not now love. We haven't made a final decision ourselves yet. I'm still not sure that it's the right thing to do. I know you're worried about Sadie and how she is going to cope but, don't forget, she's got Lisa living nearby. I'm sure she will be only too glad to help her out whenever she can and David won't be working all the time. She won't be on her own."

Mary decided not to pursue the conversation any further. She could see that Rob didn't really want to discuss it although, for her, she thought of little else. She enjoyed her job and she loved living in Scotland, but her daughter would always be her first priority and, try as she might not to, she was worried for her. She wasn't convinced that David would be around much and Lisa had her own problems. She was a sweet girl and a good friend to Sadie but her life was complicated and her own relationship was far from stable.

Sadie decided that it was time to tell the children in her class about her pregnancy and that she would be leaving the school in a few months. She had received some good news from the Head Teacher, Wendy. She had been contacted by Laura, the teacher that Sadie had replaced. Laura and her husband had returned to the UK. They hadn't settled in Germany so they made the decision to come back. Laura's husband had already secured a job in London and she had telephoned the school to see if there were any vacancies. Wendy was delighted to hear from her and told her about Sadie's pregnancy and that she would be taking maternity leave in a few months.

"I can only offer you a temporary contract Laura, "she informed her. "Sadie is intent on coming back to work when the twins are a few months old and I will be honouring her decision. I hope you understand?"

"Of course," Laura replied. "That's amazing news. I'm so happy for her. She is such a sweet girl and a great teacher. I would be delighted to cover her maternity leave, if that's agreeable with both you and her."

"Well, that's settled then," said Wendy. "Why don't you come into the school in a few weeks and then you can get together with Sadie and talk about dates, only I'm not quite sure exactly when she intends to leave."

"Yes, I'll do that Wendy. Thank you so much for this opportunity. I've really missed being here. If nothing else, our move to Germany has shown me that there's no place like home!"

Sadie took a deep breath as she walked into the classroom. Now was the time to speak to the children. She had noticed that some of them had been giving her quizzical looks over the last couple of weeks.

"Good morning children," she said. "Good morning Mrs Burns," they answered in unison. Before she could speak, Isobel, one of the little girls that Sadie was particularly fond of, put her hand up.

"Mrs Burns. Have you got a baby in your tummy?" Some of the other children started giggling and seemed embarrassed.

"Yes, Isobel. Well actually I have two babies in my tummy. I was about to tell you all anyway." Isobel's little face was a picture as she struggled to understand what her teacher was telling her.

"Two babies! Have you got room in your tummy for two babies?" The other children laughed and Sadie couldn't resist joining in with them.

"Yes, I have just about got room Isobel, although it's a bit of a squeeze. What I wanted to tell you all, is that I will have to leave the school in a few months to have my babies - but - I will be coming back when they are a few months old. By that time, you would have moved up to the next year and you will have a new teacher anyway. But I just wanted you to know that I will come and see you all and find out how you're getting on in your new class. I am really proud of all of you and I have loved being your teacher. But for now we've got lots to look forward to, so shall we get on with our lessons? I've got something really exciting for you to work on."

Sadie was relieved that she had managed to speak to the children without getting emotional. It was hard for her to think that she would only have a few more months with them. They had been a joy to teach and, as her first class, they would always have a special place in her heart. They would always be her little sponges!

Chapter 14

Sadie looked around at her beautiful kitchen and dining room as she prepared for her dinner party later. She loved her kitchen. It was the heart of the house and where she spent most of her time. Since she had left work, it had become her happy place. Much to her surprise, she had developed a love for baking. She had always enjoyed cooking, but baking was new territory. Any attempts that she had made in the past to bake a sponge or make her own pastry for a pie had always been a disaster. But now, with patience and a good recipe book, she found herself producing the most amazing cakes, biscuits and pastries.

As the mouth watering smell of beef roasting in the oven wafted throughout the room, she thought about her guests who would be arriving in a few hours. She was looking forward to seeing Lisa and Alan. She hadn't seen either of them for a few weeks. But the fact that she would have to pretend to be pleasant to Mark for a few hours was not something she was looking forward to.

Her thoughts turned to the last time she had seen Lisa at her leaving party at the school. On behalf of the staff, she had presented her with a generous gift voucher for Mothercare. Lisa had told Wendy the Head Teacher, that her and David needed to buy two car seats, and that a voucher would go a long way towards covering the cost. She was overwhelmed with their generosity and thanked everyone for their kindness. Little Marcus had volunteered to present her with a huge bouquet of flowers from the children, and most of them had made her little cards saying how much they were going to miss her. It had been difficult saying goodbye to the children in her class. It touched her heart to see how much they cared for her.

At the end of the afternoon, Wendy gave a short speech to wish her well and thanked her for all her hard work, and said that she looked forward to Sadie's return to the school in the near future. It was an emotional but very happy day that she would always remember.

Her thoughts returned to the food preparation as David walked into the room. "Mmmm, that beef smells delicious," he said. "What can I do to help?"

"You can peel the potatoes and prepare the vegetables, and there's also the seafood starter to do. "I've made an apple pie - my pastry", she said laughing. "And I'm just about to do a Pavlova."

"Aren't you the clever one?" he answered. "You're quite the baker now aren't you? Our guests are going to be very spoiled."

"I'm really looking forward to seeing Lisa and Alan", said Sadie. "I just wish that Mark wasn't coming. I hope that he doesn't do or say anything to upset Lisa. I don't trust him."

"'Well, like it or not, sweetheart, Mark is her partner. Where she goes, he does too. So we'll have to at least, try and make him feel welcome." Sadie shrugged her shoulders and carried on making her Pavlova. David was right, they would have to make the effort with Mark for Lisa's sake.

She decided that she would go upstairs and get changed soon. She wondered what she would wear. She felt like the side of a house now and was struggling to get into any of her clothes. Even the maternity clothes that she had bought recently were getting a bit tight. She patted her growing tummy as she felt yet another strong kick inside her. She had noticed much more movement lately. It was difficult to detect whether it was a knee or elbow that was jabbing at her insides but it was reassuring. The babies were certainly very active.

As she was getting changed, David called up the stairs to say that he had finished preparing the vegetables and that he had made the starter.

"I've taken the beef out of the oven. It looks lovely. Shall I put the potatoes in now?" he asked.

"Yes please, darling. I'll be down in a minute. Just looking for something to wear that fits me." She eventually settled on a loose maxi dress which, before she was pregnant, was much too big for her. She congratulated herself on not having given it to a charity shop. It fitted her perfectly now.

Their three guests arrived on time at 8pm. Alan was the first to come through the door. He walked over to Sadie first, hugging her tight. "Goodness, you've grown since I last saw you," he said laughing as he stood back looking at her tummy.

"Haven't I just?", she said. "It's so good to see you Alan. You're looking well."

"Yes, I am, thank you - very well." He turned his attentions to David shaking his hand. "Good to see you David. The house is looking great by the way. You've done a lot since I was here last."

"A lot of it is down to Sadie," he answered. "She's the one with the artistic flair."

"Hi Lisa, Hi Mark," said David as they walked in holding hands. "Good to see you. Come through to the lounge. We'll all have a drink before dinner."

Sadie hugged her friend warmly but cringed inwardly as Mark leant forward and kissed her on the cheek.

"You look lovely, Sadie. I like your dress," said Lisa. "There's a story behind this dress," she said laughing. "I'll tell you later."

When it came to the seating arrangements around the table, Sadie had made a point of sitting Lisa next to Alan with Mark opposite her. She guessed that they would have plenty to talk about and, whether Mark liked it or not, she wanted to give them the opportunity to have a proper catch up. She looked at Mark's face as she guided him to where he was sitting. He was obviously unimpressed that it was Alan sitting next to Lisa and not him. Throughout the meal he hardly said a word other than exchanging polite pleasantries about the food. His eyes were fixed on Lisa and Alan as they chatted happily about the latest Sci Fi book they were both reading. They were so relaxed in each other's company. Once again, Sadie thought what a lovely couple they made. She refrained from further thoughts on the subject, remembering what David had said and reminded herself that she had promised to make Mark feel welcome.

"We haven't seen you since you proposed to Lisa, Mark. It sounded very romantic, and the ring is beautiful. Congratulations. You're a lucky man. Lisa is a beautiful girl" she said smiling at her friend.

"Yes, same here," said Alan. "I meant to congratulate you earlier - sorry. Your lovely lady here distracted me talking about the book that we're both reading," he said laughing.

"Thank you," Mark answered as he glared at Alan. "I know how lucky I am. Lisa is my world and she knows that, don't you honey?"

He looked at Lisa as he attempted to smile but Sadie was looking beyond his false platitudes. His eyes were cold and almost menacing. His smile was fake and frozen. He wasn't fooling anyone.

"Thank you all. Yes we're very happy. I'm a lucky girl. The next step is to arrange our wedding. Hopefully Spring next year," said Lisa. Sadie couldn't believe how her friend was getting sucked in by this guy. If she could see through him, then why couldn't she?

After dessert and coffee, everyone went through to the lounge as Sadie and Lisa cleared the table. When they got in the kitchen, Lisa quietly closed the door behind them. "I've been waiting for an opportunity to get you on your own Sadie. I've got something to tell you." Sadie felt her heart sink. She sensed this wasn't going to be good.

"I'm seven weeks pregnant. I've known for a week or so but I wanted to wait and tell you when the time was right. I didn't want to say anything at your leaving party. It was your special day and I wanted you to enjoy it without having anything else to think about."

Sadie looked at her friend. It wasn't often that she was lost for words. But this was one of those times. She took a deep breath as she said "Oh Lisa. I hoped that you would wait, at least until you got married and you were absolutely sure that you and Mark were really going to make your relationship work."

"It is working," answered Lisa. "We have been getting on really well for a long time now."

"Lisa, I've been watching him tonight. He's absolutely furious that you have been talking to Alan over dinner. He hates anyone else paying you attention. How do you think he will be once the baby is born? Can't you see that he wants you all to himself? He is never going to share you with anyone, even your own child. What did he say when you told him you were pregnant?"

Lisa looked downwards and hesitated as she answered, "He doesn't know yet. I haven't told him."

"You haven't told him!" she exclaimed. "Why not Lisa? Is it because you know what his reaction will be? I can't believe that you would be so irresponsible." Sadie was angry now. What on earth was she thinking?

"I'm going to tell him in a few days, I promise. I just need to wait for the right moment."

"I don't think there will ever be a right moment. He is not going to react well - you know that. I'm worried for you. What if he hurts you again?"

"He won't hurt me. He promised that would never happen again and I believe him. He will be surprised but once he gets used to the idea, he will be as happy as I am. I'm sure of it."

At that moment, David opened the door and walked into the kitchen.

"What are you two whispering about? Come and join us in the lounge. I thought we could have a game of cards. Alan and Mark are up for it."

"Ok, we'll come in a minute - just clearing away the last of the dishes," said Sadie as she tried to compose herself. She had to admit that she felt shaky and upset but she needed to pull herself together before the others noticed.

"We'll talk about this tomorrow Lisa. Don't say anything to Mark in the meantime."

"No, I won't. Thanks Sadie. What would I do without you?"

The rest of the evening was a bit of a blur for Sadie. She joined in with the card games but her mind was elsewhere. She longed to go to bed. She was tired, physically and mentally. It had been a long day - perhaps everything would seem better in the morning. Fortunately, it wasn't long before everyone decided it was time to say their goodbyes and head home. As Lisa left with Mark, Sadie whispered to her that she would call her in the morning.

"Thank you both for a lovely evening and an amazing meal," said Mark as he ushered Lisa out the door. "We'll see you again soon."

Not if I can help it! thought Sadie to herself. Tonight hadn't done anything to help change her mind about him. She just hoped that Lisa wouldn't say or do anything to antagonise him when they got home.

Alan was the last one to leave at midnight.

"You could have stayed the night Alan. It's really late for you to be driving back to London," she said. "It's been so lovely seeing you. Don't be a stranger will you? Come and see us again soon." "I'll be fine. I don't mind driving at this time of night anyway. There's not much on the roads. I should be home in no time and, yes, I'll come and see you soon. Certainly before the babies are born."

"Bye David," he said as he stepped forward and shook his hand. Look after your lovely wife. She is going to need you more than ever now." Sadie thought that he sounded sad.

David smiled at him and looked at her. "Always," he said wistfully. "Always."

After an unsettled sleep, Sadie woke up in the morning to find David packing his overnight bag. She had forgotten that he was going to Manchester today and that he wouldn't be back until tomorrow.

"Oh sorry, darling. I completely forgot that you were going away. Let me make you a nice breakfast before you leave."

"A bacon sandwich will do me sweetheart. You did enough cooking yesterday. "It went really well didn't it?" she said. "Apart from the obnoxious Mark."

"Oh he wasn't that bad Sadie. He joined in well when we were playing cards. He opened up a lot more. I just think he's a bit shy that's all," he answered.

"I don't think he is shy at all. I think he is an arsehole and I wish Lisa would dump him."

"That's a bit harsh sweetheart. I thought we agreed that we were going to try and get along with him for Lisa's sake." She decided not to pursue the conversation any further and that she wouldn't tell him about Lisa's pregnancy. As soon as his taxi arrived to take him to the station, she was going to ring her and see how she was before she left for work.

David managed to finish his bacon sandwich just as the taxi pulled up outside. He kissed Sadie goodbye and promised that he would call her as soon as his meeting in Manchester was finished. As he ran down the path towards the taxi, he turned to look at her and called out

"I love you Mrs Burns. Take care. I'll see you soon." Sadie blew him a kiss and shut the front door. She suddenly felt a strange feeling washing over her – one of fear and uncertainty. She shivered inwardly. She experienced a weird sense of foreboding? It freaked her out. I must ring Lisa, she thought to herself. Something might have happened to her.

Lisa answered the phone quickly sounding slightly out of breath.

."Lisa, are you ok? It's me, Sadie."

"Hi Sadie, yes I'm fine. I'm just running late for school that's all. I've been rushing around. I'm a bit out of breath."

"Yes, I can hear that you are. Are you sure you're ok? Nothing happened with Mark last night did it? He didn't kick off, I hope."

"Well, we did have a bit of an argument but that's all. He is convinced that I fancy Alan. I've told him so many times that Alan and I are just friends, but he just doesn't believe me. He thinks that, if I speak to another man, it's because I'm coming on to them. Nothing will persuade him otherwise."

"That's what I mean by him not wanting to share you with anyone else, Lisa. He is controlling and manipulative and he is never going to change."

"I think he is trying hard to change. We argued, yes, but he calmed himself down. He didn't touch me, honestly. That, in itself is a step forward."

"Well, I hope you're right, I really do. Anyway, I'd better let you go now or you'll be late for work. Say hi to everyone for me won't you?"

"Yeah sure. Thanks for ringing Sadie. See you soon."

She ended the call hoping that her friend was right although she still hadn't been able to shake off this feeling of apprehension that was troubling her. She remembered her Mum saying that she wouldn't be working this week, so she decided to give her a call. Mum will reassure me, she thought to herself. She always knows the right things to say.

"Hi Mum. Are you enjoying your week off." "Hi love, yes it's been nice. I've managed to catch up on a lot of jobs that have been piling up so I'm really pleased." "Anyway, never mind me. How are you doing? Did your dinner party go well last night?"

"It was lovely Mum. The food was great, although I say it myself. Everyone seemed to enjoy themselves. It was a bit awkward with Mark being there and he obviously wasn't very impressed with me sitting Lisa next to Alan for dinner. He glared at Alan all the way through the meal and hardly said a word. Poor Lisa got it in the neck when she got home. He's convinced that she fancies Alan. They had an argument apparently but Lisa assures me that he didn't touch her and he had calmed down by the time they went to bed. She went off to school this morning as usual and she sounded ok when I spoke to her, so hopefully she's alright. I just don't trust him though, Mum. He's a control freak and he can obviously be violent. I just wish that she would dump him. She'd be much better off with Alan and I know he likes her."

"Oh Sadie. You do worry about everyone don't you? You're such a sweet girl but there is only so much you can do. Lisa is a grown woman. If she wants to stay with Mark, then it's her decision. You can't get involved. You have got those two babies to think about. Your own family must come first." said Mary. "

"Yes, that's what David says too. I know you're right, but Mum

I've had this strange feeling today that something bad is going to happen. I can't shake it off. That's why I wanted to talk to you. What does it mean?"

"It means that you are already too involved in Lisa's problems. That's what it means. It's affecting you Sadie. You have got to take a step back for the sake of your own well-being." Mary felt worried about her daughter. It was times like this that she wished she lived closer so that she could give her a hug. The idea of moving down South was still uppermost in her mind. She wouldn't say anything to her yet but she had decided that she would speak to Rob about it again tonight. They needed to make a decision, one way or another.

Sadie felt better after her conversation with her mum. She always knew what to say and despite her disagreeing with her involvement in Lisa's relationship, she did understand. She decided that she should talk to her more often. She had a calming influence on her that nobody else, not even David, could give her.

After she had eaten her evening meal and spoken to David, she had a shower and put her dressing gown on. As she was on her own, it seemed the perfect opportunity for an early night. There was nothing on the TV that she wanted to watch so she decided to take one of her baby books from the lounge and read in bed.

Just as she was climbing into bed, her phone rang. She knew it wouldn't be David. She had just spoken to him and it wouldn't be her mum again. She felt herself tensing as she saw that it was Lisa calling. "Hello Lisa - you ok?" she said nervously.

She could barely hear Lisa's reply. Her voice sounded faint and weak. "No, Sadie, I'm not. Help me. Please help me!" Sadie was really worried now. This didn't sound like Lisa at all.

"What's the matter love? What's happened? "

"It's Mark. He's driven off in the car. I don't know where he's going."

"Has he hurt you? What has he done?" Her heart felt like it was pumping out of her chest. She just knew that something bad had happened. This was what she had felt all day. Lisa's voice was trailing off as if she was losing consciousness. She managed to hear the words "He punched and kicked me, and I'm bleeding. I think I'm losing my baby."

"Hold on Lisa. I'm coming over right now. Can you still hear me?"

She could hear her breathing but there was no other sound. Perhaps she has passed out. Please God that's all it is, she thought as she quickly took off her dressing gown and threw on the clothes she had been wearing earlier. She raced downstairs and grabbed the car keys. It was pitch black and raining heavily. She had never liked driving at night - especially when it was raining, but all she could think about was getting to her friend as soon as possible.

Thank goodness that she doesn't live far away, she thought as she pulled away from the house. It was only about ten minutes away but it felt like an age. It seemed as though she caught every traffic light on route. The rain was getting heavier and heavier. It was a struggle to see through the windscreen even though the wipers were going at full speed. It was the longest ten minutes of her life. She pulled up outside Lisa's flat hoping that the front door would be unlocked. She thought how Mark must of left in a hurry as the door was still ajar. She called out to Lisa but there was no reply. As she walked into her bedroom she stopped in her tracks. She felt like her feet were glued to the floor at the sight before her. Lisa was sprawled on the bed. Her eyes were swollen and shut. Bruises were already showing on the tops of her arms and she was clutching her stomach crying and moaning.

"Oh Lisa, my lovely girl. What on earth has that monster done to you?" She rushed to her side and cradled her in her arms. She flinched with pain at her touch. She wondered if he had broken or bruised her ribs.

"My baby, my baby," Lisa cried. "I'm bleeding down below Sadie. I think he's killed my baby."

"Are you able to sit up? I'm going to take you to the hospital. They'll know what to do." "No hospital Sadie. I don't want to go to hospital. They will ask awkward questions. They'll want to know what happened. I don't want to talk about it with anyone,"

"I'm not leaving you here. You need medical care. If you are having a miscarriage, the doctors will know what to do. You don't have to tell them anything until you feel able to. The main thing at the moment is to get you some help. Please, think about your baby if nothing else." That seemed to do the trick as Lisa tentatively lifted herself off the bed and leant on Sadie's arm.

"Come on my love. It will be alright I promise. We'll take the back road to the hospital and avoid the hold ups. It won't take long," she said. With her very large tummy managing to get in the way at every turn, she struggled to get Lisa into the passenger seat. She was in a lot of pain and not making much sense. She kept mumbling about Mark – that he didn't mean to do it, he was upset about her being pregnant. Was it his baby or Alan's?

Sadie couldn't believe what she was hearing. She felt so angry. She wanted to shout at her – what on earth made you get pregnant with that man's baby! But now wasn't the right time for recriminations. She needed to get her to hospital as soon as possible.

The rain hadn't eased and the roads were beginning to flood as Sadie started her journey towards the hospital. She was pleased that she had chosen to take the back roads. It was quiet with very little traffic and she anticipated that they would get there quicker than driving through town. She looked across at Lisa who had stopped crying and seemed a little calmer. Her heart went out to her. She was such a sweet girl. How could anyone do this to her, especially someone who professed to love her.

What happened next was like she was being propelled head first into a horror movie. Sadie felt a loud bang from underneath the car. Suddenly, they were skidding all over the road. The car started spinning and tumbling out of control. She stamped on the brakes and grabbed the steering wheel in desperation as her body shook and battered against the driver's door. She remembered the sound of glass breaking and then there was darkness. She opened her eyes but nothing made any sense. She could hear voices, there were flashing blue lights and sirens. Where am I? she thought. Am I having a bad dream? She reached across to the passenger seat.

Where was Lisa? Her eyes went to the shattered windscreen as she felt the blood running down her face. She tried to move but she was trapped. Just as she was drifting off to sleep, she heard a friendly voice. "Don't try and move love. The fire brigade are here. Try and stay awake. They're going to get you out. You'll be ok. We're going to take care of you."

That was the last thing she remembered.

Chapter 15

It was six days later before Sadie woke up. She opened her eyes through a mist of bright lights and blurry faces looking down at her. There were beeping sounds coming from the monitor next to her bed. She struggled to focus still not knowing where she was.

The faces were talking to her. Their lips were moving but she couldn't understand what they were saying. She focused on one of them.

"Is that you Mum?" Her smile and warmth was familiar and comforting.

"Oh my darling, you've woken up. I can't tell you how worried we have all been," Mary said as she wiped the tears from her eyes.

"Where am I and where's David? She started to be aware that something bad had happened. Her hands instinctively went to her stomach.

"My babies. Where are my babies?" she cried.

"David has just gone for a coffee", said Mary. "He'll be back in a minute. Me and your dad are here with you.

"Where are my babies?" She screamed. Why wasn't anyone telling her where they were? "They're fine darling. David will tell you what happened when he gets back. Just rest for now. You've been through a terrible trauma. Let's just take things a step at a time," said Mary.

She hated not being able to say any more but she had promised

David that he must be the one to tell her what had happened. She needed to respect that. The police had been unable to contact David after the accident. He had been with a client and didn't see the message until the next morning.

Luckily, Sadie had her mum and dad's contact details in her purse, so they telephoned them straightaway. Mary answered the phone. She felt the colour draining from her face as the policeman told her that Sadie had been in a serious accident and that they should get to the hospital as soon as possible. He told her that she had been taken by air ambulance to the Major Trauma Unit at Addenbrooke's Hospital in Cambridge. Rob took the phone from her hand and steadied his wife as she crumpled to the floor.

"Oh Rob, our little girl. We've got to get to her."

"We'll leave straightaway love. Try not to worry. She'll be fine, I know she will. She's a fighter." Rob heard himself say the words but he was just as worried as his wife. The thought of anything happening to their little girl was beyond comprehension.

They arrived at the hospital a couple of hours after David. As he sat at Sadie's bedside holding her hand, he told them that he was waiting for Alan to arrive. He had been distraught when David had phoned him to tell him about the accident. His mum and dad were also waiting anxiously by the phone for news. Mary noticed that he was white as a sheet and had obviously not showered or shaved for the last 24 hours. She walked towards him and put her arm across his bowed shoulders. She felt him shudder as the tears he had been holding back since he had arrived at the hospital, began to stream down his face.

"Oh Mary, this is my fault. I shouldn't have gone away. If I had been at home, I would have stopped her. She's seven months pregnant for god's sake. What on earth possessed her to drive in the dark and in heavy rain? She hates driving in the dark, and where was she going?"

"It's not going to help Sadie to start apportioning blame now son. We've got to see her through this," said Rob.

"What have the doctors said? Is it serious?" Mary grabbed Rob's hand. She was terrified at what David might say.

"She has a head injury and they're worried about the babies. They have been showing signs of distress, so the doctors are talking about giving her a caesarian later today. I'm just waiting for them to come back and they will tell us what they're going to do."

"But it's too soon," cried Mary. They might be too little to survive. And what have they said about Sadie's head injury. She's going to get better isn't she? Please tell me she is going to be alright." Mary was crying now. She had managed to hold it together up until this moment, but this was too much to bear. She could be about to lose both her daughter and her grandchildren. She was terrified. She walked around to the other side of the bed and looked at Sadie's beautiful face. Apart from a bruise on her forehead and cuts on her face, she looked peaceful as if in a deep sleep. Mary felt her warmth as she curled her fingers around her limp hand. She squeezed it hoping for a response. But there was nothing.

At that moment, two doctors walked into the room looking very serious. "Mr Burns, Mr and Mrs Connel, can you follow us into the family room. It will be easier to talk there?"

They followed the doctors, lost in their own fearful thoughts of what they were going to say. The older one of the two invited them to sit down.

"As you know", he said "Sadie has a head injury. This has caused some swelling on the brain. In order to rest the brain and help the swelling to subside, we've had to put her in an induced coma. I know this sounds alarming but it's the best option for her recovery."

"What are her chances doctor?" asked Rob nervously.

"We are cautiously optimistic but we won't know if there has been any permanent damage until we wake her up. At the moment, we are more concerned about the pregnancy. The babies are continuing to show signs of distress so we will need to do an emergency cesarean this afternoon. They appear to be a good weight for the number of weeks gestation so they have a fighting chance. Once they're delivered, they will be transferred to the neonatal intensive care unit where they will be monitored and cared for around the clock. Can I also ask you all – were you aware that there was another young lady in the car with Sadie?"

They all looked at David for an answer but he was as shocked as they were. David turned to Mary first.

"Do you think it was Lisa?" he asked. "Did Sadie say anything to you about going out with her that night? I know that she has spoken to you a lot about how worried she has been about her lately."

Mary remembered the conversation she had with Sadie a couple of days ago. "Yes, she did tell me that she was concerned about her again. I'm afraid that I gave her a bit of a telling off. I felt like she was putting her own health at risk by getting too involved in her and Mark's relationship."

"I've told her the same so many times," he said. "But why would she be out in the car with her at that time of night? It doesn't make sense."

"I'm afraid that the police will want to speak to Sadie when she wakes up to get the full story," added the doctor. Regrettably, the young lady died at the scene. They are going to need details of next of kin etc."

The eerie silence in the room was tangible as the words 'the young lady died at the scene' hung in the air as if frozen in the horror of the moment. It couldn't be true. They must have got it wrong. Not Lisa. Not beautiful Lisa. Rob put his arm around his wife as she sobbed into her handkerchief. David sat still, open mouthed, trying to take in what he had just heard.

"I'm so sorry," said the doctor. "You obviously knew this young lady. Are you aware of who might be her next of kin?"

"She lived with her partner Mark. I suppose he is registered as her next of kin. But I can't be sure," said David. I do know that she was an orphan. Her parents died some years ago in an accident. She does have a brother but he lives in Australia and I don't think they keep in contact."

"Would you be kind enough to give me the young lady's address and I'll pass it on to the police. They will want to inform her partner of her death," added the doctor. David agreed that he would, but he felt the police should be made aware that Mark had abused Lisa in the past both mentally and physically, so he turned to the doctor and said

"I think there is a strong possibility that he might be involved in what happened. That could be why she was in the car with Sadie." "If he is behind all of this, I swear I will kill him!"

"I can understand your anger Mr Burns but this isn't going to help your wife. Let's just leave it to the police shall we," said the doctor.

"Come on David. Let's go and have a coffee." said Rob. "We've all had one hell of a shock. We need to sit down quietly and take it in. Getting angry isn't the answer. If Mark is responsible for any of this, then the police will make sure that he pays for it. Let's just leave it to them."

Mary's thoughts turned back to Sadie. She knew how much she loved Lisa. She was going to be absolutely devastated. Then there was her two little babies. What was going to happen to them? She felt she was living in a nightmare that she couldn't wake up from.

She followed Rob and David in a daze into the lift and down to the floor of the restaurant. Rob said he would get the coffees as her and David found a quiet table in the corner.

"I can't believe what's happening," said David holding his head in his hands. "It's so much to take in. Sadie with a head injury, our babies in danger and Lisa dead! If that man is responsible for this, I'm going to make him pay, whatever it takes." Never before had he felt such anger.

"I understand David and I agree with you but we're all in shock and it's not easy to think clearly," said Mary. "The doctor was right. We've got to leave this to the police. In the meantime, we're here to support Sadie. When she wakes up, she is going to need all of us to be strong. I'm going back to the ward when I've finished my coffee. If she is having the caesarean this afternoon, then I want to be there. Are you coming?'

He nodded and said "Yes of course. You're right Mary. I can see where Sadie gets her sensible head from now. We've got to concentrate on her and the babies. I must ring mum and dad too and also see if Alan has arrived yet. They were all so upset. Mark will get his comeuppance I'm sure. I just wish that I had taken Sadie more seriously. I thought she was overreacting and getting too involved but, she was right wasn't she? If only I had listened and supported her more , then perhaps we wouldn't be where we are now. I'll never forgive myself for that."

"Nobody is to blame for this other than that horrible man." said Mary. "Just remember that. None of us knew what was really going on. I'm sure that Sadie didn't even know the half of it. He was calculating and manipulative and he probably fooled a lot of people, He knew exactly what he was doing and now it appears that he has caused the death of one of the sweetest girls I have ever met. He's a monster and deserves to be locked away for a very long time. When Sadie wakes up, we'll find out exactly what happened and then I'm sure justice will take it's course. Until then, I'm focusing on the here and now. I know how hard it is, David but that's what we've got to do."

David smiled kindly at his mother-in-law. He thought what a wonderful woman she was. She was devastated at what had happened to her daughter and her best friend, yet she still she retained her dignity and strength in what was undoubtedly one of the worst times of her life. As David, Mary and Rob made their way back to the ward, they saw that Alan was just ahead of them and about to enter Sadie's room. David called out "Alan hang on mate. I'll just fill you in before you go and see Sadie. We've just been talking to the doctors." David guided him to the family room as Mary and Rob went in to sit with Sadie.

"What happened? You just said there had been an accident. Is Sadie going to be alright?"

"She's got a head injury and she is in an induced coma", he answered. "But right now the doctors are worried about the babies. She is having a Caesarean this afternoon." He then proceeded to tell him that they thought Lisa had been in the car with Sadie.

"Until she wakes up we don't know the whole story, but it seems like she was taking her somewhere, we're not sure where, but we're convinced that it's got something to do with that bloody Mark. The tragic thing is" - David hesitated as he spoke the words that he had been dreading. "Poor Lisa died as a result of the accident."

Alan gasped. He felt numb. He found it hard to comprehend that such a beautiful young woman's life had been snubbed out, just like that. He thought of how they had been laughing and chatting to one another only a short time ago. How was this possible?

"I know it's a shock," said David. "We couldn't believe it either, but I'm afraid it's true. Apparently her injuries were so severe that she died at the scene."

"That poor girl," said Alan. "She had her whole life in front of her. Do you really think that Mark is behind it?"

"Yes, I do. Sadie has been worried about Lisa for a long time now. She never trusted Mark, and she was right. I should have taken her more seriously."

"I'm sure we'll find out what happened when Sadie wakes up. Until then, is it ok if I go and see her?" Alan asked. "Yes of course. We'll both go now. I want to be with her when she goes to theatre anyway, and hopefully that will be soon."

As they both made their way back to the ward, one of the doctors was just leaving Sadie's room. "Oh, Mr Burns, good I wanted to see you. We're going to take Sadie down to theatre in about fifteen minutes. If you come with me, we'll get you in your theatre scrubs so that you are ready to be by her side when the babies are delivered. I'm assuming that you want to be there?"

"Yes of course," said David. "I want to be there every step of the way. I'll just go and tell my in-laws and I'll follow you down."

Mary and Rob watched nervously as Sadie was wheeled out on a stretcher to go down to theatre. Mary wished that she could be with her but the doctor had said that it would be better if only one person accompanied her. She accepted that it had to be David. He was the babies father. He needed to be with his wife.

Time seemed endless as they anxiously waited for news. Alan had taken himself off for a walk to clear his head. He was clearly in shock after hearing about Lisa's death. Mary and Rob felt for him. He had been very fond of Lisa. It was a lot for him to take in.

About an hour after Sadie had been taken to theatre, David appeared back in the ward. He was red in the face and looked very emotional. Mary could see that he had been crying. Her heart skipped a beat. Was something wrong?

"David, how is she? Please tell me that our little girl is ok?" she cried.

"She's fine. She's still unconscious but her vital signs are stable. The babies have been delivered. They're tiny but they're strong and they're putting up a good fight. They have taken them to the Neonatal Unit. The doctors think that they've got a good chance. The little girl was just under 4lbs and the boy was 4lbs 2ozs. They are absolutely beautiful, just like their Mummy."

David was crying again as Mary jumped up and hugged him. She looked across at Rob who was just standing still, tears running down his face.

"Oh Rob, love", she said. "I'm forgetting about you in all of this. You've been so strong. I've taken you for granted. This has been just as hard for you. I'm so sorry."

"That's ok love. It's difficult for all of us. But it's going to be alright. I just know it is. Sadie is a strong girl. She's going to get better and she's going to take care of those two little babies." He had been trying to put on a brave face all day for the sake of his wife. He knew how much she was struggling, but he couldn't hide his emotions any longer. The thought of those two little souls struggling to survive was the catalyst for the tears that he had been holding back all day.

Sadie was brought back to the ward after a short time in recovery. The doctor reported that the caesarean had gone to plan. The babies were small but they were doing well. He said that Sadie would be kept sedated for the rest of that day and they planned to try and wake her up tomorrow. He suggested that everyone went home and got some sleep. There was nothing else that they could do and it was important that they were rested and prepared for what the morning would bring.

They all agreed to book in at a nearby Premier Inn for the night. Mary wanted to stay with Sadie but Rob said she looked exhausted and that a good night's sleep would do her the world of good. David was also worried about his mum and dad. They were anxiously waiting for news. They didn't even know that the babies had been born yet.

"Oh poor Susan and Colin," said Mary. "They must be going out of their minds with worry. I'll ring them as soon as we get to the hotel." Luckily the hotel had a couple of double rooms available for the rest of the week. Mary and Rob booked one of them and David booked the other. He suggested that Alan stay with him for at least one night. He looked absolutely exhausted and David wasn't happy about him driving back to London when he was still so upset. Lisa's death had hit him hard.

"I'll sleep on the couch and you can have the bed," he said to Alan. "You look done in. Alan agreed, albeit reluctantly. He would have preferred to drive home but then he wanted to be with Sadie when the doctors woke her up so he conceded that it was probably more sensible to stay at least for one night.

Susan answered her phone straightaway as she noticed that it was Mary calling. "Mary is that you? We've both been so worried about Sadie. Colin and I wanted to come to the hospital but David didn't think it would be a good idea for too many people to be around her at the moment. How is she Mary?"

"She's still unconscious but the doctors are hoping to wake her up tomorrow, she answered. "I've got some more news. You and Colin are grandparents! The babies were delivered by caesarean section this afternoon. They're small but they're strong and, so far, they are doing well."

"That's fantastic news, Mary. I have been really worried about them too. It's been an absolute nightmare hasn't it? Are you and Rob ok? What an awful shock it must have been for you. Do you know what happened yet?'

"We're hoping that Sadie will be able to tell us when she wakes up –

only - Mary hesitated as she delivered the news about Lisa dying at the scene of the accident. Susan gasped and her voice faltered as she said "Oh no, that poor girl. I can't believe it. She was such a lovely person. Sadie is going to be devastated isn't she? What a terrible tragedy."

"We're all still trying to get our heads around it Susan. We don't know why Lisa was in the car with Sadie at that time of night or where they were going, but we suspect that she had been attacked by that boyfriend of hers - Mark. Sadie was aware that it was an abusive relationship. She had tried countless times to get Lisa to leave him but she was determined to stay. He controlled her and made her believe that he was going to change, but, clearly, he never was going to. Sadie saw through him almost from day one, but he was very convincing. Goodness knows what that poor girl went through."

"Well the truth will come out Mary. I'm sure of it. The main thing at the moment is for Sadie to recover. Those two little mites are going to need her," said Susan. "Will you ask David to ring me tomorrow and let me know how her and the babies are? Colin and I would love to come and visit but we'll hold fire until he thinks Sadie is up to it. In the meantime, you and Rob take care of yourselves and, if you get the chance, give the babies a kiss from us. Do you know their names yet?"

"David said that they had decided on Mia and Matthew before they were born, but Sadie might change her mind when she sees them. We'll let you know, and I promise we'll keep in touch with you every step of the way," said Mary.

She was pleased that she had taken the time to speak to Susan. She had obviously been very worried too. She knew how much her and Colin loved Sadie.

In the depths of tragedy, the bond that they already had would be stronger than ever now. As well as their much loved children, they shared a new responsibility - their two precious grandchildren.

Chapter 16

David and Alan returned to the ward carrying four cups of coffee, a few minutes after Sadie had woken up. Alan took a seat in the corner of the room as David went to her bedside and held her hand. He turned to Mary.

"How long has she been awake? I wanted to be here with her."

"Just a few minutes," she answered. "The doctors have only just left. She's very disorientated David. We need to take things gently and not expect too much from her yet. The doctors are coming back soon. Hopefully they will be able to tell us more."

Meanwhile, Sadie was trying to make sense of it all. Where was she? What had happened? Try as she might, she couldn't remember anything. She did remember that she was pregnant, but where were her babies now. She looked at David's concerned face. She knew that he was her husband. Perhaps he knew where her babies were.

"Have you got my babies?" she asked. David gripped her hand tightly and looked straight into her beautiful blue eyes.

"Your babies have been born, sweetheart, and they are absolutely beautiful, you clever girl," he answered with tears in his eyes.

"Mia and Matthew are here?"

"Yes, they are here and they're doing well. When you feel a bit better, I'll get a wheelchair and I'll take you to see them."

Sadie looked at her parents and at Alan sitting across the room.

"Have you all been here with me the whole time?" she asked.

Rob stepped forward and looked at his precious daughter. "We've never left your side darling. You were in a serious accident. Do you remember?" he asked.

Her hand went to her head. It was hurting. She must have been knocked out. That's why she couldn't remember anything. At that moment, the doctors came into the room.

"Hello Sadie. You're back with us, that's excellent. How are you feeling?" one of them asked.

"My head really hurts and I'm struggling to remember what happened," she answered.

"It will take time for your memory to come back – perhaps a few days – and in the meantime we'll give you some medication to help with the pain. I want you to rest now. You've suffered a severe brain trauma. It's important for you to get some proper sleep. I'm going to ask your visitors to leave now. They can speak to you in the morning when you have rested. Sorry folks, I'm sure you would rather stay, but it's important for Sadie to get some rest now."

David agreed and said that they would all say their goodbyes to her and come back in the morning. He looked at her beautiful face. She was already closing her eyes and seemed much more peaceful. He bent and kissed her lips.

"Sleep tight, sweetheart. We'll see you in the morning." Mary, Rob and Alan also said their goodbyes and thanked the doctors for taking such good care of her.

As they all left the ward to go back to the hotel, no one spoke. The last few days had been such an emotional rollercoaster, it was difficult to find the words. Alan was the first one to break the silence.

"Sadie did really well didn't she? I'm sure she is starting to piece it all together. I'm optimistic that after a good night's sleep, she will be feeling much better and her memory will come back."

"In one way, that will be fantastic, Alan", David replied. "But how is she going to cope with the news about Lisa? It's going to break her. I know Sadie, she's going to blame herself. That could set her right back again,'" he said.

"Let's not jump too far ahead," said Mary. We all need to rest tonight and we'll face whatever we have to tomorrow."

"Mary's right guys. Let's get something to eat and grab an early night. We're no good to Sadie or those two little ones if we're dead on our feet," added Rob.

David suggested that they all meet up later and go to one of the many pubs near the hospital for dinner. Meanwhile, he said that he needed to make some telephone calls. He hadn't spoken to the Head Teacher, Wendy, at the school yet and he wanted to check in with work to let them know that he wouldn't be back for a while. He also realised that he hadn't spoken to his mum or dad since Mary's call with them yesterday. Alan had decided earlier that he would go back to London but David persuaded him to stay for another night.

"If Sadie is well enough tomorrow," he said "I would appreciate you being there when we break the news to her about Lisa. You mean a great deal to her. She will appreciate your support."

"Ok," said Alan. "If you think it will help, of course I'll be there. I'm going to take myself off for a bit while you're making your calls. Perhaps a walk and some fresh air will clear my head. It's been a stressful couple of days. I admire you David and how you have dealt with this ," he added. "You've been so strong. I don't know that, in your place, I couldn't have coped as well as you have."

"I'm not really coping," he answered. "I'm putting on a brave face as much for Mary and Rob's sake as I am for mine. Sadie is their world. They must be in bits, but they are so thoughtful and caring of others. They are wonderful people."

"I agree. They are the best. No wonder Sadie is the person she is. I wish I had parents as loving and supportive as they are," said Alan sadly. David looked at his friend and resisted the urge to put his arms around him. He wished that he hadn't been so unpleasant to him in the past. He had always been there for him and Sadie.

He deserved to be happy. Once again, he thought how difficult life could be. His emotions were all over the place. His mind was in turmoil, but he knew that, right now, he must forget his own issues and concentrate on his wife and children.

David found the telephone call with Wendy really difficult. He could hear the emotion and shock in her voice as he told her about Sadie's injuries, the birth of the babies and finally Lisa's sad death. She said that she would pass the news on to Sadie and Lisa's colleagues on his behalf. She understood how hard it must have been for him to deliver such tragic news to everyone.

"David if there is anything - and I mean anything - that I can do, you will let me know won't you?" "Yes of course, Wendy, thank you."

"I assume that Lisa's partner has been informed?" she asked.

"We don't know the full story yet. but we're hoping Sadie will remember and be able to tell us what happened. We think that he did something to Lisa and that Sadie was taking her away somewhere. The police have been informed that Lisa was the victim of domestic abuse, but they can't do anything about it without evidence. They will want to speak to Sadie when she is well enough. But until then, I assume he is hiding himself away like the coward he is."

"It's beyond belief David. Lisa was one of the sweetest people I have ever met and she was a great teacher. We are all going to miss her very much."

At this point, Wendy started to cry softly. David spared her having to talk any further and said that he would keep in touch and update her on Sadie's progress.

After he had made his other calls, he felt exhausted. The effort of having to keep repeating the horror of the last couple of days drained him. It had been especially difficult to dissuade his parents from coming to the hospital. They were anxious to see Sadie and to meet their new grandchildren. He understood, but it was too soon. They didn't even know how Sadie was going to recover yet and whether or not she would regain her memory. He promised them that, as soon as she was showing real signs of improvement, they would be welcome to come and see her, but now wasn't the right time. He heard the disappointment in his mum's voice. He felt guilty but it was the right thing for Sadie. That was what was important right now.

The next morning, he was about to have a shower and get ready to visit Sadie when his mobile rang. He saw that it was an unknown number and wondered if it was the hospital.

"Hello, is that Mr Burns?" said a voice he didn't recognise.

"Yes it is. Who's speaking?" he asked.

"My name is Detective Sergeant Russell. I'm sorry to hear of your wife's accident and the death of her friend Lisa Martin. I'm sure that you are aware that we will need to speak to your wife when she is ready to do so. We need to clarify exactly what happened on the night of the accident and why Miss Martin was in the car with her. Her partner has identified the body and, as I'm sure you will understand, he is totally devastated. I understand that Miss Martin had only recently informed him that she was pregnant and that they were planning to get married. He claims that he has no idea why his fiancé would have been in the car with your wife. He said that he had popped out to get a bottle of wine and that when he returned, Miss Martin had gone."

David couldn't believe what he was hearing but also realised that he had to be very careful about what he said to the police at this point. Until he could speak to Sadie, there were so many unanswered questions. The last thing he wanted to do was to complicate things for her.

"I appreciate your call Detective Sergeant but I would rather not make any comments at this stage. Not until my wife is more stable and able to remember what happened. She has been through a terrible time and hasn't even been able to see our twin babies yet. I will say this one thing - do not trust anything that Miss Martin's so called partner is telling you."

"Thank you for your time Mr Burns," said the detective." Rest assured that we will find out the truth and if anyone is responsible for Miss Martin's death, I an promise you that they will find out. I will speak to you again soon."

David went through to the bedroom where Alan was just waking up from his night on the sofa.

"Did you hear any of that?" he asked. "It was the police. They've spoken to Mark. Apparently he identified Lisa's body. Predictably, he is denying all knowledge of why she was in the car with Sadie when the accident happened. But one thing I did learn, Lisa was pregnant. If Sadie knew, she certainly didn't tell me. I'm wondering if it's connected in any way with what happened."

"Pregnant!" That's a surprise," said Alan. "Why would Lisa choose to have a baby with that monster?"

"I don't know. I will never understand why she was with him in the first place," David answered. I think we should get ready and give Mary and Rob a knock. The sooner we get to the hospital, the better. I want to go and check on the babies too. I'm hoping that Sadie will be well enough to see them. It will give her the incentive she needs to get better. They're going to need their mummy."

David knocked on Mary and Rob's door but there was no answer.

"It looks like they have already left to go to the hospital," he said. "Let's go downstairs and get a taxi. I should be with Sadie. That bloody policeman has made us late now." Sadie was just waking up as her parents came into her room. They had checked with the nurses first to make sure that it was alright for them to go in. The Sister on the ward reported that she had a peaceful night and had only woken once to take her medication. She also advised that they didn't ask her any questions about the accident until the doctor had been in to see her.

"Is she well enough to go and see her babies?" asked Mary.

"Yes, we were going to suggest that. Her husband has just phoned to say that he is on his way so when he gets here, we'll get a wheelchair and he can take her to see them. You and your husband are also welcome to visit them afterwards. They are both doing really well. They're feeding well and they're breathing on their own now. Apart from being small, they are absolutely perfect."

"That's such a relief," said Mary. Sadie is going to be so happy to see them and let's hope it will give her that extras push to get better."

"Thank you Sister," said Rob. "You have all been so kind. It's a huge comfort to know that our daughter and grandchildren are in such safe hands."

As they approached Sadie's bedside, she smiled. "Mum, Dad, I'm so pleased to see you. I'm sorry that I wasn't making much sense yesterday. I feel a lot better today. I can remember bits and pieces of what happened so I'm sure it will all come back to me in time. "That's good darling," said Mary." But let's not talk about the accident now. We've got some good news! The Sister said that you can go and see Mia and Matthew. She is going to get a wheelchair and David is going to take you. He's on his way with Alan now."

"Are they ok?" she asked. "I've been thinking about them. I can't believe that they have been born and that I don't remember a thing about it. I've also been worrying about Lisa. Nobody has told me how she is. Is she in this hospital too?"

Mary and Rob looked at each other in stunned silence. This was the one question that they had dreaded having to answer and one which they felt David should respond to. Rob was the first one to gather his thoughts as he said

"Let's just wait for David darling. He wants you to go and see the babies first and foremost. We'll talk about everything else afterwards. You're still recovering. We don't want to overload that poor brain of yours now do we."

"Ok Dad. But I do need to know how she is. I'll ask the doctors when I get back."

"That's fine love. Just concentrate on seeing your babies for now, ok". Mary smiled at her husband. He had come to the rescue once again. What would she do without this wonderful man.

David and Alan arrived just as the Sister came into Sadie's room with the wheelchair. "Hi David. Hi Alan. I'm going to see Mia and Matthew. Isn't it wonderful?" she said as the Sister helped her to sit up, swing her legs round to the side of the bed and guide her into the wheelchair.

"Well you look much better sweetheart," said David.

"I've got a bit of a headache but otherwise, I'm fine," she answered. He bent down and kissed the top of her head.

"Right, let's go and see our babies. Wagons roll," he laughed as he took the wheelchair and began to push it towards the door.

"We'll come along later," said Mary. "Let's go and get a coffee," said Rob. "We'll give them some time on their own with their little family."

When they all sat down with their coffees, Rob told Alan that Sadie had asked them how Lisa was. "It was a question that we expected at some point but we weren't prepared for it this morning," said Rob. "I think I managed to avoid answering it for now but after she has seen the babies and she knows they are doing well, she's going to ask again. I just think that David should be the one to tell her. What do you think?" he asked Alan.

"Yes, I agree, but I think it would help David if we were all there too. He's going to need our support. Sadie is going to be devastated. She is also going to have to speak to the police. This Detective Sergeant rang David this morning before we left for the hospital. Apparently, Mark identified Lisa's body and he also told them that she was pregnant. She had only recently found out. We don't know whether Sadie knew or not but she certainly didn't tell David.

Did she say anything to you Mary?"

"No, not at all. I'm shocked. I didn't expect that," she said.

"Well Mark is denying any knowledge of why Lisa might have been in Sadie's car that night. He claims that he went out to get a bottle of wine and that when he got home, Lisa had gone. David doesn't believe a word of it and quite honestly neither do I. Whatever happened that night, then I'm sure he is behind it. Hopefully Sadie will be able to tell us."

By the time the three of them got back to the ward, Sadie and David were back. They were both smiling ear to ear and sitting together on the bed.

"Well", said Mary. "Tell me all about my lovely grandchildren then."

"They're beautiful Mum. Aren't they David? They are so tiny but absolutely perfect. I held them and the nurses said that in a couple of days I can have them beside me here and feed them myself."

"They are pretty amazing, I have to say," agreed David. "Why don't the three of you go and see them now. We'll be fine here, won't we darling?" "Don't go yet," said Sadie. I want to talk to you all. I can remember everything now. Everything that happened the night of the accident. I want to tell you before I have to speak to the police."

"Are you sure sweetheart?" said David. "There's no rush. We can do this in a couple of days when you are feeling a bit stronger."

"No, I don't want to wait. It's time that you all knew the truth."

Sadie told them how she had found out that Lisa was pregnant just a few days before the accident. And how shocked she was that Lisa could have been so irresponsible. It was clear though that Mark was never going to be happy about it. She tried to make her see how controlling and manipulative he was. How jealous he was of anyone else in her life. How he was convinced that she was having an affair with Alan. How he was never going to change. She begged her not to tell him about the pregnancy until she was sure that she was going to go ahead with it.

She told them that despite her protests, Lisa did tell him and the inevitable happened. She described how she had rung her on the night David was away on business. How she was practically incoherent and begging for help. "She told me that she was bleeding and that he had killed their baby. Her voice faded away at one point. I honestly thought she was dying. I had no choice but to go and help her. It was dark and raining heavily but I was just focused on getting to her as soon as possible.

When I got to the flat, the door was open. Mark was gone and I found Lisa sprawled on the bed covered in blood and almost unconscious. He had obviously punched her in the face too. Her eyes were puffy and bruised. She was in a dreadful state. I managed to get her into the car. Her injuries were so bad that I felt I had no alternative but to drive her to the hospital. By then it was clear, to me that she was suffering a miscarriage but I just concentrated on trying to keep her awake and telling her that everything was going to be ok.

Then, there was this almighty bang underneath the car and this is where everything is still a bit hazy. I remember lots of blue flashing lights and people talking to me, then waking up here. Nobody has mentioned Lisa. Is she ok? Is she here? Can I see her?"

At that point, one of the doctors entered the room. He smiled at everyone and turned to Sadie.

"Hi Sadie, Sister tells me that you have been to see your babies. That's really good news. I also understand that you are beginning to remember what happened on the night of the accident. How is your pain now?"

"I feel a bit bruised and battered doctor and I've still got a headache, but otherwise much better, thank you," she answered.

"Well I think you should rest now. You've had a busy morning. We're going to take you down for a scan tomorrow just to make sure that there are no further complications from your head injury. If all seems well, then I don't see any reason why you can't go home in a few days. Apart from your husband, have you got anyone who can stay with you for a couple of weeks? You're going to need some help to begin with."

Before Sadie could answer, Mary replied. "I'm going to stay with her doctor. My husband and I had already discussed it and agreed that it would be the best thing for Sadie. David has to go back to work at some point and, like you say, she is going to need a lot of help. I'll speak to my employers and arrange an extended leave of absence. They are aware of what's happened and have been extremely understanding."

"That sounds splendid," said the doctor. "How do you feel about that Sadie? I'm sure you will be glad to get home won't you?"

"Yes, of course, and thanks Mum. I was hoping that you would be able to stay and help me for a bit. I don't know where to start. I haven't got any nappies or formula. There's so much to organise."

"I'm afraid the babies will have to stay in hospital a little longer Sadie, "said the doctor. "We would like to see them putting on a bit of weight before we discharge them. Once they get close to 5lbs and they are continuing to feed well, then they can come home and join you. But it's early days. We still need to monitor them for a while longer. Now, I must insist that you get some rest. I'm sure your visitors will understand."

"Yes, I promise I will," answered Sadie. "But first, can you tell me how my friend Lisa is? Is she still in hospital? I really want to see her. Nobody has given me any news of her."

The doctor looked at David and then again at Sadie. He hesitated, moved forward and took one of her hands. "I'm so sorry my dear, but your friend is dead. She was killed instantly in the accident.

Sadie stared at him and snatched her hand away.

"No, she can't be dead. I'm alive so she must be. You've made a mistake. She was sitting right next to me in the car. She was in pain. She was having a miscarriage and she had been beaten by that bastard Mark but she was alive!"

She looked at the solemn faces around her and focused on Alan. "Tell me it's not true Alan. I know you would never lie to me."

He felt sick to his stomach. He had been dreading this moment with every fibre of his being.

"I'm so sorry my lovely girl but it is true. Lisa is gone." As Alan said those words, she let out a loud scream and started sobbing uncontrollably. David went to her side and took her in his arms.

"Let it out darling. Let it out. I know how much you loved her. This is the most devastating news. I understand. We're all in shock. Lisa was a wonderful girl. It's so unfair."

"She begged me not to take her to hospital. I should have listened to her and she would still be here today. It's all my fault," she cried.

Mary and Rob felt helpless as they looked at their daughter breaking her heart in front of them. This had to be the worst day of their lives. They had no words to say that would make her feel better. They looked at the doctor hoping for reassurance.

"I'll give Sadie something to calm her and help her sleep. Try not to worry. She needs time to process this news. It's been a terrible shock for her," he said smiling kindly. "Give her a few minutes alone with her husband and then I think it would be advisable to leave her to rest. You can telephone the ward later to see how she is."

As they walked towards the door, Sadie called out "I don't want my mum and dad to go. I want them to stay with me, please."

"Ok", said the doctor. But only for five minutes. I'll get Sister to come in shortly and give you something to help you sleep."

She was till sobbing. She couldn't take anything in. How had Lisa died ? Nobody had told her what had happened. There were so many questions in her head she was finding it difficult to focus. She looked up at her mum and dad and saw that they were fighting back the tears.

"What happened?" she asked. How did I crash the car? How could I have killed Lisa? I was trying to save her and now she's dead."

Rob answered. He could see how Mary was struggling to hold it together. "We don't know, sweetheart. The police have made a full report. They were just waiting for you to come round and then they were going to speak to you. We don't know anything more at this stage."

"What about Mark? I take it that he knows?" she asked.

"Let's not talk about Mark now, sweetheart, said David. "The police will deal with him. The doctor is right. You need to get some rest. I'm so very sorry that we have had to give you such bad news. But the one thing you mustn't do, is to blame yourself. You were a really good friend to Lisa. You did everything you could to help her. It was a tragic accident – no fault of yours. She would want you to concentrate on getting better so that you can take care of your babies."

Sadie heard his words but it made no difference. It was her fault. She had virtually forced Lisa to go to hospital. She was driving. Perhaps she wasn't concentrating hard enough on the road ahead? How could she move on from this. Her best friend was dead. She had her whole life in front of her and now it was gone - because of her. She knew that she could never forgive herself. Why Lisa, why not me?

Her thoughts returned to the image of Lisa lying on the bed, her body battered and bruised. "Why didn't I call an ambulance?" she cried out loud. "She would still be alive now. I was stupid to try and take her to hospital myself.'"

"You did the right thing at the time, darling," said Mary. "You wanted to get her there as quickly as possible. You were thinking of her and her baby. An ambulance might have taken a while to get there. You had an accident. Nobody could have predicted that. You must stop blaming yourself. It won't bring Lisa back and she wouldn't want you to think like that."

Sadie looked at her mum. She was always so wise but not even she could say anything that would make her feel better. The tears continued to course down her face. She didn't think she would ever stop. She had never before felt such heartache.

"I'm going to see if the Sister can come in and give you something to calm you down a little bit," said David. "I'm worried about you sweetheart. You're taking all the responsibility for what happened, and it's not your fault. The only one to blame is that arsehole who beat Lisa up. None of this would have happened otherwise. When you feel a bit calmer and able to speak to the police, we'll make sure that he gets put away for this."

David was really angry. He hated to see Sadie so upset She was such a sweet and thoughtful girl. She didn't deserve it. Now, more than ever, he was determined to make sure that the police heard the truth about Mark and what an evil monster he was.

Chapter 17

Sadie spent another three days in hospital. The repeat of the scan had shown no further concerns so the doctors agreed that she would fare better at home with her family to continue with her recovery. Mary and Rob spoke to David about their plans to take early retirement and move down south to be closer to Sadie. He agreed, that in the circumstances, it would be a good idea. He knew that his job was going to become more and more demanding and that he wouldn't be at home as much. He was concerned that Sadie would find it difficult looking after the twins, certainly in the early months and especially now, after the accident. She was obviously very fragile since the news of Lisa's death. To know that her parents were going to be closer would give him peace of mind.

Mary and Rob decided to head back to Scotland before Sadie was discharged from hospital and start the process of speaking to their respective schools regarding their intentions to retire. They also wanted to list their house for sale with one of the local estate agents. It was especially hard leaving Sadie. She was still very distressed and begged them not to go. Mary promised that she would be back in a few days and in time for her coming out of hospital.

"Dad is going to stay on in Scotland for a few weeks and then he will join us. We've decided to take early retirement and sell the house. We're going to look for a little bungalow close to you and David. We've been thinking about it for a while but we didn't definitely decide to go ahead until we had spoken to David. He thinks it's a good idea. It will mean that we can help you with the twins and support you if David is away on business. Are you pleased?" she asked.

Sadie started crying again as she thought about Lisa and how she would never get the chance to be a mum and have the loving family that she was so lucky to have.

"You would do that for me? Give up the jobs that you love and move away from everything you're familiar with?"

"We're close to retirement age anyway, sweetheart." Said Rob. "You and the twins are more important to us than anything else, so yes, we're happy to do it. We nearly lost you in that accident. It puts everything into perspective and makes you realise how precious life is. Please don't cry. I promise you we'll get through this awful time in our lives together. That's what Lisa would have wanted. She wouldn't want us to be sad. Let's try and remember her for the lovely person she was."

Mary and Rob hugged their daughter one last time before they left for Scotland. She was still crying when they went but she promised that she would ask one of the nurses for something to help her sleep. Whilst she was awake, thoughts of the accident continued to haunt her, at least, lost in sleep, it gave her respite from the heartache for a few hours at least. David had told her that the police were waiting to speak to her. He had managed to put them off for a couple of days but they were persistent. He told her not to be surprised if they turned up at any time. She knew that she needed to speak to them. She wanted justice for Lisa. Mark had to be punished. But - it would mean going over all the details of that dreadful night again. She wasn't sure how she would cope with that.

Sure enough, the police turned up at her bedside later that day.

Sadie had calmed down a bit after a couple of hours sleep and David was sitting with her when they walked in accompanied by the doctor.

"Sadie do you feel able to speak to the police? If you're not up to it, they can come back tomorrow," he said.

"No, it's ok, doctor. I'll speak to them now," she answered. The detective introduced himself "I'm Detective Sergeant Russell. I spoke to your husband the other day. We were wondering if you could tell us everything that you remember on the night of the accident," he said. "I apologise for you having to relive the details, Sadie. I understand that Miss Martin was a very close friend of yours."

"Yes, she was my best friend. She was being abused by her partner. I was trying to help her, and now she's dead." Sadie could feel the tears coming again. She tried to pull herself together. It was important that she told the police everything if she was to make sure Mark paid for what he had done. She took a deep breath and started at the beginning. She told the Detective of when she first became aware of what Mark was doing to Lisa and how she had begged her, time and time again, to leave him. She told him about the bruises she had seen on her body, the number of times that she wasn't able to go to work because of what he had done to her, and the night that he had raped her.

"He controlled her every move and if she stepped out of line, then he beat her. He was a monster but Lisa just couldn't see it. She told me that he was always sorry afterwards and made promises that he was going to change. She did leave him for a few days and came to stay with me. That was after the night he raped her. But he sweet talked her round again, making promises that he would see a counsellor and attend anger management classes. For a while, it looked like things were better between them. They even went off on holiday together and that was when he proposed. Lisa was blinded by his fake promises. God knows why, but she loved him and would always make excuses for him.

Then she told me that she was pregnant. I couldn't believe that she could be so irresponsible. I told her that Mark would never accept anyone else that she loved in her life - not even their own child. I begged her not to tell him about the pregnancy until she was absolutely sure that she was going ahead with it. I prayed that she would change her mind and realise that she had made a terrible mistake, but she told him about the baby on the night of the accident and that's when he nearly beat her to a pulp. He accused her of having an affair with a close friend of ours and questioned whether the baby was really his. He kicked her in the stomach and beat her around the face and body.

Lisa phoned me. She could barely speak. She told me that Mark had killed their baby. She was bleeding and in pain. Looking back, I should have called an ambulance, but I honestly thought that she was dying. I needed to get to her as soon as possible. When I arrived at their flat, Mark had gone. I found Lisa sprawled on the bed. She was in a terrible state and it soon became obvious to me that she was suffering a miscarriage. I managed to get her into the car and told her that I was going to drive her to the hospital. She didn't want to go but I told her that she needed to see a doctor if she wanted to save the pregnancy. That seemed to do the trick and she agreed to go. It was an awful night. The wind was howling and it was raining really heavily. I remember a loud bang underneath the car and then we were skidding and tumbling over and over. What happened after that is very hazy and then I woke up in hospital."

"Thank you Sadie. I understand how difficult that must have been for you. Would you be prepared to sign a statement? I think we need to pay her partner a visit. He will be arrested and charged with

Grevious Bodily Harm with intent to procure a miscarriage for the time being. There will be a post mortem. If Lisa's death can be proven to be caused in part by the injuries sustained in the attack on her, then we could be looking at a charge of Manslaughter," said the Detective.

"That's no more than he deserves," said David. "If Sadie hadn't gone to her that night, then she may have died anyway."

"Yes, you're quite right," said the Detective. "You did the right thing for your friend in the most difficult of circumstances, Sadie. I understand that you have recently had twins, so you were obviously heavily pregnant on that night. You were selfless. You put her needs before your own. The accident was something you could never have forseen."

"Do you know what actually happened, Detective?" David asked.

"It looks like the car hit a huge pot hole on the side of the road. Sadie wouldn't have seen it. It was dark and the heavy rain had filled the hole. It sent the car out of control. It rolled over several times before it landed on it's roof in a ditch. Lisa was found in the road. We think that she went through the windscreen."

"Oh no!, poor Lisa," cried Sadie. I had no idea. I could have helped her."

"She died instantly Sadie. There was nothing you could have done. Don't blame yourself. It was a tragic accident." said the Detective. Sadie started to cry softly as David put his arms around her.

"The Detective is right, sweetheart. You've got to stop blaming yourself. Mark will be punished for what he did to Lisa. He's the culprit, not you. You did everything you could to help her, just remember that." The policemen left thanking Sadie once again for her help and promising that they would keep both her and David in touch with further developments.

"I hope you don't mind sweetheart, said David, but you will be having some visitors this evening. They're coming to see you and the twins."

"That sounds nice. Is it your mum and dad?" she asked.

"Yes, they have been so worried about you. They wanted to come straightaway after the accident, but I asked them to wait until you were feeling better and the twins were getting stronger."

"It will be nice to see them," she answered. We'll take them to see Mia and Matthew. They must be desperate to meet their grandchildren."

"Yes they are," he said, "but they really want to see you too. You know that they think the world of you, don't you?

"I'm so lucky to have such a lovely family around me. I couldn't get through any of this without all of you," she said. She started to cry again. "Poor Lisa will never know what it's like to be a mum or to have people in her life who love her. I've got to live with the fact that, because of me, she lost that opportunity. No matter what anyone else says, I will never forgive myself for that."

David looked sadly at his wife. He knew that whatever happened now, she was never going to be the same again. There were no words to comfort or convince her that it wasn't her fault that Lisa was dead. She was lost and helpless, trapped in a dark place which offered no respite from the pain and self blame. He hoped with all his heart that their two precious babies would be the ones to release her from that dark place and give her hope for the future.

By the time Susan and Colin arrived, with David's help, Sadie had managed to have a shower and wash her hair. One of the nurses brought the twin's cots to be close to her bedside and she had fed and changed them. She looked at their little faces and their tiny feet and hands. She couldn't believe that through all the heartache of the last couple of days, she had managed to produce two perfect little human beings. It didn't seem real. She wondered how she was supposed to feel – what was expected of her. She loved them, of course, so why wasn't she deliriously happy. She knew that she should be, but all she could think about was that while she had made it possible for two new lives to be born, she had been responsible for the loss of another.

When they arrived at the hospital, Susan and Colin were relieved to find Sadie sitting up in bed and looking much better than they had expected. They had bought chocolates and perfume for her and lots of lovely gifts for the twins, including a couple of hand knitted matinee jackets - one in blue and one in pink that Susan had made herself. They looked at the sleeping faces of their grandchildren in wonder.

"Oh Sadie, they are beautiful," said Susan. I can't believe they're here already. I expected them to be a lot smaller than they are. They are absolutely perfect. I think that Matthew looks like David and Mia looks like you," she added.

"Do you think so?" said Sadie. I can't see either of them like us yet. They spend most of the time asleep so it's difficult to tell. Thank you both for coming. It's really good to see you and so kind of you to bring so many gifts. You really shouldn't have."

"We have been so worried about you Sadie," said Susan. We would have come sooner, but David wanted us to wait until you were feeling stronger. You must be devastated about Lisa. She was such a lovely girl. We are both so very sorry.'"

Up until that point, Sadie had managed to hold it all together but just the mention of Lisa's name prompted the tears to flow once again. "I'm so sorry, I didn't want to cry in front of you. This is supposed to be a special occasion for you to meet your grandchildren," she said.

Susan stepped forward and put her arms around her daughter in law. "Don't apologise, sweetheart. You have been through so much in such a short time. This should be a happy time for you and David too. You must be feeling stuck in the middle of all sorts of emotions right now. Colin and I understand and I want you to know that we are here to help you through this difficult time. I've spoken to your mum. She's told me about her and your dad's plans to move down here. Between the four of us, we will support you and help you with the twins for as long as you need us to."

"Thank you so much. I'm so lucky to have such a wonderful family. It means everything to know that you will be there for us. Doesn't it David?

"Yes it does," he answered. "Thank you both. We really appreciate it. Susan could see that Sadie was really struggling to talk through her tears so suggested to Colin that they go and have a coffee and leave her and the twins to rest.

"Do you want to join us David?" she asked. "We can give Sadie some time alone. Hopefully she will have a little sleep." "Yes, I think that's a good idea," he answered. "Will you be ok sweetheart?" Sadie nodded.

She was relieved to have the opportunity to have some time on her own. It had been lovely seeing her in-laws but it was proving to be increasingly difficult to put on a brave face in front of everyone.

"I'll be fine," she answered. The twins are due a feed soon and I expect they will need changing. I'll settle them down and then try and get some sleep. I don't know why but since the accident, I feel really tired all the time."

"Don't forget, you had a serious head injury Sadie," said Colin. "It's going to take time for you to be back to how you were. You mustn't expect too much of yourself too soon."

As they all left her room, Sadie gave a sigh of relief. She hated feeling this way but all she really wanted was to be alone with her thoughts. She was going home tomorrow. In some ways, she was looking forward to it. To be surrounded by everything that she was familiar with and to sleep in her own bed would be nice, but it also meant that the horror of what had happened since she left to go to Lisa's that night would become a reality.

Whilst she was in hospital, she could convince herself that she had just had a bad dream. Nothing seemed real. She looked at her sleeping babies. She was even finding it hard to believe that they were hers. She had no memory of their birth. They were suddenly just there.

Her thoughts were interrupted by Matthew who started wailing for his bottle. She pressed the buzzer beside her bed and one of the nurses entered her room. "I think the babies are waking up for their feed. Shall I feed them or have they got to go back to the ward?" she asked.

"You look tired Sadie. I'll take them back to the unit and we'll feed and change them. I suggest that you take this opportunity to have some rest now."

As two of the nurses wheeled the babies away to be fed and changed, Sadie closed her eyes and drifted off to sleep. She remembered nothing until the next morning when she was woken by one of the catering staff bringing her breakfast. "Hello sleepyhead," she said. Do you know that you slept through supper time last night? You must be starving." Sadie rubbed her eyes and looked at the woman's kind face.

"No, not really. But I'm sure I'll enjoy my breakfast. It will be my last meal here. I'm going home today."

"That's good news, love. You've had a tough time of it. I'm sure you'll recover much better in your own home," said the woman.

"My husband should be here soon, so I need to get up, have a shower and get dressed," she answered.

"I'll go and get one of the nurses to help you. Don't try and get up on your own. We don't want you falling over now do we?"

After she had breakfast and the nurse had helped her shower and get dressed, Sadie's consultant knocked at her door with one of his registrars in tow.

"Good morning Sadie. So you are going home today. How do you feel about that?" he said.

"I'm ready to go home doctor. Apart from feeling tired all the time, I'm much better. My mum is coming down from Scotland later today and she will be staying with me and looking after me until I feel stronger."

"That's good. You are going to need some help for a few more weeks yet. We need to get you better in readiness for your babies coming home. They are doing very well, by the way. You should be able to take them home within the next two weeks," said the Consultant smiling broadly. "Thank you so much doctor. You have all been really kind. Can I visit the twins while they are still here?" she asked.

"Yes, of course, but I don't suggest that you come in more than a couple of times. I understand that you live in Chelmsford. I wouldn't want you driving yet and even if someone else brings you in, the journey will be very tiring for you. The babies will be fine. We will take good care of them until the time comes for them to come home."

Sadie knew the doctor was right. She would miss her babies but it was only for a short time and then they would be home with her. She acknowledged that she still had a lot of healing to do, both physically and mentally. Everything that had happened still seemed surreal. She wasn't ready to look after her babies yet. She had to learn to look after herself again first.

When David arrived to collect her, he was pleased to see her sitting in the armchair next to her bed dressed in jeans and a crisp white blouse. She looked fragile but much better than he had expected.

"Oh you're ready sweetheart. I wasn't expecting that. I thought you would have to see the doctor and be discharged first."

"I've already seen him," she said. "He says I can go home now. He knows that mum is coming later to look after me, otherwise I'm sure that he wouldn't have let me go home yet."

"Are you sure you feel ready?" he asked. "Yes, I'll be fine, honestly. The babies have got to stay in for a while longer but the doctor said I can come and visit them. Can we go and see them before we leave?"

"Yes of course, I was going to suggest that," he said.

"Mum and dad have gone home now but they told me to tell you that they will come and see us soon. Mum is going to speak to your mum when she gets here and they'll work out some kind of rota once the babies come home. They really want to help you Sadie. They know that I've got to go back to work and they don't want you to be on your own."

"That's so kind of them", she said. "I'm going to need help, I know that. I'll be much better when I can get over this overwhelming tiredness. The doctor said that it's quite normal to feel like this after a head injury. He said it will pass and I'll gradually feel stronger, but it's obviously going to affect how I'm going to be able to look after the twins. Our parent's offer of help is going to be a lifesaver. We are so lucky to have them in our lives."

"Well young lady, let's go and see our babies and then get you home - ready?"

"Yes, I'm ready," she said as she stood up shakily from her chair and held her husband's arm. As she took one last look at the room that had been her safe place during the darkness and horror of the last two weeks, she sighed and thought of Lisa. My poor dear friend. I'm going to miss you so much. My life is never going to be the same again without you in it.

Chapter 18

Six weeks had passed since Sadie had left hospital. She was overwhelmed with the amount of cards, flowers and good wishes that she received from everyone she knew and even some that she didn't know, who had heard of what happened. Wendy, the Head Teacher, visited on behalf of everyone at the school and told her how everyone was thinking of her and sent their love. They had been shocked to hear of Lisa's death and were anxious to convey their sympathies to her.

By now, it was common knowledge what had happened on the night of the accident. Most people knew that Mark had been arrested and stories were rife about the abuse that Lisa had suffered at his hands. Nobody blamed Sadie, in fact she was considered a hero for rescuing her from his violent attack on that fateful night. She was grateful for the support that everyone was giving her, but nothing, as far as she was concerned, would exonerate her from the overwhelming feelings of grief and guilt that haunted her day and night.

The twins came home after three weeks. Sadie felt ready. She was regaining her strength day by day thanks to her Mum who was a constant support. However, their sudden presence was like a tornado hitting the house at full speed. Even with her mum's help, she felt that she didn't have enough hands to deal with the huge amount of washing, feeding, bringing up wind, and changing nappies that took place every day and half of the night. She soon learned that they both had a good set of lungs. If one wasn't bawling then the other one was. She cherished the moments when they were quiet and asleep, but it seemed like those times were few and far between. David was the only one who seemed to escape the onslaught. His work kept him away for most of the week and at weekends he always seemed preoccupied with paperwork.

Rob planned to drive down and join everyone after his final day working at the school. The house was up for sale and it looked like they might already have a buyer. It was time to start looking for a new home for him and Mary close to Sadie and David. He knew it wasn't ideal for them to continue living with them. They needed their own space although he knew it would be difficult for Mary to leave Sadie. She was loving the fact that she was so involved with the twins and equally Sadie would find it difficult not to have her mum on call 24 hours a day,. But he also recognised that they all had their own lives to live too.

Rob hired a van and loaded it up with everything they would need to start again in their new home. Mary said that she would rather sell the house with most of the furniture. It was big and bulky and quite old fashioned. He agreed that, if they were going to be looking for a small bungalow, nothing they had in their house would be suitable. Apart from a few sentimental pieces which they couldn't part with, everything else was left behind. As he left the house that had been their home for so long, he had a last look round remembering all the happy times that him and Mary had enjoyed there. He felt sad but he knew that they were doing the right thing for their daughter. She needed them more than anything now and for as long as fate allowed, they would be there for her.

Mary and Sadie were enjoying a cup of tea on one of the rare moments that the twins were fast asleep when there was a knock on the door. It was Detective Sergeant Russell who was accompanied by another female officer. As Sadie opened the door, one of the twins started crying.

"It's ok, Sadie, I'll see to the babies," said Mary. "Thanks Mum. Come in Detective. How can I help you?" she said.

She led them into the lounge and invited them to sit down.

"Can I get you some tea?" she asked.

"No it's fine Sadie, thank you but we've just had lunch," he answered. "We have come to tell you the results of Lisa's post mortem. It seems that her death was due to a catastrophic internal bleed. She did have some injuries from the accident - a broken leg, some cracked ribs and multiple cuts from the glass, but that wouldn't have caused her death. Apparently, the injuries to her stomach were so severe that the amount of blood loss led to organ failure. She was probably already unconscious by the time the accident occurred. We're going to charge her partner on two counts – Grievous Bodily Harm and Manslaughter. Her death was not your fault Sadie. I hope that now you can start to forgive yourself."

Sadie sat in stunned silence as she listened.

"So she did die because of him. Is that what you're telling me, Detective?"

"It looks like it could have been, but we'll need to prove it in a court of law. Will you be prepared to give evidence for the prosecution when it comes to trial?" he asked.

"Yes, of course. I just want justice for Lisa. I'll do whatever it takes to get that monster locked away."

At that point Mary came back into the room cradling Matthew in her arms. Sadie looked at her mum with tears in her eyes.

"He killed her Mum, he bloody killed her." The detective looked at

Mary who was trying to console Matthew.

"Hello Mrs Connel. I'm sorry to come here unannounced. I an see you're busy with the little ones. But I wanted to let Sadie know the outcome of the post mortem as soon as possible."

"Please don't apologise," said Mary. It wouldn't matter when you came, it's usually chaos here at any time of the day," she laughed. "As for Mark, it sounds like he is going to get what he deserves. It's good news but it won't bring Lisa back. I'm just relieved that my Sadie doesn't have to blame herself anymore."

Sadie looked at her Mum as the tears began to fall.

"How could he do that to her Mum? He kicked and punched her so hard that he killed her and the baby. She loved that man despite everything he did to her. I've going to make sure that he gets locked away for a very long time. It's the last thing I can do for Lisa now. I'm going to stand up in that court, look him in the eye and tell the jury everything."

"Please don't upset yourself again, darling," said Mary. We have to be patient. It may be quite a while before the trial and you've still got a lot of healing to do. Mark will get his punishment. I don't want you to waste any more of your time thinking about him or talking about him until you have to. He's not worth it."

The detective agreed with Mary, shook Sadie's hand and said that he would keep in touch and inform her as soon as he had any further news. As he left with his colleague apologising once again for the interruption, Mary handed Matthew to Sadie for his bottle. By now he was crying hysterically and had woken Mia who was now equally distressed. Sadie looked at her Mum who was smiling at her fondly.

"I think you've got enough on your plate for the time being don't you? Let's get these two little tikes fed and changed and then hopefully we'll get some peace. I want you to put all thoughts of getting revenge on Mark on the back burner for now. Your Dad will be here tomorrow and I'm sure he will agree with me, as will David. We all want what's best for you and these two little ones. It's the only thing that's important at the moment."

Rob arrived early the next morning. He had driven overnight to avoid the traffic and had already taken the few pieces of furniture and keepsakes from the house to a local storage company. He had also arranged for the hire company to collect the van later in the day. He was tired and hungry and ready for some sleep but he was also anxious to see Mary, Sadie and the twins.

Mary rushed to the door as he pulled up on the drive. She ran straight into his arms. She had missed him so much. "Oh Rob, it's so good to see you," she said. "I've really missed you. How was the journey love?"

"It was fine. There wasn't much on the road. It was a good idea to travel overnight. I've missed you two love. Are you alright? You look tired.

"Yes, I am. It's full on here. You might change your mind about staying and turn round and go back to Scotland after you've been here for a couple of hours," she said laughing.

Sadie came through to the hall carrying Mia.

"Dad! I'm so pleased to see you. Mum and I have been really looking forward to seeing you. Here you are, take your granddaughter. I'll just go and get Matthew. You've arrived just in time. They're about to be fed."

Sadie kissed him and handed over Mia as she turned tail into the lounge in response to Matthew's hungry cries. "See what I mean?" laughed Mary. "It's like a madhouse. We're constantly feeding and changing them. They are beautiful but they're hard work. It will be good to have another pair of hands."

Rob looked fondly at his wife. "It will get easier love. They are still very small and probably need feeding more than the average new born to start with."

"Yes, that's what the midwife told Sadie. She told her just to feed them whenever they need it which, at the moment, seems to be every couple of hours."

Rob followed Mary into the lounge. "Right love, you go and make a cup of tea and I'll feed this little one," he said.

"I'm going to make you some breakfast too. You must be starving," said Mary. "I certainly am," he said laughing. "Just like these too!"

David arrived home from work earlier than usual to welcome Rob's arrival. He decided it would be good to have another male for company and not have to listen to endless baby talk from Sadie and Mary. He loved the twins and he helped out with them as often as he could, but he had to admit that he looked forward to them growing out of the baby stage and the time when they could all finally have an uninterrupted night's rest.

After Mary had cooked a delicious dinner and they had finally got the twins to sleep, Sadie told Rob and David about the visit from Detective Russell and the findings from Lisa's post mortem. David could see how much the news had upset her but tried to make her see that, tragic though it was, she wasn't in any way to blame. He hoped that, at last, she could try to move on with her life and banish the feelings of guilt that still seemed to haunt her.

"Mark is likely to be charged with Manslaughter. He is responsible not only for Lisa's death but also that of her unborn child. I hope they throw the book at him," she said. Detective Russell asked me if I would be willing to testify in court and, of course, I agreed. I owe it to Lisa to expose him for the monster he is."

"I told Sadie that it might be a long while before it comes to court David", said Mary. "What do you think?"

"'I don't really know", he answered. "I'll have a word with Alan. Criminal Law is his bag. I'm sure he will be able to tell us more about how it works. The main thing is that he is being charged. With Sadie's evidence, I'm sure he will be sentenced. Let's hope that he will be in prison for a very long time."

Mary looked across at her husband who was now struggling to keep awake. "Oh I'm sorry love, you must be exhausted. You were up all last night. You go up to bed and I'll bring you a hot chocolate."

"You spoil me, thank you sweetheart. I must admit that I'm feeling pretty exhausted now, so if you'll all excuse me, I'll see you in the morning." "Thanks for everything, Dad - you too Mum. David and I wouldn't be able to manage without you both. I don't know how we can ever repay you," said Sadie.

"Don't be silly, darling. You don't have to thank us," she answered. You can pay us back when we are old and decrepid and we need you to push us around in our wheelchairs!" she said laughing.

For the next few weeks, Mary and Rob were out and about looking at bungalows in and around Chelmsford. The estate agent dealing with the sale of their house in Edinburgh had contacted them to say that a couple had put in an offer and they had accepted. It was a little lower than they would have liked but the couple were first time buyers so there was no chain involved. Rob figured it was worth taking a slight drop in the asking price if it meant the sale would go through quicker. It was becoming more and more difficult living with Sadie and David. They were both so busy and whilst it was lovely spending time with them and the twins, they were all beginning to get under one another's feet.

Sadie had changed in so many ways. She had always been so relaxed and laid back and always had a smile on her face. Since the accident and the birth of the twins, she seemed permanently stressed. As well as Mary always being on hand to help and support her, she had lots of offers of help from neighbours and colleagues from school. Some of them said they would babysit so that she could go out on her own for a couple of hours, but she always refused saying that she couldn't leave the babies.

Mary tried to encourage her to take some time out for herself and advised her that she would feel so much better if she had a break now and again, but there was no convincing her. As Mary had always feared, David wasn't much help at all. He was always working, even when he was at home. She wondered if a visit from Alan would cheer her up and suggested it to her one day.

"I haven't seen him in months Mum. He's like David, always working," she said.

"Well why don't you invite him down next weekend?" said Mary. Susan and Colin are visiting on Sunday aren't they? I could do a lovely roast dinner and, if it's a warm day, we can all go out for a walk with the twins in their new pram. It will be nice for all of us to be together again. What do you think?"

"Yes, that sounds nice Mum. I'll ask David to give him a call and see if he can come next Sunday."

"Good, that's settled then," said Mary. I'll get a piece of beef from that lovely butcher shop that I came across the other day. Dad and I were viewing a bungalow and it was just round the corner in a little parade of shops. We were going to tell you and David later but I might as well tell you now. We loved the bungalow and we're going to view it again tomorrow. It's been completely renovated and in immaculate condition. It's got three bedrooms, two bathrooms and an open plan lounge diner. The kitchen is brand new, Sadie. It's really lovely." "Oh Mum, I'm so happy for you. It sounds perfect for you and Dad. How far is it from us?" "It's in Chelmer Village, quite close to the flat that you used to live in", said Mary.

"Well that's a good omen. We loved living there. It's a really nice area. How exciting!" Mary was so pleased to see how Sadie's face had lit up at her news. She hadn't seen her like this for a very long time. More than anything, she hoped that this would be a turning point for her – that she would feel safe in the knowledge her family would always be close by.

Alan was pleased to accept Sadie and David's invitation to Sunday dinner. He was looking forward to seeing how much the twins had grown and, more importantly, David had asked him to speak to Sadie. He told him that she was very fragile mentally. Any mention of what happened to Lisa still reduced her to tears. The hate and the obsession she had for exacting revenge on Mark consumed her very being. She was convinced that by her testifying in court, Mark would be sent to prison and she would have kept her last promise to Lisa.

David wanted Alan to explain to her that the complexity of the law didn't always go the way one would expect it to. There was always the chance that Mark's solicitor would find a way of getting a Not Guilty verdict, especially if Sadie's evidence was questioned and found to be insufficient to warrant a charge of manslaughter.

He reassured David that he would take Sadie to one side when there was an opportunity for him to talk to her. He agreed with David that it wasn't a given that Mark would be found guilty of Manslaughter when it came to court. She needed to move on with her life. He thought how ironic it was that her need for revenge on Mark was controlling her in the same way that he had been controlling Lisa.

It was just after dinner on Sunday that Alan found the perfect opportunity to speak to Sadie. David was in the kitchen washing up and the two sets of parents had gone out for a walk with the twins.

"This is nice, isn't it?" he said, as Sadie poured them both a glass of wine. "It's been ages since you and I sat down quietly and had a chat."

"Yes, it is nice Alan. I've missed you. In fact I've missed life as I knew it," she said sadly. "Nothing feels the same anymore. I love my babies and I wouldn't be without them, but I feel empty inside. I miss Lisa so much and I just can't shake of the feelings of guilt that I have. I know it's not my fault that she died. Nothing I did caused her fatal injuries, but I should have got her away from that man. I wanted to believe her when she told me that he had changed, but deep down, I knew he never would. I should have insisted that she left him, went to the police and reported him. She could have got a restraining order against him and moved in with us until she found a place of her own. She had no family looking out for her. I was the only one who knew what was going on and I did nothing about it."

"Now, hold on, stop there!" said Alan. "You were a great friend to Lisa. You were always there for her when she needed you. Nobody ever knows what goes on behind closed doors. Lisa had choices. Her choice was to stay with Mark despite his abuse. I don't pretend to understand it. I don't think I ever will, but she was a grown woman and nothing you could say or do was going to change her mind about him. For some weird reason, she wanted him in her life. Perhaps it was her own insecurities. Perhaps in a strange way, his controlling behaviour made her feel safe. I really don't know Sadie. But what I do know is that if you continue to persecute yourself like this and fill your heart with hatred and thoughts of revenge, you will destroy your life. Lisa loved you. She would be heartbroken to know how much you are punishing yourself."

She thought how Alan had a way of making everything feel better. He was such a dear friend. She moved towards him and hugged him as the tears flowed once again.

"Thank you for your wise words Alan. Do you know how many

times I wished for you and Lisa to get together? You would have made the perfect couple. If only things could have been different."

"We would never have been more than friends Sadie. She was a beautiful girl inside and out, but her heart belonged to Mark and we need to accept that," he said.

By now David had finished the washing up and entered the room just as Sadie and Alan parted from their embrace. "Oh, sorry, am I interrupting," he said sarcastically.

"Don't be silly David. Alan was just trying to comfort me," she said as she wiped her eyes.

"Yes, that's his specialty," he said equally sarcastically.

At this point, she felt angry. David was being naïve and immature.

"What on earth do you mean by that? Grow up David. Alan is our friend. If I can't hug a dear friend without you coming out with silly remarks like that, then it's a poor show." Alan looked surprised and embarrassed and sat down to drink his wine.

"I'm sorry David. Sadie was upset. I was just trying to make her feel better. You would have done the same in my place."

"Let's just forget it," said David sulkily. "Have you spoken to her about what to expect from the trial when it comes to court?"

"I was just about to," he said.

He sat down opposite Sadie and began. "First of all there will be a plea hearing. Mark will be asked to submit his plea of guilty or not guilty. I suspect that he will plead not guilty which means that the case will have to be heard in the high court. It could be quite a long time before a date for trial is set Sadie. It certainly won't be any time soon. When the time comes, you will be called as a witness to testify for the prosecution. If Mark is found guilty of Manslaughter, the typical sentence varies between 2-10 years in prison. If the jury finds him not guilty of Manslaughter but guilty of Grevious Bodily

Harm which caused a miscarriage and Manulipative and Coercive Behaviour, he may still face a prison sentence but it's difficult to predict what that will be.

You just need to put all thoughts of a trial out of your mind until the time comes, Sadie. It's likely that Mark will be out on bail so I suggest that you keep well away from him and, please, don't attempt to make any contact with him as this will have a negative impact on your statement when you testify.

Have you any idea when Lisa's body will be released. I'm sure you will want to arrange her funeral won't you, or is her brother coming over from Australia to do that?'

"Nobody knows where he is," said Sadie. "And anyway, Lisa had no contact with him. She hadn't heard from him in years. I don't think she even liked him that much. As far as I know, there is no other family. David and I will organise the funeral. I'm sure that's what Lisa would want. I can't believe that we're even talking about her funeral, Alan. It seems no time since we were both out together shopping for dresses for my wedding."

She started crying again at the memory of Lisa standing in the bridal shop looking absolutely beautiful in her pale pink dress.

"I know, life is not fair", said Alan. She had her whole life in front of her. That's why we have to do everything we can to make sure that Mark pays for what he's done. But it mustn't be at the cost of your own mental well-being, Sadie. In the meantime you've got to try and move on with your life, hard though it may be." David had been very quiet up until then but as Alan said these words, he stepped forward and took Sadie in his arms.

"Alan is right sweetheart. I'm sorry I was a bit snappy earlier. It's just that I hate to see you like this. I feel helpless. I don't know how to make things better."

"It's ok. I know I haven't been easy to live with lately. I haven't been fair to you or the twins. I promise I will try and be more understanding of how you are feeling. I know it's not just me, you're hurting too." she said as she buried her face in the warmth of his chest. I'm so lucky to have you and our little family. I'm so sorry."

Alan stood up and looked out of the window as he heard voices outside. "Your parents are back with the twins. Do you want them to know what we have been talking about?" he asked.

"No I don't want to spoil the day. If they know how upset I've been, they'll only worry. I'll go through to the kitchen and make them a cup of tea. Mum made a lovely fruit cake so we'll all sit down and enjoy that. The twins are due a feed anyway so it will be all systems go when they get in," she said, trying desperately to smile through her tears.

Luckily, nobody seemed to notice the tense atmosphere in the room. Both grandmother's were completely fixated on taking the twins out of the pram and giving them their bottles which Sadie had prepared. Rob and Colin were deep in conversation about the new bungalow that Rob and Mary were planning to buy. Sadie was relieved that they were all distracted and that she wouldn't need to talk about her conversation with David and Alan.

She thought again about how David had reacted when Alan had been comforting her. He had apologised, but sometimes his attitude puzzled her. There were certain aspects of his personality that she didn't understand. She remembered her mum's concerns about David from the very beginning. Had she been right? Was there something that he was keeping from her? Was it something from his past?

She dismissed her negative thoughts as Matthew started to cry. He had finished his bottle but was obviously looking for more. Susan, who had been feeding him looked across at Mary who was winding Mia. She had finished her bottle too but seemed quite content.

"I think your son is still hungry Sadie", she said.

"Yes it's usually him who is looking for more. Mia is never as hungry as him. I'm going to have to make up another 2ozs for him from now on. Sorry Susan , I'll go and do it now if you don't mind trying to placate him in the meantime."

"He's a typical boy, they're always hungry," laughed Susan. David was the same when he was a baby. "He's much the same now," she said laughing.

"Did I hear my name mentioned?" said David as he walked in from the kitchen smiling. "I've been cutting the cake ready for our cuppa. It looks delicious."

"See what I mean?" said Susan. "Always hungry!"

The rest of the day passed pleasantly and the twins slept soundly all afternoon. The combination of a generous feed and a walk in the fresh air seemed to do the trick. Alan was the first to leave saying that he had work to do in preparation for court the next day. As Sadie and David went to the door to say goodbye, he spoke softly to Sadie.

"Now don't forget, you mustn't worry about the court case. As soon as you get a date, let me know and I'll go through your statement with you. But until then, just concentrate on that little family of yours. The twins are absolutely gorgeous. Just enjoy them and forget about Mark for now."

"Thanks, Alan I will. I'll also let you know when Lisa's funeral is. We're going to organise it as soon as we can, aren't we David."

"Yes, of course. It's the least we can do for her. She would want you there too Alan."

"Just let me know. I'll be there," he said.

Chapter 19

Over the next few weeks, Sadie was busy planning Lisa's funeral. Her and David had discussed it with both sets of parents and they had all agreed to share the cost. Attempts to trace Lisa's brother had come to nothing. She had no other close family and they had all loved her. It was the last thing that they could do for her. Sadie was determined to make it a day to remember – a memorable day. A celebration of her life. She didn't want people to be too sad and also to wear brightly coloured clothes, rather than the traditional black. She had already chosen a selection of Lisa's favourite pop songs to play at the ceremony. All her friends and colleagues at the school, plus a lot of the parents said they wanted to come as well as Wendy, the Head Teacher, and her husband.

As Alan had predicted, Mark had pleaded not guilty at his preliminary hearing so she had heard that he was out on bail until the date of the trial was set. Sadie hoped that his bail conditions would ensure that he wouldn't come to the funeral. She had promised everyone that she would put all thoughts of him out of her head. Her focus had to be on saying a final goodbye to her friend. But it was hard. She had never felt such hate for another person in her entire life. How dare he be walking around free, when Lisa was lying on a cold slab in the funeral director's Chapel of Rest. It dominated her thoughts day and night. Both Alan and David had told her that there would be no way that he would show up and that she mustn't even think about it. She just hoped and prayed that they were right.

Although they had obviously never discussed it, Sadie felt sure that Lisa would not want to be buried. She knew that would be the last thing she would want for herself ,so decided on a cremation ceremony. The chapel in the local crematorium was really nice and set in beautiful gardens. The funeral directors said that she could pay for a plot for Lisa's ashes and have a rose bush planted in memory of her. She thought how lovely that sounded. It would give her a special quiet place to visit her.

On the day of the funeral, the hearse arrived with Lisa and pulled up outside Sadie and David's house. They had asked for a wreath with white roses to be placed on her coffin. Lisa had loved roses. As Sadie looked out of the window at the hearse, the enormity of the day suddenly hit her. She thought to herself how this shouldn't be happening. How unfair it was. Lisa was a young woman who was expecting her first child. She had a long life to look forward to. The pent up emotion of planning this day over the last few weeks, suddenly overwhelmed her. As David heard her racking sobs from the kitchen he came running in and took her into his arms.

"Oh sweetheart. This is so difficult for you. I know how very sad you are but, remember we promised ourselves that there wouldn't be any tears, just smiles and happy memories ." He took a handkerchief from his pocket and wiped away her tears. "You've smudged your make up now". he said smiling.

"I'm sorry. I really didn't want to cry. I just can't believe that she is lying all alone in that coffin. It suddenly seems more real."

"I understand," he said. "It's tragic, it really is but , we promised her a great send off and that's what we're going to do . He took her hand and looked down at her tear stained face.

"Are you ready?" he said.

Colin had kindly offered to stay behind at the house and look after the babies so that Susan Mary and Rob could attend the service. As they all arrived at the crematorium , Sadie was amazed at the number of people who had shown up. Most people were wearing something bright as she had asked and were standing around in small groups chatting. Sadie recognised some of the parents not only from Lisa's current class but also from classes that she had taught in previous years. There must have been at least 40 people there. She thought how that reflected on the love everyone had for Lisa. It was very touching.

"Look, there's Alan," said Rob as he spotted him standing quietly on his own near the entrance to the chapel. "I'll go and tell him that we're all here."

"Thanks Rob", she said. She thought what a sad figure he looked standing alone. His head was bowed and his shoulders hunched as if he was fighting back the tears. He was always so strong for everyone else, it was easy to forget that he was hurting too. He looked up and smiled as Rob approached him.

"Hi Rob, good to see you. I wish it was in happier circumstances though."

"Yes, it's a sad day but Sadie wants us all to remain as upbeat as possible. She sees this occasion as a celebration of Lisa's life and doesn't want people to be too sad. Personally, I think she is going to struggle with that but I understand her sentiments. Come and join us Rob. We need to be standing by when the hearse arrives."

Sadie and David were talking to Wendy and her husband and Peter and his wife as Alan came over.

"Hi Alan, do you remember Mr and Mrs Marshall from the school and Peter and his wife Kate? You met them on our wedding day," said Sadie. "

“Yes of course”, he said. It’s good to see you all again. I just wish that it was in happier circumstances.”

“We still can’t believe it,” said Wendy. Lisa was a lovely girl and a great teacher. Everyone loved her.”

“That’s plain to see,” he answered. “There are so many people here. Such a shame that she didn’t seem to have any close family,” he added. “Yes, she lost both of her parents in a motorbike accident and her only brother lives in Australia, I believe. I understand that they were estranged but I have no idea why,” she said.

At that moment, the hearse appeared through the gates of the crematorium. There was an instant hush as the little groups of people who had been chatting, parted ways and stood either side of the gravel drive as it made it’s way slowly to the entrance of the chapel. David, Alan, Rob and Peter had agreed to be the pall bearers so as the Funeral Director manouevered the coffin from the hearse he directed each of the four men to carefully lift and shoulder it’s weight before they walked slowly and steadily towards the front of the chapel.

Sadie had chosen “Angels” by Robbie Williams as the music for the funeral procession. Lisa had loved that song. Sadie often heard her singing it softly to herself when she thought nobody was listening. She thought it was the perfect choice and embodied everything that was special about her.

The service was everything Sadie had hoped it would be. It was led by a Celebrant who had been recommended by the Funeral Director. She knew that Lisa wasn’t religious and this lady had been really helpful in guiding Sadie through the day and helping her with the eulogy. Thanks to her advice and guidance, she managed to deliver it without breaking down.

Wendy had also prepared a lovely tribute and spoke about Lisa’s time at the school and all the wonderful things that she had achieved over the years. There were lots of tears but also moments of humour. Wendy recalled the time that one of the children had put a very realistic toy spider on her chair before class started. It was a well known fact that Lisa was terrified of spiders. Wendy said that her screams could be heard right down the corridor. Lisa being Lisa, saw the funny side of it and insisted that the child shouldn't be chastised. In fact, it turned out that her screams frightened him so much that it proved to be punishment enough!

For Sadie, the hardest part of the service was the committal. The final goodbye. She had been dreading it. As the coffin slowly disappeared through the curtain, 'You raise me up' by Josh Groban was playing. It was the perfect song. It afforded everyone that special moment where they could concentrate on their own private thoughts. The sound of weeping could be heard throughout the chapel. Sadie couldn't contain her emotions any longer. She leant on David's shoulder as the tears rolled down her face. She took a last look as the curtain closed and whispered

"Goodbye my darling Lisa. I will never forget you. I love you. Sleep tight."

Everyone had been invited back to Sadie and David's house for a drink and something to eat after the service but it was only Wendy and her husband and Peter and his wife who accepted. Sadie was quietly relieved. She really wasn't in the right frame of mind for entertaining. It had been an emotional and tiring day and she felt sure that the twins would be playing up. Poor Colin had been left alone with them long enough. She thought that he was probably more exhausted than she was! As she approached the front door, she could hear one of the babies crying. "Please come in everyone. David will get you all a drink. Forgive me if I disappear for a while, but it sounds like either my son or daughter is playing their poor

Grandad up. I had better go and rescue him," she said laughing.

She made her way upstairs to the twin's bedroom and found Colin pacing back and forth with Matthew trying to pacify him. Mia was fast asleep in her cot.

"I might have known it would be Matthew," she said. "He is always hungry."

"I didn't know what to do Sadie. He was only fed an hour ago. I wasn't sure whether I should give him another bottle or not. Little Mia settled nicely after her feed. She has been asleep since."

"I'm so sorry Colin. I should have warned you about Matthew. It's not unusual for him to have a few more extra feeds than Mia. I think he must have hollow legs," she said laughing.

"How did it go Sadie? I've been thinking of you all. Did Lisa have the send off that you wanted for her?" he asked.

"Yes, it was perfect Colin. But to be honest, I still feel like I am dreaming. It's hard to explain but I don't think I have even started to accept what happened. Maybe I never will," she said sadly.

"It will take time love. You will probably never accept it, but you will learn to live with it and you've got these two to help you do that."
"Thank you Colin, and thank you for looking after them for me. Now I think you deserve a drink. Everyone is downstairs. Go down and join them, have a drink and something to eat. I'll see to these two and I'll join you all shortly."

Once Sadie had settled the babies, she made her way downstairs to find everyone tucking into the buffet that Susan and her mum had prepared. Alan was sitting with the Marshalls and both set of parents were chatting with Peter and his wife. David was in the kitchen opening a couple more bottles of wine.

"Have they gone to sleep now?" he asked.

"Yes at last. Mia always settles quicker than Matthew. He always seems so hungry. I've already increased the amount of milk he is on. Perhaps I'm doing something wrong. I think I'll have a word with the midwife and see what she thinks."

"I wouldn't worry too much," said David. He is just making up for being born early. They are both doing really well. You're a great Mum, sweetheart. You mustn't doubt yourself."

"I feel like I'm running on autopilot David. I was just saying to your dad that nothing seems real. It's like it's happening to someone else. To be perfectly honest, I don't feel like I'm coping as I should be. I know I said I wouldn't think about Mark or talk about him before the trial but It's on my mind all the time. I'm scared that he is going to get away with it. I'm the only one that Lisa confided in. It's going to be my word against his."

"All you can do is tell the truth," he answered. "If there is any justice, then he will be found guilty but we have to wait and see. There's nothing to be gained by worrying about it now. Let's go through to the lounge and make sure everyone is ok. It's been a tough day for all of us but especially for you. You must be exhausted."

"Yes, I am. But I'm the lucky one aren't I? Lisa is the one who has paid the ultimate price, "she said sadly.

She was quietly relieved when people started to make their way home. David was right. She was exhausted and looking at the clock she realised that it would soon be time for the next feed. After the Marshalls and Peter and his wife had said their goodbyes, Colin and Susan were the next ones to leave promising that they would visit again soon.

"Thank you both so much for coming today and helping me make it such a special day for Lisa," she said. "Colin, I hope it didn't put you off babysitting again."

"Not at all. I enjoyed it and happy to do it again anytime. I just want to say that Susan and I are really proud of you. You've been through so much and yet you never stop thinking about everyone else. You are an amazing young lady."

As Colin said those words, Sadie could feel the emotion rising in her chest. She was really struggling to hold it together now. Mary stepped forward and put her arms around her daughter. She had been keeping a close eye on her all afternoon. She had noticed the pain in her face, her trembling hands and the wavering forced smile. Her heart went out to her. If only she could stop her hurting. She thought how she longed to have her happy beautiful daughter back again, and tried to ignore the gnawing fear inside her that it might never happen.

Alan took his cue from Susan and Colin. As he hugged everyone and said his goodbyes, he took a last look at Sadie as she went back upstairs with her mum to feed the babies. He had also noticed how much she had been struggling throughout the day and yet had managed to do everything she could to make it the perfect farewell for Lisa. Colin was right. She was a remarkable young woman. He hoped that they would set the date for Mark's trial soon. The sooner this tragic episode in her life was behind her, the sooner she could start to heal.

Sadie woke up the next morning to the sound of her mum hoovering downstairs. She looked at the bedside clock. It was 11am. She remembered feeding the babies at 2am and wondered why they hadn't woken her since. She jumped out of bed and into the nursery. They were both sound asleep. Surely they hadn't slept through. She called out to her Dad who she could hear whistling in the spare bedroom.

"Dad, did you and mum feed the twins this morning?" "Oh morning love." said Rob as he wandered out the room pulling his jumper on. "Yes we fed them at 8 this morning. We didn't want to wake you. You deserved a bit of a lie in after yesterday. Did you hear David leaving for work?"

"No, I didn't hear a thing and the babies are still asleep. That means they only had one feed during the night. That's got to be a first. Thanks Dad. I must admit I was really tired. I feel much better this morning. I can hear mum hoovering downstairs. I thought you were both going to see the bungalow again this morning?"

"Yes we are but not until 12," said Rob. "Why don't you get the twins ready and come with us?"

"No, you don't need us tagging along Dad and I'll probably be feeding them around that time anyway. I'll come and see it once you've decided to go ahead and you put an offer in. I'll keep my fingers crossed for you."

Mary and Rob were back by 1pm. They had loved the bungalow even more seeing it a second time and had already contacted the estate agent and submitted an offer. Sadie had just finished bathing and feeding the twins and was sitting having a coffee as they walked in with huge smiles on their faces.

"Well," she said. "How did it go?"

"We absolutely love it," said Mary. "We've put an offer in and we're waiting to hear back from the agent."

"It's going to be perfect for us," added Rob. "The couple that are in it at the moment are moving up to Yorkshire and they're going to rent somewhere to start with so they are ready to move asap. "If our offer is accepted, we could be in within 6-8 weeks." "Wow, that's quick," said Sadie. "I'm going to miss having you here but I'm really happy for you. It sounds perfect." Mary looked at the sadness in her daughter's eyes. "I'm not going to abandon you sweetheart," she said. I'll pop in every day and you can come and visit us too. We'll make it work."

Sadie smiled fondly at her mum. She knew it was important for them to have their own home just as it was for her and David, but she was going to miss her constant support and help with the twins.

David did try but he was completely wrapped up in his work. That was never going to change. She had to accept that it was a trade off for their comfortable lifestyle.

She thought about the new car that he had just bought and his plans for extending the house. Before the accident, this would have excited her but her priorities and dreams had changed. She would swap it all to have the simplicity and joy of her old life back. She couldn't see herself going back to the school and teaching again. It could never be the same, because she wasn't the same.

As the familiar feeling of tension and sadness started to overcome her, Rob's mobile phone rang. As he ended the call, he looked excitedly at his wife and daughter,

"It's ours!" he cried. "They've accepted our offer!'

Chapter 20

Four months had passed. It was the morning of the first day of Mark's trial. Sadie had been summoned to appear at Chelmsford Crown Court at 2pm by the prosecution lawyer. She had been waiting for this day for so long. It was going to be her chance to expose Mark for the bully he was. She felt a mixture of emotions as she carefully selected one of her smart suits and a white blouse to wear from her wardrobe.

The twins were in the bedroom with her sitting in their little swing seats. She smiled at them as they gurgled and pulled faces at one another. They were her absolute world. Over the last month or so, they had become two quite distinct little characters. Mia was the quiet delicate one, very chilled and contented. Matthew was quite the opposite. He was loud and demanding and completely focused on when his next meal was going to be. He was already 3lbs heavier than Mia, and had a distinctive giggle that melted Sadie's heart. The twins had been her saviour since the accident. They gave purpose and meaning to her life. She couldn't imagine being without them now.

Mary and Rob moved into their dream bungalow six weeks after their offer was accepted. It was just ten minutes in the car from Sadie and David. Just as they had promised, they popped in every day to help her in any way they could. Rob spent a lot of time working in the garden while Mary just enjoyed having time with the twins to give Sadie a break. She looked forward to their visits so much. Although

David was making the effort to be at home more often, she could never completely rely on him. He loved the twins but he found it difficult keeping them entertained and it would usually end up with either her or Mary coming to the rescue. She concluded that he was one of those people who felt awkward around babies. She hoped that, as they got older, he would find it easier.

David had managed to take a day off work so that he could drive Sadie to the court and be there for moral support. Mary and Rob were staying behind to look after Mia and Matthew. As she climbed into the car next to him, she felt the nerves creeping in.

"I hope I can do this David. I'm really nervous now."

"Remember what Alan told you. Just start from the beginning and tell the truth. You'll be fine sweetheart. I'm rooting for you."

She remembered Alan's advice after he had read her statement. He warned her that when it came to her being cross examined by Mark's barrister she would need to be prepared for him to find holes in her story. His job was to defend Mark and therefore he would do whatever it took to discredit her testimony. He told her not to let him bully her, to stick to the truth and stay calm and focused.

His words were uppermost in her mind as her and David entered the courthouse. A court official showed them where to sit and told Sadie that she would be called into the witness box when they were ready for her. David said he would make his way into the court and take his seat in the public gallery.

"Good luck, sweetheart, I'll see you in there," he said as he made his way towards the entrance to the courtroom.

Sadie was summoned and called in after ten minutes. As she walked in, she felt an icy chill going down her spine as she spotted Mark sitting in the dock. Her eyes met his. His cold dark stare bore into her very being. It was quite clear just what he thought of her, but she didn't care. He was dressed in a smart navy blue suit with a white shirt and striped tie. He looked the epitomy of the upstanding citizen.

She knew different - he was a wolf in sheep's clothing and she needed the jury to see that too. She was directed towards the witness box and asked to swear on the bible that she would tell the truth. The barrister for the prosecution asked her to confirm her name and address.

"Thank you for coming today Mrs Burns. I understand that you and your husband were good friends of the defendant and his late partner."

"Lisa was my best friend. The defendant was her boyfriend but I wouldn't describe him as a friend, quite the opposite." she said.

"Can you please explain what you mean by that, Mrs. Burns?" he asked. "He abused Lisa for years. I hated him for what he did to her."

At this point the Defence Barrister stood up and protested. The judge agreed and said that the jury should disregard the remark.

Sadie looked across at David who was smiling at her but gently shaking his head. She realised too late that she had overstepped the mark. She would need to be more careful how she responded to questions from now on and just concentrate on presenting the facts.

"Mrs Burns, could you kindly tell me about your relationship with the deceased, Lisa Martin, and what happened to her during the time you were friends?" said the lawyer.

Sadie started her story from the very beginning. She glanced across at the faces of the jury as the facts of Lisa's abuse unfolded. Mark remained still and tight lipped. His face gave nothing away. She noticed that some of the women in the jury were looking upset as she described Lisa's injuries on the night of the accident and her subsequent miscarriage. She had promised herself that she wouldn't cry but as she recounted the final moments of the accident and the day that she found out that Lisa had died, the tears began to flow.

One of the court officials handed her a tissue as the barrister spoke "I can see how difficult that was for you Mrs Burns. Thank you." With that, he turned to face the judge and said "No further questions my Lord." As he sat down, Mark's barrister stood up and faced her. She looked at his stern expression. She felt the tension building inside her.

"Good afternoon Mrs Burns. Can I ask you if you were the only person that Miss Martin confided in with regard to the alleged abuse?"

"Yes, as far as I know," said Sadie. Mrs Marshall, the Head Teacher at the school where Lisa and I worked was aware that she was in a difficult relationship. Lisa had many absences due to various little unexplained 'accidents' throughout the two years she worked for her. She never spoke to her about it but she did fear that she was being abused."

"So, let's make it clear for the members of the jury. Mrs Marshall just assumed that she was in an abusive relationship. There was never any real proof of that. Is that correct?" said the barrister.

"Yes, I suppose so as far as Mrs Marshall was concerned. But I saw Lisa's injuries. I confronted her and that's when she told me that they were due to 'rough sex' with her partner. I didn't believe her. The marks on her body were not consistent with her explanation. Eventually she told me the truth and from that moment on, she confided in me."

Sadie was asked to explain again in detail what happened on the night of the accident. The barrister questioned why Sadie hadn't rung an ambulance if Lisa's injuries were as bad as she said they were. He inferred that she was exaggerating. He said that Lisa could have naturally suffered a miscarriage. He tore apart everything she said. She looked at David. His eyes were pleading with her to carry on and be strong. She remembered Alan's advice and suddenly felt the anger welling up inside her that this man in front of her was making out she was a liar. She looked up at Mark's smug face. There was no way that she was going to back down. Not now.

She took a deep breath and looked into the face of the barrister.

"I have told you the absolute truth. Lisa was in denial and that's why she kept so much of what happened to herself. For some unknown reason, she loved Mark and she hoped that he would change. There were short periods of time when he didn't hurt her, for instance when he asked her to marry him. But it never lasted. He was insanely jealous of anyone else who loved and cared for her. He even tried to put a stop to our friendship but that didn't work. Every time he felt threatened in terms of her showing affection to anyone else, he would beat her. She came to stay with me for a few days after he had raped her, but as usual, he sweet talked her round and she went back to him. On the night of the accident, She told him she was pregnant. He accused her of sleeping with a friend of ours and then kicked and punched her in the stomach. That's how she lost her baby."

"Can I just interrupt you there, Mrs Burns?" said the barrister. "You were not a witness to this attack I presume?"

"No, I wasn't but Lisa phoned me begging for help just after it happened."

"So you only have her word for it?" he asked.

"There was no other explanation. Mark did it to her. I had no reason to disbelieve her," she said, feeling frustrated.

He then asked her to recall her memories of the accident and commented on the seriousness of it. He suggested that Lisa died because of the injuries sustained in the crash. At this point the prosecution stood up and said that there would be further evidence to substantiate her claim from the pathologist who conducted Lisa's post mortem. He would testify that she died from internal bleeding due to trauma to the stomach. Sadie was relieved to hear that there would be further evidence to back up her testimony.

"I have one last question, Mrs Burns," said Mark's barrister

"At any time during the period of Miss Martin's alleged abuse, did she ever approach the authorities to report it, or speak of it to anyone else apart from yourself?"

"No, I told you. She was in denial. She couldn't see how he was controlling her. Deep down, I think she was scared of him."

"Once again, Mrs Burns, this is supposition on your part. Did she ever tell you that she felt she was in danger?"

Sadie thought of the night that Lisa had phoned her after Mark had raped her.

"Not at first, no. But the night he raped her, she was terrified. That's why she came to stay with me and my husband."

"Don't you think it's strange that she didn't report this incident to the police?", he asked.

"I wanted her to. I begged her to leave him, but he convinced her that he was sorry, that he wouldn't do it again, that he was going to change."

"Is it correct then that Miss Martin returned to the defendant and reassured you that she was happy in her relationship and that she was going to get married?"

"Yes, that's true. But I didn't believe that he would change and I was right," said Sadie.

"I think you have made quite a lot of assumptions, Mrs Burns. I suggest that your dislike for the defendant clouded your perception of their relationship and that you have exaggerated the facts." Before Sadie could answer, he said, "Thank you Mrs Burns. I have no further questions. You can stand down."

The judge smiled at her and said, "you are free to leave or you can take your place in the public gallery."

Sadie stepped away from the witness box and looked at David. He gestured for her to come and sit in the empty seat beside him. As she sat down, he took her hand and whispered in her ear. "Well done, darling. He gave you quite a grilling, but you remained calm and positive."

"I just hope it's enough", she answered.

The trial continued for a further two days. David wasn't able to get any more time off work, so the next day Rob accompanied Sadie to the court whilst Mary stayed at home with the twins. Today was the day that Mark was going to give his evidence. She wondered how he was going to react when he was cross examined by the prosecution. Knowing how devious he was, she felt sure that he would deny everything. She hoped that the jury would see through him.

The testimony from the pathologist the day before hadn't gone as well as she had hoped. The defence's claim that Lisa's injuries could be consistent with being thrown from the car and her body hitting the hard road service, was recognised and acknowledged by the pathologist. He also concluded that a blow or kick to the stomach would have caused similar injuries. He confirmed that the official cause of death was due to a catastrophic internal bleed. He also conceded that, in the circumstances presented, it was difficult to provide a definitive answer as to the exact cause.

Sadie was amazed at how the defence seemed to twist everything. She hoped that today, after Mark's evidence, the prosecution would get to the truth. She couldn't even consider the possibility of him getting away with it.

Her heart was pounding and her stomach in knots as Mark took to the stand. He glanced at her briefly before he took the oath. Rob whispered in her ear.

"Whatever he says, don't say anything sweetheart. We know he is going to deny everything but don't let it get to you. Let the prosecution do their job. They know what they're doing."

Sadie smiled at her dad. She knew he was right. It was going to be difficult listening to his lies but she didn't want to say or do anything that would jeopordise the case against him.

The defence began by asking him to describe his relationship with Lisa.

"She was my partner. I loved her. We were planning on getting married."

"How do you feel about the claims from the prosecution that you abused Miss Martin throughout your time together?"

"It's nonsense," Mark answered. "Lisa was very vulnerable. She had lost her parents in a tragic accident. She was estranged from her brother. She relied on me to give her stability and to protect her. She didn't make friends easily. I took care of her and provided her with a safe environment."

"How do you explain the bruises that Mrs Burns saw on Lisa's body?"

"We had a very physical sex life. We both suffered bruises from time to time after rough sex. They were superficial. It was never anything serious."

"Would you agree with the claim that Miss Martin accused you of raping her?" Mark looked suitably shocked as he answered.

"I didn't rape Lisa. Our sex was always consensual. We had an argument that night. She was just lashing out. She was prone to temper tantrums if she didn't get her own way. She was just trying to punish me. Lisa was very difficult to live with. Her moods were erratic. I never knew where I stood with her."

"Yet you asked her to marry you?", said the barrister

"Yes, despite our problems, I loved her. I hoped that once we were married she would feel more secure in our relationship."

The barrister then went on to ask Mark to describe what happened on the night of the accident. He claimed that Lisa had started an argument because he hadn't taken the news of her pregnancy well. He said that they had both agreed not to have children until after they were married. Unknown to him, Lisa had stopped taking the pill. He admitted that he was angry and accused her of sleeping with someone else. He said that Lisa lashed out, hitting and kicking him. He admitted that he fought back but that he hadn't kicked or punched her in the stomach. He said that he managed to calm her down and said that he would go out and get a bottle of wine. It was then that she started screaming, telling him that she was bleeding and that he had made her lose their baby. He told the barrister, "I just couldn't take anymore of it. I left the flat and jumped in the car. I hoped that by the time I got home, she would be calmer and that we could talk."

"What happened when you got back to the flat?" asked the barrister.

"The front door was open and Lisa had gone. I didn't know what to think. She didn't have the car and I couldn't imagine her walking anywhere. That's when I wondered if Sadie had anything to do with it."

"Is it true that you didn't approve of her relationship with Mrs Burns?"

"No, I didn't. She obviously didn't like me and would do everything she could to come between me and Lisa. She was a negative influence on her. I think she was jealous of our relationship."

Sadie was amazed at how she managed not to shout out at this point. She expected Mark to lie but this - it was beyond anything that she could have imagined. He had turned the whole story on it's head. He was the abuser, the one who had controlled Lisa and yet here he was trying to blame her. Rob could feel the tension in her body as he squeezed her hand and looked into her eyes pleading for her not to say anything. She knew she had to remain calm. The prosecution was going to cross examine him next. She had to have faith in the process, hard though it was.

The Defence Barrister smiled at Mark as he said, "Thank you Mr Taylor. No further questions."

"Good afternoon, Mr Taylor" said the Prosecution Barrister. "Would you say that your relationship with Miss Martin was a volatile one?"

"Yes, at times it was. She had a short fuse. It didn't take much for her to lose her temper," said Mark.

"I find that very confusing, Mr Taylor. Mrs Burns description of her friend is the polar opposite. She claims that she was sweet, very gentle and kind. She was loved by everyone who knew her. The head teacher at the school where she taught young children, spoke very highly of her. She was highly respected and a great teacher.

"She was good at hiding her true personality," said Mark looking a little flustered.

"I believe her and Mrs Burns were extremely close friends for a few years. I find it difficult to believe that she wouldn't have noticed if Miss Martin had the tendencies that you describe during this time. I put it to you, Mr Taylor that it is you who has a temper. It is you who was controlling and abusive throughout the relationship and now that Miss Martin is not here to defend herself you are laying the blame at her door. Mrs Burns has absolutely no reason to lie. She has nothing to gain from it, but you do Mr Taylor."

"Objection!" shouted the Defence Barrister. The judge responded immediately.

"Overruled. Please continue."

The defence continued to attack Mark's testimony. Sadie noticed how his earlier bravado started to crumble. She looked across at the jury. They were listening intently. She wondered what they were thinking. Rob smiled at his daughter. He was so proud of her. Having to sit through Mark's evidence and listen to his lies couldn't have been easy for her.

After the prosecution had completed their cross examination, Sadie listened as both barristers presented their closing speeches As they concluded their respective arguments, the judge looked across at the members of the jury for his summing up of the case. He pointed out that with regard to the two charges of Manslaughter and Grevious Bodily Harm, each one should be considered separately and based only on the evidence presented in court. He reminded them that they should only vote for a Guilty verdict if the evidence given satisfied beyond a reasonable doubt. If there was reasonable doubt, they must aquit. Whatever the decision, there must be a unanimous verdict on each of the charges. If they failed to reach a verdict by the end of the day, they would be sent home under oath and would continue with their deliberations the next morning.

One of the courtroom officials then asked for everyone to stand as the judge left the court. Sadie turned to Rob and said "Well, I guess we just have to wait now. Let's go home Dad. I think we can both do with a stiff drink." "Sounds a good idea, sweetheart. There's nothing else we can do now. It's in the hands of the jury."

When they arrived home, Mary was waiting anxiously for news. She had bathed and fed the twins and they were sleeping soundly in the nursery.

"Oh you poor things, you look exhausted," she said as Sadie and Rob walked in and sank down on the sofa. "How did it go?"

"Well, as we expected, Mark lied all the way through his testimony. He made out that Lisa was the crazy one, that she caused the arguments between them. He even blamed me for being jealous of their relationship! Can you believe it?!" said Sadie.

"He denied ever having hit her and that she was the one who caused the fight between them on the night of the accident. I knew that he would deny everything but I never imagined how far he would go."

"Sadie was amazing, love," said Rob. She handled the defence barrister like a pro. He did his best to discredit her, but she stood firm and didn't let him get to her. I looked across at the jury while she was being cross examined. They believed her, I'm sure of it."

"Well, let's not speculate Dad. Mark put on quite a performance. Let's hope that we don't have to wait too long before we know one way or another."

By the time David had returned from work, there was still no news from the court. He could see that Sadie was feeling anxious. He told her not to worry and that It was just an indication that the jury were divided and hadn't yet been able to reach a unanimous decision.

"It will probably be some time tomorrow before we know, so I think you should get an early night, sweetheart. I've taken the day off, so I will come with you when they deliver their verdict. Alan is going to try and get some time off too. He wants to be there to support you."

"Oh, that's great darling. To have both of you there with me, means a lot and you're right, I should get some sleep. Tomorrow is a big day."

The next morning after what turned out to be a restless night, Sadie went through to the nursery to get the twins ready for the day ahead. Their other grandparents were coming to look after them so that Mary and Rob could attend court. She knew that they would have a fun day. They loved the attention from their grandparents. They were always thoroughly spoiled and Sadie had peace of mind that they would be well looked after. She had arranged for her and

David to meet Mary, Rob and Alan at the court. As she looked at her reflection in the mirror, she could see the tension in her face and felt the familiar feeling of panic starting to overwhelm her. David appeared behind her and took her into his arms.

"Don't worry sweetheart. It's all going to be fine. Mark will get what's coming to him today and then all of this will be over. We can start living our lives again." Sadie looked into his face.

"It will never be over, David. Whatever happens to Mark, Lisa is never coming back is she? I have to live with the fact that she died when I was supposed to be protecting her. Nothing is going to change that."

Alan had already taken his place in the public gallery by the time they arrived at the courthouse. Sadie hugged him quickly before she sat down next to him and David.

"Thank you for coming," she whispered "It means a lot." She looked up at the dock and saw that Mark was sitting alongside a prison officer. She could feel him watching her but made a point of avoiding eye contact. Rob and Mary entered the courtroom and, as they spotted her, she gestured for them to come and sit beside her.

She turned to her dad, "You're just in time. We've been told that the jury has reached a verdict and that they will be called back in a few minutes."

"'That's good, love," he said. "Not much longer and we'll know." As the judge entered there was an eerie hush of anticipation in the courtroom. The members of the jury followed on, their faces showing no emotion. Sadie felt her heart beating in her chest. This was it. The moment she had been waiting for.

The Clerk of the Court then asked the spokesman for the jury to stand. "Has the jury reached a unanimous verdict on each of the two charges?" he asked. Sadie looked at the kind face of the man standing in front of them and willed him to deliver the answers she was looking for. He spoke without hesitation.

"Yes we have." "Regarding the charge of Manslaughter, do you find the defendant Guilty or Not Guilty?" Sadie held her breath as she waited for his answer.

"Not Guilty!"

There were gasps and mutterings throughout the public gallery. Sadie suddenly felt icy cold throughout her core. She was numb with shock and disbelief. This couldn't be happening. She knew that Mark had caused Lisa's death. Why couldn't the jury see that? She looked up at the dock. Mark's smug expression sickened her. Just as she was trying to process what had just happened, the Clerk of the Court asked, "regarding the second charge of Grevious Bodily Harm, do you find the defendant Guilty or Not Guilty?"

"Guilty!"

David leant across and took Sadie's hand. He was smiling from ear to ear.

"It's great news, isn't it sweetheart?" She felt confused and lost for words as she nodded to her husband. She looked at her Mum and Dad and Alan. They were smiling and hugging each other as if they had won the lottery. Why didn't she feel the same? Her thoughts were broken by the sound of Mark shouting at the jury.

He was furious and pointing towards Sadie, he said "It's all lies. She made the whole thing up. I didn't hurt Lisa. I loved her."

Order!" shouted the judge. "Sit down and be quiet or you will be removed from court."

Mark sat down but continued to glare at Sadie. "Just ignore him," said David. All he is doing is making things worse for himself. Let's just hope that the judge gives him the maximum sentence for what he's done, then we'll never have to see his miserable face again."

Sadie smiled but inwardly she was trying to make sense of it all. She was struggling to believe that he hadn't been found Guilty of Manslaughter. He had got away with it as far as she was concerned.

He wasn't going to get the punishment he deserved. The judge asked for silence as he began his explanation and reasons for the sentence he was about to impose. He concluded his summing up by looking directly at Mark.

"The deceased was a young woman who had her whole life in front of her. The historical abuse that she suffered at your hands was cruel and manipulative. You had many opportunities to tell the truth but you have continued to lie and attempt to shift the blame on to others including your deceased partner. There has been no indication of remorse on your part and you have said nothing which makes me believe that you recognise the seriousness of your actions. Therefore, you leave me with no alternative but to impose a custodial sentence. You will be sent to prison for four years.

Please take the prisoner down."

There were more gasps from the public gallery. Sadie put her head in her hands trying to overcome the feeling that she was going to faint.

Four years! Was that all Lisa's life was worth?! He would probably be out after two years. How was that justice?

Mary looked across at her daughter with concern.

"Sadie are you ok love?" You are very pale. Let's go outside and get some fresh air. In fact, I think we could all do with some air." She looked at Rob who nodded in agreement.

"Yeah come on lads. Let's get Sadie out of here. We'll get a coffee somewhere." The five of them followed the members of the public who were already leaving. Some of them were muttering and questioning the sentencing.

Sadie heard one woman who turned to her husband and said, "He got away lightly didn't he? I reckon he was responsible for the death of that young girl. Four years in prison isn't much of a punishment, is it?" Her husband looked at her crossly. "Be careful what you are saying. People will hear you. It's not our place to question the jury's decision."

Sadie felt a strange sense of comfort. She wasn't the only one then.

As she left the courtroom holding on to her Mum's arm, she wondered how she was going to move on from this day. She'd made a final promise to Lisa that she would make sure Mark would pay for everything he had done to her.

She had let her down. That man was still going to have the opportunity for a long life despite having robbed Lisa of hers. In that moment she was lost. She feared that she would never be the same person again.

Chapter 21

2018

It was the day of the twin's fifth birthday party. Sadie had spent all morning blowing up balloons and hanging birthday banners while her mum was busy in the kitchen making sausage rolls and little triangle sandwiches for the ten children who were coming later. David and her Dad had prepared some games for after tea. Sadie could hear them giggling and laughing out loud in the lounge. It sounded like they were probably going to enjoy the party more than the kids! She looked around at her handiwork. The new extension leant itself well to parties. It was a big spacious room with a long dining table to seat twelve people. The long floor to ceiling windows looked out on a huge garden with immaculate lawn, fruit trees and pretty flower beds. Right at the back in the corner, David had built a tree house for the twins and there was another area with swings and a slide.

The house was all but finished now. It was everything they had hoped for and more. David worked very hard and would still be away from home for a few days during the week, but he was earning a lot of money and they enjoyed a comfortable lifestyle. Sadie was so proud of how hard he worked. He was also a great dad. Now that the twins had outgrown the baby stage, he spent all of his spare time with them. He would take them swimming and play with them for hours in the garden. She would smile to herself as she watched them running around and having fun . She felt blessed to have such a lovely family. She thought of Lisa every day. It still hurt. She knew it always would, But she had learned to live with it. She had to, for the sake of David and the kids.

Shortly after the court case Sadie had a breakdown. She was diagnosed with anxiety and depression. Looking back on that dark time in her life, she could understand why It had happened, but she hadn't seen It coming. There were months of deep sadness and negative thoughts. She was unable to care for the twins. She lost interest in everything and everyone around her.

David was lost. There was nothing he could do to make her feel better. As had often happened in the past, her Mum and Dad were her saviours. They moved back in. Mary took care of the twins and Rob became her strong shoulder to lean on. Gradually with the help of medication and counselling sessions, she started to recover.

Once she felt better and the twins were less of a handful, Sadie's thoughts returned to the possibility of going back to teaching. Wendy Marshall from the school had asked her if she would like to return to her old job on a part time basis. She had considered It for a while but decided that it would be too upsetting. She would always associate Lisa with the school. It could never be the same for her again. Wendy understood but urged her to think about taking a job at another school. She had always considered Sadie a wonderful teacher. It would be a waste of her talents if she didn't think about it seriously.

Sadie and David had already discussed the path that they would take when it came to the twin's education. David was insistent that, now they could afford it, they should go to private school. Sadie wasn't so sure. The state run schools in the area all had a good reputation.

However, after some investigation, they found a private pre-prep school for 3-7 year olds which had an impressive reputation. The school was 10 miles away in Brentwood. It was further than Sadie would have liked but, after visiting the school with the twins one day, both her and David were convinced that it would be perfect for them. The headmaster was a very well spoken man in his early sixties who had previously been a university lecturer. He explained that to start with the twins would do a few hours each morning until they were four years old, after which they would attend full time. Sadie couldn't imagine her babies going to school at just three years old but the programme of activities and the pre school education was first class. They wanted to give them the best start in life that they possibly could and this school seemed to have it all.

Over the next two years, the twins became two very different little individuals although they both shared the same thirst for learning. They continually asked questions and were never happier than when someone was reading them a story. Both Sadie and David's parents were the best grandparents they could ever have wished for. The twins simply adored them. Mary and Rob were Nanny and Grandad and Colin and Susan were Grandma and Papa. They were all frequent visitors so Sadie was never short of help.

Life was beginning to settle into some sort of normality although she still had days where a black mist seemed to envelop her and she felt herself slipping back into depression. The doctor had prescribed anti-depressants when she had her breakdown. She hoped that she would never have to rely on them again but when she recognised that her dark days were becoming more frequent, she made an appointment to see him again. He explained that these relapses were not uncommon and suggested that she start to take the medication again. Reluctantly, she had to accept that she may have to live with the possibility of always feeling this way.

She rarely discussed these feelings with David. He tried to be patient with her when she was feeling down but she sensed that he didn't really understand. As far as he was concerned, the past was gone. He struggled with the fact that Sadie even thought about Lisa now. She decided it was better to keep her thoughts to herself.

She hardly ever saw Alan now. Like David, he always seemed to be really busy. She spoke to him on the phone occasionally but she felt that he was keeping his distance. David hardly ever spoke of him either. She wondered if they had fallen out again. Theirs was a relationship that she could never understand. It would always puzzle her but she had responsibilities now. She wasn't going to waste her time trying to work out what might be going on between them. They were grown men. They could sort it out themselves.

Just after their third birthdays, the twins started at their new school. As David and Sadie had hoped, they settled in really well, very quickly. As lively three year olds it provided them with the stimulation they needed. They were both popular and soon made lots of little friends. Their teacher loved their cheeky characters. She told Sadie that they were a joy to have in her class.

She was so proud of them. They were her pride and joy. There was never a day that passed without her feeling grateful for having them in her life. It was times like that when she would think of Lisa and her unborn child. She would never know what it was like to be a mother. She had been robbed of the most special relationship you could ever have with your child. It was cruel and so unfair. She despaired of ever being able to come to terms with it. Try as she might, she would always blame herself for letting her down.

She had already lost her belief and trust in the judicial system but never more so when she heard that Mark had been released after serving just three years of his four year sentence. When she thought back to that last day in court, the feelings of intense anger and disbelief came rushing back. He was free to carry on with his life. It made her sick to her stomach. She hoped that Karma would prevail and that he would get his punishment in some way and at some point in the future. She clung to that hope with every fibre of her being. Thankfully, she heard that he had moved away from the area and was living in Yorkshire. She took some comfort in that. At least she would never have to see him again.

Now it was the day of the twins first proper birthday party. Sadie and David had decided that five was a good age to start on what would probably be an annual event for the next five or six years at least. They had pulled out all the stops to make It a day to remember. The twins didn't know but, as a surprise, they had arranged for a magician who was a children's party entertainer to come after tea and all the children who were coming had party bags to take home with little gifts and sweets inside. There was a lady who lived in their road who had a little business making celebration cakes. She had made the most unbelievable chocolate birthday cake and decorated It with Toy Story figures. Sadie knew the twins would love It.

After she had finished decorating the party room, Sadie walked into the kitchen to see how her mum was getting on.

"How's It going Mum? Can I help? I could do with a break from blowing up balloons. I'm out of puff!" she said laughing.

"Well done love," she answered. "You can finish those sausage rolls. They just need a lick of egg wash and then they can go in the oven. Where are the twins? I haven't seen them for the last few hours".

"I told them to play upstairs in their rooms," said Sadie. "I didn't want them seeing all the surprises that we're planning for them. Dad and David are in the lounge sorting out some games. All I can hear is them laughing, so god knows what they're up to. They're worse than the kids."

"That's typical", said Mary. "Men never grow up. They're boys all their lives. Now, while I've got you on your own, tell me how you are love. I can tell that you are still suffering deep down. You try not to show it, but I'm your mum and I know when you're not yourself."

Sadie looked at her mum's concerned face. She didn't want her worrying. "Oh, I'm ok Mum. I have the odd day where I feel a bit down, but on the whole, I'm doing ok. The kids help. There is always something going on with them that takes my mind off things."

Mary wasn't convinced. She had noticed that Sadie had lost weight and didn't seem to be as concerned about her appearance as she used to be.

"Have you thought about going back to teaching? You could get something part time. There are so many schools in the area, I'm sure one of them would have a position available."

"I have thought about it" said Sadie. "But I'm not ready yet. Maybe when the twins are a bit older. David isn't keen for me to go back to work. He says we don't need the money so he can't see the point."

"It's not about the money, Sadie. It will give you purpose and some independence. It will be good for you. You're a great teacher. Surely David understands that, doesn't he?" Mary asked. "I think there is a lot about me that David doesn't understand," she said sadly.

"What do you mean love? Isn't he being supportive? You've been through so much in the last few years. If your husband doesn't understand, then who on earth will." Mary felt herself getting angry. Even after all these years, she still didn't fully trust David.

"He tries Mum but I know that I can be difficult to live with sometimes. He is a good husband really, and he adores the kids. I'm lucky to have such a wonderful life. I just need to stop feeling sorry for myself and move on from the past."

"That's easier said than done Sadie. You are a caring and sensitive girl. It's little wonder that you have the odd bad day. David should be mindful of that."

At that point, Sadie heard the patter of footsteps running down the stairs.

"Sshhh. Let's not talk about this anymore, Mum. I can hear the kids coming." Mia was first. "Matthew keeps cheating Mummy. We're playing snakes and ladders but he goes up the snakes instead of down, that's cheating isn't it?" she cried.

"Well perhaps Matthew doesn't understand that. I'll explain it to him. I'm sure he doesn't mean to cheat," she said.

Matthew put his head round the door. "I heard that Mia. You're telling lies. Honestly Mummy I'm not cheating. She just doesn't like it because I keep winning." Sadie sensed the tension and could see an argument brewing between her children. Most of the time they got on really well, but now and again there would be a bust up which would usually lead to them being sent to their bedrooms. But not today. Today was a special day and she didn't want to spoil it for them or their little friends who would be arriving soon.

"I tell you what, you two. Let's put the game away for now. Your friends will be here soon and you need to get changed. We'll talk about the game tomorrow and perhaps we can all play. How does that sound?" said Sadie.

Matthew was the first one to relent. Mia was still sulking. "Ok Mummy, I'll put the game away." "Good boy. I have laid your clothes on your bed so why don't you go and put them on and get ready for your party.

You too, Mia."

She watched as they both left the room and made their way upstairs. Mary smiled at her daughter. She really was a good mum. The twins were a credit to her. As for David, she wasn't convinced that he was as good a husband as Sadie had portrayed. She had stopped voicing her thoughts regarding her son-in-law to Rob. He was completely smitten by him. He could see no wrong in him and couldn't understand why Mary didn't feel the same. Mary hated arguing with her husband, so for her, It was easier to keep her thoughts to herself. She wondered if that was what Sadie was doing too.

The twin's birthday party was a monumental success. The children loved the magician and Rob and David's party games had them all rolling around the floor laughing. They ate all the food which was perfect but that left Mary worrying that she hadn't prepared enough! Mia and Matthew's faces were an absolute picture when Sadie brought out their birthday cake adorned with five pink and five blue candles.

As all their friends and family sang Happy Birthday, Sadie felt herself getting emotional. Her babies were growing up. She wondered what the future would hold for them. Would they have their own dreams, just as she had? Would they be happy? Looking at their little faces on this special day, she knew that, no matter what, they would always be her priority. The love she felt for them was pure and unconditional . Her children had saved her. They had given her purpose and guided her through the worst time in her life. In that moment, she vowed to always be there to protect and care for them, just as her parents had done for her.

Chapter 22

2023

Sadie woke up feeling strangely apprehensive. David was due back from Paris today. She hoped that he would be pleased to see her. The day before he left, he had been very quiet and preoccupied. She assumed it was because he was stressed about his meeting. She realised how serious he was about his work and how important the meeting in Paris was.

She could hear Mia and Matty chatting excitedly in Matty's bedroom about dad coming home. They missed him so much when he was away. She slipped on her dressing gown and went into the room. "Good morning you two. Fancy you being up before me," she said laughing.

"What time will dad be home Mum?" said Mia.

"He should be here when you get back from school but he may have to go into the office when he gets back. So we'll have to see." She looked at their eager little faces as they suddenly looked sad.

"He is always at work. It's not fair," said Matty sulkily.

"I know darling but he works hard for us all so that we can have a nice life. Anyway, don't worry. I'll persuade him to stay at home today. He will be tired after his trip. Right, let's get you dressed ready for school and then come down for your breakfast. The sooner you get to school, then the sooner you will see dad' she said, hoping desperately that David would be at home later. She hated to see them so disappointed. It made her more determined to dissuade him from going in to work today. He needed to spend some time with his children – and her!

When she got home after dropping the children at school, she ran herself a hot bubble bath. David had texted her to say that his flight was on time and that he should be home around lunchtime. That would give her enough time to enjoy her bath and get herself ready. She wanted to make a special effort today. She had her new make up, her new clothes. It was time to show her husband that she was still attractive, that she could still excite him as she always used to. She vowed to pull herself together. To be the old Sadie again. The Sadie that he had fallen in love with all those years ago.

She was just making the finishing touches to lunch when she heard his key in the door.

"I'm home!" he cried. Sadie ran into the hall and straight into his arms. He held her away from him looking her up and down.

"Wow! You look lovely Sadie." "Well, thank you kind sir," she answered. "I've missed you. I wanted to make a special effort for your homecoming."

"Well you've certainly done that. You look stunning," he said kissing her on the cheek. She wondered why he hadn't kissed her passionately on the lips. That was what she was hoping for. But perhaps he was just tired.

They both sat down to lunch. Sadie was eager to hear about his trip and whether his meeting had gone as well as he had expected.

"It was really successful," he said. "It went even better than I expected. There should be a big bonus coming my way after this."

"Well done, darling," she said. "I'm very proud of you."

"How are the twins?" he asked.

"Dying to see you. I had a job getting them to go to school today. You will be here when they get home won't you?" "Yes, of course," he said. I'm not going in to the office today or tomorrow, so I will be able to spend quite a bit of time with them."

Sadie's face lit up at the prospect of him being at home for a couple of days. It was the news she had hoped to hear.

She looked across at his handsome face. The butterflies in her tummy started stirring. She always felt them when she wanted him to make love to her.

"We've got a few hours before I have to pick up the kids. Do you fancy coming upstairs and then I can show you how much I've missed you?" she said, her voice shaking with desire. There was a moment's silence before he replied. "I would love to darling, but I've got a report to do which I need to email to the office this afternoon. If I'm going to be off tomorrow, I need to get it done before the kids come home."

She felt like she had been slapped in the face. She felt humiliated. Her husband had just refused to make love to her in favour of writing a report! What on earth was she supposed to think? She got up from the table without saying a word and went upstairs to the bedroom. She tore off her new dress, wiped her face free from make up, tied her blonde curls into a ponytail and put on a pair of jogging bottoms and one of her baggy sweatshirts. It was too early to go and pick up the kids but she just wanted to get out of the house. She decided to jump in the car and go and visit her Mum. She knew that her Dad was at his bowling club this afternoon. It would give her the opportunity to talk to her Mum alone.

She called out to David who was already busy typing on his laptop in the lounge.

"I'll see you later. I'm going to see mum and then I'll go and pick up the kids." Before he had a chance to answer, she was out of the front door and in the car. As she pulled out of the drive, she saw him looking at her through the venetian blinds. She didn't care what he thought.

'Let him stew', she mumbled to herself. She was so angry at that moment. He had really hurt her. She had made so much effort and he had thrown it all back in her face.

She pulled up on her mum and dad's driveway without even remembering how she got there. Her head was all over the place. She didn't want to upset or worry her mum but she needed to speak to someone. Mary opened the door, surprised to see her daughter standing there.

"Oh this is a surprise. I didn't expect to see you today, love. I thought David was coming home."

"He is home, Mum. I just wanted to talk to you. Is Dad here?"

"He's bowling this afternoon. He won't be home until about five o'clock. Are you ok? You look upset." she asked.

"I just needed to talk to you Mum", said Sadie holding back the tears.

"Sit down love. I'll go and put the kettle on and you can tell me what's happened."

As Mary clattered around in the kitchen, she sat on the sofa, trying to pull herself together. She really didn't want to worry her mum unduly. She was beginning to wonder if she had overreacted.

"Right," said Mary as she walked in with a tray with two mugs and a plate of biscuits, "Tell me what's wrong. You're as white as a sheet."

"I'm not ill Mum. There's nothing wrong with me. It's just David. He really upset me this afternoon."" What's he done?" said Mary. She had already guessed that it might be something to do with him.

Sadie had never discussed her sex life with her Mum. It was

something that made her feel a bit uncomfortable. She was unsure how to explain her conversation with David. She decided to tell it as it was. There was no point skirting around the issue.

Mary listened intently as Sadie described not only what had happened this afternoon, but her fears in general regarding the future of their marriage.

"Do you think that he is seeing someone else sweetheart? "she asked. She hated seeing her daughter so upset. It was hard to resist the temptation to tell her 'I told you so.' She took no pleasure in knowing that she had been right to doubt David's integrity.

Sadie hesitated before she answered. Yes, she did suspect that he was seeing someone else, but the idea of admitting it to herself, never mind her Mum, was something she just wasn't ready to do yet.

"I'm sure that he isn't Mum. In fact, I think it's probably me. I'm so sensitive since the accident, Lisa's death and the trial. I think it has all affected me much more than I realised. I'll speak to David this evening when the kids are in bed. I'm sure we can work it out. We love each other."

"It's nothing to do with you Sadie. If David was really true to you then he would understand that you are feeling vulnerable. He is the one who should be making more effort. I know he is a good provider. He works hard. Goodness me, your Dad never stops telling me what a great guy he is in looking after you and the twins. But he should spend more time with you. He is always working and goodness knows what he gets up to on all these business trips!" Mary was feeling angry now. She knew her words were upsetting Sadie. But they needed to be said.

"Honestly Mum. It will be ok. David and I will sort it out. I don't want you to worry, and please don't tell Dad. Promise me?"

"Ok, I promise. But you mustn't keep anything else from me. I'm here to support you love. I'm not judging you. You have to do what you think is right for you and the twins."

Sadie finished her tea and hugged her mum. "Thanks Mum but I had better go and collect the kids now. They will be waiting to see their dad. They were so excited this morning. They have really missed him. I'll give you a ring tomorrow. Please don't worry."

Mary watched her daughter drive off. Her heart was breaking for her. Something told her that this situation with David wasn't going to end well. It was going to be difficult for her not to tell Rob when he came home. He could always tell when she was upset. But she had promised Sadie. She wasn't going to break that promise.

Just as Sadie had guessed, Mia and Matty were waiting by the school gates as she arrived. 'You're out early," she said.

"We asked our teachers if we could leave five minutes earlier", said Mia. "We told them that we hadn't seen dad for weeks and weeks and if we didn't get home early today then we would miss him," said Matty.

"Well that was a bit of a white lie wasn't it?" said Sadie stifling a laugh. "Never mind, I forgive you and I've got some good news. Dad will be at home all day tomorrow, so you will see him in the morning and again when you get back from school."

"Brill!" said Matty. "Can we stay at home tomorrow Mum? Do we have to go to school?" added Mia.

"Yes, young lady, you have got to go to school. Dad wouldn't want you missing out on your education. You'll see him tonight as well. So you'll have plenty of time to spend with him."

The twins knew better than question either of their parents about going to school. From the age of three they had been taught the importance of having a good education. They accepted it and thrived on it. But they did miss seeing their dad. All their friends seemed to have fathers who spent a lot of time at home. It made them sad sometimes but it also made the times they did spend with him very special.

Sadie was well aware of how difficult David's absences were for Mia and Matty. As she drove home, listening to their excited chatter in the back seat, it made her determined to try and build bridges with him. They had to be strong and protect their relationship for the sake of their little family.

"Dad, Dad, where are you?" called Matty excitedly as he ran into the house, Mia hot on his heels.

David appeared from the lounge, a huge smile on his face and his arms outstretched as both children flew into his arms.

"Hello my darlings. Oh I've missed you so much," he said "We've missed you too Dad," said Mia. David glanced towards Sadie who was standing awkwardly in the hallway.

"Did mum tell you that I'm going to be home for a couple of days. We are going to have so much fun, aren't we Mum?" he said smiling at Sadie.

"Yes, of course. I'm going to get some dinner ready, then we can all play a game. Anyone fancy Monopoly?" she said.

As Sadie was preparing dinner in the kitchen she could hear the twins pleading with David to play with them in the garden.

"Come on Dad", said Matty. We can have a kick about while Mum is getting the dinner ready."

"Oh no not football, answered Mia. I hate football."

"I'll tell you what we'll do so that it's fair for both of you. How about hide n seek?" said David.

"Yeah" cried the twins in unison. "I'll hide first", said Mia.

She smiled to herself. It was lovely to hear the children so happy. She decided that until they went to bed, she would put her own feelings to one side and enjoy the evening just being together. She decided she would speak to David tomorrow once they had gone to school.

It was nearly 10pm before the children finally relented and went off to bed. Had Sadie not put her foot down, she felt sure that they would have stayed up all night! It had been a lovely evening, full of fun and lots of laughs. Sadie cherished these times. It was all she had ever wanted. Her perfect family. More than anything, she hoped that her and David would be able to resolve their differences.

He had tried to speak to her about what had happened in the afternoon a couple of times during the evening, but she was determined not to talk about it until the twins were safely out of the way. They were bright kids. She knew that they would pick up on the tension. She had to protect them.

As they climbed into bed later, David tried to bring it up again.

"Sadie, I'm so sorry about this afternoon. The last thing I wanted to do was to hurt you."

"Well, you did hurt me David. But I'm not talking about it now. I'm tired and the twins might hear us. We'll sit down and have a proper chat tomorrow once I have taken them to school."

"They asked me if I would take them to school. Is that ok?" he asked.

'Yes, of course it is. You don't need my permission to take your own children to school. We'll talk when you get back. I'm going to sleep now. Night Night."

Sadie closed her eyes hoping that she would be able to sleep but her head felt scrambled. The man she loved was lying beside her but it felt like there was this invisible wall between them. They should have been in each other's arms making love like they always used to. Whatever was wrong, she feared that it might never be the same between them again.

Memories of Lisa invaded her thoughts. Now, more than ever, she missed her friendship. She would have supported and advised her what to do. She turned her back on her husband so that he couldn't see the tears that were starting to fall as she felt an overwhelming sadness washing over her.

The next morning she was woken by the sound of the twins chattering downstairs with David. He had obviously decided not to wake her and was getting them some breakfast. She had lain awake trying to ignore his snoring until the early hours of the morning so she was grateful for the extra hour or so of sleep.

She went to the bathroom, put her dressing gown on and made her way downstairs.

"Hi Mum" said Mia, as Sadie walked into the kitchen. "Dad got us up this morning and he has made breakfast. Matty is already on his second boiled egg and toast!" Sadie looked at Matty smiling.

"Well done Matty. You love your dippy eggs don't you?" "They're yummy," he answered with his mouth full. Dad makes lovely dippy eggs."

"Sit down darling," David said to her. "I'll do some for you."

"No, it's ok. I'll just have cereal and a slice of toast. You need to get going soon, otherwise the kids will be late for school." He looked at the kitchen clock.

"Mum's right kids. I didn't realise how late it was. Finish up your breakfast and go and get your shoes and blazers on. Say goodbye to Mum too. Remember, I'm taking you to school today."

As usual, this precipitated the last minute flurry of rushing around, packing school bags, cleaning teeth, brushing hair before, finally, they left.

Sadie looked around at the mess in the kitchen. Suddenly it seemed so quiet and still as if the life had gone out of the house. She shivered inwardly at the thought of what today's conversation with

David would bring. She cleared the kitchen and went upstairs for a shower. She was just finishing getting dressed when she heard the car on the drive. David was home.

He was sitting in the lounge looking very serious when she came downstairs.

"Would you like a coffee," she asked.

"That will be great. Do you want me to make it?"

"No, it's ok. It won't take a minute, "she said "Were the kids ok?"

"Yes they skipped into school happy as Larry. We are so lucky to have found that school for them. They're both doing really well aren't they? They've made some lovely friends too. It's great to see them so settled and happy."

Sadie paused before she answered, "They are happy now, yes. I just hope that whatever is wrong between us can be sorted out David. They would be devastated if we were to split up."

She waited for the denial from him that there was anything wrong but it didn't come. He looked downwards before he finally lifted his head and looked into her eyes. She saw that he was blinking back the tears. His lips were quivering. His hands were shaking.

"What on earth is wrong David. Are you ill?" She felt scared now.

"Come and sit beside me Sadie," he said. As she sat down next to him, he took her hand in his.

"I need to tell you something which is very difficult for me. You know that I love you don't you?" he asked. "I loved you from the first moment I saw you and that hasn't changed."

"I love you too, so whatever is wrong we can fix it. I really appreciate how hard you work for our little family and I know that I don't always show it. I also realise that these past ten years since the twins were born have not been the easiest for you. I know that I have changed since the accident and Lisa's death but, I promise you, I'm going to make more effort from now on. I want to be the same girl that you married."

"You are the same girl sweetheart. You are the sweetest, kindest person I know and you're an amazing mum. Don't ever doubt that. It's not you that's changed. It's me."

"What do you mean?" she asked. He looked at her lovingly and answered,

"Let's have that coffee first and then I promise I will tell you everything right from the very beginning."

Chapter 23

Sadie remembered looking at the clock. It was 10.30am when David started to tell his story.

She listened as he explained how, as a young boy, he felt different from the other kids of his age. He found It difficult to make friends. The other boys picked on him because he wasn't interested in playing any sport and told him he was a cissy because he liked reading books. He was a loner but he was extremely bright. Academically, he breezed through school but he struggled with any form of social interaction with his peers. He knew that his parents – his mum in particular - worried about him. She would question him as to why he never wanted any friends round to play with. Why he spent so much time alone in his bedroom reading books. She felt it wasn't 'normal' behaviour for a young boy.

"I guess I realised that I wasn't like the other kids, but I was happy in my own little world. I decided by the age of twelve that I wanted to be a lawyer. I fixed all of my hopes and dreams on it. Nothing else seemed important.

When I started at Uni, I felt like a fish out of water. I enjoyed the work, the lectures, all of that, but I shied away from the social scene that seemed so prevalent at that time. I liked girls but I wasn't really attracted to them. This was when I questioned myself. Was there something wrong with me? All the other guys did nothing but brag about their sexual conquests. They teased me because I didn't have a girlfriend. Then, I met Alan and everything changed. I had found a friend. A really good friend. We got on well. Before long, we were spending all of our spare time together.

I wasn't entirely naïve. I guessed early on that Alan was gay. He didn't make any advances towards me but we had several in-depth discussions about our sexuality and he suggested that I might be gay too. He asked me why I had never had a girlfriend, why I avoided social situations where there would be girls.

I didn't know how to answer. I felt confused about my feelings for him. I thought about my hopes and dreams to be a lawyer, what my parents would say, would people judge me if they thought I was gay. I decided in that moment to change my life. To be the man that I should be. I wanted a wife and a family. I wanted to be 'normal'.

It was shortly afterwards that I met you Sadie. You blew me away. I had never seen such a beautiful girl. I fell in love with you and I knew then that, one day, I would marry you."

Sadie sat open mouthed. Time seemed to stand still. She couldn't believe what she was hearing. This was her husband, her soul mate, the love of her life and he had used her. Used her to hide behind his true self. She felt sick to her stomach.

"What are you telling me?" That I was nothing more than a trophy wife? A convenience for you to continue with your clandestine affairs with men? You're nothing but a coward. You disgust me."

"Please Sadie, let me explain."

"I think you've said enough don't you?" She spat out the words, fighting back the intense anger that was rising in her chest.

"Please Sadie." he said. "Can I explain?" By now, she had heard enough but she nodded weakly, avoiding eye contact with him.

"Go on. It can't get much worse."

David continued. "After I met you, I told Alan that I was falling for you and that I didn't want to see him anymore. He pleaded with me not to have a relationship with you. He was afraid that you would get hurt. He told me that I wasn't being honest with myself or with you. That it would end badly. It just made me more determined to make it work. To make you happy. To have a normal life.

Sadie interrupted. "A normal life! How could it ever be a normal life? You were just pretending. How could you do that to me? To our children?"

It's all starting to make sense now. The awkwardness between you and Alan. Your strange moods when he was around. I thought he was my friend. I confided in him. Why didn't he tell me the truth? I'll never forgive him for this."

"Alan only ever had your interests at heart. He became very fond of you, you know that. He thought the world of you and your parents"," he said

"So why did he let this happen? I don't understand any of this."

"Alan begged me not to marry you but I wouldn't listen. I really loved you Sadie and I wanted to marry you. It was only when I found out that you were pregnant that I started to worry about the promises I had made to you. We were going to have a family. That put more pressure on me to face up to who I really was. I was on the verge of telling you, when you had your accident. Then everything happened so quickly. It was never the right time after that."

"And Alan. What was your relationship with him at this time?" she asked.

"We became close again - very close. He was my rock and my support at a very difficult time for me. You were so badly injured Sadie. I thought I was going to lose you."

She could hardly contain her anger at this point.

"It was a difficult time for YOU! It's always about you isn't it? What about how I felt. How my parents felt? Am I missing something here? Are you trying to tell me that you and Alan became lovers when I was lying in hospital, when my best friend was killed. This is unbelievable!"

"We didn't want to hurt you Sadie, we really didn't. I had to admit to myself and to Alan that I had always loved him, but I was torn. I loved you too – very much. We decided not to tell you. You had been through so much. We agreed to see each other whenever there was an opportunity and I that I would continue to be the best husband that I could to you and a father to our children."

"You've been lying to me for all these years. I can't believe that you have been sleeping with me, making love to me and then doing the same with Alan – our friend! It's sick David. You're sick. All those business trips. Is that when you saw each other? And what about Paris? Is that why you didn't come home that night? My God, Mum was right about you. I should have listened to her. From the moment she met you, she knew that you were hiding something. I can't even look at you. I want you to leave. Pack a bag and get out before the children come home."

She was shaking with anger and fighting back the tears. She had never felt so humiliated. He had made a fool of her. There was no coming back from this.

"What about the twins?" he said. "Won't they wonder where I am? I told them I would be at home tonight."

"I'll think of something to tell them for now but they are going to find out what's been going on. How do you think they are going to feel when they discover their precious daddy isn't who they thought he was. You've hurt me, that's bad enough, but our children. How could you do this to them? Just get out David. Run off to your lover. You deserve one another!' "I'm so sorry Sadie." He was crying now.

"Can't we try and make this work somehow. I don't want to leave you and the kids. I love you all so much."

She looked at his tear stained face and realised for the first time what a pathetic and selfish man he really was. He was expecting her to agree with continuing their sham of a life while he sought his sexual pleasure elsewhere with another man.

At that moment, she lost all respect and love that she had once had for him. She dried her tears and stood up and faced him. She felt the strength flooding back into her body.

"Get out! You can take the little car. I'll need the Range Rover. Come back for your things in a few days. Our marriage is over and you can tell Alan that I never want to see him again either. I'm going upstairs now. I expect you to have gone by the time I come down."

She looked back at the clock. It was 11.25am.

It had taken less than an hour for her whole world to collapse.

She came back downstairs half an hour later. David had gone. She noticed a scribbled note on the telephone table. It read 'I'm so sorry. Please tell the kids I love them. I'll call you in a couple of days xx'

She picked up the note, tore it into little pieces and threw it in the bin. She had to concentrate on Mia and Matty now. She had already decided to tell them that dad had been called away for work and that he was going away for a few days on a business trip. That would give her enough time to sort out what she was going to do.

After she had composed herself, she rang her mum. "Hi Mum. Can I ask you a big favour?"

"Oh hello love. Yes of course you can. Is everything alright?" Mary had been thinking about her daughter all morning and hoping that her and David had sorted out their problems. "I need to speak to you and dad. But for now do you think you could have the kids tonight and take them to school in the morning? I can pack them an overnight bag and drop them off this afternoon after school if that's ok."

"Yes of course it is," said Mary. You know we love having them. I'll cook them a nice meal and then we can all watch a film. Are you and David off out somewhere?"

"No, he has been called back into work and then he's off on another business trip for a couple of days." Sadie hated lying to her mum but she just wasn't ready to tell her what had happened yet. She needed time to process it herself.

"Oh no, he's going away again? He's only just got back from Paris! I hoped you were going to spend some time together. It's really not fair on you love," said Mary feeling concerned.

"It's ok Mum. I've got plenty to do here and if I don't have to keep the kids entertained, I can get on much better. Don't worry, I'll be absolutely fine. I'll see you later with the kids.

Bye, love you."

Mary stared at her phone as Sadie ended the call. She sensed something was very wrong. She didn't ask her how her and her dad were – she always did that. And she couldn't remember the last time she had asked them to look after the twins. Sadie treasured the time that she spent with them, especially when they had been at school all day. It didn't make sense. Mary decided that she wouldn't say anything to her when she saw her later. Whatever was wrong, she knew that Sadie would tell her when she was ready.

Mia and Matty were waiting at the school gates full of expectations and excitement to see their dad. They ran towards Sadie, puzzled expressions on their faces. "Hi Mum where's dad?" asked Matty. "We thought he was coming."

"I'm so sorry both of you, but dad had to go back to work unexpectedly. He has got to go away again for a couple of days. He said to tell you that he is really sorry and that he loves you very much."

The words almost got stuck in Sadie's throat as she said them. David didn't deserve her excuses but she couldn't bear to see how upset they were. From now on, she would do whatever it might take to protect them.

"There is some good news though," she said smiling and clapping her hands. "You're going to spend the night with Nanny and Grandad and they are going to take you to school in the morning. How does that sound?" " That's brilliant Mum" said Mia. "I love going to Nanny and Grandad's house. They let us eat lots of sweets if we finish our dinner and they let us stay up late too."

"Well, there will be no late night tonight young lady. You've got school in the morning, but Nanny did say that you could watch a film after dinner."

This brought a big smile to their faces and the disappointment of not seeing dad was soon forgotten. They skipped off ahead towards the car, discussing what film they were going to watch and wondering what Nanny was going to make them for dinner. Sadie felt relieved. It would give her more time to prepare herself for what was going to be an extremely difficult conversation with them.

They were just ten years old. How was she going to explain to them in a way they could understand that dad loved Uncle Alan and wanted to be with him and not her? She hated David at that moment. How could he do this to her and their children? She would never be able to forgive him. She had never felt so alone. In a heartbeat, he had shattered all her dreams for the future.

After she had dropped Mia and Matty off at her mum and dad's house, she made her way home. Luckily, they barely gave her a backward glance as, excitedly, they ran into the hallway calling for Grandad. She was grateful for the distraction. It also avoided the possibility of any awkward questions from her mum. She was sure that she had already guessed that there was something wrong. She would have to tell her and her dad soon but for now she just wanted to be alone.

She had only been home for five minutes when her mobile rang. She looked at the screen to see who it was calling. She really didn't want to speak to anyone right now. It was a number she didn't recognise. She hesitated before she finally picked up.

"Hello. This is Sadie Burns. Who is this please?"

"Sadie, it's me, Alan." Instinctively, she went to end the call.

"Don't hang up please Sadie. I really need to talk to you," he said.

"Well, I don't want to talk to you. I can't believe that you thought I would after what you and David have done to me." She was shaking with anger. How dare he ring her?

"I understand, I really do. But we can't leave things as they are. Like it or not, Sadie, we all need to sit down and talk about what's happened and where we go from here. We have to think about Mia and Matty in all of this."

"Don't you dare even mention my children's names. You lost any right to do that, the day you started sleeping with my husband." She was really angry now.

"Can David and I arrange to meet you. Please Sadie. I know you are angry. You have every right to be. This is a difficult time for all of us. But we do need to talk."

She took a deep breath. She knew he was right, but the thought of facing him and David knowing what they had been doing behind her back for years, sickened her.

"I'll meet with you but it will only be to discuss the practicalities. The divorce and the sale of the house. I have no interest in your relationship. Personally, I wish that I never had to see either of you again. However, sadly, I have to accept that David has the right to continue seeing Matty and Mia. He is their father. My only concern now is to protect them. I want to make this awful situation as painless as possible for them."

"Thank you Sadie. I am so sorry that it has come to this. I really care for you. I always have. It breaks my heart that we have caused you so much hurt. Please believe me."

"I'm not interested in your platitudes Alan so save your breath! I'm going to end this call now. My mum and dad don't know yet. I've got to tell them as well as thinking of a way that I can tell my children that their daddy is leaving us. I've got enough on my plate right now. Tell David to come and collect his things as soon as possible. Make sure he texts me first. I don't want to be at home when he comes."

"Yes, I will," he answered. I'll also be in touch to arrange a time and place where we can all meet up."

Sadie didn't answer. She ended the call and walked into the kitchen. She looked around at the beautiful home that her and David had created together. What had it all been for? Was this really how their relationship was going to end? She thought back to their first home together and how happy they had been planning their future. But it had all been based on lies and deceit. It was all too much – like a nightmare that you never wake up from. She sat down, put her head in her hands and cried until there were no tears left.

After a restless night, she woke up feeling stronger. Today was a new day. She thought of the twins and how they were going to need her now more than ever. It was time to put aside her own feelings of hurt and concentrate on building a new life without David. She always used to be a strong independent woman. She told herself that she could do it again.

After she was showered and dressed and had eaten a small bowl of cereal, she set off in the car to see her mum and dad. They would have dropped the twins off at school by now. It would be a good opportunity to speak to them on their own. She wondered if David had told his parents yet. She was really fond of Susan and Colin. She knew that they would be shocked and saddened by the news. He had let everyone down.

Her hands were shaking as she knocked on her mum and dad's front door. Rob came to the door first.

"Hello love. Your mum and I were just wondering if you would pop round. We've just got back from dropping the kids off at school. They've been really good. I think they enjoyed staying here. You know what your mum is like. She spoiled them rotten. Did you enjoy the peace and quiet and get everything done that you wanted to?"

"Sort of Dad. I just wanted to talk to you and mum without the kids being around," she said.

"That sounds a bit ominous. Is everything ok?" he asked.

"No not really," she answered. Mary appeared from the kitchen. She had heard what she had said. "Has something happened between you and David?" she asked.

"Yes it has. Can you both sit down and I'll tell you everything."

Mary and Rob sat in shocked silence as Sadie told them exactly what David had said to her about his feelings for Alan and how they had been meeting secretly since the twins had been born. She watched as her Dad's face gradually turned from pink to bright red as the anger building inside him began to spill over.

"You mean he is gay? Is that what you are telling us Sadie? He has lied to you – to all of us – from the very beginning. I'll bloody kill him!"

"You will do no such thing Rob," said Mary. "He isn't worth it. I wish I could say that I'm shocked, but I'm not. I told you that he seemed secretive about his past, didn't I? I didn't know what it was, but looking back, it all makes sense now. Susan told me that, even as a young boy, he wasn't like the other kids."

"Why did he have to lie about his sexuality?" said Rob looking at his daughter "There are plenty of gay people living openly, proud of who they are. So why did he marry you? Why did he choose to have a family with you? He knew who he really was. He's nothing but a weak, pathetic coward. I welcomed him into our family. I treated him like my own son. Sadie, you are the most beautiful girl, inside and out. How could he do this to you and those two lovely kiddies? I'll NEVER forgive him for this."

"I know you're angry Dad. I am too. But I guess I have had a bit longer than you to process it all. He has broken my heart and he has destroyed the love and respect I had for him, but I need to be strong for the twins. I'm going to tell them this evening. It wont help if I'm an emotional mess, and it won't change anything."

Mary looked fondly at her husband. "Sadie's right love. The twins have to be her priority now. She turned to Sadie. "What about Susan and Colin? Do they know?"

"Not unless David has told them," she answered.

"They are going to be heartbroken. They love you and the twins so much," said Mary sadly. "It's not their fault Mum. I have no intention of losing contact with them just because their son is a low life. They are the twin's grandparents. Mia and Matty love them. They will always be a part of our lives and yours too, I hope. I know how close the four of you have become. Don't let what David has done spoil your friendship,"

"We won't love. I promise," said Rob. "They are good people. I feel sorry for them. David has hurt all of us – just because he wasn't brave enough to admit to himself and his loved ones who he really was. I actually pity him. He might be a successful lawyer, but he is a weak and spineless human being. What about Alan in all of this? Have you spoken to him?"

"I didn't want to," said Sadie. "But he called me from a number I didn't recognise. I was going to end the call straightaway but he pleaded with me to listen to what he had to say. I got the usual platitudes of 'We are so sorry. We didn't want to hurt you' blah blah' then he suggested that the three of us meet up to talk about where we go from here. He said that they were concerned about the twins!"

"It's a big late for that!" said Mary angrily. He wasn't thinking about them when he started sleeping with David all those years ago."

"I know Mum. I agree. But like it or not, he has the right to see his children. I can't stop him while they are so young. Once they are eighteen, they can make their own decisions. Until then, I have no choice. I agreed to meet up, but only to discuss the practical issues. I'm not prepared to listen to anymore of their excuses or explanations for their behaviour. I'm not interested. The only thing I care about now, is doing the right thing for our children. I will file for divorce, sell the house and start my life over. I'll go back to teaching. David always tried to dissuade me. But I was good teacher and I've missed it. I'm not going to let what has happened spoil my future."

"Good for you, love," said Rob. "I'm really proud of you and how you are dealing with all of this and, remember you're not alone. Your mum and I are here to support you. We will always be here to fight your corner." Sadie looked at their concerned faces and for the first time she thought about their mortality. They were growing older. They woudn't always be in her life.

She felt the pain of her realisation in that moment. She pushed her dark thoughts away and smiled lovingly at them both. They were her rock. They always had been. She loved them so much.

Chapter 24

Sadie listened to the excited chatter of her children in the back seat as she drove them home from school. They were so happy. It was Friday afternoon and the weekend was just around the corner. Matty was playing football for the school team in the morning and Mia had been invited round to her best friend's house for lunch. She wondered how she was going to have the conversation she knew she had to have. The last thing she wanted to do was to burst their happy bubbles. She decided to wait until Sunday morning. They had no plans. It was going to be a quiet day at home.

"Mum, are you coming to watch my match tomorrow?" Matty asked.

"You bet I am, and guess what? Grandad is coming too. We'll go out for a burger afterwards and then we'll pick Mia up from Jessica's house."

"Will dad be home tomorrow?" he asked.

"I'm afraid not darling. He is still away."

"He is never here when I play in a match. It's not fair," he said sulkily.

"I know but he can't help it if he has to work Matty. I'm sure he would rather come and watch you playing football." Sadie hated lying to her son. He looked so sad. Her heart went out to him.

Mia sat quietly. She was thinking that she didn't mind that dad wouldn't be home. She loved going to Jessica's house. Jessica had so many toys to play with and her mum had just bought her a puppy. She was going to wait until dad came home and then she would ask if she could have one too.

After the twins had gone to bed, Sadie sat down with a glass of wine. It had been a difficult few days but she feared that the worst was yet to come. Thankfully, she hadn't heard from Alan again and there still hadn't been a word from David. She was going to have face both of them soon but for now she needed to plan what she was going to say to Mia and Matty on Sunday. As she was pouring a second glass of wine, her mobile rang. She saw that it was Susan's number and her heart skipped a beat.

"Hi Susan," she said.

"Sadie I've heard from David. I'm so shocked. I can't believe what he has done to you. I'm so sorry love. I am disgusted with him I really am. I know it's a stupid question, but are you ok?"

"I'm as ok as I can be in the circumstances, Susan. I admit that we haven't been getting on so well lately, but I didn't see this coming. It would appear that both him and Alan have been lying to me for years. I know he is your son, but I will never forgive him for what he has done to our little family."

"I quite agree Sadie. If only he had admitted that he was gay right from the start – not only to himself but to all of us - I'm sure we would have accepted it in time. I always suspected that he was hiding who he really was, even as a young boy. I blame myself for not confronting him about it back then."

"You weren't to know Susan. It's not your fault. It's nobody's fault except his. He acted like a coward and we are all casualties of that."

"Colin has disowned him. He won't even hear his name mentioned. I'm really worried about him, Sadie. It's destroyed him," said Susan.

"Why don't you both go and see mum and dad? You have all become such good friends. It might help if you support one another," Sadie answered.

"I didn't think they would ever want to see us again after this."

"Don't be silly Susan. You know mum and dad aren't like that. They're not going to judge you for David's actions. They are really fond of you and I think they will be pleased if you go and see them. It will help all of you to be able to talk about it together."

"I knew from the day I met you that you were a very special human being, Sadie. I loved you from that moment. I was so happy that David had found you. You were going to be the daughter that we never had. Now he's thrown it all away. He doesn't deserve you. He doesn't deserve to be happy. I'm ashamed of him – not because he is gay – but because he didn't have the guts to be honest about it. What about the twins? Do they know yet?"

"No, they've got a fun day planned for tomorrow. I don't want to spoil it for them. I'm going to speak to them on Sunday," she said.

"That's going to be difficult for you. Would it help if me or your mum were there too?" "It's kind of you Susan. But this is something I need to do on my own. I hope you understand?"

"Yes of course. I'm so sorry Sadie. You shouldn't have to be dealing with all this. You've been through enough. Just know that Colin and I are always here for you and the twins. We always will be."

"Thank you. I really appreciate that. Now don't forget, give mum a ring. She really will be pleased to hear from you. Come and see the twins too. They've missed you."

"Thanks, love, we will. I'll be thinking of you tomorrow. You are an amazing mum. You'll find the right words. Take care of yourself too. I'll speak to you soon."

Sadie ended the call promising that she would keep in touch and thanking her mother in law for her support. Her heart went out to Susan. She could hear how much she was hurting. David had really let his parents down, so much so, she wondered if they would ever be able to forgive him.

Sunday came round all too quickly. It was 10am. Mia and Matty were still sleeping after their busy day on Saturday. Matty was exhausted after his football match and the excitement of being voted man of the match for scoring two of the three winning goals. Mia had spent all afternoon and part of the evening at her friend Jessica's house. She decided that they deserved a lie in. It also gave her the opportunity to prepare herself for the conversation she was going to have with them.

Half an hour later they both wandered downstairs rubbing their eyes "Hello sleepyheads," she said. "Ready for breakfast?"

"Yeah, I'm starving," said Matty.

"You're always starving," said Mia laughing.

"Right," said Sadie. "You choose what you would like. You were both so good yesterday. You deserve a treat." Almost in unison they both turned to Sadie and shouted - "pancakes with lemon!"

She laughed at their eager little faces. "Pancakes with lemon It is then. Go and get dressed and they will be ready when you come back downstairs." She watched them as they tucked into their pancakes and then asked for more. Luckily she had made enough batter mix!

"What are we doing today Mum? Are we going out?" said Mia.

"We will probably go to Nanny and Grandad's for tea later, but this morning I want to talk to you both about something really important."

She cleared up the breakfast dishes and walked into the lounge where they were playing a game of Pictionary.

"Can I speak to you both now and then afterwards perhaps I can play too?" she said.

"Yeah. You can play too Mum!" said Mia excitedly.

"What do you need to talk to us about?" said Matty looking puzzled. Sadie took a deep breath. She had no idea where to start. She hadn't planned it at all. She just hoped that it would come naturally.

"It's about me and dad You know how much we both love you, don't you? That will never, ever change. But dad has decided that he can't live at home anymore."

"Is that because he is always away working?" asked Matty.

"It's part of it darling, yes. But Dad wants to live in London with Uncle Alan. He loves all of us very much but he loves Uncle Alan too, so he had to choose."

She looked at their faces. They didn't understand. How could they? She waited for a response but they just continued to look at her.

"I know how difficult this is for you to understand. But sometimes, mums and dads split up and choose to live a different life. That doesn't mean that they have stopped loving you or that it's your fault. It's the same with me and dad. Just because we won't be living together doesn't mean that anything will change for you. Dad will see you as often as he can. In fact you will probably see him more than you do now and you will be able to have lots of fun with him and Uncle Alan.

She wasn't prepared for what Matty said next.

"Is dad one of those men who wants to be married to a man? We learned about It at school didn't we Mia? They're called gay aren't they? There is a boy who goes to our school. He has got two mum's. They're called gay but they're really nice. I've seen them when they pick him up from school."

She hadn't expected that. The twins were only ten years old. She hadn't imagined for one moment that they would know what 'gay' meant.

She recovered herself quickly. "Yes Matty that's what 'gay' means. But dad doesn't necessarily want to get married to Uncle Alan. He just wants to be with him but it's important for you to know that he is still your dad and he always will be.

Sadie looked at the sad face of her daughter. She hadn't said a word. "Do you understand Mia? Is there anything you want to ask me?"

"You promised me that you wouldn't get a divorce like Jessica's Mum and Dad. You promised me!"

"I'm sorry darling but I didn't know then that this was going to happen. You know that I would never lie to you don't you?" Mia was sulking now.

"It's not fair, I was going to ask dad if I could have a puppy. Jessica's mum has just bought her one. It's so sweet Mum. I really want one and I promise I will look after it and take it for walks. Once again, Sadie was lost for words. She had expected floods of tears that dad was leaving home, but it appeared, as far as Mia was concerned, she was more upset at the prospect of not being able to have a puppy!

"I think you and Matty are still a bit young to have the responsibility of looking after a puppy, darling. I'm not saying that you can't have one, but let's wait a while. I'm going to be busy looking for a new house and a new job. I want to start teaching again. Do you understand?"

Mia was still sulking but she nodded her head and looked at her brother. "Shall we finish our game Matty? Are you going to play too Mum?"

"Yes, I'll have a game with you. I've just got to give Nanny a call to say that we will be over for tea later. I won't be long."

Sadie walked into the kitchen. She was still trying to get her head around the twin's reactions. It was not what she had expected at all. She wondered if it would take time for the news to sink in. But she also knew how resilient children could be to bad news. They often handled it much better than adults. Perhaps this was an example of that. She really hoped so. It would have broken her heart to see them upset. All she could do was to wait and see and to be on hand if they had any more questions over the next day or so.

The rest of the afternoon passed with no further conversations about David until it was time to get ready to go to Nanny and Grandad's house. As they were all getting their shoes and coats on, Matty turned to Sadie. "Do Nanny and Grandad know that dad is going to live in London with Uncle Alan?"

"Yes they do Matty. So if you want to talk to them about it, they won't mind."

"No, it's ok. I just wondered if it was a secret. Shall I tell my friends at school tomorrow?"

"You don't have to do that, darling, but if you think it will help you to talk to your friends, then that's ok too," said Sadie. "It's nothing for you to be ashamed of, or to feel afraid to talk about. It's the same for you too Mia. You can tell your friends if you want to, but you don't have to do anything that you don't want to."

"I'm going to tell Jessica. Her Dad left home too. We're going to be the same now." said Mia. Sadie thought that she almost sounded proud that she had such an important thing in common with her best friend. For now, she was just relieved that both her children appeared to be coping much better than she had expected them to.

Mary and Rob were anxious to see Sadie and the twins. Sadie hadn't given any clue as to how Mia and Matty had taken the news when she had phoned.

"I hope the children are ok," Mary said to Rob. "I don't know what to expect when they get here." "I think if they had taken it badly Sadie would have told you and they probably wouldn't have come anyway", said Rob. "Let's just carry on as we would normally with them. I'm sure Sadie will tell us what happened whenever she gets the opportunity. Try not to worry love."

Mary was pleased to see that Rob had been right in telling her not to worry, The twins appeared to be their normal happy selves and Sadie seemed relaxed.

"What's for tea Nanny?" said Matty. As usual, he was always thinking ahead to the next meal.

"I've made a nice shepherds pie and, guess what? I've made a treacle sponge for dessert," said Mary. She laughed as both him and Mia danced up and down clapping their hands. They always loved her treacle sponges.

"'Nanny said tea wouldn't be ready for about an hour," said Sadie. "So why don't we ask Grandad if he can find a film for you to watch in the lounge and I'll help Nanny."

"Good idea," said Rob smiling at Sadie. He guessed that she wanted to speak to Mary without the children being there. "Come on kids. Help me find something on Netflix for you. I could do with a sit down so I'll watch it with you."

This seemed to please them. They loved their Grandad. He was good fun and he would probably let them watch something that they wouldn't be allowed to see at home.

"The chilcren seem fine Sadie," said Mary when she joined her in the kitchen. "I expected them to be a bit quiet at least." "I didn't know what to expect Mum. I'm surprised that they took it as well as they have. They were a bit upset at first but when I explained it to them, they just seemed to accept it. They even new what 'gay' meant. Apparently they have learned all about it at school and Matty has a friend who has two mum's. It all seemed quite normal to them. I think that they will be fine as long as they can still see David. I'm going to meet up with him and Alan soon. We'll talk about it then."

"How are you coping though love? It must have been such a shock."

"Yes it was at first, she said "but looking back over our years together, there were signs. I just chose to ignore them. "He told me that him and Alan didn't get together until after my accident, but I don't believe him. There were so many occasions when he was supposedly away on business. But was he? I just don't know. Perhaps there were other men before Alan. It makes me feel sick to think that he might have been having sex with random men and then coming home and sleeping with me."

"I know. It makes me so angry to think how he has deceived you, how he has used you and humiliated you," said Mary. "I spoke to Susan this morning. Her and Colin are devastated. She thought that we wouldn't want to see them again after this. I hope I managed to convince her otherwise. They are a lovely couple and both me and your Dad consider them good friends. We promised each other that we would get together soon. I don't want this to destroy our friendship."

"I'm glad that you feel that way, Mum. After all, they are a big part of our lives and the kids love them. They shouldn't have to suffer for what their son has done. As for me, I'm going to start divorce proceedings straight away and I'm going to sell the house. I don't want to live in it anymore. There are too many memories. I'm ready to start my life over. I'm definitely going back to teaching. In fact, I'm going to speak to the headmaster at the twin's school. He might know if there are any opportunities, teaching the little ones at the pre-prep school."

"One step at a time love," said Mary. "I admire you for dealing with this in such a mature and positive way. But it's early days. I don't want you rushing to sell the house. You need to make sure that you see a solicitor first and are aware of your rights. That applies to the divorce too. Just get some advice first. I know that's what your Dad will say too. What I will say is that you should have this meeting with David as soon as you can. You need to put some arrangements in place for him to see the children and make sure that he isn't going to upset them. If he is living with Alan now, he needs to know how to behave in front of them. They might know what 'gay' means but you wouldn't want them exposed to anything inappropriate."

"That's what worries me too Mum. To be honest, I would rather that Alan wasn't around at all when he sees the children. But you're right. It's something we need to discuss. If I haven't heard from him by tomorrow, I'll ring him and arrange where we can meet. I don't want him coming to the house. It will probably have to be in a pub somewhere."

After she had dropped the twins off at school the next morning, she thought about the conversation she had with her mum. Much as she dreaded the thought of it, she needed to speak to David. There were a lot of practical things to sort out but, more importantly, she felt concerned about how his access to the children would affect them in the long term. She really didn't think it would be appropriate for Alan to be a part of the process, certainly while they were still so young.

Hands shaking she took a deep breath and dialled his number.

"Sadie, I'm so glad that you have phoned. I hated the way that we left things. Are you and the twins ok?"

"What do you think David? How am I supposed to answer that? Look, I don't want to get into anything over the phone. I'm ringing to arrange a meeting. Not at the house. What about that pub in Chelmsford that we used to go to? I'll ask mum and dad to pick the children up from school and they can stay the night with them. They love spending time with Nanny and Grandad, so they'll be quite happy.

"Whatever is best for you Sadie," he said. "Have you told the kids yet?' ' "Yes, I've told them. They took it much better than I thought they would. They're fine. Like I said, I don't want to talk about any of this on the phone. I'll see you at the pub tomorrow at 4pm. Don't bring Alan. This is between you and me, ok?"

"Ok, I understand," he said. "I'll see you tomorrow then."

Sadie didn't give him the opportunity to say anything else and ended the call. She felt anxious about the prospect of meeting him. It all still felt surreal. But she had to stay strong. From now on, she was going to put herself and the twins first. David had betrayed her. She owed him nothing.

As she expected, the twins were excited when she told them that they would be staying at Nanny and Grandad's house again. Mary and Rob were only to pleased to have them and happy that Sadie had arranged the meeting with David. Rob could sense how anxious Sadie was, although she was putting on a brave face.

"Don't let him intimidate you love. He is a lawyer, he can talk the talk. But you stick to your guns and make sure that he will continue to support you and the twins financially."

"I don't want his money, Dad. I don't want anything from him. He has a duty to support Mia and Matty until they are eighteen. That's the only thing that's important. When I get the money from the sale of the house, I'll buy something smaller. I'm also going back to work. I will be fine financially."

When Sadie arrived at the pub the next day, David was already there. He was sitting in a quiet corner. She was relieved to see that he was on his own. She had wondered if Alan would still come despite her saying that she didn't want him there. He smiled at her. He was looking very sheepish. She guessed he was probably feeling as nervous as she was.

"Hello Sadie," he said. "What can I get you to drink?"

"Just a lemonade please, I'm driving," she answered." Of course.

I'll get myself a shandy and then we can talk."

Later, when she got home, she couldn't remember who had spoken first, but unlike the last conversation they had, this time it was polite and a little distant. It was almost like they were a couple of strangers who just happened to have had children together. He seemed different. He openly admitted that he had treated her badly. That he had hurt everyone he loved. But he seemed more relaxed somehow, as if a huge weight had been taken off his shoulders.

She listened to his apologies. His regrets about how he had handled it all. He spoke about Alan fondly. It saddened him how he had treated him too.

"I've made such a mess of my life Sadie. I don't expect you to ever forgive me, but I hope, in time, we can be the friends we always were, even if it's just for the sake of the children. I have, and I always will, love you very much. You are the sweetest, kindest and most genuine person I know." She looked deep into his eyes and remembered the first time that they had met. The attraction had been instantaneous. He was still a very handsome man. She had to admit that there would always be a part of her that loved him too. But, their marriage was over. It was time to let him go. She took a deep breath before she answered.

"I appreciate your honesty David. I'm just sad that you couldn't have confided in me from the beginning. I would have been devastated of course, but I would have got over it in time. Look how many people you have hurt now? Just because you weren't brave enough to face up to who you really were.

I have also wondered whether there were other men before Alan? Were there? I think I deserve the truth this time."

"There were a few but, honestly Sadie. They meant nothing. I had pushed Alan away. I thought I had lost him for good."

"How do you think that makes me feel?" she said. "You're a coward and a hypocrite David. That's why I can never forgive you. However, I agree, for the sake of the children, we must try to maintain some sort of amicable relationship. Certainly until they are old enough to make their own decisions."

Inwardly, she felt disgusted at this new admission of his infidelity. But she wasn't going to let him see how she really felt. She felt sick. It was the final nail in the coffin.

Before they left, she agreed to his suggestion that he saw the children for one day every weekend. She also stayed firm on her request that Alan would not be around on his access days. David agreed that, to start with, he would respect her wishes but he hoped that she would reconsider after a few months when the twins were settled into a routine. She was careful not to make him any promises and told him that she would be seeing a solicitor with regard to the sale of the house, the divorce and maintenance for the children. He agreed to it all. She had expected some sort of negative response but it didn't come.

He spoke about his Mum and Dad and thanked Sadie for her understanding and kindness towards them. It felt strange, but as he was speaking, she suddenly felt awkward and uncomfortable in his company. She resisted the urge to get up and leave as she answered

"I have no reason to change my feelings towards your parents David. None of this is their fault. They are lovely people and they are Mia and Matty's grandparents. They will always be a part of our lives.

I'm going to go home now. I don't think there is anything else to say. I'll contact you when I think the twins are ready to see you."

As she stood up, David moved towards her as if he was going to hug her. She moved away. The thought of him ever touching her again made her flesh creep. As she made for the door, she didn't look back. From now on, she would only look forward.

Chapter 25

Nearly a year had passed. The house had been sold and the divorce almost finalised. The twins never spoke again about the day she told them that David was leaving. They had adapted well to the new routine of seeing him at weekends. She had to admit that he always made a special effort to make sure they enjoyed their visits with him. She had finally relented to his constant requests for Alan to be a part of his time with them. Although it was a bitter pill to swallow at first, she had to admit to herself that Mia and Matty were always happy and upbeat after their visits. They talked a lot about how Uncle Alan made them laugh and played lots of games with them. It seemed to be working well.

She had also bought a little Victorian terraced house close to where her mum and dad lived. It was situated in a lovely tree lined road in a quiet area. The twins had already made friends nearby and spent lots of time playing outside with them. Mary and Rob were constantly on hand to help her if she needed them and Susan and Colin were also regular visitors. Life was beginning to settle down.

Sadie often thought of Lisa. She still missed her so much. Although she had got to know some of the other mums at the school, she hadn't met anyone like Lisa - someone that she had that special connection with. She visited her special place in the crematorium most weekends and left a spray of flowers by her headstone, talking to her as if she was still here. It gave her some comfort knowing that she could still have that connection with her.

She still had nightmares about the accident. It was difficult to erase the dark thoughts that still haunted her. But day by day, she was learning to live with it. She knew that's what Lisa would have wanted.

Her thoughts turned to the here and now. She was ready to go back to work. She had really missed teaching. The time seemed right. She telephoned the headmaster of Mia and Matty's school to enquire whether there any positions available either there or at the pre-prep school. He knew Sadie and was aware of her teaching history. He sounded quite disappointed as he told her that unfortunately, although they were looking for a teaching assistant at the pre-prep school, there were no vacancies for a teacher with her qualifications. She was realistic. It had been a bit of a long shot. But nothing would deter her now. She decided to take her time in looking. Something would turn up.

One day she decided to go for a walk before she picked the children up from school. She chided herself often enough for not getting enough exercise. Today there was no excuse. It was a lovely afternoon. The sun was shining in a blazing blue sky. She looked at the beautiful trees, the gardens full of colour and felt the warmth of the gentle breeze on her face. She felt lighter somehow as if the dark cold blanket of depression that had enveloped her for so long, had finally been lifted. She found herself reaching the park and made her way towards the lake. She noticed a small boy standing at the edge of the lake throwing bread to the ducks. He looked about three years old and he was holding a man's hand. She assumed it was his daddy. As she approached slowly, the man turned around and looked at her.

"Sadie, is that you?" he said. She recognised him immediately. It was Peter, one of the teachers from Hill Park School.

"Hi Peter, yes it's me. I thought you looked familiar from behind. Is this your little boy?" she said smiling at the face of the little blonde haired boy.

"Yes, this is Oliver. Say hello Oliver. This is Sadie. She is an old friend of Daddy's. She used to teach at the same school Daddy does."

"Hello," said the little boy looking very shy. She thought he looked adorable and very much like Peter.

"Goodness, how long has It been Sadie - ten or eleven years?"

"Yes, I guess it has," she answered. "Time goes so quickly doesn't It?" "So you're still teaching at Hill Park then?" she asked.

"Yes, I'm still there, but just part time now. I've got this little one to look after," he said smiling at his son. She wondered about his wife. He hadn't mentioned her. She thought that perhaps she was working full time and wasn't able to look after Oliver during the day. As if he was reading her mind, he added.

"Sadly, my wife Kate died from cancer just after Oliver was born. We don't have any other family nearby so, I am his sole carer." Sadie was lost for words. She remembered meeting his wife at her and David's wedding. She couldn't have been much older than she was.

"Oh, Peter, I am so sorry. How tragic. What a terrible shock that must have been for you. She was so young."

"Yes It was Sadie. I didn't think I would ever get over it but having Oliver helped me to heal. He needed me. I had to be strong for him. He has been such a blessing."

She felt her eyes beginning to fill with tears as she reached out and put her hand comfortingly on his shoulder. "You are so brave. Oliver is a lovely little boy. He is a credit to you."

"Enough about me. How is David and what about those twins of yours? I bet they're a handful aren't they? But in a good way I'm sure," he added.

"The twins are good, thank you. They go to private school. David insisted that they have a private education. I have to admit that they are both doing really well. Matty is a keen sportsman. He plays for the school's football team. Mia is the academic one. She loves languages. I'm very proud of both of them."

"And David? Is he the big shot lawyer that he always wanted to be?" he asked. "Yes, he is. He's done very well. He lives in London now. We're separated."

Sadie saw the shock on his face as he answered. "Oh I'm so sorry to hear that. I thought you two were the ideal couple. You looked so happy on your wedding day. Kate and I both said how well suited you seemed to be.

"Yes, I thought so too," she answered. "Things changed sadly."

"I didn't mean to pry Sadie. I'm so sorry." She could see how genuinely he meant that. He was still the nice person that she remembered him to be.

"You weren't prying Peter. It's fine, really. She looked at her watch, "I'm afraid that I must go now. I've got to pick up my car and then collect the twins from school. It's been so nice to see you again and to meet your little boy. He's adorable."

"Perhaps we could meet up for a coffee one day if you have time," he added.

"That would be really nice. I'm sure we will bump into each other again," she answered. She bent down and took Oliver's hand. "It's been lovely meeting you Oliver. Take care of your daddy won't you?" The little boy nodded and looked up at Peter. "Can we go on the swings now Daddy?"

As she turned and walked away she heard Peter saying to his son. "She is a nice lady isn't she? Let's hope we see her again. That would be nice wouldn't it?"

As she walked home she thought about his words. It had just been a chance meeting with an old friend. That was all. So why did she feel so cheerful suddenly. She started humming a song she had heard on the radio earlier. She couldn't remember the last time she had done that. She felt she had made a connection with Peter. They had both suffered tragedy in different ways. She questioned whether that was the reason she felt drawn to him, or was it something else?

After she had collected the twins from school, she decided to drive past Hill Park School on the way home. It looked just the same as she remembered it. She wondered if Wendy Marshall was still the Head Teacher, whether the classrooms were still the same, whether any more of her past colleagues, apart from Peter, were still there. In that moment, she thought of the happy times she had spent teaching 'her little sponges.' It was as if Lisa was telling her to go back to her happy place.

After the twins had gone to bed, she decided to telephone her mum. She was such a good listener and would advise her whether or not it was a good idea to contact the school. Firstly, she told her about her chance meeting with Peter and his little boy.

"Do you remember Peter, Mum? Him and his wife, Kate were at our wedding." "Yes, I do. They were a nice couple. Very quiet, if I remember correctly," said Mary.

Sadie then proceeded to tell her about Kate's death and how Peter was left caring for his little boy alone.

"Oh, dear," said Mary. That's so sad. She couldn't have been much older than you Sadie." "No, I don't think she was. I don't know any details, just that it was cancer."

"Did you tell him about you and David?' said Mary.

"Only that we are separated that's all. I didn't feel it was the right time to go into detail.

I know I'm changing the subject Mum, but I've got something on my mind and I wanted your advice. You know that I want to go back to teaching. Do you think it's a good idea for me to contact Hill Park to see if they have any vacancies? Would I be making mistake if I went back? I drove past today and I felt that Lisa was talking to me – telling me to go back – that I belonged there. Does that sound stupid Mum?"

Mary had always hoped that her daughter would want to go back to teaching one day. She had been through so much pain that she was afraid she wouldn't want to re-visit anywhere that would remind her of the past.

"Oh love. I am so happy to hear you say that. You were a great teacher and you worked so hard to get where you wanted. I think Hill Park will welcome you back with open arms. Go and see them. Hopefully Wendy Marshall is still the Head Teacher. She will be so pleased to see you."

"I should have asked Peter. He is still teaching there part time but he didn't mention Wendy. She may have retired by now," said Sadie.

"Well there is one way to find out," Mary answered. "Why don't you go there tomorrow after you've dropped the twins at school?"

"Yes, I think I will. Thanks Mum. What would I do without your words of wisdom?"

'I just want you to be happy again love. This could be a fresh start for you – a chance to regain your independence and become the strong woman that you always used to be. Don't let what David did to you destroy your confidence. You are beautiful and brave and you have the kindest heart. He is your past. Now it is time to start looking forward to your future."

Sadie knew her mum was right – she always was. She decided that she would call in at the school in the morning after dropping the twins off.

Chapter 26

The next morning held the promise of yet another beautiful day. The air was warm and still as Sadie drove into the car park of Hill Park School. She looked around at the familiar sights. The pretty rose gardens and the green and lush playing fields. Nothing had really changed. Then she spotted a Magnolia tree near the entrance to the main building. She didn't remember it being there before. She noticed a brass plaque in the ground in front of it. As she bent down to read the words, she felt a shiver up her spine. It was for Lisa.

It read:

This tree has been planted in loving memory of Lisa Martin. A much valued teacher at our school and a beautiful human being, loved by many. Her light will always shine bright in our hearts.

Sadie felt the emotion rising in her chest and the tears filling her eyes. It was a beautiful tribute to her friend. She knew in that moment that this was where she belonged.

Just as she was making her way through the main doors towards the Head Teacher's office, she saw Peter coming down the corridor towards her.

"Sadie! Fancy seeing you here. I didn't think that I would see you again quite so soon," he said smiling broadly.

"Hi Peter. I promise I'm not stalking you," she laughed. I didn't have the chance to tell you yesterday but I want to come back to work. I was on my way to Wendy's office. Do you think there is any possibility there will be a place for me here?"

"It's strange you should ask me that question now, Sadie. We didn't have much time to talk yesterday but I was going to ask you if you would be interested in coming back. As I told you, I can only work part time because of my son. I work three days and the other two days are covered by one of the new young teachers who joined us last year. She would ideally like a full time position so she has applied for a job at another school. She is just waiting to hear if she has been successful or not. If she does leave us, then we will need another teacher to work on Mondays and Fridays. Would that interest you?"

"That would be perfect for me Peter. I didn't really want a full time position anyway. It must have been fate that I bumped into you yesterday. Up until then, I wasn't really sure what I wanted to do, but now that I'm back here, it feels like home. I feel closer to Lisa too. It just feels right somehow," she said.

"I understand," said Peter. "I remember how close you two were. I used to laugh to myself in the staff room as I listened to you both chattering away. What happened to her was beyond tragic. Did you see the tree we planted for her on the way in?"

"Yes I did. It's absolutely beautiful. That was a lovely thing to do for her."

"It was Wendy's idea. She was absolutely devastated when she died. "We all were," he said.

"How is Wendy? Is she still the Head?" she asked.

"Wendy retired three years ago. Mr Marshall had a stroke so she took early retirement to look after him. Sadly, he died last year,"

"Oh no", said Sadie. "He was such a lovely man. Do you still hear from her?"

"Occasionally," he said. "She moved away to be closer to her daughter. We have a new Head Teacher – a man this time. He is very nice. The kids love him. His name is Martin Davies. I'll go to his office with you and I can introduce you."

"That's very kind of you Peter. Thank you," she said.

Sadie was pleasantly surprised when she met Martin. As Peter said, he seemed a very nice man. He had a small goatee beard and she thought he was probably in his late fifties. He smiled kindly at her as Peter explained how Sadie had taught at the school before her children were born and that she was looking to come back on a part time basis if possible.

As he introduced her to Martin he suddenly realised who she was.

"Are you the Sadie Burns that Wendy Marshall told me about?" he asked.

"Yes - well for now anyway. My divorce will be finalised soon and I will be going back to my maiden name of Connel," she answered.

"Wendy spoke very highly of you. She always hoped that you would come back one day. I am aware of the tragedy involving you and Lisa Martin. I'm so sorry. It must have been very traumatic for you. Lisa was well thought of here. Wendy was extremely fond of her. It affected her very deeply when she died."

"Yes. It was an awful time. Lisa was very special." Her eyes started to fill with tears again as she thought of the wonderful tribute the school had written about her friend.

"I'm sorry Sadie. I didn't mean to upset you," he said.

"It's fine. I'm sorry" she said wiping her eyes "I have just seen the tree and the lovely tribute to Lisa in the school grounds. It's just made me very emotional."

"Of course. I quite understand. Please don't apologise. You must had many fond memories of your time here."

"Yes, I do. It's a lovely little school and if possible, I would love to come back," she said.

"I believe that Peter has told you that there is likely to be a part time position available teaching his class on Mondays and Fridays. Is that something that would suit you or were you looking for something full time?" he asked.

"Part time would suit me fine. My children are still quite young so I would prefer not to work every day."

"Well that sounds ideal," he said." We will know definitely by early next week. Is it ok if I give you a ring then?"

"That would be lovely. Thank you Mr Davies," she said.

"Please, it's Martin. We don't stand on ceremony here, do we Peter?"

Peter shook his head and smiling at Sadie he said, "It will be great to have you back again Sadie. We are a very tight team and the kids are great."

"Thank you – both of you. I couldn't be happier. I'll look forward to hearing from you next week Martin." She stood up and shook his outstretched hand.

"It was lovely meeting you Sadie", he said smiling broadly.

Peter opened the door for her and followed her into the corridor.

"Well, what do you think of our new Head then?" he asked.

"He seems really nice. Very kind and understanding. Thank you so much Peter. I probably wouldn't be here if I hadn't bumped into you yesterday. I really didn't know what I wanted to do. Now I feel that I'm where I'm meant to be. Please let me take you out for a drink to thank you." The words seemed to leave her mouth before she really thought about it. Would he think she was being forward?

He looked deep into her eyes and laughed before he said "You beat me to it. I was about to ask you out for dinner. Will you come. Please?"

"That would be lovely, Peter but I've got a better idea. Why don't you come round one evening and I'll cook? It's been ages since I cooked for anyone else. it get's a big boring making fish fingers and chicken bites all the time!" she said laughing. "Would you be able to find a babysitter? If not you are welcome to bring Oliver too."

"I have a very good next door neighbour. Her husband sadly died last year. She loves looking after Oliver. He's like another grandson to her. I'll ask her if she wouldn't mind babysitting. I'm sure she will be delighted to. But are you sure about cooking? I wanted to take you somewhere special as way of a celebration," he said.

"I'm absolutely sure. I love cooking anyway. It will be my pleasure."

"Well as long as you're sure. I'll look forward to it", he said. "I'd better get back to my class now. I've got your number. I jotted it down when you were giving it to Martin. I'll give you a ring next week and we'll fix a date, if that's ok."

"That's fine. Thanks again, Peter," she said as she headed towards the car park.

On the way home, she found herself planning a menu for Peter's visit. She felt excited at the prospect of male company once again and couldn't deny that she felt attracted to Peter. In the past, she had considered him a friend, nothing more. But seeing him again had made her realise what a good looking man he was. She wondered if it was too soon to be thinking of starting another relationship. He had lost his wife. She was in the throws of a divorce. Was it really the right time, she wondered.

After a few days, much to her delight, she received a phone call from Martin. He confirmed that the young teacher who had been job sharing with Peter, had handed in her resignation. She had been offered a full time position at another school to commence in one month's time.

"Is that too short notice for you Sadie?" he asked.

"No, not at all, Martin. That's perfect for me. Thank you so much. I'm really looking forward to coming back."

"It will be great to have you on board," he said. Might I suggest, in the meantime, that you get together with Peter to discuss how you are going to move forward in terms of planning your lessons etc? He will probably want you to come in and meet the children too. I'll leave that with you to sort out with him," he added.

Sadie ended the call on a high. She couldn't wait to tell her mum the good news.

"Mum, it's me. Guess what?" she said.

"Oh hello love. You sound very bubbly. What's happened?" said Mary.

"I've been offered a part time job at Hill Park. I will be job sharing with Peter two days a week."

"That's brilliant news, love. I'm so happy for you. I just knew that things were going to get better for you. You deserve some good luck. Your dad will be thrilled too. He's out bowling again. I can't keep him away at the moment! Mind you, he does love playing and it gives me a bit of peace too," she said laughing.

"And there's more, said Sadie. "Peter is coming to dinner next week. He asked me to go out for a meal but I said I would rather cook for him. I know it's early days, Mum, but I really like him. He seems such a genuine guy and he's pretty good looking too!"

"Wow, it's all happening isn't it?" said Mary. "Good for you love. You're far too young to be on your own. Peter sounds nice. And you seem excited and very happy for the first time in a long while. I hope I'll get to meet him soon so I can give him the once over!"

Sadie laughed at her mum's suggestion but knew she was only kidding.

"Let's see how we get on first Mum. I don't even know yet whether he is looking for a relationship. He might be quite happy living on his own with his son."

Sadie looked at her phone and could see that someone was trying to ring her.

"I'll have to ring off now, Mum. Someone is trying to get through. I'll speak to you soon. Love you."

"Hi. Is that you Sadie?" said a familiar voice. She recognised that it was Peter. "Yes, it is. Hello Peter. How are you?"

"I've just heard from Martin and he tells me that he has offered you the job. I'm so pleased Sadie. I really am. It's brilliant news."

"Thank you," she said. "I'm pretty pleased too."

"How about we arrange that dinner date now," he said. "We need to celebrate."

"Are you free tomorrow?" she asked. "I hope you're not a vegetarian. I've got a couple of fillet steaks in the freezer just begging to be eaten," she laughed.

"No. Definitely not. I love steak. It sounds great and I am free tomorrow. Are you sure you don't want to go out?"

"I'm very sure. It will be nice to have a cosy night in."

"Well, if you're sure. I'll bring a bottle of bubbly so that we can make a toast to the future," he answered.

Sadie felt her heart skipping a beat. He had mentioned the 'future'. Could it be that he felt the same attraction for her? She ended the call feeling like a giggly teenager. It reminded her of the first time she had met David. The desire and affinity towards that person which overwhelms and excites you. She didn't think that she could ever feel like that again. Perhaps this was going to be her second chance to find real happiness again.

Peter didn't disappoint. He arrived the next evening right on time. She thought how handsome he looked. He was dressed in casual jeans with a pale blue denim shirt and was clutching a bottle of bubbly and a huge bunch of flowers. He moved towards her and kissed her on the cheek.

"Wow, you look absolutely stunning Sadie."

"Thank you," she said. "The flowers are lovely Peter. You shouldn't have gone to that trouble." "Beautiful flowers for a beautiful lady," he answered. "It's my pleasure. Thank you for inviting me."

Sadie suddenly felt a bit uncomfortable. They were making polite conversation but there were so many things that they still didn't know about each other. She decided that she needed to tell him about David and Alan. It might change things between them. But she had to be honest. It was a chance she would have to take.

"Before we sit down to dinner, I feel I need to be honest with you and tell you why David and I split up."

"You don't have to Sadie. Whatever happened between you is not my business and it won't make any difference about how I feel about you.I always thought how beautiful you were. I was married and I loved my wife. I would never have cheated on her. But I was always really attracted to you."

"Oh Peter, I had no idea. I'm so sorry."

"Please don't apologies. How would you know? You were engaged to David. I would never have said or done anything that would jeopardise your relationship. I was devastated when Kate died. For a long time I blamed myself for having feelings for someone else. It felt like a punishment.

After we got married, we started trying for a baby but Kate had problems. She had four miscarriages before, eventually, we were offered IVF. It worked! We were so happy. We had almost given up on having our own child. About five months into the pregnancy, we found out that she had breast cancer. It was very aggressive. The doctors wanted her to start chemo straightaway but she refused to have any treatment.

She was terrified that the chemotherapy would affect the baby. The doctors assured her that it would be fine but there was no way she was going to change her mind. She had waited so long to have a child. She was terrified that she might lose it. By the time Oliver arrived, the cancer had spread. She started treatment. It gave her another year. She passed away two weeks after Oliver's first birthday."

"Poor Kate. It's so sad. She sacrificed her own life for the sake of her baby. She must have been a remarkable woman."

"Yes, she was," said Peter. She was really brave right to the end. I talk to Oliver about her every day. I want him to know what a wonderful mummy he had."

He looked across the room and saw that Sadie was wiping away a tear. "Please don't be upset Sadie. It's ok now, really it is. Oliver and I are fine. We'll always keep Kate's memory alive but she would want me to move on. To be happy again. I don't know what happened between you and David, but whatever it was, he really hurt you didn't he?"

"Yes he did. I don't think that I will ever find it in my heart to forgive him. I thought we would spend the rest of our lives together but he betrayed me. He used me and he destroyed our marriage. "

She felt that now was the time to tell Peter everything. He sat in stunned silence as she told him the whole story. He felt angry that this beautiful woman sitting in front of him had been treated like this by her husband.

"You deserved so much better than him Sadie. He was a coward. He should have been honest with you from the start. I promise I will never let anyone hurt you like that again."

He walked towards her and took her in his arms. She looked up at his kind handsome face and she knew that this was the man who would always be there for her. The man who could teach her to trust again. To love again.

Their lips met in a soft kiss as she felt the spark of desire stirring inside her. This was her future. The happy ever after that she had dreamed of....

About the Author

Carol is Mother to three children and Grandmother to five. At the age of 76 she made the decision to write her first novel. When she left school, she was fortunate enough to find her dream job on Woman's Weekly Magazine in London. At the age of 17, she was employed as Junior Secretary to the Knitting Editor. By the age of 21 she was promoted to Assistant Fashion Editor. She left at the age of 22 to start her family but always dreamed of returning to Journalism.

After raising her children, she followed a career in Mental Health and in later years, worked for a local Hospice in supporting bereaved families. Her love of writing was always uppermost in her mind and she always dreamed of writing a book. But there was never enough time to make that commitment until she finally retired at the age of 75. She hopes that it will prove , no matter what your age, there should be nothing to stop you from following your dreams.

Printed in Great Britain
by Amazon

62486698R00201